THE CHINESE TAKEOUT

Josie Welford, wealthy widow and licensee of the White Hart gastro-pub, is attending morning service in her quiet country church when a filthy Chinese youth flings himself into the church and demands sanctuary. Josie supports Father Tim Martin's decision to protect Tang, but it's not long before the media are involved, bringing fatal results not just to the priest and the refugee, but to St Jude's itself. Police investigations are strangely slow, so Josie takes matters into her own hands, assisted by no less a personage than the rural dean ... who is alternately entranced and repelled by Josie's methods.

THE CHINESE TAKEOUT

THE CHINESE TAKEOUT

by

Judith Cutler

Magna Large Print Books
Long Preston, North Yorkshire,
BD23 4ND, England.

British Library Cataloguing in Publication Data.

Cutler, Judith
    The Chinese takeout.

    A catalogue record of this book is
    available from the British Library

    ISBN   978-0-7505-2802-3

First published in Great Britain in 2006 by Allison & Busby Ltd.

Copyright © 2006 by Judith Cutler

Cover illustration © Brighton Studios

The moral right of the author has been asserted

Published in Large Print 2007 by arrangement with
Allison & Busby Ltd.

Magna Large Print is an imprint of Library Magna Books Ltd.

Printed and bound in Great Britain by
T.J. (International) Ltd., Cornwall, PL28 8RW

Acknowledgements

Thanks to Keith Bassett, David Houston and Margi Walker for their help: any mistakes are mine, not theirs.

Dedication

For Marion Roberts,
dear friend, fellow writer and inspiration

Chapter One

My boredom threshold is pitifully low. I've always regretted it, but then, I am a Gemini. Mine isn't the sort of boredom that has you staring into the middle-distance sucking the end of your ballpoint or playing endless hours of Patience on your computer when you ought to be doing your accounts. Not usually. It's the sort that makes you look back on what you've just done and realise that, while it might have seemed an achievement at the time, you now feel absolutely flat: fulfilling one ambition just means you have to find another ambition to fulfil.

Father Martin's sermon was inducing yet another sort of boredom, the sort that enables you to turn off your brain and reflect on what you'd rather be doing, such as work – in my case preparing for the fast-approaching lunchtime and the fully-booked restaurant awaiting me back in Kings Duncombe. But I could tell myself that my staff had everything under control, and so my thoughts turned back to ambition, and to what I'd be doing this time next year. Where did I see myself? Would I still be the landlady of the White Hart, juggling the needs of local

11

drinkers and the discriminating palates of a choosy restaurant clientele? Although it had once tickled me pink to see (over the door) *Licensee, Josephine Welford,* now it barely moved me. I needed a new venture, and with all my late husband's ill-gotten fortune still largely untouched, I had enough money to do what I pleased. How would a possible new venture, up here at Abbot's Duncombe, work out? Would the natives of this hamlet be any friendlier than those at the mother village, where I'd brought hostility upon my head by, amongst other things, usurping others' flower-arranging rights?

That was one reason for my starting to come to St Jude's; the other was a sort of cultural tourism. I'd often seen the church when I was out on one of my long walks – indeed, its position on the top of a hill meant it was something of a landmark – and had wanted to see inside. These days even in the country churches had to be kept locked, so that meant a Sunday call. And since I didn't have any floral (or other) history with the members of the congregation, it had become my regular church. No one from St Faith and St Lawrence had called into the pub to ask why I'd absconded. I'm not sure if I'd have been entirely frank if they had. You soon learn that in villages certain things are best left unsaid. Since Father Martin operated out of (there's bound to be a proper technical term for that) four or five churches, he at least wouldn't see it as any sort of snub.

I could sneak a look at my watch.

Come on, Josie. Poor Father Martin can't help being a kid young enough to be your son, with the most active Adam's apple that's ever joggled its way through a Church of England service. It's like a mouse running up a stocking leg. The mole in my herb patch escaping from the Olbas Oil I've poured into its hill. A baby ferret in a tiny sack.

Josie! If you listened attentively, you might be able to give the sort of intelligent praise he so obviously needed.

That was how I always sugared the pill of my inevitable criticisms, which he unremittingly sought out. He had a problem, of course, being, like me, an incomer and therefore regarded with suspicion if not outright hostility. Grockles were never welcomed with open arms, though their money was so vital to the community. So maybe that was why he chose me as his most unlikely mentor.

Off I was going again. I could barely remember the text that the sermon was related to, pretty shameful considering he'd been speaking a bare ten minutes. Perhaps it was a sign of incipient senility – decidedly premature, of course. They said that ballroom dancing and bingo were some of the best preventatives. Bother those for a game of soldiers. The latter at least. I wouldn't mind swanning round an old-fashioned ballroom in the arms of a handsome man. The trouble was, now I could afford the most swish of dresses, I no longer had the figure for it. I'd done my best with WeightWatchers, and had been featured nationally as one of their great successes, but that left me as a slim and svelte fifty-something, not a slim and svelte twenty-something with a chance of looking chic in acres of tulle.

Enough!

Perhaps I'd do better to look at the church itself. The solid shell itself was twelfth century, possibly earlier, not cruciform in shape, more like a lower case *t*, the dash on the *t* being a minute lady chapel, no more than three yards by three. With its small windows and huge, solid pillars, it was old enough to inspire, even if the Victorian improvements were not. A subsequent, but not consequent, fire had undone some of the damage and caused a lot more, to be honest. All the pews and the pulpit had gone, and what had once been fine medieval glass had been replaced by uninspired modern stuff, with a few fragments of the original gathered in a central panel in the east window. Both the east and the west windows cried out for some really fine contemporary work, but there hadn't been enough insurance money. As for the sixteenth-century pews, their replacements were some individual seats, refugees from some defunct Baptist chapel now no doubt a bijou yuppie residence. They had come complete with book-holders screwed to the back. No human form that I knew would fit them. At least the gaps between the rows were narrow enough to deter kneeling, a mercy to older knees, even though Father Martin was high church enough to have liked us to genuflect and cross ourselves at every opportunity – perhaps in rhythm with his Adam's apple. There were persistent mutterings about the possibility of bells and smells, largely from a resentful choir.

In St Jude's, the choir didn't sit where you would expect them to sit, in the choir, that is, the area between the pulpit and the altar. It was equally correct and much clearer to refer to it as the chancel, anyway. Thanks to a quirk in the acoustics, it wasn't possible to hear the poor, clapped-out organ once you got beyond the hideous Victorian rood beam, supporting a crucifix the Vatican might have turned down as too garish for the most exuberant Mexican church. So now, before each service, the three men and eleven women constituting the choir processed not up the aisle to the front, but down from our tiny lady chapel on the right of the chancel to the rear.

I usually sat as near them as I could, not least because I couldn't hold a tune in my head and needed all the support I could get, and some of the singers were more in tune than the organ, which occasionally emitted those bum notes musical types call dominoes. And, of course, I could people-watch unseen.

The rest of the congregation – some sixteen in total – stared, as far as I could see, stolidly in front. Some might have been nodding, if not in agreement, but Father Martin, high in his pulpit, was in the best position to judge. They were mostly so old as to make a fifty-something like me seem youthful, generally farmers or stallholders, plus a few villagers. Occasionally there'd be the excitement of a holidaymaker. Children were invited to special monthly services, with a couple of pop-type hymns everyone was too embarrassed by to try to join in the syncopation. Very few children came a second time, despite, or perhaps because of, Father Martin's acoustic guitar.

He was clearing his throat, working up to his denouement. No, wrong term. That OU course I'd taken was beginning to wear off and you don't often use literary jargon in the kitchen. Tony would have been ashamed of me. For an old lag, veteran of no end of jail-terms, he'd had an amazing vocabulary,

16

honed with a daily attack on every news-
paper crossword he could lay his hands on
in the confines of the prison library. Come
on, Tony: what's the word I'm after? Peror-
ation, that's it. The climax of his sermon.
'Love thy neighbour as thyself. And I tell
you–'

What he had to tell us we never knew. For
even as he primed his epiglottis, the church
door crashed open and a figure hurtled up
the aisle, tripping over the shallow step into
the chancel, and landing, like a rugby player
scoring a try, at the foot of the altar.

'Sanctuary!' the intruder shouted. 'Sanctuary!' Or something close enough.

To my amazement – was it the age of the
congregation, or the fact that some might
well have been asleep? – there was no immediate action. A trendy film-maker would
have frozen a succession of frames to show
how slow we all were. Father Martin was
hampered by his inevitably overlarge cassock
and the steepness of the pulpit steps. Anyone
else wanting to join his investigation of the
still prone figure was hampered by the tight
ranks of chairs, handbags, kneelers and other
people's knees. In a row to myself, I was at a
distinct advantage, legging it the length of
the aisle before some people had properly
registered what was going on. I'm not sure
what propelled me – my innate nosiness or a

17

belief that a life mixing with violent criminals had qualified me to deal with potential crises. Then the church wardens, who would have liked to exercise authority over the interloper, bustled up, one yelling in the sort of voice a farmer catching scrumpers would use: 'Hoy! You there! You can't do that.'

Father Martin – such a mouthful, and much easier to call him Tim, which I did in private – always more wrists, elbows and knees than was convenient, hovered in anguish, not knowing whether to exhort like his wardens or kneel beside the visitor to comfort him, as I was doing. In vain, I have to say. My gentlest touch was enough to have him trying to burrow under the altar, which as stone was impervious to his efforts.

He was bird thin, with filthy black hair below his shoulders. Until I could see his face I could no more than guess at his origin, but I thought perhaps Chinese or Malaysian. He smelt quite rank – not just in need of a shower, but unpleasant. One or two politer noses were pulled sharply away. For by now he was quite surrounded, and I had a sudden image of how it must seem to him – like a fox surrounded by baying hounds.

'Call them off, Tim!' I hissed. 'Let the poor kid breathe. Hey, what are you doing?'

The church wardens were ready to manhandle him.

18

He scrabbled to his feet, hand out-stretched, the other gripping the altar cloth. 'No!' I shouted. 'Back. He's got a knife!' And might be prepared to use it, he was so terrified. Getting to my feet faster than my knees enjoyed, I shooed the others away. And damned soon joined them myself. 'Everyone – back. And be very quiet.'

A bit of silent prayer might be a good thing, but it was hardly my place to suggest it. So now four of us – Tim Martin, William Corbishley, Geoffrey Malins and I – stood in a loose ring, just as the four knights must have surrounded Thomas Beckett. The difference was, of course, that in our case the majority were unarmed.

Father Martin, every inch a Father, with no scrap of everyday Tim in evidence, stepped forward and, with a stern smile, held out his hand for the knife. The young man, scarcely more than a boy, brandished it more fiercely, making jabbing movements that could have spelt evisceration to any of us. Three of us made little pacifying gestures. Father Martin didn't. His right hand, veins in his thin white wrist perilously close to the surface, stayed where it was. Not a shake, not a tremble. His face was calm, compelling. The only sign that he shared our terror was the convulsive yoyo in his neck.

It seemed the church was full of the sound of breathing: the young man's gasps, Father

19

Martin's, which tried to be calm and relaxed, but ended with quick jerks, as if the muscles would hold out no longer, my own panting. There were audible sobs from some of the congregation, but I didn't turn to see whose.

I sensed, rather than saw, Geoffrey Malins muscling up to speak. 'I say–'

'Leave it to Tim,' I said from the corner of my mouth.

'But he's no right–'

'Do as she says,' Corbishley said, as the blade jagged in his direction again.

Neither of them should have been involved in these heroics. Neither would see seventy again, and while Malins was stringy thin, Corbishley was carrying a couple of stone more than he should, and his cheeks, though pale now, were normally reddish blue, as if neither he nor his doctor had heard of preventing heart disease.

'Why don't you two back off and sit down?' I murmured. 'Looks less intimidating if you do.'

'Give in to that oick? Never!'

That augured well, I didn't think.

Malins added, 'And leave it to a lady?'

'All my years in the hospitality industry,' I said, using the politest term, 'I've had a few knives pulled on me. And Tim's doing very well.'

One reason the kid might be dithering,

adrenaline apart, was the damp creeping up through the tiled floor. As the men backed away, I increased my surrender gesture, then, crossing my hands across my chest, mimed cold. I had his interest. I gestured again: would he like my coat jacket?

Assuming he would, I peeled it slowly and bunched it, ready to lob it to his other hand. Instead, I hurled it at the knife, which clattered across to Tim. Screaming, the kid fell to his knees. Slowly and deliberately Tim kicked the knife away, and bent to pick up my coat jacket. Instead of returning it to me, he passed it to the youth.

I nodded enthusiastically – he should put it on. Two hundred and fifty quid's worth of cashmere! Why not?

There was movement at the back of the church, and then hesitant footsteps. I risked a look – after all, the lad had no more of a weapon than my coat. It was one of the choir ladies, bearing a cup of tea in her free hand.

'Plenty more in the pot,' she announced cheerfully, in a voice surprisingly free of the local Somerset burr. 'Would you like a cup too, Father Martin?' She slopped a little as she struggled with the step, but made her way straight to the boy. 'Go on, love: you try a drop of that.'

'I think we all would,' Tim declared, his voice as uncertain in register as if it were only now breaking. 'And biscuits, if we may.'

There was more movement. At the back of the church, in what was once presumably the vestry, there was a minute kitchen, just large enough for a kettle and tea-urn and a cupboard holding disposable cups and equally plastic teabags and coffee. There was no running water, just a standpipe outside. Father Martin had introduced the idea of a communal drink after the service, the ladies taking it in turns to provide cakes and biscuits, so that people who had made in some cases a considerable effort to get here should be refreshed before they set off home again. It was a nice idea, somewhat undercut by the fact that the church had no lavatory.

'Annie,' the tea lady declared pointing at herself. 'Annie.' She laid a finger on his chest. 'And you are? Annie,' she repeated. 'And you? No? Ah, well, you get yourself round that, and you'll soon feel better. Why don't you sit yourself down?' The only chair was the sanctuary chair, reserved for visiting bishops, but she ignored the niceties and pushed him into it. 'Sorry, Tim,' she said, over her shoulder.

'I won't tell if you won't,' he grinned. Then he donned a more official face. 'He's an honoured guest anyway. Why not?'

'There you are, then.' She passed the lad his cup of tea. 'Now, where are those biscuits?' Her accent was distinctly Mancunian.

'Annie. Tea.' As the plate of biscuits arrived, complete with paper doyley, she pointed again. 'Biscuit.' Then she pressed his chest, raising her eyebrows.

A syllable emerged. Tang? It might have been. At least he had spoken. He drank the disgusting tea in one medicinal draught and fell upon the oversweet biscuits, supermarket bourbons, as if they were manna.

'He'll make himself sick if he has too much sugar on an empty stomach,' a fragile male voice came from the back. 'And I reckon we could all do with a biscuit – the shock, you know.'

A locust cloud of hands descended. Tang was left with four. He did not need to speak to tell us what he thought of that.

Annie patted his hand. 'Never you mind. I'll nip and get you some proper food in a minute. A nice slice of chicken, how about that? Good. I'll see you soon!'

He grabbed her wrist and held her.

With infinite gentleness, she unprised the fingers. She gestured again, walking from the church, and then, after a pause filled with gestures he might or might not recognise as cooking, walking back in again with something to eat. She looked around. I would do as a substitute. She put my hand into Tang's, patted his cheek and set off.

'Josie.' Then I pointed to the others I could name. 'Father Martin. Geoffrey. William.'

Neither ever used the shorter forms of their name. I ground to a halt. I knew the others by sight only: these country people weren't as free with first names as they were in cities.

One or two took the hint.

'Mrs Rose. And this is my husband Mr Rose. Ted, really, I suppose.'

'Mrs Gray...'

'Mr Heath...'

Our conviviality was suddenly interrupted by a thunderous banging.

'Oh, for goodness' sake,' Mrs Rose expostulated gently, 'don't whoever it is know we wouldn't lock the door during a service?' She set off down the aisle to admit the disturber of the peace.

Assuming the worst, Tim followed, at first at a scuttle, but breaking into a dignified stride.

'Stay where you are!' His voice was rock steady, as he leaned his full weight against the door. 'Leave your weapons outside. And then one of you may come in. I said leave them! You do not enter the House of God with batons and gas!'

Chapter Two

Tang watched the proceedings with horrified eyes, his hand gripping mine as if he would collapse without me. His nails were long and filthy. As he got warmer, the smell grew. But I wouldn't permit myself so much as a twitch of a nostril, not until the police had left us. Instead, I used my free hand to pat his shoulder.

Bathos. Pure bathos. It was only Mrs Mills, who lived next to the church. She had scuttled off to bring a travelling rug for the poor kid. The tartan clashed hideously with the cerise of my jacket, but we all appreciated the gesture. And were relieved that it had not been the police. How would we have reacted? How much support would Tim have got for his spirited stance?

As if in response to the unasked questions, Tim swallowed convulsively and coughed for silence. 'Now, as soon as possible I must speak to the rural dean,' he said. 'And we all – thank you so much, Annie and Mrs Mills and Josie, for setting an example – have to care for Tang's needs.' He wrung his hands. 'If only this were a modern building, with all mod cons.'

Corbishley's eyes bulged. 'But he's not staying here!'

'What else would you suggest?'

'He – he's not even clean!'

'Damn it, he stinks to high heaven!' Malins added.

'Why doesn't Mrs Welford take him back to her pub? There'll be food and drink there, and plenty of bedrooms and bathrooms,' Corbishley continued.

'She can't possibly – not with all those children living there!'

I didn't like Malins' excuse. It was true I had a family staying in the pub long term, the siblings of my head waitress, soon to be my trainee manager. But I objected to the implication that Tang must be a danger to children, simply because he was seeking sanctuary for crimes unspecified.

'Josie can't possibly offer him hospitality,' Father Martin cut in. 'Any more than you or I can, much as I am sure we would like to. As I understand it, if the laws of sanctuary still apply, and it's a big if, they protect the claimant only as long as he is within the church's precincts. In other words, as soon as he steps outside the police can pick him up.'

'But we have no ... facilities!'

'It can't be beyond us to find anything he needs,' I said, perhaps trying to make up for not immediately seconding Corbishley's proposals for Tang. 'He'll be roughing it here for a bit, obviously, so we must try to make his life bearable.' In my opinion nothing less than a four-star hotel constituted bearable, but let that pass. 'Do any of you own camping equipment?'

Father Martin stepped into the growing puddle of silence. 'I'm sure the Scouts have practically everything.'

'I thought they usually camped in proper sites, these days – with shower and toilet blocks,' Malins added, significantly.

'Not to mention camp-fires for cooking.'

Father Martin didn't even need to look at me.

'Food's no problem,' I said. 'He can have his own takeouts, by courtesy of the White Hart. And if the wiring's up to it, I'll donate a microwave,' I added. Not the restaurant one, no way, but the little one in my own kitchen. If necessary I could replace it tomorrow.

A couple of people slipped quietly away, not relishing the horn-locking, no doubt. Or perhaps their Sunday roasts were demanding to be basted. Thank goodness for my wonderful crew. Robin had introduced his cousin Pix into the kitchen, and Lucy's sister Lorna was deemed old enough to waitress, provided she had nothing to do with the serving of alcohol. That needed me. I flashed a look at my watch.

Father Martin caught me at it. 'I know you have work to do, Josie,' he began sadly, 'but–'

'But I will be back as soon as I've supervised lunch. And, Father, whatever you do, I'm sure you'll have the absolute support of both the congregation and the parish as a whole,' I lied. 'Tang – I am going away.' My fingers walked in front of his face. 'But I will be back.' They made a return journey. Did he understand? 'We need an interpreter, Tim. Shall I get on the phone to a friend of mine who runs a Chinese restaurant?'

'Probably won't speak the right sort of Chinese,' Malins muttered.

'He'll know a man who does,' I said, crossing my fingers behind my back.

I patted Tang's hand and touched his cheek with my finger, smiling positively, and started down the aisle. The door swung open before I reached it. In came Annie, with a tray covered with a bright check tea towel. The smells were such I wondered if I could recruit her to my team.

I watched with pleasure as she presented the plate of roast chicken with all the trimmings to our guest. And in disbelief as he dashed it from her hand, shouting hysterically. After a moment, he sank to his knees, scooping into his mouth with those filthy hands all the vegetables. But the breast, glistening in its beautiful coat of gravy, might have been purest poison. He backed away from it, shuddering. Then he retreated to the sanctuary chair, huddling up against the viciously carved wood as if to a comfort blanket.

'OK, no chicken then,' I said, and set off.

Nick Thomas, my other lodger, had to have chosen this weekend to go and visit his daughter up in Birmingham. I was glad for his sake there'd been some sort of reconciliation, Elly understanding at last that her father's erratic behaviour had been a result of mental trauma when he'd been a policeman back in Birmingham. She might understand, but it seemed to us both that forgiveness was some way off. While he was building bridges, of course, he wasn't doing his usual casual bit of bar work for me – he was actually a full-time inspector for the Food Standards Agency – and Lucy was run off her feet.

I couldn't have anything to do with food till I'd stripped off any clothes that had been in contact with Tang, and my hands would take a week to feel clean, despite the antibacterial scrub I assailed them with. But I was on duty within ten minutes of getting back, presenting the smiling, confident face you need front of house. Mentally I was reviewing what I could immediately provide for Tang, besides my little microwave.

29

During lunch I realised I had to put the morning's doings firmly to the back of my mind. There were regulars to talk to, and newcomers: not many of those because all tables tended to be booked from week to week these days – hence the possibility of an Abbot's Duncombe venture. Some were becoming friends, including one couple I had to phone up to put off if there were going to be nuts in any of the recipes. Already there were gluten-free items on the regular menu. John Oakham, who was waving me over now, had to exist without dairy products, and not because he was watching his weight, either.

'So what's my special dessert this week, Josie? This is the wonderful landlady Daisy's been telling you about,' he explained, rather unnecessarily, to his guests, a couple, like the Oakhams, in their sixties. 'She does something special for me every week, bless her. And it doesn't feel like worthy good-for-you food, either.'

'Pears in red wine,' I said. One of my staples, and a boon if you were busy. All you needed were Conference pears, still as hard as the devil's head, a sprinkle of sugar, a little water and enough red wine to cover them. Once they were in a slow oven you could simply leave them to it. Some people added cinnamon or cloves, or mulled wine spices: I trusted them as they were. After eight hours, they'd be a wonderful mahogany brown, sitting in a wondrous liquor that cream or ice cream positively demeaned.

'Do I pick up a familiar accent?' one of their guests asked. She had a trace of Brummie, so I hammed up mine to sound like Frank Skinner on speed.

'Ar. Nice to see you, me wench. How's the metropolis?' I added, in my usual voice.

'Bustling. Vibrant. Dirty. Business as usual, in fact. Do you miss it?'

'She lives here in Paradise and you expect her to miss a place like that?'

I laughed. 'I don't often. Just sometimes.' I thought of the people I'd left behind. People who'd taught me everything about cooking. 'There's something special about a multicultural community...'

'Absolutely! I'm a cricket freak, Josie, and there's nothing better than going to Edgbaston and sitting with people from half a dozen different places all yelling for England!'

I nodded. 'And the food! And Diwali and the Chinese New Year and Eid!'

The Oakhams were almost scratching their heads in bemusement. 'But we have foreigners here too,' Daisy said. 'In Exeter.'

Their friends and I exchanged a look. Somehow and quite unwittingly Daisy had made our point for us. And the Oakhams were enlightened, generous-minded liberals. If their first reaction to Tang would be that he was foreign, it wasn't hard to predict the reaction of the more insular villagers.

I had no sooner parked by the St Jude's lychgate and started to unpack the Saab I currently favoured than an estate car pulled up, driven by Aidan Carr.

I could have hugged him – did in fact. His preference might be men, but we got on very well, and he'd put one or two very good antiques my way.

'What are you doing here?' I asked.

'News spreads fast in villages, Josie! As a former outcast myself, I thought I should help the poor boy. He might need this to keep out those raging draughts,' he said, dragging out a screen covered with unlikely Victorian women. 'Should be Chinese, of course, but I thought this old thing would be better than nothing. See – someone's cut all these pictures out of magazines or whatever and pasted them on. Collage, we could call it, if we wanted to be pretentious.'

'We could. I'd call it a godsend, myself – the church is like a wind-tunnel. Here, let me give you a hand.'

The door was locked, and it took a few moments for Annie to admit us. She pounced on the screen with glee. 'The very thing to create a little bathroom – Mr Barnes has leant us a new plasterer's bath and he's just gone to get a chemical toilet. Quite urgent, that,' she added, lowering her voice. 'We had to let him use a flower vase. Not very sanitary, of course, but there you are. We can use the tea-urn to boil water for a bath, too.'

In fact Tang needed very much less than I'd expected. The people I'd suspected of supine escape had in fact been using their initiative too. I spotted pillows, a bedroll, and a couple of those director's chairs complete with a ducky little drinks holder. And if church fêtes were anything to go by, those biscuit tins would harbour the sort of delectable cakes that figured in my weight-watching nightmares.

'There's a jogging suit of mine in the car,' Aidan said, waving at Tang but not approaching. 'And some new undies. Then we can burn that awful stuff of his.'

Tim overheard and shook his head. 'It's just possible that the Bishop will insist we hand him over to the police and that he'll have to be tried...' His voice faltered. '...for whatever it is he's done. If we keep his clothes, then maybe his defence can use them.'

I pulled a face. 'Or more likely the prosecution.' I have to admit that the trials that saw Tony sent down for all those stretches generally brought in the correct verdict –

guilty that is. But I had seen entirely innocent men fitted up, either by their so-called mates or by the police. Maybe the clothes would provide indisputable evidence. 'I've got a roll of bin liners in the car. Everything can go in one of them.' Returning, I said, 'As far as an interpreter's concerned, I had to leave a message for my restaurateur friend, I'm afraid. But you seem to be communicating without his assistance.'

'I wish. Now, Josie, can you stay with him for a bit? I've got early evensong over in Duncombe Minimus, and since they only see me once a month, I can't let them down.'

'And you need a shower first.' I grinned. 'What have you and the church wardens decided about a rota for keeping an eye on things?'

'The church wardens and I!' he snorted. He looked at his watch. 'I'll be back by five-thirty, Josie.'

By now the whole church smelt bad. True, it wasn't a large building, the aisle about the length of a cricket pitch, the sanctuary only three or four yards, and overall it wasn't much wider than, say, two buses, side by side. The trouble was that Tang was now toasting himself over a single-burner butane cooker. Who could blame him? Late February it might be, but it was bitterly cold in here, despite the wall heaters Tim had left on, and he still wore only the clothes he'd arrived in, plus my cashmere jacket, of course.

As I stepped forward to greet him, Malins, who contrived to look straight through Aidan, intercepted me. I produced a deceptive smile: if Aidan was good enough to ring Kings Duncombe's church bells, he was good enough to be treated politely.

'Geoffrey, you know Aidan Carr, don't you? Where's the best place for this screen, do you think? In the Lady Chapel? Or nearer the kitchen?'

'I'm sorry to see you're party to this sacrilege,' Geoffrey hissed, spraying us equally in his fury. 'This is an abomination! Letting a criminal stink out an historic building like this: it's intolerable!'

'My understanding,' Aidan said, drawing himself up to his full five foot five, 'is that the dear boy is a fugitive, not a proven criminal. We don't even know what he's fleeing, do we? So let us give him at least the benefit of the doubt. Now, the sooner we can get him into that bath, the better. Ladies, given my proclivities, it might be better for the poor lad's reputation if I were not present. What about you, Geoffrey? Are you an old queen too?' And he tucked his arm into Malins' and led him from the building.

Annie seemed more than capable of taking charge, so I left her to usher Tang into his new boudoir while I fetched towels, soap and a manicure kit from the car. On reflection, I removed the scissors, just in case. Tony reckoned no one had ever managed to top himself with clippers and emery boards.

Having to refill the tea-urn from the standpipe was a pain, because we had to do it jug-kettle by slow jug-kettleful and I could see that bailing out the bath wouldn't be easy, but at least, as Annie and I sat sipping our tea – I'd brought along a rather better class of teabag – we congratulated ourselves on doing our best. The incident of the chicken still puzzled us.

'Do you suppose he's vegetarian?' she asked.

'I can't imagine even a devout vegetarian making such a fuss. Damn it, most vegetarians I know would have stuffed it down, if they were as hungry as he obviously was. What about religion?'

'China? I thought they were officially atheists? And they'd be Confucians, wouldn't they? What does that mean, dietwise?'

'I've never known a vegetarian Chinese restaurant,' I said. 'And I certainly don't know any religion that bans chickens.'

'Halal? Is there a Confucian version of halal or kosher?'

We shrugged in unison, and fell into a quiet gossip. It turned out that Annie had been a teacher before she retired some sixteen years ago. At first she'd thought the life of a hermit would be ideal after all her years being at other people's beck and call, but she'd realised how much she missed her fellow men and now worked a couple of days a week in Exeter in the Citizens' Advice Bureau.

'So you're better able than most to advise Father Martin?'

'I wish I were. Telling folk how to re-schedule debts and deal with bad landlords doesn't help when it comes to ecclesiastical law. Or criminal law. Or, come to think if it, immigration and labour law. Tang could have problems with all of them. Tim's first job is to establish as best he can that Tang is innocent of anything. Only then can he tell the rural dean and then the bishop he has to keep him here.'

'So it's the bishop's decision?'

The heavy door opened and slammed shut, as Malins and Aidan returned. 'The bishop's? Dear me, no. At least, not entirely,' Malins corrected himself. 'The church is in the jurisdiction of its wardens: Mr Corbishley and my good self. And we have an appointment with the rural dean – it's to him we report in the first instance – at nine-thirty tomorrow.'

In which case I would be with him at nine. I'd no idea which dean, of course, or where he might hang out, but Tim ought to know.

I nodded noncommittally, however, and

merely asked, 'That bath: it's too heavy for us women and it would take forever to bail it out. You couldn't recruit a couple of younger men to carry it out?' Given his age, I certainly wouldn't have asked him to help.

'Bailing's the only answer.'

'In that case, I hope it doesn't take too long.' I pressed an empty vase into his nerveless hand.

Aidan soon appeared with a full bucket in one hand and the bag of stinking clothes in the other. At least it was tied so tightly it emitted fewer noxious odours.

'And all this will have to be stored somewhere?'

'Anywhere. So long as it isn't the White Hart.'

'Quite. I'll leave it in the porch for the nonce. By the way,' he added, as casually as if he were reporting an early spring daffodil, 'did you hear? Snow's forecast. Just what you need.'

I checked my watch: if Tim's service was over, it would be good to warn him. But there was no mobile signal up here, as I found when I perched on the highest grave. Aidan offered a gentlemanly hand to help me down. 'Any idea who will stay and care for Tang tonight?'

'You're right: we need to make sure he doesn't try to break out and run for it. For his sake.'

'And ours, Josie.'

'Because we mustn't be seen to be aiding and abetting if it does turn out he's a serial killer or a child-molester?'

'Quite.'

I looked at him from under my lashes. 'I could always get some of my late husband's mates to spring him. It's nice and close to Dartmoor and I'm sure some would oblige.'

He steadied me as I descended. 'The less you refer to those connections the better, I suspect.' He wrapped his arm round my shoulders, leading us back to the church, and asked, 'Do you still miss him?'

'I spent most of my life missing him when he was banged up. But I miss him even more now.'

'So there's no truth in the persistent rumour that you and our Food Standards Inspector friend, Nick Thomas, are an item?'

'Absolutely not. He's got too much baggage, has Nick.' Not to mention that as an inspector with the West Midlands Police he was the man chiefly responsible for sending my beloved Tony down for the last time.

'And that steely-eyed Devon detective? The one who helped sort out the bombing?'

'We had our little moments,' I conceded. 'But he's taken a promotion in Liverpool, and we hardly bother to email each other now. Brrrh. Let's go in.'

By the time it was dark, soon after five, Tang was equipped with a camp-bed, an arctic quality sleeping bag, food, chocolate, bottled water, several changes of clothing and a pile of books.

Tim's appearance in a full-length black clerical cloak – was that what was called a cope? – certainly impressed Tang, who seemed inclined to kiss the hem. Tim raised him quickly, however, with a smile I thought was forced.

'You've heard from our church wardens?' he asked me quietly.

'Indeed. Can you possibly pre-empt them, Tim? Get the bishop out here to see the situation for himself?'

'The bishop won't overrule the rural dean responsible for our area. I've already phoned him, Dean Braithwaite. He'll be working this evening, of course,' he added, with a rueful smile that made him look about twelve.

'I'd still prefer him – the bishop, anyone! – to see the situation himself before the terrible twins get at him. And that doesn't give you much time: they've got an appointment at nine-thirty.'

'I don't have much time anyway. I've still got to take evensong in Kings Duncombe. Where you no longer worship, I see.'

'It's a good job, all things considered,' I parried. 'Off you go, Tim – I'll hold the fort here till you come back, having had, I hope, a good supper first. Plenty of stodge to keep you warm.'

'I shall need it if I'm staying overnight. No argument, Josie. You can see someone has to and that someone must be me.'

'Well, if Tang needs an arctic sleeping bag, you'll need one too. I mean it! Don't play the martyr till you need to. And phone the rural dean again! Beg him to come out – think of the impact on him if he has to drive out here in the dark through the snow! Quite Biblical!'

He managed a grin. 'You know something, Josie? You remind me of my godmother.'

'I shall take that as a compliment. And don't forget that sack of clothes!'

Chapter Three

Annie decided it was time to teach Tang more English, which was something she could manage very well without me. Better. While she saw the slowness of his progress as a challenge, I was dispirited. I didn't want him to catch my despair, so, as the two heads, his black, hers white, bent over a child's book she'd found somewhere, I looked round for something else to do. One possibility, and I must have been out of my mind to consider it, was to climb up the tower to see – well, just to see, really. I'm approaching the age when physically I shan't be able to act on impulse, so occasionally I do things people consider plain daft. OK, things I consider afterwards, when all my muscles are screaming and my joints are on fire, plain daft.

If I needed an excuse it was that mobile reception might be better higher up. We really did need to get hold of an interpreter I could trust. There were well-documented cases of police interpreters being distinctly bent. If one came via Nigel Ho, my fellow restaurateur, then I thought that might improve the odds in our favour.

And I could still do ladders – just. Actually, they were easier than narrow, steep staircases, because I could legitimately come down backwards, so I would risk this one. I couldn't fault the church wardens' attitude to health and safety: the steps had their own set of very bright lights, and the handrails didn't even flinch at my weight. Perhaps they thought their responsibility ended there. The door at the top was magnificently warped, with half an inch or so in places between the door and the frame, which explained why even the fiercest heaters couldn't conquer the chill. But, hinges well oiled, it opened outwards quite easily, and I stepped out into the night. Tony had always daydreamed about us taking up stargazing together, probably because when you were in jail you didn't get much of the wide open sky, free from light pollution. Abbot's Duncombe was too small a village, with not even a shop, for the county council to consider streetlighting. Most of the inhabitants eschewed security lights, and drew their curtains tightly, especially on a night as cold as this. If you wanted to walk between the scattered dwellings, you took a torch. I'd have to consider that before I put in a firm bid on the pub. No point in spending a lot of money on a building people wouldn't feel safe reaching – after all, I wanted more than clients on wheels.

Up on the tower, the air was icy, but pure: Tony'd have relished that, too. It would be nice to share things again, wouldn't it? I didn't mean just sex: there were a couple of men in my life who'd be more than happy to supply that side of my needs. I meant love – the sort of thing Tony and I had shared for all those years. Preferably without the enforced periods of celibacy. Near celibacy, in my case, if there is such a thing. While he was doing bird, Tony was prepared to accept the odd fling – I was young enough to be his granddaughter, really, and he thought that keeping me on too short a rein might cause problems. But if things threatened to get serious – well, so did he. And since he was so powerful, he had any number of minions still outside ready to change my mind. At last he and I both understood that things would never get serious with anyone else because he was truly the love of my life.

That life, the old life.

During the last few years I had changed so much, not just in appearance but also in achievements and now aspirations, that I wondered if our marriage would have survived. These days I certainly wouldn't get involved with anyone I suspected of being a criminal, and not just from fear of retribution, either. To tell the truth, apart from when I was bored, I was beginning to want a nice, straightforward ordinary existence. Perhaps for a moment I might have considered embarking on a relationship with Nick Thomas. He'd drifted into my life in a most unpromising way, and now lived permanently at the White Hart, as a quasi-uncle to the brood of Gay children left orphaned by a horrible accident last autumn. But he had his quarters, and I had mine, and although we met all the time, it was never carnally.

Nigel Ho was someone I had met carnally once or twice, but we were chiefly just fellow chefs and possibly becoming friends: hence I could happily ask him for a favour. I'd rather Tim didn't know about our intermittent moments together, not because I was ashamed, but because I didn't want to let down a man who'd compared me with his godmother. In any case, once something was pretty well over there was no point in shouting it from the rooftops – or even the church tower top.

I left another message for Nigel but, despite the sting of what I supposed were snowflakes on the wind, I didn't return immediately. After all, I was well wrapped up. Tang might be wearing my warmest smart outfit, but I still had my heavyweight walking gear: I had hunched myself into the thickest fleece and waterproof I could find, and was doing a fair imitation of a perambulating duvet.

Headlights were picking out the road from Kings Duncombe: could this be Tim returning? If it was, I'd better scuttle down again to unlock the door for him. The tower door opened beautifully, and closed equally sweetly. The steps gave not so much as a wobble under my weight. I set to and brewed some tea.

As if he was playing the lead in *Swallows and Amazons*, Tim gave a cloak-and-dagger-ish drumroll on the door – three short knocks, three long, three more short. SOS? At last, for good measure, he identified himself.

Tang was able to say 'hallo' and then, as I pressed mugs of tea into everyone's hands, 'thank you,' an achievement Tim greeted with lavish praise. But his face became serious. Turning to Annie, he said, 'I think you should push off as soon as you can. There's already an inch of snow on some of the higher moors, and promise of more to come.'

Annie nodded, gathering her things to-ether and repeating the walking finger gesture Tang now clearly understood to mean *au revoir*. He smiled and bowed, and though my jacket was overlarge, and the fuchsia pink definitely not one he should pick out for his spring outfit, especially not combined with Aidan's turquoise jogging suit, you could see that in other circumstances he might be a personable young man.

'I'll be back in the morning,' she said, waving as I locked the door after her.

'So will I,' I said, preparing to get my things together and follow.

Tim's throat bobbled. 'Er, actually, I was wondering if you wouldn't mind waiting a bit. I did talk to the rural dean again. He's coming down in about half an hour.'

'That's excellent!'

He shook his head sadly. 'I'm not so sure. He said there should be two people with Tang all the time, so that if he tried to escape he could be intercepted. A belt and braces man.'

I said bracingly, 'At least he's going to see

how things are before he listens to your dear church wardens.'

'I think he's had an earful already. He wasn't best pleased, Josie.'

I hugged him. 'You couldn't have done anything else, Tim. Could you?' I demanded.

'No. Not at the time. But I suppose I could have insisted on taking him to the police and stuck to him like glue to make sure nothing went wrong. Maybe I should have done.'

It would certainly, I reflected, have made for a much less stressful Sunday afternoon. On the other hand, a lot of people had had the opportunity to show how generous they were. But he was waiting for reassurance. 'Maybe you still can. If that's your boss's advice, then we'll both go.'

'The trouble is, Josie, which boss?' He didn't need to look skywards to make sure I understood.

'Look, Tang realises there's something worrying you. Just go and do your best with him while I heat up some soup. Did you eat?'

'I thought my place was back here.'

'Tim!' I sighed. 'All right. There's enough food here for three. Enough for an army, actually. And bread and cheese and cakes and home made jam and a wonderful look-ing treacle-tart.' It was like Ratty and Mole's first picnic, except that that hadn't come with a microwave and a proper four-burner camping stove. 'I'd say the vast majority of your little flock are behind you here.'

He raised an eyebrow, not quite cynical but certainly questioning. 'What proportion of my "flock" comes to church, ever? What proportion comes when it suits them? What proportion happened to be here today? And with the church wardens against my decision, how can I say I have majority backing?' On the last question his voice cracked.

'People from St Faith and St Lawrence were among those who gave.' I wasn't ready to concede. 'And folk from other churches within the benefice.'

'Stop being kind, Josie. Please. Let's face it, I'm out of my depth. If not now, when the church hierarchy start arguing, when the media get hold of it, when the lychgate holds back satellite vans and reporters stand on graves and police spokesmen with loud-hailers give out warning messages. Where will I be then?'

Tang was now very agitated, pulling on Tim's cloak. Absently, Tim patted his newly clean and manicured hand, as one might pat a fretting puppy.

'Look,' I said, going into my inevitable bossy mode again, 'you can't talk to each other but there's one way you can both at least pass the time.' I produced a Sainsbury's carrier someone had donated full of things to while away vast stretches of hours: cards, jigsaws, chess, draughts, Monopoly. 'What do you fancy?'

Tang grabbed the chess set, grinning happily. I hoped Tim was a better player than I expected him to be or that his ego was more resilient.

Perhaps I wouldn't have made such a bad mother. While the young men played, I sorted through the bags of clothing people like Aidan had donated, suitable stuff going into one pile, the bizarre going into some spare black sacks for Oxfam. Surprisingly – he was such a fey man, always claiming to be incompetent in all practical skills – Aidan had made the best choice, including, as he'd said, new underwear and socks. He must have made a special trip into Taunton for them. He'd also brought along the flip-flops Tang was now wearing, but another carrier produced something more practical for the chilly church, a pair of leather-soled slippers with bright knitted tops that covered the calves too. I tiptoed over and placed them by Tang's feet. He nodded absently to acknowledge them, then realised they were worth more than that, and, even as he re-moved Tim's bishop from the board, slipped them on. He got up and did a little shuffling dance. Without prompting, he said something that might have been 'thanks'. Well done, Annie. And then, still dancing, he took the pawn Tim had just moved.

So when would the dreaded dean get here? We'd been waiting well over half an hour. Had he been fobbing us off, or was he delayed by the snow I should be trying to avoid? Opening the door an inch, I peered out. It was inky black out there now, of course, since the clouds had moved in. I couldn't even see my car.

To save Tim's face, I insisted that the boys eat before Tang submitted Tim to another ritual humiliation, the whole game being over in less than half an hour. They were just clearing their soup bowls when someone rapped on the door, in the Morse code Tim had used. Another boy hero, no doubt, enjoying a pre-arranged signal.

Tim dragged at the door, flushing like a schoolboy and breaking into a stammer of welcome, not to an elderly ogre, but to a man in his earlier fifties sporting one of those wide-brimmed waterproof hats. To my disappointment, he didn't wear a cloak, in which he'd have looked really striking, but a Barbour. And I was surprised he didn't even wear a dog-collar, just a fine-knit polo-neck sweater under a leather jacket.

'Dean, this is Mrs Welford, and our friend Tang.'

The dean gave a smile that lit up his whole face. I'd never seen eyes so dark a blue and so piercing. His glance round the church encompassed everything from the makeshift boudoir to my Michelin woman outdoor gear. I'd rather he'd seen me in what was now Tang's jacket, but he smiled gravely at Tang and took in the direction of the buttoning and flicked a glance at me, so maybe he'd got a fair idea of what had gone on. Possibly Tim had poured out an account of the whole incident over the phone.

'Josie,' I said shoving out a hand at the end of the giant sausage of my sleeve.

'Andy,' he responded, with what I'd describe as a professional smile, the sort I use for new customers. Andy, not Andrew. Now, that was interesting for a start. And how on earth did he contrive to have warm hands on a night like this?

'Andy, Tim's been heroic and organised all this support. And food. Would you like some? There's plenty left.' There: Mary would have been proud of me. Or was it Martha? I stirred the fragrant saucepan to demonstrate.

'Please.' He pulled up another chair to our little circle and took the bowl and spoon. 'Let me get this straight, Tim: you don't need my permission or the bishop's to go ahead with this. Not so long as you're convinced your guest is innocent.'

'Innocent of what? We don't even know what he's supposed to have done!'

I got the impression the dean didn't like

being interrupted.

'When and if you come to suspect he's guilty, you become an accessory after the fact, and might well see the inside of a jail yourself.'

Tim paled. 'But how do I know he's innocent if I can't communicate?'

'Talking to the police might help,' I said. 'But I'd go with a solicitor – someone who'd know what questions to ask.'

'And, moreover, someone who would know Tang's rights – and yours.'

I couldn't recall ever having heard anyone use the word 'moreover' in conversation. It sounded very classy. But then, I'd never met anyone as senior as a dean. Prison chaplains – oh, I could almost have written a *Rough Guide* to them. I'd met unctuous replicas of Obadiah Slope; red hot evangelicals rolling the word 'sin' round their mouths as if it were a particularly toothsome Belgian praline; ordinary decent men and women who did their best to control floods of despair with practical kindness. None of them was quite like this dean.

'Not many solicitors would be qualified for something like this, would they?' I asked. Come to think of it, I'd come across even more solicitors than chaplains, half of whom I'd have trusted no further than I could have thrown the altar.

'I know a couple who might make a decent

fist of it, if Tim wanted me to ask them.'

'We want more than "might", Andy,' I said firmly.

He turned those blue eyes on me. 'You're as convinced as Tim of Tang's innocence, are you?'

Half of me wanted to jump up and down yelling, 'Yes, yes, yes!' The other asked coolly, 'How can I be convinced of anything when we can't exchange more than two words? All I know is that I saw a very frightened boy asking for sanctuary this morning, and, like a lot of people there, I simply responded to his plight.' I gestured round the church.

'Josie's trying to find an interpreter. She's got a friend who runs a Chinese restaurant. She's asked him. Any news yet, Josie?'

'I have tried. But the only way I can communicate by mobile from here is by standing on top of the tower. I'll have to have another go from the landline back home. Unless you think that we need two people here overnight, Andy?'

'You're prepared to stay?' I couldn't decipher Andy's expression or his tone of voice.

'I'd rather sleep on my zillion spring mattress, but if you think it's necessary I'll stay.'

'Your zillion spring mattress it shall be.' Andy nodded. 'My sleeping bag's in the car.' He went up in my approval by about seventeen notches. 'And some bottles of water:

isn't your only water from a standpipe? If that freezes, we could have problems. And there are a couple of Calorgas cylinders, too. Would you mind staying just a few more minutes, Josie, while Tim and I bring everything in?'

'Not at all. In fact, since Tim's so good with Tang, I'll be the beast of burden.'

We only needed a couple of journeys. When we'd dumped the last items, Andy motioned me back into the porch. 'What do you really think?' Andy asked.

I squared my shoulders. 'I'd hate him to be turned in to police custody without adequate support. Even if he hasn't done anything, there's no saying they won't find evidence that he has. There have been miscarriages of justice before. Think of the Birmingham Six, the Guildford Four, and so on and so on.'

He shook his head, dropping his voice. 'This is out of my range, Josie.'

'I can't say it's something your average publican comes across every day.' Why did I choose such a pejorative, indeed, old-fashioned term? I usually described myself as a chef or a restaurateur. Weren't publicans usually bracketed with sinners, come to think of it? And I couldn't for the life of me recall the approved attitude to them.

'The later translations refer to publicans as tax-gatherers,' Andy observed, to my surprise.

'And if we're flummoxed, what about Tim?' I continued. 'Especially when some people who should be supporting him aren't.'

He shook his head. 'The church wardens are entitled to be anxious. The building is their legal responsibility. Yes, really.'

'So tomorrow's meeting should be interesting.'

'But I have asked them not to call the police till we've had our meeting. It'd be good to keep it low-key, and come to a joint decision when we do act.'

'I'm sure you're right. Now, unless I'm mistaken that's snow. I'll just say goodnight to the kids and then I'll head off home.'

'Back to your zillion springs,' he agreed.

Chapter Four

Although no bed was ever involved, I often invited Nick Thomas, my lodger and guardian extraordinaire to the Gay children, to breakfast. He'd suffered from a stomach ulcer for years, but never quite got the knack of eating regularly and sensibly. Since I'd put myself in charge of as much of his diet as I could control, he'd been able to reduce his medication and his cholesterol and blood pressure had dropped convincingly.

I put it down to the porridge I was serving this morning.

'If only it didn't look so grey and dreary,' he sighed, taking a reluctant mouthful.

Since his at least had a swirl of maple syrup on it, I wilfully misunderstood, looking at the dismal sky. 'You want more snow? I know slush is horrible but for a time last night I was afraid we might be snowed in.'

He regarded me balefully, but nodded. 'The local radio people say the motorways further east are bad. It might be a work from home day today: I've got a forest of paperwork to do and a virtual forest of emails to deal with.'

I smiled at his pale joke. Everything about Nick was pallid. He looked a bit better since I'd confiscated all his beige and greeny-yellowy clothes for a charity appeal and made him replace them with tones of blue, even if he did insist on the grey end of the spectrum. But even his new open-air life had done little more than make his white cheeks sallow, though it had bleached his hair to a salt and pepper with a hint of French mustard.

'Do you have much to do with meat processing plants?' I asked bluntly.

'There's meat processing and meat processing.' He put down his spoon with a suspiciously final air, and reached for the toast, only to find it was wholemeal. 'So you mean stripping all the meat off the bones, or the actual cooking?'

'I've no idea. It's just a hunch of mine – the sort of thing you chew away at in the wee small hours. During morning service at St Jude's we had an unexpected visitor.' I explained.

'Chinese labourer? I don't like the sound of that, Josie.'

'Meaning?'

'If he doesn't speak English he could be an illegal. Illegal immigrant,' he corrected himself, with one word returning Tang to the human race. 'Subject to all sorts of bother if the police get hold of him. Like deportation. And the people smugglers who got him into the country won't like that, because it means they won't get their evil paws on the money they'll have charged him for his journey.' He spread some cholesterol-reducing margarine. 'Actually, I'm surprised the police have let him get away with it.'

'Er – they don't actually know about him yet. Church politics, Nick. Some say he should be allowed to stay, some insist he go. We can't communicate with him to find out what he has or hasn't done.'

'Has, if you ask me. Like simply being here. He may have committed some other low-grade crime that won't bring the police out anyway – which explains why they haven't got the place surrounded with a team of negotiators in place – but if they get him on a plate they'll deal with it. Or maybe he's being framed for something. Whichever it is, you've got a bit of a problem. There's no such thing as sanctuary, not any more. Not as a legal concept, anyway.'

'When was it abolished?' I was ready to write to as many MPs as I could think of to protest.

'Must have been back in...' he scratched his head, '–oh, something like 1534, whenever the Reformation was.'

'But I thought – wasn't there some case of a Sri Lankan asking for sanctuary, back in the Nineties?'

'He got it too. But that was probably because the police didn't want to outrage public opinion by raiding a church. It didn't stop them a couple of years back from breaking into a Black Country mosque, though, did it, to get hold of a little Muslim family? Sending the family to Germany for some reason, as I recall.'

We sucked our teeth and shook our heads, liberal Derby and Joan both craving justice and marmalade, which I had deliberately run out of, my final few pounds being extremely stubborn. I passed good-for-the-heart bananas.

'Seem a long time ago, a long way away, the Midlands, don't they?' he observed, reminding me of Eeyore, wanting to return to look for his tail.

I spouted a few clichés about never going back, and prepared to load the dishwasher, taking his plate from under his nose. Like all the restaurant vegetable peelings, the banana skins went into my green bucket. I had enough land to grow a handful of organic herbs and vegetables and everything compostable went into one of my converters.

Nick might be working from home today; I certainly wasn't. On Mondays we offered cold lunch only, and no dinners, so we didn't have a major meeting about menus and specials, nor did I have to go and shop. Not that I did every day anyway, since I could leave everything to Robin and his cousin Pix. Could, but usually didn't. I tried to be a very hands-on boss. Although we now had a couple of lads Robin would keep referring to as the scullions, we all mucked in with even the end-of-session scrubbing down.

'Why were you asking about food processing plants, by the way?' Nick asked, making me jump. I hadn't realised he was still in the room.

'A couple of things. The first was the smell of the man. It really was stomach-churning.'

'And that's from someone who can joint ripe game!'

'I wash afterwards. And change my

59

clothes. The second – this was weird, Nick – was his reaction to chicken. One of the congregation brought him this lovely plate of chicken breast, and damn me if he didn't literally throw it down in front of her.'

'What about the rest?'

'That went down double-quick, as if he was starving. But he wasn't starving enough to touch perfectly good free-range chook. So I was wondering, you see, if he might have had something to do with poultry that wasn't hand reared in a back garden pen.'

'So it's not just the official, regularly inspected places you want me to look at? It's ones that are just rumours between me and my Trading Standards mates?'

'Exactly! Oh, why weren't you here yesterday?' It was meant to be a purely rhetorical question, but he managed a smile.

'Because I was busy watching West Brom beat Blues. Elly had got tickets. To please me!'

I squeezed his arm. 'You'll get there yet. I know you will.'

He swallowed a couple of times. 'Meanwhile, the less publicity this Tang case gets the better, I'd say. People like a bit of Law and Order, and if it gets out that the church is going easy on an illegal immigrant the story'll get bigger and bigger. And the bigger it gets, the more inevitable it is that the police will be involved. And the harder for the police to do what they'd like, and get him to turn Queen's Evidence against the gang masters and people smugglers. They'd much rather give one lad witness protection and nail a whole gang than have to make a very public show of deporting him, which the press will no doubt be howling for, and letting the main men escape scot-free.'

I nodded sombrely. 'The trouble is, the news is out already. Half the village seemed to be donating clothing and stuff yesterday.'

'I'll bet the other half are already dipping their pens into venom. I wouldn't be too high profile if I were you – not after last year. I wouldn't want you to be the next woman tarred and feathered.'

Mindful of his advice, which was often good, when I called in at the village shop on my way to St Jude's, I carefully bought nothing unusual in the way of provisions and didn't raise the topic of Tang. Since everyone was talking about someone's missing dog, I could probably have bought the Great Wall of China and no one would have remarked on it.

'It'll be them Gyppos,' someone was saying.

I bit my lip. I hadn't been meant to hear, and as far as I knew no one down here suspected my Romany roots, but I hated that sort of assumption. Only Nick's advice to maintain a low profile made me button my lip. Still wondering whether I was simply being supine, I loaded my bag.

'Or else one of them bogus asylum seekers. My friend down Plymouth way lost everything in her garden shed last week. One of them foreigners.'

This time I couldn't resist chipping in. 'Back in Birmingham most of the petty crime seemed to be committed by people feeding their drugs habit. I suppose...' There were some pretty rough parts of Plymouth, probably with the same social issues.

But my hint was ignored. The other customers were well into the rights and wrongs of foreigners equally taking our jobs and living off our social security. My own status as an incomer was pretty tenuous, and like Nick I'd seen what they could do to women they disapproved of. Just at the moment it seemed better to help Tang than to make a general point. But that might have been cowardice.

The straggle that was Abbot's Duncombe was completely inert as I drove through. There was no sign of anyone by the church either, but I parked neatly between Andy's Ford and Tim's Ka. Noting with irritation that the black sack of discarded clothes still lolled in a corner of the porch, I did the silly SOS knock to be admitted by Andy, flourishing without embarrassment a battery shaver with which he attacked a crop of designer stubble. Today he sported a clerical shirt in a flattering dove grey. One day I'd ask Tim what, if anything, dictated the colour. He of course wore perpetual black, reminding me, now I came to think of it, of a latter-day Hamlet in a long skirt.

In hushed tones, as if he were an invalid, I asked about Tang.

Andy replied in kind. 'He had a good night. Better than me.' Raising his voice as he grinned, he added, 'I envied you your mattress with the zillion pocketed springs, believe me.'

Anyone else, and I'd have said, 'Come and join me tonight.' But he wasn't just a clergyman, he was a senior clergyman, and some primitive part of me wanted to tug my forelock or curtsey. An even more primitive part was quite in favour of making the offer: bright sunlight made him look remarkably personable.

'What about poor Tim? I wish I could tell him the right thing to do.'

'He's supposed to be the one offering you spiritual guidance,' Andy objected, amused.

'I'm sure he will one day. And it'll be good, too. But calling himself Father when he's – what? Thirty?' I shook my head. 'It brings half the villagers out in a rash, same as me when I come across those teenage

Mormons who call themselves Elders!'

'You think wisdom can only come with age?'

'Sometimes I think rank stupidity comes with age. Think Malins and Corbishley.' There were footsteps and voices in the porch. 'And here right on cue they come.'

'Tim! Your guests are here! You wretch,' I added, 'leaving that sack of stinking clothes where everyone can fall over it!'

'Sorry. I'll shift it later – promise!' he called over his shoulder as he flung open the door as they announced their presence. No "secret" knock for them!

'What a good idea to have your meeting here, Andy,' I continued in a much lower voice.

'That was Tim's. Having to keep an eye on Tang as well as having meetings meant spreading himself rather thin.'

'The poor kid has to do that anyway, running five churches. And it's not just churchgoers that claim his time: all the villagers use him as a social worker. And that's five villages, remember.'

'You're preaching to the converted, Josie! Overworked and underpaid. And living in a tied house everyone regards as an extension of the village hall. Blamed for everything from child abuse to the Decline in Moral Standards, but howled down for dropping the mildest hint that parents should make some token attendance at church if they want their child baptised. And if they want a church wedding themselves, of course.'

'And if priests are married they're neglecting church duties and if they're not they're gay. OK, Andy, I get the point. I'm a fan of Tim's. I was a fan of Sue, his predecessor, until she made a couple of really bad mistakes. And I believe she got promoted as a result,' I added more bitterly than I meant.

'I'm sorry if my colleague got it wrong. But I don't know the case. I was wrestling with problems in London at the time. I've only been here five minutes. I haven't even finished unpacking my books yet.'

I wasn't entirely happy with the conversation, either side of it, actually. I shouldn't have raised the spectre of Sue, and he seemed remarkably quick to distance himself from any wrongdoing. What we should have been doing was making ourselves a team to face Corbishley and Malins, both of whom had studiously ignored all of us as they entered the church and were now ostentatiously kneeling at the altar rail, deep in prayer. Who was it Christ bollocked for praying in public?

'Pair of Pharisees,' Andy muttered, as if in response to my mental question. That was the second time he'd done that.

Tony had done it all the time, but we'd had practice.

I braced my shoulders to show I was ready for action. 'Shall I make some coffee?'

'There's no reason why you should always be the one to brew up. I can boil a kettle pretty well. Tim and I filled the tea-urn from the standpipe a while ago. And we managed breakfast, thanks to someone's toaster.'

'Golly, you didn't use that old thing? One Noah threw out of the Ark? I thought it was an offering from those two to solve the problem in one fell swoop by setting the place on fire!'

I followed him into the kitchen, gathering up mugs to wash them outside. 'Hunt out some biscuits, will you? A few always sweeten a meeting. And some of that treacle tart.'

'Three men into one treacle tart equals none for anyone else, I'm afraid.'

'I'd better make another one then.' Better still, get one of the lads to. Pix was an angel with desserts. 'Or just wait and see what the other women come up with. One of them does a lemon drizzle cake to die for. Even looking at it gets me a WeightWatchers' fine!'

I hadn't been invited to the meeting, but there was nothing to stop me playing chess with Tang and listening intently to the arguments. It meant I would inevitably lose, of course, whereas thanks to Tony, I might have given him a bit more of a game than

Tim. OK, not much more.

By the time we settled, Andy had already opened the meeting, and had invited Tim to explain his actions. Every time one of the wardens attempted to interrupt, he was chaired firmly into place.

Then it was Corbishley's turn. I've no idea what his background was, but he was a pedant, in the pejorative sense. The first point he made was the one Nick had put to me earlier – that in law there was no such thing as sanctuary, the concept having been abolished by Henry VIII. Actually, I'd have said that was pretty irrefutable, and if only he'd had the sense to shut up he'd have had my reluctant vote. But he got more and more involved with detail.

'Now, technically the young man should hold the knocker on the front door to claim – you may have seen those still extant at Durham and on St Gregory's, Norwich. Or he should sit not in the sanctuary chair, but a frith-stool.'

'What's one of those?' Tim put in, sounding genuinely interested.

'St Jude's doesn't have one so you don't need to know,' Malins snapped. 'Furthermore, if you do want to keep him on church land, he doesn't have to stay within the church itself. He's allowed to roam the precincts.'

I thought I sniffed a bit of slick Internet

research here.

'You mean he's free to walk round the graveyard – to get some fresh air? Excellent,' Tim said.

'In fact, there's no reason for him to be in the church at all,' Corbishley declared, 'where we really have so few facilities–'

'Fewer than in the graveyard?' Andy asked dryly.

'We could rig up a perfectly capacious tent. Or maybe get a caravan–'

'–Through the lychgate? My dear sir, that really would be like trying to get a camel through the eye of a needle,' Andy drawled, in a tone designed to irritate the socks off anyone unfortunate enough to be on the receiving end. 'But I'm afraid I can't follow your logic. Why is it acceptable to protect Tang outside, in the cold and the wet, but not inside, in the cold and the dry?'

'It may have escaped your notice, Dean, that this is an historic building, untouched for centuries. It should be preserved.'

Untouched? What about all the improvements perpetrated by the Victorians? I wanted to yell my objection but Andy was already there.

'Like the blood and custard tiles in the sanctuary itself? Come, Mr Malins, you know as well as I do that they're an abomination in the face of – if not the Lord, then at least any decent church architect. You must do better than that.'

'I don't need to. As church wardens, Mr Corbishley and I have undertaken to do all in our power to preserve the fabric of this ancient establishment. It is a trust that we have kept for years. Who do you think refurbished the place after the fire? Who cares for the graveyard? Who maintains everything about St Jude's?' He spoke with what I was sure was genuine passion. 'In our view, allowing such a hallowed place to turn into a cross between a soup kitchen and a kindergarten is detrimental and we can put a stop to it.'

I could imagine Tim's throat in full bobble. 'And how do you propose to do that?'

'We shall certainly see the bishop,' Malins informed him. 'And we shall tell the media what we're doing. You'll see who the public support.'

Tim's voice again, getting higher and more strained: 'It isn't a matter of public support or even the bishop's support. It's a matter of doing God's will.'

'As interpreted by a pimply youth who calls himself Father and dresses like a Catholic priest? I don't think so! And nor will others.' I hadn't realised that there was a faction against young Tim. If he could irritate someone like me who found so much to like in him, it was hardly surprising that he'd got up hierarchical noses. But this seemed serious – serious enough to put another young man's life at risk. Malins' voice rose in proportion with his anger.

'Mr Malins!' Andy kept calm but even from where I sat I could hear the steel in his rebuke.

'Ask him why there's no congregation worth speaking of! Ask him what's happened to the choir. Ask him why there's been a mass exodus to other churches. Ask him why we may have to deconsecrate some of the churches in the benefice! He can't lead his flock, all he can do is bleat at them in the most tedious of sermons. He's a waste of space!'

There was a terrible silence. Tang's hand hovered in mid-air, as if he didn't dare break the silence by so much as a click of plastic on wood. What did he make of it? It must be like being a small child whose parents were having a row: he didn't know the words, but the sounds were angry and threatening. I took his spare hand, squeezed it reassuringly, and managed a smile. If anyone could tear holes in that tissue of prejudice, Andy could.

Surely.

'We are not discussing the performance or otherwise of your parish priest, gentlemen. And if we were, I would not listen to you until you could moderate your language and demonstrate the truth of what you are saying.'

Good on you!

'Meanwhile, let us return to the question before us: what do we do with the young man who has availed himself of the age old *custom* of sanctuary?'

'We keep him here until we can hear from his lips what he has – or hasn't – done!'

'That may take some time, Tim, but it's the option I personally favour. Then, if it's clear he has deliberately committed a crime, we must insist he hands himself over to the police. The Church has never been in the business of protecting malefactors. What we need is an interpreter.'

'Mrs Welford has a contact–' Tim began.

'One of her fancy men? Surely we can do better than that,' Malins sneered.

Andy's turn. 'And would your choice be honest, trustworthy and discreet?'

'Would Josie Welford's paramour be?'

Tang was peering at my face like a puppy who knows his owner is upset. I smiled, determined to convince him that I wasn't both furiously angry and deeply hurt.

'Josie is a good woman!' came Tim's furious voice.

'More like the woman of Samaria, if you ask me!'

Andy's voice again. 'And it was she, and not Nicodemus, who listened to Christ's

71

words and spread the good news.'

'Oh, good news isn't the only thing Josie puts around, believe me!'

Many years ago, I had cursed Nick Thomas. It was a Romany curse, ill-wishing him for sending my Tony down for the last time. Life hadn't exactly been kind to Nick himself since then, and I often lay awake wondering to what extent I'd been responsible for his suffering. That was one of the factors that stopped me stepping forward now, and repeating the performance. The other was the company – visible and Invisible. Should I simply step into their circle and see what effect that had on my accusers, or let the other men defend me?

Andy spoke very sternly. 'I will not listen to you! You have denigrated the skills of your priest, and now you assassinate the character of a good friend to this congregation. Leave this place immediately. And before you present yourself for Communion again, study the advice in the Prayer Book. Good day to you, gentlemen.'

There was the sound of chairs being pushed back.

'You haven't heard the last of this, young man!' Corbishley's threat came as a hiss. It was transformed into a gasp as he strode out of the Lady Chapel and realised that Tang was not alone.

Would he offer an apology? He turned on his heel and approached us as if he might. But as he came within range, he leaned forward and, his spittle flying on to my face, declared, 'Listeners never hear any good of themselves – do they?'

Quite inadvertently, as I flinched, I turned the other cheek. But I said, as quietly as I could, 'And I suppose you are fitted to throw the first stone?'

I suppose it was better manners than cursing. But it turned him a purplish-red, and I was afraid for a moment he would have a heart attack. As for Malins, he went greenish grey.

I didn't let my gaze drop.

Tony had instilled into me that in the face of criticism or hostility I should never betray my feelings. I was to remain calm, my face impassive, trying not to let my breathing speed up. Keeping the outward and visible under control, he said, would help with the inward and private. I'd used the technique with success time and time again during police questioning or in the witness box. I never thought I'd have to use it in circumstances like this.

The church wardens gave one more apoplectic glare apiece and stomped off. After the slam of the heavy door, you could feel the silence.

There was a sudden scurry.

Tim had gone. And where was Tang? Andy was turning tail and dragging open the church door, as fast as he could. I followed, my adrenaline taking longer to flow but at last unlocking torpid limbs.

Tim brought Tang down in a rugby tackle just inside the lychgate. Andy gathered them both up, propelling them back towards me to be shooed back inside and cosseted.

'He knows he's got us into some sort of trouble,' I said, holding him tightly and patting his back. All I could feel was bones. 'You should have seen him while Corbishley and Malins were ranting.'

Tim might have been grinding his teeth, he looked so angry. As for Andy, he had disappeared into the kitchen, and soon emerged with mugs, which he parked on a chair. Nodding almost apologetically, he withdrew to the Lady Chapel.

Still holding Tang, I stretched out an arm to include Tim. I ached with pity for him. During his tenure as priest in charge, he'd done his very best with limited experience and probably sketchy support, and now he'd got that sort of criticism.

As for me, I'd never had a best to do as far as men were concerned. I'd embraced the menopause as an opportunity to enjoy a side of life denied me for thirty-odd years. I saw my no strings sex as simply a source of pleasure, and while I'd never made a song and dance about my choice, had never made any particular effort to keep it quiet. Now it had blown back into my face. I must learn to live with it.

Tim, on the other hand, had learned that in some people's eyes he had failed not in his career, but in his calling. Tony would have told him he'd had a learning experience (wherever had the old devil picked up such lingo?) and that he was young enough to benefit from it.

As for Tang, he had done his best to save us from further internecine strife, even at the risk of his own life: he was the hero of the moment and somehow I must tell him so. Pushing away from them, I embarked on a complicated little mime Marcel Marceau would have applauded, telling him he was kind, but mustn't do it again. How much did he take in? He was as inscrutable as any clichéd Chinaman.

Andy came back into the nave as we were in the middle of our group hug. He might have been about to join us, but there was another knock at the door. This time it was Annie, who had somehow laid hands on a huge quantity of paper and fat felt pens and what looked like a Chinese-English dictionary.

'I don't know whether it's the right sort of Chinese,' she apologised, 'but it's the best Taunton Oxfam can do. The other thing is, perhaps he can draw pictures to convey what made him come here.'

They withdrew to what had become Tang's corner, close to both the altar and the Calorgas heater.

'Do you think we could switch off the wall-heaters to save the church some money?' Tim ventured. Did he think that would appease the church wardens?

'It won't be the church paying: it'll be me,' I said. 'And I like my warmth, thanks very much.'

'You're being very generous,' Andy began. His throat moved as convulsively as Tim's. This wasn't going to be an easy five minutes for either of us, was it?

'It seems to me that my being here isn't helping Tang's cause,' I said briskly. 'If I go back to the White Hart, I shall be able to give Nigel Ho another shout. Now, in that little kitchen you'll find there's pasta sauce for an army, and plenty of pasta. Salad to go with it – I've already washed it, so there's no need to venture out again – and a jar of dressing. There's cheese and fresh bread for afters.' It was some of the local cheese for which the White Hart was justly renowned, but let them discover the quality for themselves. 'And you could open a market stall with all the fruit you've acquired. I wasn't sure about wine? In church?' I held up a corkscrew by way of temptation.

76

Andy took the corkscrew from my hand and his cue from my neutral tone. 'Bring it on!' He added, *sotto voce*, 'You're not going to let a couple of unpleasant old men get to you?'

'On the contrary,' I said, 'I shall be trying to find out exactly why something I said got to them.'

Chapter Five

Half of me wanted to hurtle into Taunton to check the local paper for references to Malins and Corbishley. But reason told me that if they had done anything I could get an angle on, they wouldn't have gone public with it. If they had, they wouldn't still be pillars of the church, rigid with respectability. The other half was reminded, by the sight of all the walkers consuming lunchtime bar snacks, the only food on offer on Mondays, that I hadn't had my constitutional for a couple of days. Obviously I'd been otherwise engaged yesterday, and Saturdays were now so busy that all three of us chefs worked throughout the day to prepare for the hordes descending on the new dining room, once the foetid snug.

As part of the refurbishments, I had

emptied an old store room, known locally as the landlord's sheep shagging den, and refurnished it as a new snug for the regulars, complete with genuine old furniture from a country inn newly become a chic holiday residence used perhaps three weeks a year. The same fate would almost certainly have befallen the White Hart had I not stepped in. My changes might not have pleased all the locals, but at least, once their excruciatingly painful old settles were *in situ*, some were grudgingly prepared to admit that a clean, warm bar, serving a wide range of locally grown food, was better than no pub at all.

I had had their old haunt completely gutted, and slung out the cast iron and plastic furniture, too tatty even to keep for use in the beer garden. I replaced it with even older, but beautiful, serviceable, elegant furniture – a couple of George II tables, for instance, which had been ridiculously cheap just because they were the wrong George. The result was a gratifying influx of older clients, the sort who came on time, chose fine wines, and left quietly at a sensible hour. To the bemusement of the old codgers, their new territory was rapidly being colonised by a highly profitable wine bar clientele. But not even for all their crisp tenners and the pleasure of their televisual faces would I apply for a late licence: my reluctant neighbours deserved to sleep at night. As did the children in what had once been B and B rooms. And me, come to think of it.

As the bar emptied, I resolved to take a walk, despite the vicious wind. A static week always saw the scales creeping up again, and that wasn't part of my plan at all. Since Nick was disinclined to exercise without company, I popped up to his room and told him to get his boots too. He hushed me with an admonitory finger.

'Come and look at this – quick!' he hissed, pointing at the television.

I sat heavily beside him.

There was St Jude's, slap in the middle of the regional lunchtime news.

Tim and Andy stood beside a pretty but frozen-looking reporter, the shot framed by the lychgate.

'Father Martin, many of your parishioners are up in arms about your decision to harbour an illegal immigrant accused of a serious crime–'

Andy stepped in. 'You are misinformed. There is no evidence that Mr Tang is an illegal immigrant or that he has committed any crime whatsoever.'

'But, Father Martin, it's clear that your parishioners don't approve of what you're doing.'

Tim said, 'For every parishioner who has

doubts, there is another who supports me. You only have to look inside the church–'

Which you won't let us do!'

'–to see how much has been done to make our visitor feel comfortable,' Andy cut in again suavely. 'Father Martin has the absolute support of the senior clergy in the diocese in offering our hospitality to this unfortunate young man. Thank you.' He smiled with finality, and withdrew into the churchyard, tucking his arm into Tim's as if companionably, but in actual fact more or less dragging him, I suspected.

Unfortunately his handsome face was replaced by Geoffrey Malins' grim facial contours. Presumably time ran out, for we were returned to the studio almost at once. Back in the studio, the newscaster promised updates in the early evening slot.

'Just what we needed,' Nick said.

I hadn't realised he intended to be part of the support team, but wouldn't deter him by pointing this out.

'No doubt it'll hit all the national networks tonight. And then the newspapers. Well, if he is here illegally, and the people smugglers who brought him here didn't know where he was before, they'll know now. Not good, Josie. Get him to give himself up now. Not that being in custody will guarantee his safety, as I'm sure you know.'

On impulse I asked, 'Would you come

with me to St Jude's and discuss it with them?'

'Glad to. We could always walk there?'

'Bit of a step. And maybe this is urgent?'

He nodded, pulling himself to his feet and shrugging on his windproof. He jiggled his car keys. 'Yours or mine?'

A voice came from below. 'Josie – you've got a visitor!'

'OK, Robin – I'm on my way!' Business, presumably: my friends used the back door, which led to my apartment. So why couldn't Robin deal with him? Mildly irritated, I ran down to investigate.

And found myself face to face with a large bunch of flowers. William Corbishley was on the far side.

'Mrs Welford. Josie. You have every right to throw me out and these with me. What we – what *I* – said and did this morning was outrageous. Unforgivable. I can't expect you to forgive or forget, but I hope you will. I'm very sorry.'

There was a long pause. I could hear Nick's breathing behind me. The colour pumped in Corbishley's face. He'd made an effort that was probably putting his heart at risk.

I ought to say or do something.

Make 'em laugh; make 'em cry; but make 'em wait! Not a Tony original, I knew. But it might have been.

I didn't take the flowers. 'You might have angered and insulted me,' I began, 'but you did it in spades to Father Martin. He is your parish priest, Mr Corbishley – a man of the cloth, who deserves your love and respect.'

His colour deepened alarmingly.

Hoping he wouldn't have an attack and die on my premises, I nonetheless continued. 'He may not be the greatest preacher in the world, but that will come with time. He may be tactless, sometimes, but that's because he's young and has high ideals. People of our generation should support him, assist him. If we criticise, it must be kindly, face to face, in private – never, ever, viciously behind his back, and especially not in public.' I paused for breath. 'Have you any idea how dangerous going to the media may be?'

'It's – it's–'

'Now,' I said, smiling for the first time, but with nothing like friendship, 'I'm quite prepared to accept your apology, but the place for those flowers is St Jude's.' For some reason he snorted, but I pressed on, overriding whatever he'd meant to say. 'Why don't you go along and make your peace with Father Martin and the dean? Mr Thomas and I will be along in a few minutes.'

I backed him out of the door, closing it quietly, and turned to Nick. 'Just leave me on my own a few moments, will you? I want to shout and swear and kick and–'

'You'd do better to get your Barbour and boots: the media aren't going to go away, you know.'

We opted for Nick's 4x4, not a vehicle I would have chosen myself, but useful, I had to concede, for his job, which involved travelling lanes best described as tracks, and tracks best described as traces. He always drove well, much better than I, though surprisingly fast in lanes I tended to creep through. At last he pulled up about a mile from St Jude's.

He broke his silence. 'Let's take that footpath that skirts the village and brings us to the back of the graveyard. I always like seeing before we're seen.'

Even as we creaked our way over a stile about an inch too high for my legs, a BBC van shot past us. I allowed myself a short sharp swear-word. I'm sure Tony, who had wholeheartedly disapproved of foul language, in spite, or possibly because, of spending so much time in an environment where it was more or less compulsory, would have forgiven me. Because I employed young people, and because of the kids now living on the premises, I tried to maintain a no-swearing policy in the pub. It surprised a lot of people, it being generally thought that good chefs can't boil an egg without seasoning it with the F word. It was probably a waste of effort, because even our sheltered village kids now used it as freely as manufacturers put salt in their crisps.

'You handled that Corbishley situation very well,' he conceded, helping me down.

'Thanks. But maybe I should have been more gracious, more accommodating.'

'What specifically did he have to apologise for?'

'Calling me a whore – though he didn't actually use that word, as I recall. But that's how he thinks of me.' I wished I could manage more than a mutter, but it was the first time we'd ever spoken openly about sex in any context. It had been a tacit agreement that we were strictly friends. OK, more a tacit acceptance on his part of my decision.

'You're a free agent, Josie. You can do what you like, when you like and with whom you like. Same as I can.'

I was intrigued. What was he about to confess? He had plenty of opportunity to meet women, his job taking him all over southern England, with lots of overnight stops. If he was courting, I'd have to take him in hand – spruce him up even more.

Meanwhile I continued uncontroversially, 'So do you think Tim Martin will accept the flowers and the apology?'

'I don't know, Josie. I certainly don't see how a vicar can work effectively knowing his church wardens respect him so very little. After a while there'll have to be a quiet resignation on grounds of health or some-thing.'

'You think the *wardens* will go? Not Tim?'

'The church isn't into conflict, is it? First I see Tim mysteriously transferred to a new parish, probably something inner-city, with lots of "challenges". But they can't keep Malins and Corbishley in place, and risk having them treat a new incumbent the same.'

I nodded, but came to a sharp halt. 'Wow! It's a good job you brought us this way, Nick: look at that lot!'

Vans, satellite dishes, a seethe of unsuitably dressed young women. All whippet thin, no doubt.

Nick permitted himself a word or two I rather envied. 'Bloody circus,' he concluded.

'And it's all Malins' and Corbishley's doing,' I added. 'I wish I'd told him to stick his flowers where the sun doesn't shine.'

'You were both firm and gracious,' he insisted. Before I could argue he set off downhill from our vantage point, the only problem being the much bigger, steeper hill that awaited us.

As I panted to catch up with him, he said, 'Imagine deciding to put a church up here. All the building materials to be dragged up. Every last bit of wood and stone.'

'And imagine how many people have died down in the village because of the graves polluting their water supply. Shades of Haworth.'

Our entry into the graveyard and then the church did not go unnoticed, of course. Even as I was bashing the Morse knocks on the door, familiar faces were charging through the lychgate. Not just familiar from the TV set, familiar as regular patrons of the White Hart. It was a good job it was Monday, or the dining room would have been heaving with them that evening, all asking questions I had no intention of answering, despite their usual extravagant choices of food and wine. Robin was rostered for the bar tonight: I'd prime him to play mum.

There was no sign of Malins, Corbishley or any flowers. Andy looked as if he might have been trying to take a nap, while Tang and Tim played another game of chess. There was a residual smell of food; unwashed plates lay in a neat heap by the door. I tutted. Surely there'd been enough water in the urn to wash them?

Deduction or accusation? 'No Annie?'

'Hospital appointment. She didn't want to go but since she'd waited three months we made her,' Tim said, sacrificing a pawn to give the information.

'That's a pity. She seemed to be able to communicate better than anyone else and Nick here needs to talk to Tang. Nick Thomas, Andy – sorry, I've forgotten your surname. And are you known by it, or by the name of your diocese?'

'That's for bishops,' he smiled. 'Andy Braithwaite. But Andy's quite enough. Hello, Nick.'

As the men shook hands, I added, 'Nick – he's one of the St Faith and St Lawrence bell-ringers – was in the police force and now works for the Food Standards Agency. He's got a take on Tang you ought to hear, and we all need to understand.'

Tim sprang to his feet. 'I know what he'll say! He'll say we should hand him over to the police. He's bound to!' He ended on something perilously like a sob.

Nick turned. 'Hi, Father Martin.' He shook his hand firmly, laying the left on top to maintain the contact. 'I'm afraid you're right. But not because I believe in Law and Order at all costs. It's because of the folk who are after him. Probably,' he conceded. He repeated what he'd said to me. 'And although one can't guarantee his safety in custody, I suspect he'll be a lot safer than here.'

Andy nodded. Possibly with relief at being spared another night camping out.

Nick pressed on. 'At the very least talk to the police: someone senior. I'm surprised they're not here yet.'

'What good will it do when they do come? After all, it's with Tang they have to talk, not us,' Tim said. 'If they find an interpreter who can say he'd be honest and trustworthy? That's why Josie was trying to get hold of her contact.'

'To be honest, now that the media have broken the story I don't think you've got any time to play with. You need to get him into a safe house. Now.'

'Then we'd have to get him out of here first,' I said.

'But how?' Tim continued. 'He's liable to arrest the moment he leaves hallowed ground.'

'I'd offer my own church,' Andy smiled, 'but unless he can fly...'

'Josie's got a helicopter licence,' Tim said.

I tried to look diffident and modest; mentally I was trying to work out the logistics of getting to Exeter Airport, borrowing a chopper, finding somewhere to land out of reach of the police, landing on the Deanery lawn and other Loony Tunes adventures. All with poor night vision, of course. Penelope Pitstop? More Josie Jetlag.

'It sounds to me as if even arrest is safer than staying,' I said firmly.

Nick nodded with fervour. 'While some people may consider the police brutal,' he insisted, 'believe me, they are mere puny beginners compared with the snakehead gangs we associate with bringing in illegal workers. And who are not bound by PACE, by Health and Safety at Work Acts and a fundamental belief in *Habeas Corpus*.'

I raised my eyebrows, which Tony used to say were the most expressive part of my face.

Tim turned on him passionately. 'So what do we do? Betray his trust believing that it's the best option? He may never forgive us. Never forgive God.'

'I think God can be relied on to forgive him,' Andy said, putting a kindly arm round his shoulder. 'How soon do you think they'll track him down, Nick?'

'They're probably on to it now. Both the police and the folk who brought him here, who, incidentally, probably have agents in the police, possibly the Home Office. These people make the Mafia look like enthusiastic amateurs, Andy. Even if they didn't know before, from the moment the media carried the story – "Illegal migrant in sanctuary bid" – his death warrant will have been written and ready for delivery.' I'd never known Nick so passionate, so eloquent. 'You have to persuade him to give himself up. And also convince the police of the seriousness of the situation. I'll try to do that,' he added, 'though whether they'll take kindly to a retired officer from a metropolitan force telling them what's what, I very much doubt.'

Tim was literally wringing his hands. Tang looked from face to face like a dog awaiting the vet's final visit. Faces that had been kind, loving even, were now clouded with concern. They boded no good.

Andy looked from one to the other, with a long appraising stare at Nick, when he thought Nick wasn't looking. Then he turned his eyes to me.

I didn't submit to inspection, not even from deans, so I asked, 'Did you have a visit from the church wardens just before we arrived?'

He looked satisfactorily taken aback. 'Should we have done?'

'Corbishley turned up on my doorstep with enough flowers for a funeral.' On reflection I wished I hadn't used that image. I wrinkled my nose: Andy nodded as if he understood. 'I told him to bring them here and ask Tim's forgiveness.'

'Did you give him yours?'

'More or less. But it came at a price – I gave him an earbashing. I told him the church needed the flowers, though.'

Did he stop himself saying something? I stepped backwards into the kitchen. 'Andy, do you think we can shift him?'

'I wish I knew. It all depends on Tim, who's taking an idealistic or quixotic stance, according to your view. I'll work on him. But he may see it as a desperate attempt on my part to sleep in my own bed!'

'Couldn't we get one of the younger men

in the parish to take your place?'

'Find one, Josie! What's the average age of the congregation?'

'Point taken. Look, Tim seems to be listening to Nick. He's very good in senior officer to rookie mode, isn't he? He might do better if we keep a low profile. Have you been up the tower yet?' I asked. 'No? Step this way. No, after you,' I said, thinking about ladders and remembering that I was wearing a skirt. 'The door opens very easily.'

We looked down on the media mob, shielded from their gaze by the thickness of the castellation.

'God's own country,' he said. 'All this lushness – so different from Dartmoor.'

'Dartmoor's granite, isn't it? And Exmoor sandstone?'

He looked almost startled. 'Is that why they have such deep lanes? They've been sort of cut into the earth?'

'I suppose so. By countless generations of farmers. It's a very old landscape. *Where every prospect pleases,*' I suggested, *'and only man is vile.'*

'The trouble is, nature needs help from man, no matter how vile, to look like this. And I never really buy the vileness of man theory. I like people too much, that's the trouble.'

Mine too. But at the moment, lest it remind him of Corbishley's view of me, I'd

91

just keep quiet about it.

We stayed where we were a few minutes longer in companionable silence, and then turned as one for the ladder.

When we got down, Nick was sitting beside Tang, sheets of paper on his lap and some of Annie's felt pens in his hand. A peer over his shoulder showed me storybook chickens and people chasing them, Prince Philip-type slitty-eyed caricatures to be precise. One had a kind smile. Tang, presumably. One, hiding behind a stone, had a very nasty expression. In the next picture, the Tang character was running hell for leather, pursued by the nasty one. Picture three was Tang in a church, with both policemen and the nasty one lurking behind headstones. The nasty one had a knife. The picture sequence involved a great deal of animated gesturing from Nick, whose histrionic talents I'd never even guessed at. He'd given the police big kind smiles. The pursuing Chinese looked positively evil. Nick gestured throat-cutting.

Tang nodded, but didn't look convinced.

In the next picture, the bad man was handcuffed, the picture of impotent rage.

Another nod.

Nick drew again, Tang and a policeman together, both smiling.

Yes? Would he bite?

For answer, Tang threw himself into Tim's

arms, sobbing a very decided negative.

'You see: we can't betray him!' Tim declared. 'Whatever the consequences.'

Chapter Six

Leaving Andy behind to try to reason with Tim, Nick and I scuttled back over the hills to the car, easily outstripping, despite our middle-aged lungs and legs, the last pursuing media kids – though that might have had something to do with the respective styles of our footwear and theirs. We even had just enough breath to agree, as Nick fired the 4x4 into action, that despite Tang's obvious reluctance – OK, palpable terror – Nick must talk to the police. Since we couldn't get a signal on either of our mobiles, we passed the time in pointless debate about whether we should simply ask for the duty CID inspector or use our limited inside knowledge.

It was a good job the police were waiting for us at the White Hart.

Actually, it wasn't 'the police' so much as 'a policeman' – our neighbourhood bobby, Ian Strand. If that term implied that every day of the week we saw him walk slowly along greeting one and all, or shovelling kids across the road into school, it shouldn't have. It meant we were one spot on a massive map, which he careered over tackling everything from cars burnt out at beauty spots to dogs worrying sheep.

'Hi, Ian – just the person we need to talk to,' I greeted him, aunt to favourite nephew style.

He always looked at me sideways, as if I were about to ask him to spit in the street. 'What might that be about then?'

'The sanctuary case up at St Jude's.'

'Abbot's Duncombe? They've got a problem way up there?'

All of four miles away. But he was a local lad. 'Yep. Serious, I'd say. But before you get on that radio thing, could you come in and give me a couple of minutes to explain?'

'I suppose it's not baking day?' He sniffed despondently in the direction of the extractor fan, which pumped cooking smells into the air, just like those at some supermarkets. The only difference was that mine were genuinely the result of baking, not some chemicals designed by scientists to tantalise and then disappoint.

'Monday: day of rest. But I'm sure Robin'll find you something. Now, come in and sit down and then you can give me your advice about a senior police officer...'

While I waited for Ian's choice of senior

officer to appear, I decided to make a few enquiries of my own. Most of the restaurateurs in the area had banded together in a mostly social group, the irony being that when we had our occasional get-togethers – which was where I'd hooked up with Nigel Ho – we endured far worse meals than any of us would dare to serve. Maybe my colleagues would have a few ideas about Tang and his chicken phobia. Were there dodgy birds about? I sent out a general enquiry to everyone on my email address list. Not wishing to lead them, I left it as general as that. Apart from adding a little *urgent* tag.

There was time for a little sprucing up. And then I remembered what Malins and Corbishley thought of me, and spruced down again.

It turned out that the senior officer responding to Ian's summons was a woman, Detective Inspector Claire Lawton. She was stern faced, in her later thirties, and could probably transform her face into something like beauty if she smiled. I'd have loved a girlie day out with her, making sure she bought a more flattering cut and colour next time she bought a business suit. And suggesting a good hairstylist.

There were days I really wished I'd had a daughter. Or a son, for that matter. And it wasn't just for the Mother's Day cards.

But I should be concentrating on the matter in hand. 'So you see, Ms Lawton, the complexity of the situation,' I summed up.

'I do. But unless we get him out of the church and into custody – even protective custody – I can't see that we can do very much. If he won't come out voluntarily, and Father Martin doesn't want us to go in and snatch him, what can we do? Especially as far as I can see there's no evidence to link him with any reported crime. Not even an overdue parking ticket.'

'A suspected immigration violation?'

'*Suspected!* That wouldn't be enough to generate the bad publicity we'd get if we went mob-handed into a church.'

'Especially with all the TV cameras outside.'

'It's as bad as that, is it? I'd better go and have a look.'

'Why don't I come along too? See if Tang will talk to you? He might find you less threatening than a man, especially as you're in plain clothes.'

'Still one problem though, Mrs Welford,' she grimaced. Those poor frown lines! 'I don't speak a word of Chinese.'

Getting back into the church wasn't as easy as getting out had been. But it wasn't the gauntlet of media people we had to run that was the problem. It was smaller, more vocal and distinctly hostile. A pair of geese.

'What the hell do we do?' I demanded, locking my car, never having come across anything like them back in Birmingham, on a roasting dish apart, that is.

'Charge them,' Nick said. He'd come along, he said, on the off chance. He didn't say of what. But he hadn't reported any useful news from his mates. 'And flap your arms and hiss back!'

'Will that work?'

'Can you think of anything else?'

So, no doubt to the delight of the media mob, the three of us hurtled up the path, pretending to be bigger, better birds.

At least it broke the ice with those inside the church. Especially when I turned back and pointed to the journalists and hissed to the geese, 'Kill!'

'Samson and Delilah,' Andy Braithwaite said, though it couldn't be classed as a formal introduction.

Once again it was Nick who took the initiative, trying to explain to Tang that Lawton was a good kind lady and a good kind cop. While he talked and drew, I strolled the few yards down into the sanctuary itself, to be joined almost immediately by Andy.

'Until Tang threw himself at this, I'd never realised that altars were made of stone,' I said, as the silence started to weigh.

'Not all by any means. Indeed, they're quite a rarity. According to the guidebook,' he said, withdrawing a folded leaflet from his inner pocket, 'there's a cross incised on it somewhere. I've explored every other corner,' he said, apologetically. 'Plenty of time on my hands.'

With what I hoped looked like reverence, I bent to lift the skirt of the altar cloth someone had ironed into box folds. More used to being on his knees than I, Andy crawled from one side to the other, peering as I hitched up fabric for him.

'Eureka!' he said, progressing from his knees to his haunches. 'Look.'

If I got down beside him, it wasn't impossible that I should need a crane to get me upright. Still, if God wanted me down there, He'd no doubt provide me with the steam power to get up again.

I traced an incised cross with my index finger. 'And that's how old?'

'Twelfth century. The idea was that the bishop made the cross in holy oil, not unlike a baptism, I suppose, and then a mason would make the exact spot permanent.'

'So eleven hundred years ago, there'd be all the solemnity of a dedication service and then some guy in a leather apron would squat down and hammer away. And then someone would come and clean up. A woman like those T S Eliot referred to as the scrubbers of the cathedral, no doubt.'

'I doubt if anyone living his rarified life would know the implications of the term,' he said, suddenly skipping back from any conversational brink.

I touched the marks in the stone one last time, and let the linen fall. 'I suppose they keep it covered so that other curious index fingers don't erode it.'

'I can't see many people bothering to touch: Tim tells me the congregations aren't huge.'

'Are they in any country church? In many respects, it's ludicrous to have so many tiny churches functioning in one benefice when people have transport and could get to a central one. It isn't as if the Church has money to burn, not after those huge invest-ment losses when the Commissioners misread the stock market. But–' I patted the altar. I forced myself upwards, hoping the creak wasn't audible.

'But indeed.' He didn't exactly spring upwards himself.

'It would look nicer with some flowers on it.'

He didn't reply. I had a sense of a bitten lip, as if I'd committed some solecism. I rattled on, 'Which is what I had in mind when I told Mr Corbishley to bring round here the flowers he'd bought as an apology for – for earlier. He wasn't best pleased.' I waited. 'What am I saying wrong?'

'Nothing.'

'Come on, Andy. I'm a grown woman. Is there some sort of shibboleth here?'

He threw back his head and laughed. 'Exactly that. You're not a Gideanite, clearly. The thing is, Josie, some churches don't have flowers in church in Lent.'

'The church's version of my giving up chocolate?'

He nodded. 'Not until Easter Saturday do they reappear.'

'No wonder poor Mr Corbishley nearly choked. The thing is, Andy, as you may have gathered, I'm fairly new to churchgoing. I trample on corns left, right and centre. Oh, dear–' I broke off, turning to see what had made Tim's voice rise in anger.

Nick, hands upraised to soothe passions, was talking. 'OK, Tim. OK. It's a fair point, Claire. I don't think you should attempt to prise Tang's story out of him until he has legal representation and an impartial translator. I'm not having any part of it, anyway.'

Lawton shook her head. 'If you want me to protect him, I need to know who from.' She set her mouth in a stubborn line. Mistake: it would cause even more lines and wrinkles if she did that very often. Still, I suppose she was one of the Botox generation.

You could see the effort Nick was making to be tactful. 'Yes and no. It'd be nice to know exactly who you were up against, but–'

She spat back, 'And of course as a serving officer you'd know!'

Children, children!

'Please don't argue in here – you can see how it upsets Tang,' I said, putting an arm round him. 'Ms Lawton, you will provide some protection, won't you? It's not as if we can dial nine-nine-nine and summon instant assistance, the nearest police station being upwards of twenty miles away, and that's as the goose flies. In any case, the only place you can use a mobile is in the far corner of the tower. And if the Assyrian is already sweeping down like a wolf on the fold, that's a bit late.'

'Though I doubt this particular one will be sporting purple and gold,' Andy chipped in.

We eyed each other in sudden appreciation. Of what, I wasn't sure, except our shared knowledge of a poem. Another time, another place, I wouldn't mind discussing with him the image of the spears resembling the Sea of Galilee.

'I'll tell you what: I'll do my best to get hold of an interpreter. Those on our official list will have been vetted, after all.'

'Soon?' I prodded.

I might not have spoken. 'Plus I'll ask Uniform to institute regular patrols. After all, he should be all right with all those cameras camped outside. And the geese'll give plenty of warning. Whose idea were they, by the way?'

'Annie Hatton's. One of the congregation. She's been trying to teach Tang some English, but she couldn't be here this afternoon. So she sent her friends.'

'If those are her friends, I'd hate to see her enemies,' Lawton said.

'So would we all,' Nick said, without a trace of irony.

Since Andy had some unspecified meeting he didn't feel he could miss, Nick insisted on staying behind with Tim. Secretly delighted at the change in him from the passive, inert man of only a few months ago into someone capable of making decisions, I stayed silent. It was a pity the White Hart wasn't serving tonight, because I would have liked to invite Andy to eat later with me, and the dining room would have been altogether more neutral than my own apartment. For the first time for years, I was bitterly aware of the effect my sexuality and my enjoyment thereof had on others who wished to find fault. If the church wardens were censorious, how much more right had a rural dean, for heaven's sake, to condemn? He'd gone out of his way, it seemed, to be friendly with me, but had been equally reluctant to embark on any discussion with me of what Malins and Corbishley had said. Thank goodness.

Or was it I who'd been reluctant to engage in anything more than social chat? I wasn't about to defend or justify myself. And I certainly didn't want any examination of my religious feelings. The sole reason I'd started to attend church was that I believed it was vitally important to keep village traditions alive. That was why the White Hart catered for the local gaffers as well as the lucrative diners. It was also why the village cricket team had received a large and anonymous cash donation for a minibus and the football team sported the White Hart sign on their strip. But that didn't mean I went to many matches. Whereas I went to church every week, pretty well. And it wasn't for the music, which was dire, or poor Tim's sermons, which were soporific at best.

'Are you ready to brave the geese, ladies?' Andy asked. 'Josie, I may have to ask you to lead me back to the main road, if you wouldn't mind. I seemed to spend most of my time on the way here reversing and going back on myself.'

'No problem. Nick, that pie will microwave in four minutes, but do make sure it's piping hot inside – give it another minute if it isn't. Could you establish if Tang likes fish? And lamb? See you tomorrow.' My wave was cheerier than I felt. I didn't like the idea of running the gauntlet of those dratted birds, especially in front of an audience.

'Hang on!' Andy said. 'Is there anyone whose cake you can't recommend? Couldn't we bribe the birds with that?'

'A man after my own heart,' I said, grabbing a few of Mrs Herbert's all too accurately named rock buns.

Although I led Andy's car to the A road, he followed me back to the White Hart, parking neatly alongside. 'I really wanted to pick your brains – ask things I couldn't in front of Tim,' he said, smiling disarmingly.

'Ask away. Or are they questions better asked with a cup of tea in your hands?'

'I'm so cold I might ask for a mug, so I could wrap my hands tight round it. Your electricity bill will be enormous – and thank you for footing it, Josie–'

'The church seems to have its own cooling system, doesn't it?' I overrode his thanks. 'Let's get into the warm, then.' I led the way upstairs.

I liked a man who wandered into the kitchen to natter while I made tea. I also liked one who looked askance at the cake I reached out, and shook his head with obvious regret.

'The thing is, with all the goodies the parishioners have donated – and, despite the dratted birds, there's been a steady stream of visitors – it's hard not to eat just to keep out the cold.'

'And boredom. Tim and Tang are strips of wind who can feed their faces all day long and not put on an ounce,' I observed, with something of a sigh. The fruit cake was calling me, but I knew to a gram how much harm a single slice might do. 'You're sure?' The lid hovered.

'Unless you–?'

'Andy, I had to shed six stone when my husband died. Six and then some, actually. I never wanted to be fat, but he liked his wife to be plump.' I snapped the lid on firmly, and led the way back to my living room.

'Was your husband in the hospitality trade, too?'

What a wonderful mealy-mouthed euphemism! Tony would have loved it. Sitting in the armchair opposite his, I smiled innocuously. 'For three or four years Tony was Britain's most wanted man. He spent most of our married life in the nick. Died there.'

To his credit he hardly missed a beat. 'He must have been older than you?'

'Old enough to be my father. At very least. But he was the love of my life. And it was he who got me on to books and poetry, so we always had something to talk about during visits, and could fill our letters with our views. And when I lost him I – yes, I was lost too. So I started to get the education I'd never had and make something of my life.'

'Hence the helicopter licence?'

Eyes full, I could do no more than nod.

'I'm sure he'd have approved.'

Sanctimonious git! I was liking him less by the minute, him and his stock-in-trade sympathy. 'He'd have hated it! Tony's idea was that I should sit back like a lady and enjoy all the money he'd made. A bit of reading, that was fine, and going to the theatre and such. But turning to and studying properly: that would have been anathema to him. Flying lessons! But even he would have seen,' I added, swallowing hard, 'that I couldn't sit on my arse all day playing Patience.'

'So he wouldn't have liked your part in the Tang campaign.'

'I don't know. I've been worrying about that. He believed in the rule of law, you see – I won't say he enjoyed doing bird, but he accepted it as the price he had to pay for doing wrong. So he'd take DI Whatshername's part–'

'Lawton.'

'Right. He'd want to know what Tang had done before he supported him. And he'd be worried about Tim getting emotionally involved with a case that can only end in tears.'

After a long silence, he grinned. 'Do you want to come to the meeting with the archdeacon tonight? As a token parishioner? Though it'll no doubt go on forever, as these things do.'

'A very junior parishioner. If they didn't like me arranging the wrong flowers last year, how would my fellow churchgoers cope with my presuming to represent them at a top level meeting?'

'Oh, it's nowhere near the top yet. The bishop will be involved before I'm much older, and no doubt a very senior police officer too. And probably the Home Secretary will shove in his unwelcome mite.'

'And the Archbishop of Canterbury?' I asked hopefully. 'I've always been a bit of a fan.'

'That beard of his, no doubt. Let's deal with things at this level first, however. Provided your prophet of doom is wrong, and we don't have Chinese gangs descending on the place, how long can Tang be supported in St Jude's, would you say? Another week?'

'So long as the police don't take it into their heads to lay a proper siege. If they stopped us bringing in food and other supplies, getting water and emptying bathwater... Not to mention if they turned off the heat.'

'And prevented your emptying – in the fullness of time – the Elsan.'

Men and their schoolboy jokes! But I couldn't help a cackle of laughter. 'It has to be finite. And the way Nick is talking, an extended stay is inviting retribution. This evening I'll do something more useful than gate-crashing your meeting. I'll move heaven and earth to get hold of my Chinese friend,' I explained, hoping I wouldn't disgrace myself by blushing.

'Thanks. Will you be going back tonight?'

'Not to stay, thanks very much! What about you?'

'Nick?'

'He has a day job: Food Standards Inspector. He was only here today because of the snow on the M3. Plus I think he'll be the one best placed to check on any dodgy food processing plants, and to do that he needs the adjuncts of the twenty-first century.'

'Looks like me, doesn't it?'

'It makes a cast iron excuse for cutting short your meeting. Tell you what, I'll come and cook breakfast for you all tomorrow. Provided you do something for me.'

He looked as suspicious as our neighbourhood bobby had.

'Just keep your ear to the ground for information about the church wardens. Something I said touched a nerve today, I'll swear. Something about their consciences and wrong-doing.'

He looked at me shrewdly. 'Know thine enemy, eh?' And it was his turn to blush.

'I'm just interested to know why they so desperately want to get rid of Tang.'

'Smuggled goods in the crypt? A bit

Daphne du Maurier!'

'And not really the right part of the world. All the same...'

'All the same it shall be.'

Which was the nearest I got to finding which part of my brains he wanted to pick.

As I waved him goodbye, it occurred to me that now the media had located St Jude's, it wouldn't take them long to discover it was within spitting distance of what had become their favourite out-of-town watering hole. And that their favourite restaurateur (their term) was deeply involved. I'd have to nip any enquiries firmly in the bud.

A few weeks back I'd had to confiscate the car keys of the head of the local BBC news, and put him to bed on my sofa, thus saving him his licence, since Ian Strand would undoubtedly have booked him. If that didn't merit a favour I didn't know what did. A phone call, in which I promised an exclusive when all was sorted out, established that he quickly agreed with me. Since he'd not been alone on the sofa, he undertook to silence his opposite number at the independent TV news. There. Job done. There was the press to deal with, but Robin was dating one of their number, and would no doubt promise a similar deal to mine. Somehow or other we'd deal with the rest. Don't think I didn't have my ways.

Chapter Seven

There was no better place for me to garner information about Malins and Corbishley than the village shop – which could, of course, provide the press with plenty of titbits about me. But at least I was now an honorary local, which might give me some protection. I wasn't, unfortunately, their most popular customer, despite trying to buy as much locally as I could and giving restaurant contracts to relatives of the proprietors. All incomers were regarded with suspicion, be they as meek and unobtrusive as a mouse. People like Aidan Carr and I attracted something like hostility, him because of his male partner and jazzy clothes, me – well, as I'd told Andy, changes to the White Hart apart, I had been promoted as flower-arranger rather too quickly, and also made a habit of sticking my nose in where it wasn't wanted. When I'd helped send one of the landed gentry down for a nice long stretch (though I'll swear nothing like as long as one of us plebs would have got), opinion had divided. Some remembered how much prosperity I'd tried to bring to the village. Forelock tuggers still thought the sun shone out of aristos' ears, to use the polite variant Tony would have preferred, although the usual one alliterated better. They considered what I'd done nothing short of *lèse-majesté*.

I didn't need to ask any questions yet, just drift into one of the little shoals of gossipers crowding the tiny aisles. There was hardly room for a bulky customer, let alone groups like this. But who could blame them?

'All this telly business – but then, you're used to that, aren't you, Mrs Welford?' a woman said waspishly.

'I'm used to serving telly folk food and waiting on them hand and foot,' I agreed, mild as milk. 'You wonder how they manage to stay so thin, those girls, don't you?'

'Perhaps it's running away from they old geese!' an old codger put in. It was Joe Damerel, an occasional, but not regular patron of the White Hart. 'Nippin' 'em on they little bums!' he chuckled, evilly.

'They'd find more to nip on mine,' I agreed. 'But I've got a secret: I fed them some of my cakes. That quietened them down.'

'They say you're feeding that lad, too.' This was Mrs Damerel.

'No pub in Abbot's Duncombe to do it,' I said. 'And Father Martin always looks in need of a good meal, poor kid.'

'Ah, only just started shaving by the looks

111

of him,' Joe chuckled. 'Well, still wet behind the ears, any road.'

'And now he's in the middle of this mess,' I sighed. If there was a hope of Tim being able to return to normal duties it might be better if people thought he'd been thrust unwilling into controversy. 'One moment he's giving the sermon, next there's all this kerfuffle. Not everyone likes it, but I can't see what else he could have done – apart from turning a starving boy out into the snow.' No one seemed to notice that I'd compressed the timescale, knocked ten years off Tang's age and eliminated possible police involvement.

'Ah, the moor can be cruel in the cold,' another old chap said.

I pressed on. 'Goodness knows where he came from, poor thing – he doesn't speak a word of English.'

Mrs Lane, Lucy Gay's aunt, joined us. Obscurely she blamed me for her brother's death, but since I'd taken in his children, hospitality she might have felt she ought to offer, she accepted an armed truce. 'Not everyone's as sorry for him as you are,' she countered. 'There's some as say the church is no place for him, smelling it out as he does.'

'The Abbot's Duncombe folk have sorted that out with an old-fashioned zinc bath. In fact, they've all been so generous it takes your breath away. Clothes and bedding and everything.' I might as well exploit the ancient rivalry between the villages. 'But you can see why people think it's the wrong place,' I conceded.

'That Mr Corbishley's worshipped at St Jude's for the last thirty years,' Mrs Lane said. 'Poured money in there left, right and centre, he has.'

'And it shows,' I said, fervently. 'And Mr Malins, no doubt.'

'Bless you, no. He's like you, a Johnny-come-lately,' Joe said. 'And like you, to be fair, he's done his best. Though not as much as you, like,' he added, in a tone that didn't make it entirely clear whether he approved of such hyperactivity. 'White Hart doing OK, I take it?'

'I shan't starve,' I agreed. 'But what about Mr Corbishley? His wallet deep enough to carry on?'

'Deeper than mine. You bet it is, isn't it, Em? Fingers in every pie going, that one.'

'And not all his own,' she said. 'They do say,' she added as a swift afterthought.

'But he's a respectable churchwarden!' I cried, eyes wide open.

'Ah, Mrs Welford, you're not telling me as you can judge a sheep by its winter fleece,' Joe said. 'There was something about a takeover a while back – no, I can't recall... As for that Malins–'

'He's as decent a man as you can find,' Em

113

corrected him quickly. 'Civil servant, very respectable. Retired down here, him and his wife. Live right out Duncombe Minimus way. Keep themselves to themselves, they do. As they're entitled,' she concluded challengingly. She pushed her way through to the till.

I'd learned something, if nothing like enough. Thirty years' input into any establishment gave you something like squatters' rights, at least in your own opinion. No wonder Corbishley was so resentful of the incursions into his kingdom. Which made his apology all the more generous. Or interesting, depending on your point of view.

I checked my watch. Six forty-five. The shop would be open till eight, but I thought I'd pretty well exhausted its possibilities. Had the owners been around, I might have questioned them, but they'd left a couple of school kids in charge, as they had to, to keep the place open the hours they did.

I thought I'd check my emails, before one last foray to St Jude's. Nick, who was depending on me for wheels, could stick it out a few more minutes. He might, with his dogged patience, have got Tang to reveal information, rather than simply react to his little sketches. He might have persuaded him to give himself up.

There was a good crop of incoming mail.

Most simply said hello, and that their chicken was fine, thank you very much. A couple moaned about the hike in prices from a Devon organic supplier, who thought he could milk a niche market for all it was worth. Nearly £18 a kilo? Where did he think we were, London? I sent them all a standard note of thanks. But what about these two? They were well out of the area but both complained about the quality of some chicken they'd acquired, pappy in texture and indeterminate in taste.

They got an immediate response from me. Was it from their usual supplier? Had they complained? What was the outcome?

Then there was another one. She'd changed supplier but would be changing back immediately: within three weeks of the change, four of her regular customers had gone down with food poisoning. It was only because they were so loyal that they hadn't gone to the public health inspectors.

Now, food poisoning isn't unusual if the chicken is inadequately cooked: check out the FSA website for the gruesome details. But I wouldn't have thought that in a completely hygienic kitchen, with thoroughly cooked meat, there should be that much of a problem. Alarm bells ringing in my head, I asked for details of the new supplier. I would get on to it tomorrow morning, feigning an interest and asking for details of sources, as well as prices.

Where the hell was Nigel Ho? I left yet another message.

Eight o'clock. Andy should be well into his meeting by now, so with luck I wouldn't have to hang around St Jude's too long.

I was taking with me the ingredients for a Thai style salmon dish, in which I poached the salmon in coconut milk flavoured with red chilli, garlic, galang galang, shallots, lemon grass, homemade red curry paste (Robin's speciality) and a little fish sauce. I added some slivers of mange tout and a few slices of courgettes with an eye less to authenticity than to getting a few vegetables inside male systems. A few noodles and a flurry of finely torn coriander and basil and we would have a feast.

I was just leaving when the phone rang. I grabbed it. It must be Nigel. 'At last!'

It was a good job I didn't add the few helpful expletives I wanted, because after all that it was quite a different voice that responded. Flirtatiously?

'If I'd realised you were poised by the phone of course I'd have phoned earlier.' Andy! 'But I'm still at my meeting. Josie, I have a tremendous favour to ask,' he said, now in what sounded a very official voice.

Not my sleeping at St Jude's, please! 'Ask away.'

Against a background of voices, he continued, 'Bishop Jonathan wants tomorrow's meeting to be held at St Jude's. I was wondering if you wouldn't mind coming along to organise coffee and so on.' He was so formal we might never have talked about deep lanes and incised crosses. So who else was in the room?

I stared at the phone in disbelief. It slowly dawned on me that among the people listening might be the bishop himself, so I wouldn't ask questions now. But we'd meet up at St Jude's when he came to relieve Nick so I would certainly ask a few then. Apart from anything else, I had the White Hart to run, and however capable and efficient my staff might be, a business was only as good as its management. Which was still me. As for Nick, he had a job to do protecting the whole country. Grandiose as that might sound, it was he and his four colleagues who had to ensure that all our food was fit to eat. Not just chasing up carcinogenic food dyes, but checking the progress of meat through the food chain. If they were neglectful, consumers – my customers and people like us everywhere – might suffer not just food poisoning but new variant CJD and other hidden diseases.

'Andy, I've been thinking. Despite what I said earlier, this really can't go on much longer,' I said. 'I won't shout my mouth off at the meeting, don't worry. But something has to be done. Soon.'

'That's exactly what I've been thinking.'

So why did neither of us have the sense to say so earlier?

'Is the meeting with the bishop maundering on?'

'You bet.'

'Trouble is, what about Nick? I promised to collect him from the church.'

'Go ahead. And would you warn Tim and Tang that if the meeting goes on any later, I may not make it out there at all?'

'Fine. No problem.'

There wasn't even any problem at St Jude's. A child had gone missing down near Teignmouth, and the media had decamped. Every last one. Well, it was warmer nearer the coast, and food and drink were at hand. Not to mention loos. With luck they'd all forget to come back.

Samson and Delilah, bored perhaps, positively welcomed me – or perhaps it was the stale petit fours I carried that they wanted. Standing on the tower, I phoned Andy and in the briefest conversation – he was still in that meeting, poor man, and I was cold – I told him the situation. 'I'm sure they can manage without you.'

'In that case, tell them to expect me in the morning. Good night and God bless you all.'

It wasn't my alarm clock waking me. It was the phone.

'I've got you at last!'

'At five in the bloody morning, Nigel!'

'Is that what it is? I'm never any good at transposing time zones. Yes, I'm in New York. You should have come with me when I asked.'

'Been a bit busy, Nigel.'

'Which is why I phoned. And so many times.'

'I've got three answering machines!'

'I don't do messages. Josie, do you know any more about that young man?'

'No. His English is minimal, and he plays chess well. That's all I really know.'

'No idea of his contacts or family?'

'He's not asked to use a phone to make contact. Not even with his Embassy, come to think of it.'

'In that case, you must turn him in. Before it's too late.'

'What?' It was one thing to think it, another to hear it.

'It's almost certain he's what I'll delicately call an "economic migrant". His family will have scraped together enough money for a down payment on the journey from China to the UK. Until he has paid off not just the down payment but the rest of the sum involved, something in the £8000 range, he is effectively the gang's possession. Escape can lead to one thing only – execution. And maybe the same for the people protecting him. Get him out now. Now, Josie. This instant.' He cut the call before I could press him on the matter of the interpreter, and didn't pick up when I tried to ring back.

I had my clothes on and had run down the corridor to bang on Nick's door without realising I hadn't done the stretches I need every morning to get me moving.

Nick was dressed and gunning his 4x4 before I even registered that he slept in the not unattractive nude. 'A nod,' he grunted as we swept on to the road, 'is as good as a wink to a blind man.' He put his headlights on main beam, as if to blast any oncoming vehicles out of his path.

The Midlands expression meaning one should always take a hint sounded weird down here. I responded with another, as we took yet another blind corner at sixty. 'Where's the fire?'

I didn't expect the answer I got. Nodding briefly at the hill ahead, topped by what looked like a beacon, he said, 'At the church.'

It was far worse that we'd imagined. We'd summoned all the emergency services while we had a signal, without knowing exactly what we needed. The best scenario, I suppose, was that Tim or Tang had somehow tipped over the Calorgas stove, or that the ages old wiring, overloaded for too long, had finally given up.

The worst: that must have been what we got.

The church door was open, wide open. Inside, nothing but flames. I could see them, hear them. Smell burning.

Tim!

I know I paused to pull my coat over my hair. I knew I had to be careful. But I plunged in, head down.

And ended flat on my back, head ringing as I tried to pull myself up. Must try harder. So why couldn't I–?

Nick, that was why.

'Let me go!'

'No. Come back.'

'I've got to–'

'No. And if I have to pull both arms out of your sockets I'll stop you.'

So that was what the screaming pain in my shoulders was. 'But–'

'Fire engine's on its way, by the sound of it.'

I couldn't hear anything, except the roar of the flames and the crackle of glass. No young men crying for help. Just the fire.

Blinded by smoke and tears, I turned, stumbling and falling again. As I tried to look back, Nick heaved me to my feet and propelled me towards the car.

'Listen! I'm going to do the fastest three point turn I've ever done, then you are going to drive back down the lane and stop anyone coming through. No villagers. No media. Just the emergency services. Get it?'

'But–'

'Just get in, woman.' He yanked my arm. But it was too late. I'd already seen the sight he wanted to protect me from.

I saw what I'd tripped over. Samson. The head was a yard or so from the body. Delilah's too.

Somehow I found myself in the passenger seat.

Nick turned the car, and left the engine running. 'Get over and drive.' He was out before I could argue.

I did. The 4x4 blocked half the lane. I got out, ready to flag down sightseers or wave through the emergency services. Already through the greyness I could see shadowy shapes, people still in their nightclothes, herding towards me.

What if they got in the way of the fire engine?

I scrambled back into the car – lights, as many as I could find. Main beam, whatever. To hell with Nick's battery and the irritating warning beep.

I flapped and waved like a windmill gone berserk. The leaders in the race fell back. And yes, here was the fire service.

In its wake came an ambulance and then a police car.

And then Corbishley, in his Jag. I stood in front of him. For a moment I thought he'd run me over. At first he contented himself with leaning on his horn. Then he got out and unleashed a stream of oaths that would have shocked even my Tony. Partly because they called into question my morals, I let him go on until he ran out of steam. Mostly though I forbore because his eyes were streaming tears that were probably nothing to do with the smoke as he watched his beloved church blaze uncontrollably.

'How much damage?' he asked at last.

'They'll tell us when they know,' I temporised.

He peered at me. 'Your hair's singed. You're filthy. And those grazes...'

Nick must have had to work harder than I'd realised to stop me. 'I tried. But it was already... I couldn't reach...' I must be crying too. Was it for the same reason as Corbishley? But at least I still had a few wits. 'Shift your car. In case.'

In case the ambulance came hurtling back, bearing someone with a little life worth fighting for? More likely for more fire appliances coming the other way, as reinforcements. And certainly police, in what passed for droves in the foothills of Exmoor, as swiftly as indifferent roads permitted.

And here came the advance guard, another ambulance, but going towards the church, not away from it.

I spotted Annie, hair like a silver halo. I could trust her. 'Tea. Get together a team to make tea. Those lads'll need it as soon as they've finished.' I pointed to another fire team. 'And the rest of us too,' I added. It would give the women something to do, get them back in the warm and clear the way.

Picking up all I'd left unsaid, Annie nodded, with a sideways glance at Corbishley. 'Poor bugger. All those years of fundraising and obduracy.' She managed a grim smile. 'Not a bad epitaph, maybe.'

While I was unofficial traffic cop – I hoped Tony was enjoying the sight! – what was poor Nick doing? Blundering round getting in everyone's way? Six months ago, maybe. Now – who could guess?

It seemed to take for ever, but at last, now dawn had truly broken, on what promised to be a lovely spring morning complete with dawn chorus, a couple of kids in a panda car replaced me. Soon they were so busy stringing crime scene tape across the road that they didn't notice me slipping away the business side of it.

Nick was talking to DI Lawton. Her body language suggested she was accepting the dressing down of a lifetime, anger being

Nick's way of venting emotion. Perhaps she needed a little consolation; after all, her hands had been pretty well tied by Tang himself.

'If you'd had a police presence here,' I asked quietly, motioning Nick aside, 'is there anything to suggest they wouldn't simply have gone the way of Samson and Delilah?' I repeated a little of what Nigel had said to me. 'After all, they wouldn't have been armed, would they? And routine body-armour wouldn't have protected them against that sort of attack.'

'All the same–'

'Do we know how the lads...?' Swallowing hard, I gestured towards the church, now awash with fire officers dodging in and out.

Lawton shook her head. 'Smoke inhalation, I should think. We won't attempt to get them out until the fire safety people OK it. Old buildings like these – no fire alarms, no sprinkler systems.'

I let her rail against the church's inadequacies, gripping Nick's arm when he tried to protest and finally drawing him to one side. 'If you're anything to go by, she'll beat herself up for the loss of those two kids' lives for the rest of her life.' Nick had killed someone accidentally, and suffered deeply for it for twenty years. 'A few minutes spent blaming something else won't do any harm.'

Nick said dully, 'I liked him. Young Tang. I liked him. And Tim. And she let them die. We let them die. I could have stayed last night. Should have.'

'And what would you have done? Ended up in there? Like those kids? Murdered in their beds?'

'It could have been an electrical fault, something to do with that camping stove.'

'And you'd still have been dead.'

At last he shook his head. 'Electrical fault be damned! Camping stoves don't cut the throats of geese. It's a classic execution if you ask me. Got to be.'

'The fire? If they're executioners, do they usually bother destroying evidence?' I objected.

'Perhaps the heater got kicked over in a struggle. The fire service'll have a forensic team on hand, which should work hand in hand with the police.' From his voice, he doubted it. As if to reassure himself, he added, 'We must trust the professionals.'

'So that's it?' I said dully. 'We pay our respects and go home and get on with our lives?'

He looked at me. 'I must have hit you harder than I meant. Knocked your brains askew.' He gave an ironic smile. 'Come on, Josie, I know you better than that.'

I wasn't sure I could say the same of him. Perhaps his half-nod acknowledged as much. 'Oh, the police'll get round to asking for my help eventually, when people talk about Tang's aversion to chicken. And by then I'll have something to tell them.'

Chapter Eight

Our unofficial roadblock was now official, augmented as it was by another police car, blue lights still flashing, of course. Behind the police tape was a little knot of villagers, many anguished, some nosy. They and a larger tangle of news reporters combined to trap a distraught-looking Andy Braithwaite, severe in dog-collar, black shirt and the most sober of clerical grey suits. Had he known in his water something was wrong when he dressed today or was this what rural deans always wore for early morning meetings? Better speculate on his clothes than on his face, which was as bleak as Dartmoor granite.

Without speaking, Nick set the 4x4 slowly but inexorably in motion, ignoring the mikes as if they were early midges. As we passed Andy, I leaned back to open the rear door. 'Best hop in,' I said, adding, as Andy did as he was told, 'We'll tell you all we can. But not here. OK?'

To my surprise Nick drove us to where we'd parked the previous day. 'Best view of the church is up that hill,' he said grimly, over his shoulder. 'They won't let you any closer, not yet. And it's best you see it for yourself.' He stopped as if he couldn't trust his voice any longer.

We set off walking in single file, no one wanting to say the wrong thing to anyone else. Nick produced a powerful pair of binoculars as we came to rest at the top of the hill. He peered first, then passed them not to me, but to Andy. 'The roof still seems sound,' he said, 'but the same can't be said for the windows.' I was used to Nick as phlegmatic as if he'd had his emotions cauterised, but Andy might not realise how deeply he was moved.

'They always were hideous,' I croaked.

'Is death by fire – quick?' Andy asked Nick.

'Smoke inhalation's very quick. It's what gets most people. They lose consciousness and that's it.' Nick was again as deadpan as ever.

I said nothing about the geese. Why had Nick chosen to censor what he'd said earlier? Sufficient unto the hour, I suppose. Which was why I had refused to identify even to myself the smell: it wasn't just burning wood, but burning flesh. I'd roasted too many Sunday joints to be able to deny it.

Tendrils of smoke apart, the scene was idyllic enough for one of those photo calendars the West Country seemed to specialise in. After Sunday's bitter cold, I was now uncomfortably warm in my heavy fleece. Any day I'd be checking my wardrobe, slinging out anything too large or too yesterday and sending my winter gear off, via the village shop, for dry-cleaning. There was one treasured jacket that was not destined for the cleaners, however. I swallowed painfully hard. I'd make sure there were some flowers exactly that colour for Tang's funeral. Or should they be white, for Chinese mourning? And Tim, poor innocent, naïve Tim: did the Church pull out all the funereal stops, as the police did, when one of their own had died in the course of duty? If Andy was praying, I was making a gritted teeth promise to bring to justice whoever was responsible for this ... this – but there I ran out of polite words.

Nick had told the police we were returning to the White Hart until we were needed, so that was where we all went now. Later on, one of us could ferry Andy back to collect his car.

It was well past breakfast time and, to stop his stomach ulcer flaring, Nick should undoubtedly eat. But Andy and I had parted on the promise of a cooked meal with the boys, and there was no way I could turn to the grill-pan now. Compromising, I raided the morning's baking for freshly baked rolls, which I laid on the coffee tray with butter – nothing frivolous like jam. I'll swear neither man noticed his hands picking up or his mouth eating them, but the linen napkin I'd folded them into to keep them warm was soon empty.

Eventually, none of us having said much, Andy announced he must go and brief the bishop. There was a tiny silence. One of us had to drive him back to his car. I had better things to do than make minimal small talk: I wanted to get amongst that dodgy chicken. But Nick had contacts to call too, and I was reluctant, now he'd overcome his terrible inertia, to stop him.

'Tell me, Josie, do you know Tim's family?' Andy asked, as he belted himself in.

'Family? I hardly knew Tim himself, services apart. Different generation, different backgrounds. I assume you know all about him?' I prompted, starting the car.

'According to the church equivalent of personnel records, he was the son of a couple of Home Counties teachers.'

'So they're in their later fifties? Early sixties?' Maybe they'd have retired by now. After all, teachers burned out quickly these days. 'Did you meet them when he was ordained? Is that the term?'

'It is but I didn't. I told you: I'm new to the job – wasn't even on the scene when he was inducted into this parish. But I shall have to get in touch with them now.'

'*Now?* Are you telling me they know nothing of this? That the first they hear about it is when they know he's dead? Good God!'

'It was his wish,' Andy interrupted me in mid-spate. 'He forbade me to say anything. Absolutely. Don't think I didn't try to persuade, even order him. He refused point blank even to give me their phone number.' His voice broke.

'You're feeling guilty, aren't you?' I asked flatly. I'm sure other people would have pussyfooted around, but to my mind it was better to bring it out now than let it fester. And perhaps talking to a driver with her eyes glued to the road had connections with a confessional.

His voice broke, mixing grief with anger. There'd be bruises where his fists struck his thighs. 'I should have been there, Josie! Of course I should!'

'So should I. And Nick. And my betting is that we'd all have been dead. I even bet that if there'd been a couple of police officers, they'd be dead too.' It was time for him to hear some of Nigel's words to me. I made my voice as flat as Nick's.

'But–!'

131

No, I didn't want to pursue the murder theme. *'But me no buts*, as someone or other said. Of course you're feeling bad: I'd think the less of you if you weren't. But we all have jobs to do. Yours is to pull together a fragmented parish and comfort the section that's in mourning, and reconcile those who hated what Tim was doing. All of it, not just the sanctuary issue.'

'Bells and smells?'

'Tim never got that far, but he would have liked to. Andy, as I told you, the curate that Tim replaced wasn't the best in the world, a bit sloppy about truth and pretty low in terms of doctrine. Then we get a Father Martin who offends all the people Sue didn't upset. Someone's got to stick his thumb in a great big hole until someone can repair the crumbling old dyke.' I added, not quite as an afterthought, 'And by that I don't mean me.'

He contrived a smile. 'You're trying to say let the dead bury the dead.'

'Am I? Andy, God's Word and all that is your department, not mine, but the only way I've ever been able to go is forward. There have been times I wouldn't want my worst enemy to have endured, but I got through them somehow. That's why I'm as tough as old boots.'

'Are you?'

Did he want tears? Breast beating? 'On the

outside, anyway. Which is all the world needs to know about. Some people will think it very weird of me to spend the rest of the day not sobbing into my pillow, but checking chicken farmers and slaughterers and packers. But that's what I'm going to do. Not to get a better price for produce for my restaurant, as it happens, though I shall encourage folk to think that, but to get a handle on Tang.'

'What's chicken got to do with Tang?'

'All that business of baths and new clothes? When Tang arrived he stank – not just unwashed, though he was filthy, but with a smell of putrefaction.'

'Putrefaction?'

If he was going to start echoing me he could have it between the eyes.

'Putrefaction. Rotting flesh. Not necessarily his. Not necessarily human.' I waited for him to question that, too, but when he didn't, I added in a less strident tone, 'When someone offered him a wonderful meal involving chicken he flipped. I'm making a bit of a jump, OK, quite a big jump, but one assisted by Nick. Think cheap illegal labour. Where would a man like Tang work? There aren't a lot of Chinese takeouts or building sites round Exmoor, Andy. Plenty of farms, mostly arable, I grant, but enough for me to have a wide choice when it comes to my suppliers. So I'm thinking chicken farms or chicken slaughterers or chicken processors.'

He twisted in his seat. 'You don't think you know them – his killers – do you?'

'Andy, all my suppliers know their chooks by name and treat them as family. They don't quite send the birds birthday cards, but they come pretty close. And they probably treat their employees just as well. They certainly wouldn't have them ranging around smelling like a charnel house.'

Out of the tail of my eye I could see his frown. 'Are you sure there's a difference? Between organic and factory chicken, I mean.'

For a moment I was nonplussed: why ask such a trivial question now? I risked a sideways glance: perhaps he was afraid of losing control. So I played along. 'Eat at the White Hart and I'll show you the difference. It's not just flavour but texture and... When you're ready to relish your food, rather than simply eat to keep going, when I'm ready to cook for pleasure rather than to pay my way, then I'll cook for you. Was the church insured, by the way?' I added, not changing the subject as much as he realised.

'Probably. But not enough, I'd say.'

'Despite poor Corbishley's shovelling cash into it?'

'"Poor" Corbishley?' he echoed in disbelief.

Should I tell him to his face how much I

disliked having my words repeated all the time? 'I saw his face this morning. Now, do you want me to wait while you turn your car round and lead you back to the main road? Or do you have to go and say all that's proper to the fire crews and police? Actually,' I continued, killing the engine and preparing to get out, 'I wouldn't mind tagging on behind – see what sort of approach they're taking. You have a right to ask questions: I don't. Then I'll lead you wherever you want to go.'

I didn't think he'd argue, but he raised a hand to stop me. Unlike Tang's, it was very well manicured, something, in a man, I'd never quite made up my mind about. 'Before I forget. Tim's parents. I should imagine they'll want to come down ... to see everything for themselves. I don't suppose ... do you do bed and breakfast?'

'I'm not exactly geared up to it. All the original B and B rooms are occupied.'

'Did I hear something about your putting up a whole family when one of the villagers died?'

'The Gays. My head waitress's family. Their mother was already dead and their father died in an accident.' He was trying to blow me up, but Andy didn't need to know that. 'Lucy wanted to keep them together, and it seemed the best way forward. The other room is still occupied by Nick.'

135

'Nick and you... He doesn't share your quarters?'

Now that was an interesting question. How long had he been saving it up? Had there been some gossip about us, or was he purely and simply interested? And if so, why? But this wasn't a time or place for personal conversations, whatever he seemed to think. 'Why should he? He's my lodger. He arrived in the floods last autumn and would have moved out except that Social Services thought he'd be useful as a father figure for the Gay children.'

'So you simply took them all in?'

'Well, their own house was uninhabitable. Don't see this as some huge act of charity! I had the space, after all. And Social Services pay me huge amounts.' Which went straight into a trust fund for them, but that was another story. If Andy and I ever got closer, I'd tell him all about my surrogate family. He might even be useful helping with their RE homework. Meanwhile, I would maintain my tough as old boots persona. 'Anyway, if you don't think the Martins will object, I've got space in my staff quarters which can be theirs. Brand new and en suite. Gratis, given the circumstances. But that's between you and me. I don't want them going round being grateful. I can quite see why they can't stay at the rectory,' I added darkly. I had seen the previous incumbent's decor, and had no reason to believe than Tim might have had any more interest in his surroundings.

Andy's dog-collar acted like an open sesame on the police tape. I kept my head down, swept along in his wake. We passed little bunches of wild and garden flowers already mourning the dead. One note read, *For Tim and our new friend: you will both be missed.*

I would point that out to him on our way out.

'I can smell – honey?' he asked.

'The bees' nests must have melted,' I suggested, pointing upwards at sticky trails. 'Apparently the bees were a real nuisance in the summer.' There seemed nothing either of us could add to that.

Someone produced hard hats. Provided we wore overshoes, we might stand in the porch and look in. There was nothing to see but stinking destruction, water having done what the fire hadn't. There were none of the chapel chairs left, that I could see, and the pulpit and font were nothing but rubble. Only the stone altar would stand for another millennium.

Always assuming the church authorities wanted the place rebuilt.

Andy touched my elbow: a fire officer was talking to us. I followed the line of his finger. The two-legged fire fighters had a canine assistant, kitted out in little boots.

'Accelerant. That's what that there dog's looking for. To see if the fire was started deliberately. But that's not for public consumption, you understand, your reverence. But we also found Calorgas cylinders, which didn't help one bit. Not one bit.'

'Why the boots?' Andy asked, again concentrating on the irrelevant.

'Boots? Glass. Lot of glass in a building. Specially a church. Stained.'

In my book it had been ripe for renewal. Properly, this time. I'd see to that. 'Why should anyone torch it?' I asked, aloud, feigning innocence.

'That'll be for the police to say. And maybe,' he added, 'for you to tell them.'

'I thought we'd agreed we would interview you back at the White Hart,' DI Lawton frowned, as she caught sight of us. I patted Andy gently on the arm. Accepting the valediction, he wandered over and spoke to tired fire fighters and a couple of uniformed officers.

There were times when the honest truth sounded like an excuse. 'The dean needed to collect his car: I brought him over. When we were told we could look into the church, we decided to do so.' As I spoke I heard Tony's exasperated words about stupid cons always returning to the scene of the crime and thus giving themselves away.

'Really?'

Oh, in years to come, she'd regret that carefully practised cynical eyebrow lift, too.

'Really.' Flat as a pancake. 'It's a pity your budget couldn't have run to round the clock protection.'

'It's a pity you didn't make him turn himself in!'

I hadn't the heart for any more jousting. 'You're right. It is. Tell me,' I added, dropping my voice, 'what's your theory about the fire? Calorgas? Or something altogether more sinister?'

'My theories are no more than that, and as such are police business, not yours. Sorry,' she added perfunctorily. 'Now, until the forensic teams have come up with evidence of what happened, I really would appreciate being allowed to get on with my work.'

There seemed to be something of a *non sequitur* there, but Tony had taught me never to expect logic from a police officer under pressure.

'Of course,' I smiled sweetly. 'And hearing my theory would be a waste of your time.'

I have to hand it to her, she looked me straight in the eye as she said it. 'Frankly, Mrs Welford, yes. It would.'

Chapter Nine

My first move was, on the face of it, silly. An extravagant waste of something I had so little of: time. OK, I wanted to be on the move, to hunt for unsafe chicken, but why I should take it into my head to drive all the way to a restaurant in Starcross, a village on the Exe estuary, when I had colleagues reporting dodgy dealing nearer to home, I don't know. Well, I wanted to get out of the village, with all its gossip and sympathetic glances. And I justified going to Starcross by telling myself that Burnham-on-Sea, where I had another contact, was hardly next-door, and that the views across the Exe were nicer than those across the Severn, especially when the tide was out. In any case, Starcross has a residual charm that Burnham indisputably lacks.

I lunched at Michael Rousdon's new restaurant, busily building its reputation on the freshest of local fish simply served. Which suited me: I didn't fancy consuming any chicken that – though I hated even thinking ill of the dead – hands as filthy as Tang's when he'd tumbled into St Jude's might have handled at some point in its progress from life to my plate.

'Samphire!' I echoed the roly-poly waitress offering the day's special. 'That doesn't sound very local!' Or, since I'd only met it on the pages of *King Lear*, where someone collected it on the cliffs of Dover, was I betraying appalling gastronomic ignorance?

'Local,' she insisted.

'Cliffs?' That would take me a few miles westward, to Dawlish and Teignmouth and beyond, all much beloved of railway photographers. I didn't see Railtrack taking kindly to people abseiling on their property.

'From the marshes.'

Ah, just along the road, then. 'So it's out there now? What does it look like, before it's cooked?'

'We don't cook it. We pickle it. Like shallots or gherkins.'

'So is it in season now?'

'Pickled this lot last July. You put it in vinegar and that and then have to leave it.'

I nodded slowly, as if hesitating. Nothing would have stopped me trying it. 'And with those prawns – you really ought to try it.'

I did. The combination was glorious. As to the source, there was no way that Michael Rousdon was going to let on.

'You go and pick your own,' he said, joining me for a coffee. There was no trace of amusement in his face. 'Make sure you don't get cut off by the tide.'

141

'Like those Morecambe cockle gatherers.' Poor Chinese kids brought in by profit-seeking gang masters. They might have been from the same village as Tang.

'As to chicken, now, that's an open book,' he said.

I smiled the sort of smile I always smile for attractive young men with information I need. Perhaps some ghost of my former self replaces what's really before them. Actually no: the thin former self that at Tony's insistence always had to lurk inside the fat one. At least they always respond as if they see someone sexy, and who am I to correct them?

Michael leaned intimately forward, allowing his knee to touch mine. 'I buy them from my cousin, up Seaton way. So when this guy came charging in offering me free-range chicken at mass-production price, I almost told him where to go. But then I thought, you know, for casseroles and pies, why not?'

I could have told him why not. If you were advertising organic or free-range produce, that was exactly what you should be selling. But I nodded understandingly and left my knee where it was. After all, it wasn't every day that a thirty-year-old schmoozed up to me, especially one with as nice a body as Michael's, which, despite his hours in the kitchen, carried not an ounce of flab and a reassuring amount of muscle. He'd shaved his head and grown a neat beard, so he was on to a loser: I didn't do beards, on account of the soreness afterwards. But he had a skull that looked good, and there was no need to buy everything in the shop window, not even when it was in the sale.

'So did you do any sort of deal?'

He shrugged. 'I bought a bit. A couple of kilos. And it was OK.'

'Were you tempted to buy any more?'

'I thought, better the devil you know. But other folk were: Kevin over in Exmouth. He says he's no complaint.'

'And, more to the point, has had no complaints?' Lord, I was sounding like Andy Braithwaite.

'Quite. So what's your interest, Josie? I thought you were totally upmarket? Rich sods of Exeter paying through the nose.'

'Like you, I always think about profit margins.'

'I don't buy that, Josie. Not you.' A hand joined his knee.

'If I told you the truth you wouldn't believe it,' I said. I tapped his menu. 'Local produce: so were the chooks local?'

'Never got an address out of him,' he admitted.

'The old mobile phone dodge?'

He nodded.

'And I do like an address. And a sheaf of

paperwork. Pity. You wouldn't have his number, would you?'

He stood up. 'What is this?'

'I told you, it's a long and boring story. Which is mostly a wild theory of mine. I'll tell you if there's a happy ending.'

'I'll get you that number.' He disappeared into his kitchen. I stood up, ready to follow.

He stepped straight in front of me, blocking the door. Shaking that elegant head, he snapped, 'No you don't. You'll nick my pickled samphire.'

There were too many people guarding it, judging by the voices I could hear. 'I don't even know what it looks like!' But I'd damned well find out. In its natural, not pickled state, too.

Robin and the team had finished the lunch session and were already deep into preparations for the evening sitting when I got back. Their efficiency posed a question: should I promote myself to manager pure and simple, leaving all the hard work to them and any other chef and dining room staff we might need, or continue to muck in, doing what I really enjoyed, cooking and talking to punters?

Most days I inclined to the latter; today, with a police car sneaking into the place beside mine, the former was in order. Of course I made a great show, for DI Lawton's benefit, of being too busy to spare her more than a few minutes, but show it was, with Pix, Robin's cousin, particularly playing a wonderful supporting lead. Robin raised the eyebrow furthest from Lawton and got on with what he was doing.

The charade over, I led her up to my quarters, offering tea, which she accepted. When she found it was green – so much better at mopping free-radicals and thus preventing cancer, I'm told – she gave an ironic smile, but then every appearance of enjoying it.

'Why did you side with Father Martin and not the church wardens?' she asked, point blank.

I'd been asking myself that question, don't think I hadn't. But it didn't seem to me that I need share with her the thought processes it had caused, many pretty uncomfortable, to do with Tony and underdogs and plum-in-mouth diction and all sorts of other stuff. I'd come up with one positive thing. So my smile was reasonably sincere when I said, 'I think it might have been something to do with Father Martin's sermon, which was about the Good Samaritan, and the concept of who was your neighbour.' The fact that my mind had wandered was irrelevant. Let him go down as a better preacher than he was.

'That sounds more like an answer for his bishop or whatever,' she said, startling me.

'In my experience, people do things like that for other reasons.'

'OK. How about this? Once I'd disarmed him, I realised Tang was nothing but a poor thin frightened boy, much the same as Father Martin, as it happens, and I suppose my protective instincts were aroused.'

'It wasn't personal animosity against the two church wardens?'

I spread my hands. 'How could it be? I hardly know them.' And what had who been saying?

'But you knew Father Martin well enough to call him by his first name.'

'We'd met at functions in Kings Duncombe. Occasionally he'd drink here. Lemonade shandy. Very rarely he'd eat in the bar. We were both grockles, which counts for something.'

'I gather there was some hostility to him in the parish.'

'Enough to burn him alive in his church? Hardly!' She didn't bite. More quietly I continued, 'There was hostility to his predecessor, too. I suspect that if Christ himself paid a return visit people round here would find something to criticise in his sermons or his habit of leaving litter after picnics. Another incomer, you see.'

'But Mr Malins and Mr Corbishley – why did you not know them?'

'They weren't part of village life. Well,

check their addresses.' Which reminded me, I'd never pursued the truth behind the village gossip, had I?

She nodded. 'Where did you spend last night?'

'Here.'

'Witnesses?'

'I live alone. My staff and my clients may have seen me buzzing around, but once my door is closed, that's it.'

'Mr Thomas?'

'Occupies a room in the bed and breakfast area. The far side of my door.'

She looked almost relieved. Hello, hello, hello, as Dixon of Dock Green might have said: was she sniffing round Nick? Well, I'd certainly spruced him up, but I'd have thought him a tad old for Lawton.

'Is this getting us anywhere, Detective Inspector? Because I can't really believe you'd think I was in any way responsible for torching that church.'

She pounced on the word, perhaps, rather than on the concept, which, after all, I'd floated only a few moments before. 'How do you know it was torched?'

'Detective Constable Dog in Boots sniffing for petrol. We kept cooking and heating equipment away from what had become the living area. We had to.' I explained about Tang's initial desire to embrace the Calorgas heater and the consequent stench. 'Tell you

147

what, we filled a black sack with all Tang's clothes in it. I told Tim to keep it. There may be something in there that could help you place his whereabouts and even identify him.'

'Very circumspect, Mrs Welford.'

It was best not to challenge the cynicism. 'If someone claims sanctuary it could imply they've committed a crime. There might be evidence on his clothing. I wanted to make sure...'

Her frown was inches deep. 'You wanted to make sure the police couldn't tamper with any evidence on it. How trusting, Mrs Welford.'

'Life has taught me never to trust anyone, not even a good defence lawyer. Anyway, the bag of clothing disappeared, and I can only assume Tim took it.'

'Any idea where it might be now?' At least she was showing more interest in the bag than in me.

'The rectory, I assume. The garage, most likely. Given the stench.'

'Any idea who the key-holder would be?'

'None. Apart from his neighbours? But surely, you people will be entitled to access since the guy's dead.'

She had the decency to look down. 'We shall need DNA to identify him. Or dental records. There's no question of anyone identifying him, Mrs Welford.' This time she looked me straight in the eye. 'Or Tang.'

The moment she'd gone, I phoned Andy Braithwaite.

Damned repetition again! 'Keys to the rectory? Not that I know of. Surely a neighbour or the St Faith and St Lawrence church wardens...' Light dawned; his voice hardened. 'Why?'

My voice epitomised innocence, and why not? 'I just fancy seeing what the police are going to see. To be honest, when they've finished with it, it'll need a spring-clean. I suspect Tim wasn't the best of housekeepers, and I'd hate his parents to see it before it's civilised. When are they coming, by the way?'

'When they get back from Australia. Imagine the plane journey back, in those circumstances... But as for cleaning the rectory,' he said slowly, 'why don't I put just that point to the police? If you're kind enough to put his effects together for his parents, I'm sure they'd be grateful.' There was a pause. I presume he was making a note. He'd assumed what was no doubt his professional voice. 'Tell me, Josie – how are you bearing up?'

I gave a conventional answer, one I'd heard so often from other inmates' wives – and, in effect, what I actually did all the time Tony and I were apart. 'I'm keeping myself busy.' Less lugubriously I added, 'I've got a possible lead on the dodgy chicken as it happens.' No need to mention the industrial espionage I'd undertaken. I returned pointedly to the previous subject. 'Just let me know precisely when Tim's parents are coming down.'

'Of course.' Another pause. 'Josie, they may be letting me back into St Jude's later this afternoon, maybe this evening. When they've ... removed the bodies, and finished with it as a crime scene. Would you care...?'

He wasn't speaking in the tone to which you could respond, *You bet I would!* So I murmured a quiet assent, and prepared to cut the call. But there was one conversational nicety I'd ignored. 'How are you coping? And with the bishop?'

'He's not best pleased, Josie. With me in particular. He feels I should have exercised more authority and compelled Tang–'

'Tell you what, you leave him to me. I presume he'll be coming over at some point?'

He chuckled. 'With that threat hanging over him, I'm not sure he'll dare.'

'He will if I hold the post-funeral wake here. The villagers will want to say goodbye. And the guy conducting the service'll have to show.'

'That will be me.'

'Sorry, Andy, and nothing personal, as you

know – but anyone other than the bishop and the people round here would be insulted.'

'I take your point. And will let you loose on the bishop if necessary. I – er – I'll see you later, then, shall I?'

We danced round another few sentences of farewell, and at last I could get to work.

If I were going to go to St Jude's with Andy, I couldn't afford the luxury of traipsing round the countryside talking to colleagues about chicken. I had to resort to phone or email instead. This message would be more specific than last, and addressed only to people who'd responded with positive information before. Had anyone been sold chicken by someone giving a mobile number only? I thought of giving the number Michael had given, but if I were going to be devious enough to sell ropey meat as good, I might well want to be as elusive as possible. This would be a busy time of day for those without a staff like mine: I couldn't expect an immediate response.

Next a check on the Internet: so many references and indeed recipes for samphire that, provided I could locate some, I could give Michael a run for his money. And why not try some other local – and free! – wild vegetables and herbs? I put it top of the agenda for tomorrow's staff meeting. The only excuse I had for never thinking about it before was that none of the chefs I'd trained with had ever mentioned wild food, except the sort of mushrooms you can buy in Italian markets. Still, one shouldn't be too hard on them: Birmingham might be at the centre of the country, but it was a long way from any really unpolluted countryside. I wouldn't fancy dandelions picked from a motorway hard shoulder.

I was just clicking on to find what sort of funeral rites we should give Tang when my phone rang.

'The bishop's coming with us to St Jude's,' Andy Braithwaite gabbled. 'I told him you'd be coming. Any chance we could eat at the White Hart afterwards?'

'What sort of time?' I knew off the top of my head we had a party of twelve booked for seven-thirty, but had no idea how the rest of the evening was looking.

'Whatever time we finish at the church, I suppose.'

The man had no idea, had he? Still, I could always seat them up here rather than in the restaurant if things were really tight downstairs. And cook for them myself.

'No problem,' I said blithely.

I was less blithe when I saw a small detachment of reporters hanging round outside. Still, it was their way of making a living, so I invited them all in, made sure they had plenty to eat and drink and, hand somewhere in the region of my heart, admitted I'd discovered the fire while out looking for wild garlic. I'd bet Tony's legacy they wouldn't know it from common weed, any more than I would. But, I added, they'd quite understand, would they, if I wanted my part kept to a minimum in their reports. After all, I'd done nothing but raise the alarm. Heads awash with champagne they nodded – well, not exactly soberly, but the nearest they could manage.

When Nick appeared he looked spent but satisfied, as if he'd just had good sex. Or, since he waved his briefcase at me, as if he too was making progress with his chicken investigation. His return coincided with the arrival of Andy and his boss, whom he introduced as Bishop Jonathan. I knew vaguely that bishops took their see as their surname, but couldn't remember for the life of me what see we were in.

Bishop Jonathan looked younger than Andy, I'd say, though that might simply be a result of the way he tilted his head slightly sideways in a way meant to be winsome. He sported a heavy wedding ring on a hand so fleshy I was instantly glad he wasn't about to embark on healing me by laying it somewhere – anywhere – on my anatomy.

'Mrs Welford – Josie!' he beamed solemnly,

engulfing my right hand in both of his. It was like being greeted by a duvet. But he had a voice I could only describe as mellifluous. If I closed my eyes the honey would certainly flow; if I opened them it went all crystalline and gungy. 'Such a pleasure ... but in such sad circumstances...'

Nick with more speed than tact bunged us all into his Honda. As he opened the door for me, he whispered, 'I'm sure I've seen the bishop's face somewhere before – like on the sex offenders' register.' But he accompanied the slander with a wink I returned.

I wasn't at all sure why we all needed to go, but there was no way I was going to let Bishop Jonathan bully Andy for supporting poor Tim's *fait accompli*. As for Nick, he seemed to have espoused the case as some sort of convalescence as he recovered from his post-traumatic stress disorder. He'd had some therapy, once it was officially diagnosed, but I swore that his recovery had started the moment he'd saved me from certain death.

In tacit agreement, we dawdled by the Honda while the two clergymen spoke to the police officers still guarding the crime scene. The younger PC backed off sharply, as if afraid of ecclesiastical interference; the other simply tucked his hands firmly behind his back.

Another car drew up: to my amazement this brought Messrs Corbishley and Malins. Who had invited them? The bishop? That would look very much like a taking of sides. Andy? In which case, why hadn't he told me?

'Does this mean covers for six? Or just for the four of them?' I whispered to Nick.

'Wherever they go, I go,' he replied. And suited the deed to the word, as he plunged into the church as if late for evensong.

When, more slowly, I joined them, Bishop Jonathan was already leading what seemed like extempore prayers. Not wishing to interrupt, perhaps, or simply finding them inadequate, I lingered behind a smoke-stained pillar until he had finished.

Let them talk man-talk. I drifted along the aisle until I reached the altar. The cloth was ruined, but the stone had withstood the assault. Using spit and a couple of tissues, I cleaned the smoke from the ancient incised mark of the cross.

Chapter Ten

We spent the majority of the meal – I'd organised a table in the quietest part of the restaurant – listening to the sad little fundraising schemes Corbishley was propounding. Poor man, they wouldn't even scratch the surface of what had to be done.

'We've done it before and we can do it again!' Corbishley declared with a fervour quite touching provided that you forgot his outburst to me. And what had he done with the flowers he'd bought me as an apology? Was his wife – if he had one – a surprised beneficiary? Or had he, in his fury, simply shoved them on to the nearest grave or even face down in a hedge?

I nodded, knowing exactly where the insurance shortfall would come from but wondering how I could ensure its total and permanent anonymity. But at last I had a chance to probe a little.

'Are we lucky enough to have a church-warden with a background in business?' I asked with a duplicitous humility I was sure Andy would see through. 'We'll need a good deal of knowledge of Mammon, won't we?'

Andy offered a serious shake of the head.

'Alas, the Church of England isn't renowned for its financial acumen.'

'All that poor investment losing millions!' Corbishley snorted indignantly. 'Mrs Welford's right. We need proper financial advice.' I tried to look demurely gratified. 'As a matter of fact I have a colleague who may be able to help.'

'Alas, all you'll be able to do is raise money and put it towards repairs, should they be authorised,' the bishop chimed in. I cursed him under my breath – he was right, of course, but he'd wrong-footed me nicely. 'There's no guarantee that St Jude's can be rebuilt.'

I overrode him as best I might. 'What was your line of business, Mr Corbishley?'

'Chemicals,' he said offhand.

'What sort of area?' Damn, Nick's question was horribly ambiguous.

'Up in the north-east,' he replied.

'I meant, what sort of chemicals? Phiz, my son, wanted to take a chemistry degree, but the department suddenly shut up shop,' Nick added. He spoke with a passion the others couldn't understand. While he and his daughter were getting on much better, Phiz had set himself firmly against reconciliation. As soon as this business was over, I was going to have to make a little trip to Birmingham to sort that one out. Elly and I had agreed this at a girlie meeting Nick

157

knew nothing about.

'Chemists are quite an endangered species, aren't they? Several universities have closed their chemistry departments,' Bishop Jonathan observed.

Which got Corbishley neatly away from our questions and on to an attack on government education policy. Drat and drat and drat. I wouldn't have minded if people had got aerated, but Bishop Jonathan decided to switch off anything painful and charm us, keeping the conversation as bland as boiled rice. I searched in vain for an opening to quiz Corbishley further.

No one noticed – or, at least, remarked on – the excellent starters and soup. No one complimented Robin on the excellence of his steaks, his fish, or the brilliant tagine. This was a quasi-North African dish of lamb, aubergines, tomatoes, onions, garlic and chickpeas, given a lovely hit of cinnamon and harissa paste. Authentically it would come with couscous, but one of my regulars had a wheat allergy so I'd tried marrying it to brown rice. The match might have been made in heaven. At last Andy caught my eye and nodded approvingly, so not everything had been gastronomic pearls cast before ecclesiastical swine.

At long last, over some blissful local artisanal cheese and a choice of home baked bread or biscuits – there seemed to be tacit agreement that desserts would be too frivolous – we discussed the funerals.

'Have you managed to contact Tim's parents yet?' I asked.

'I only got their answerphone, and – to be honest, I couldn't think of a halfway appropriate message and I gave up. I've asked their local vicar to go round,' Andy said.

'What a job!'

'All part of a parish priest's daily round,' declared the bishop.

'Telling parents their son had been roasted alive? It's usually the police that get that job,' Nick muttered, with such fury we all ignored the inaccuracy.

'It will be good to meet them when they come down for the funeral,' Bishop Jonathan continued, undeterred.

'Surely they'll want Tim's at their local church,' Nick said. 'I know if anything happened to my son I would.'

Bishop Jonathan quivered with potential affront.

'A funeral there, and a memorial service in one of Tim's own churches?' I suggested quickly. 'St Faith and St Lawrence might just be big enough.'

'Or even the Cathedral,' Andy said, roused from wherever he'd been.

'Of course. Absolutely. We could ask the choir to do something major: what about Faure's Requiem, for instance?'

'And Tang?' Nick pricked the funereal balloon. 'What about him?'

Malins, who'd doggedly and silently eaten everything put before him, suddenly spoke up. 'That's a matter for his Embassy. In these multicultural days, you daren't offend anyone. There'll be a Confucian temple or whatever. I know they wear white.'

At least I'd been right on that. Encouraged by my ecumenical success, I said, 'Hang on! Isn't there a Chinese Christian community? There's a church near the National Portrait Gallery. Though I can't for the life of me remember which denomination.' These senior moments! Baptist or Catholic? Some difference!

'Josie's right. He sought sanctuary in a Christian church,' Nick continued, growing in passion. 'And in the very short time he was with us, he and Tim had become inseparable. I'd hate to think of two funerals, a Premier league and whatever the old first division calls itself these days. Unless we could prove he'd have wanted otherwise,' he added, suddenly retreating into his old Eeyore self.

His gloom fell even on Bishop Jonathan, who evinced an aversion to coffee, even decaffeinated, after eight.

As people were getting to their feet, Andy said quietly, 'Bishop Jonathan, I think we should anticipate all these grander services with a very simple one tomorrow. Evensong. At St Faith and St Lawrence.'

To do him justice, the bishop nodded. 'Of course. I'll clear whatever's in my diary and take it, if that's agreeable to everyone.'

It was. The party broke up very swiftly.

'Prosy buggers,' Nick said, stomping off to his room with no further ado. I popped into the kitchen to thank Robin and Pix, not to mention the scullions.

'Tomorrow morning's meeting still on, gaffer?' Pix came from near Birmingham, and apparently enjoyed puzzling the locals with his native lingo. Though I dimly recalled the old geezers in Hardy sharing the honorific, I'd stopped reading him after the hanging in *Jude the Obscure:* perhaps I should start again.

'Don't see why not. I know I've been lead-swinging since Sunday, and I know you could run a place this size blindfold and with one hand tied behind your back. But I like to stay involved,' I finished mildly. 'And I've got an idea I want to run by you. OK?'

'Just the one?' asked Robin, eyes twinkling.

'One good one's better than two average. Or three boring.'

'You sound like that woman in *Emma:* you know, that picnic,' Pix said, almost leaving me gaping.

'On Box Hill?'

'That's right. We did this adaptation and toured it for a season round village halls.'

'In your actor phase, yes?'

'I was Mr Knightley,' he said, ageing ten years and looking down his nose.

'You two and your books,' Robin grumbled. He yawned and stretched. 'See you at this 'ere meeting, then.'

'Samphire? Round here?' Pix demanded, stifling a yawn, as he always did at our nine-thirty get-togethers.

'I'm not suggesting you scale up and down Hartland Point and gather it yourself,' I said, pouring more coffee, but eschewing pastries at the very pinnacle of the points scale. 'And I don't even insist on samphire, delicious though it is. There are all sorts of herbal miracles in the hedgerows, according to the Internet. We're not close enough to the sea to get all of them, but how about dandelions for starters? And chickweed? Bitter cress? Ivy toadflax? Goodness knows we're awash with enough weeds in the herb garden.'

'I suppose you couldn't get much more organic and natural than that,' Robin conceded. 'What about other things, though? And once you'd weeded the herb patch, where would we get more?'

'You're the walker, gaffer.' Pix leaned pointedly back in his chair. 'Who better than you to source the stuff?'

'I'll do my best. There's this book I saw on the Internet that tells you all about it. I've sent for a copy. Now, Robin, could you check out the laws applying to foraging? There are bound to be some.' He'd dropped out of a Law course and occasionally fingered his books. It'd be a total pain if rereading them made him go back to Uni, but that was a problem I'd just have to deal with. I might find some way of helping with those huge student debts he'd end up with, too.

'Like all wild swans belonging to the Queen, you mean?'

'Exactly.'

Robin donned his sober face. 'Why this sudden enthusiasm, Josie? Are we going into the red, or something?'

'You know we're not!' I shared the books with them every week. They knew to the last penny how much we had in the current account. About the rest, of course, zilch, and that was how it was going to stay, or I would have Tony's hands reaching down from heaven to box my ears.

'So why the sudden yen for freebies?'

'It's not the cost. It's the flavour, the texture, the exquisite flavours you can't get from polytunnel produce, no matter how good the producer.'

The lads stared at me. 'Oh, ah,' Pix

grunted, the two syllables epitomising extreme cynicism. 'You've been reading too much bloody Wordsworth, gaffer.'

'One of the worst poets ever to write some of the best poems,' I snapped. 'Or the best poet to write the worst poems.'

'Unless it was his sister?' Pix suggested.

But we mustn't get diverted into Eng. Lit. I knew our discussions could while away hours. 'Poetry apart, though, think of the cachet. Think of the publicity.'

'Think of the egg on our faces if we served someone the wrong sort of something. I mean, we all know about mushrooms turning out to be toadstools – whoops! – so are any of these precious weeds of yours poisonous? And what if you got poison ivy instead of ivy toadflax? We wouldn't know till the punters keeled over.'

'Quite,' Pix nodded. 'So we really might need to recruit someone with a real knowledge of the local fauna to scavenge for us, rather than doing it ourselves.'

My joints thought of all that bending and stretching and fervently agreed. In any case, I had a pub to run, another to think about buying and dodgy chicken to investigate. We adjourned the meeting, promising to consider, if I still wanted to poke my nose into other things, a third qualified chef whom we could train up to take over the Abbot's Duncombe place if we took it on. I rather thought Robin and Pix would want him or her to specialise in the free herbal side.

Time for dodgy chicken, then. Phoning the mobile number Michael Rousdon had given me, I hung on and on. No voice mail, no messaging service. I fizzed, slapping the desk in frustration. I was just about to go and walk it off when Pix called up. We'd had a sudden lunch booking for eight, in addition to our usual regulars. I wouldn't care to give a hand, would I, since Robin was still shopping for tonight? Excellent! What better than a good session with a vegetable or two to rid oneself of frustration?

Hell, I was so tired. The lunchtime special salad – chicken, bacon and avocado – had leapt out of the kitchen. I think the reason lay in the houmous dressing I used. The salad and a light soup and the ploughman's platters. More and more people had crowded in. I suppose it was the suddenly warm weather that had brought them out. Yes, now I came to think of it, it was positively summery. Look at the sun on the forsythia.

How dared those kids have died when they had this to look forward to? Had they fought? Had they hurt their assailants? For a moment I thought hopefully of DNA, but then I recalled the means needed to identify them. There'd be no traces under anyone's fingernails. And no trace in the gutted church.

How long had I stood with my forehead against my bedroom window? Long enough to leave a little patch I religiously polished off. The White Hart now ran to a cleaning lady, but it was imperative she spent most of her time in public areas, not chasing round after me.

Time to blow some of these damned cobwebs away. The tougher the walk the quicker they flew, so today I rooted out heavy trousers and jacket, and boots, rather than shoes. I even found my gloves.

Pix was standing at the reception desk staring in disgust at the phone. 'You've got an answerphone – why don't folk use it? Three times someone's tried and not left a message. And then when I grabbed the phone, they put it down at the other end.'

'You gave the name of the place, did you?'

'As per your training, gaffer.' He gave a mock salute, softened by a smile you'd call affectionate.

'And the answerphone message is clear enough – thanks to you and your school of Olivier enunciation. Weird.' I shrugged it off, but something in my bunion twitched. 'I suppose,' I added, turning back, 'you didn't try 1471?'

'I did, as it happens. In case whoever it was just didn't like answerphones and might have gone elsewhere. But they'd denied their number. Some poor sap in a call centre trying to make up his quota, maybe.'

'Sure,' I said, easily, as if I meant it.

I'd gone no more than a few yards before noticing Corbishley deep in conversation with a man in a metallic blue 4x4, clean enough to suggest he wasn't a genuine farmer needing four wheel traction to get himself up his front drive – some round here were two miles long, and bore as much relation to your average block-paved path as St Jude's bore to St Mark's, Venice.

As I passed, Corbishley straightened, pointing strongly northwards, and stepped back, apologising at nearly treading on me.

'These townies,' he complained, as the vehicle pulled swiftly away. 'Coming down here with their big cars and lacking the most basic maps. Weekend sailors too – did you see the coast guards Plymouth way had to rescue a man trying to navigate with an Ordnance Survey map?'

'Putting everyone else's life at risk,' I said, as he presumably hoped.

'Quite so. And now I must hasten away. My wife, you know?'

My headshake was designed to express both my ignorance and my potential sympathy.

'Virtually crippled. Arthritis. And the

167

drugs she takes for the pain – took, I should say! – seem to be implicated in the strokes she had last year. She's virtually house-bound these days, especially when the wind comes in from the east.'

'I'm so sorry.' That might explain his crankiness, too, of course.

'But on a good day – I see you've installed ramps and a disabled – er – cloakroom. Perhaps we may...'

'You'd be most welcome.' Even if, as I strongly suspected, he wanted another freebie. 'As you saw, we get very busy some nights. Could you just phone beforehand to make sure we have a table?'

He was clearly taken aback. Should I gab on about making sure I could organise a table with easy wheelchair access? On the whole, Tony's dictum about never giving more information than necessary, especially if it sounded like an apology, ringing in my ears, it was better simply to offer an affable smile.

It seemed we were going our separate ways when he suddenly stopped. 'Have you heard ... is there any news? About the young men?'

It was a very good question, and inter-estingly expressed. Particularly neutral, one might say. As for information, DI Lawton wouldn't rush to share any gems with me. But she might well talk to Nick, if her prickliness with him were indeed a sign she was attracted. It wasn't the best of odds, though. Andy was a more likely conduit of information. A phone call to him was certainly in order. Or so I told myself. Unless I could grab him after this evening's service.

'Nothing, I'm afraid,' I replied. 'Of course, the fire service, the police – they probably have different protocols.'

He snorted. 'These big organisations. All red tape and not letting the left hand know what the right is doing.'

'You sound as if you speak from bitter experience,' I prompted.

'Indeed I do. All my years in industry ... government here, Europe there. Couldn't turn round without falling over some sort of inspector.'

'Of course, in the chemical area ... but you'd have to be very careful with pharmaceuticals, wouldn't you?' I rocked back on one hip, folding my arms loosely and nodding in readiness for a comfortable gossip. No response. 'Or petro-chemicals?'

'Heavens above! Look at the time! Can't leave my poor lady wife on her own any longer. She'll think I've run away to sea. Good day to you, Mrs Welford.' He felt for a non-existent hat to doff, and compromised with a half-salute.

Damn and blast. But I saw him off with a neighbourly wave, hoping he would think

I'd been after no more than a casual chat. Had I pressed too hard? But I still didn't know how he'd earned his crust.

My feet were much more inclined to take me back to the village shop to see what a bit of a natter would unearth than to stride out into the country for some real calorie-burning, muscle-hardening exercise. As I dithered indecisively on the edge of the pavement, I felt rather than saw something approaching me fast, and simply reeled out of the way. I think my hand on part of the vehicle might have helped propel me. As it was, I went base over apex over the artistic line of potted daffodils and jonquils I brighten the White Hart's boundary with. And someone switched off the sky.

Chapter Eleven

No, there it was. It was covered by a black-ish-red mist, which thinned as I blinked. Blood? I must have hit my head on one of the dratted pots. At least bleeding meant I wasn't dead. I mopped with a tissue. There: I'd live.

What now?

Scrabbling to my feet and giving chase was not an option. Not at my age. What I needed was more a period, as Jane Austen might have said, of quiet reflection.

Were all the bits and pieces in the right place and preferably in working order?

Possibly.

Yes, of course they were! Don't make such a fuss, woman.

At least my walking gear of heavy trousers and quilted jacket would have saved me from gravel rash: I'd have hated playground knees. And that thought did bring me up fast. It was chucking out time at the school. What if the maniac continued his progress down the village street at that pace?

OK. I was sitting up. What about the next move? Standing up?

No, nothing seemed to be broken. I could walk. Run? Come on: all that adrenaline pumping through the old veins was supposed to aid fight or flight. It might permit an ungainly jog.

Was I aiming to prevent a disaster? Even if I could have taken wing, it might have been too late. Would have been.

Then I realised I could hear no screams. Perhaps he'd dropped speed enough not to be lethal. All the same, a couple of mums might have noted the make. I hoped so. Because – and I hang my head to admit it – I couldn't recall a single thing.

Of course I could, I told myself as I puffed onwards. It was big. A people carrier? It could have been one of those frog-eyed Italian jobs. No. It was even uglier than that. A ubiquitous white van? They always bullied their way around. One with bull bars? It was 4x4s that needed bull bars, to fend off the herds of wild cattle rampaging through our lanes – or not. So was it a 4x4 that had driven at me?

The thought processes were as tedious as that. I'd been run down – yes, it had been driven straight at me – by a damned great 4x4. A metallic blue one. And only slowly did it dawn on me that it could have been the one that I'd seen Corbishley leaning up against, affable as you like, for all he'd huffed and puffed about the driver after-wards.

Suddenly my bumble to the school picked up pace. If I'd wanted information before, now I'd get it or die.

It was only as I gazed at the world through a forest of legs that I realised that there is only so much that mind can achieve over matter. It was as if my matter gave out when it was clear no kids had been involved. My legs had folded all on their own, the rest following. Now, over my head anxious Mummerset voices were talking about the relative merits of first aiders and ambulances. One of the schoolteachers had train-ing, it seemed, and she was getting the first aid box right now. Others opined that a dressing on that poor head was all well and good but what if I had concussion?

A sharp new voice – also female – broke through the whispers. 'There's an ambulance on its way, Mrs Welford. It's DI Lawton here. Can you hear me? No, don't try to move.'

'I'm fine,' I insisted. But my voice let me down. And I realised I was perilously close to tears.

For some reason A and E at Taunton was deserted – they almost welcomed someone to fuss over. Truth to tell, I almost welcomed being fussed over. Especially when every last test proved negative, and the cut that had produced a quite disproportionate amount of blood proved to be so far up my forehead that my hair would certainly cover it and any subsequent scar.

The bonus was that I suddenly had an interested police ear. Not DI Lawton. She was well above such mundane things. But an obliging girl, PC Bernie Downs, who asked careful questions and didn't mind waiting while I sorted out sensible answers. I didn't actually implicate Corbishley in the incident, except to say he'd been talking with the driver of a similar 4x4 only a few minutes before. Let the police talk to him: just at the moment I couldn't. There was talk of keeping me in, for what they tactfully called 'observation', for heaven's sake.

'You mean you want to watch the bruises coming out!'

'And one or two other things.'

'No can do. I've got ... there's a short service at church– I have to–' Aware that my incoherence wasn't doing my cause any good, I shut up.

But it was no good. Despite my fretting – what would people think if I missed an evensong dedicated to Tim? – the medics took ages to find painkillers and the paperwork to set me free, and it was only when I threatened to discharge myself that they shifted up a gear.

The police girl, kind and solicitous as if I were her mother, offered me a lift but I took a taxi, wanting to be as unobtrusive as possible, a vain hope, of course, given the efficiency of the village jungle drums. There was already a little bunch of flowers where I'd been hit and a couple by the back door of the White Hart. Weird. I thought people only left them when there'd been a fatality. As soon as I'd paid the driver, I forced my clanging head groundwards to have a look at the one on the verge. It was either that or bend the knees and pick it up, not a serious possibility at the moment. I wished I hadn't bothered. RIP, indeed. Anonymous, of course. I got the message. To be fair, those by the door were altogether nicer, and signed, to boot. It seemed I did have some well-wishers in the village. I just hoped someone remembered to tell Andy why I'd skipped his and the bishop's gig. Meanwhile, I phoned PC Downs to tell her about the wreath. I had to leave a message, but I hoped for the best.

'If you really want instant dismissal, without references, you make a fuss,' I told an anguished-looking Robin when he started to flap. 'Just get on with your work and leave me to do my best. I've got both Lucy and Lorna to help out. For God's sake, if you have me at death's door, you'll put them into a panic, too.'

Robin at last seemed to understand and let himself out of my flat. But the look he shot over his shoulder was distinctly old-fashioned. 'It's no use pretending nothing happened, not in a village,' he said.

'Just play it down,' I said. 'Stupid grockle clocks elderly licensee. That sort of thing.'

'As opposed to – hang on, Josie, you think this is connected to the St Jude's fire, don't you?'

I jabbed with a minatory digit, which was turning into an aubergine. 'One word to anyone but me and you're out. Tonight!'

'Not if you're expecting Pix to tackle the turkey Marsala – you know he always overcooks it.' He returned fully to the room, and squatted beside me. 'You'll tell Nick?'

'I suppose.' This was what it must be like to be old. Taking orders – for your own good – from kids.

'No suppose about it. It's better to tell him than leave him to work it out.'

'OK. On one condition. You go and get that RIP wreath and shove it – put some gloves on first, mind – shove it in the shed. I don't know what they can and can't get DNA off these days. Besides which, it's untidy, littering the place up like that.'

'So you will tell the police?' Robin insisted.

'Already have.'

'And Nick?'

We exchanged old-fashioned looks, well tempered with affection that was certainly genuine on my part, and he slipped out.

Nick. Yes, Nick. As I struggled into the shower and thence into some clothes that didn't demand I wriggle to get into them, I gave him some thought.

Why had he looked smug yesterday? I'd never got a chance to ask him. I probably wouldn't this evening, not unless bell-ringing practice was cancelled as a mark of respect. And then it'd be him doing the interrogation, wouldn't it?

Hell: more and more bruises were coming out. I did my best, with several layers of foundation and a magic pen designed to cover blemishes, but it wasn't a very good best. Earrings? My lobes winced at the thought, though not as much as my fingers at the prospect of rings. And there was no way I could crush my hand through my favourite bangle. OK. I'd have to admit it. I'd been in a road accident. But as far as my clients were concerned, that was it. Full stop.

Shoes. Oh, my God.

What I really wanted to do was sink in front of the TV news with a glass of wine and baked beans on toast, but that wasn't how it worked in – what was it Andy had called it? – the hospitality trade.

The news! I ought to catch the news for the latest take on St Jude's. But all I was in time for was a weather man so miserable he made Nick look positively joyous telling me it might be fine tomorrow.

Shrugging metaphorically – my shoulders weren't up to the literal kind – I put on a smart front-of-house smile and went down to do my job. Lucy Gay had laid up, and would currently be feeding all her brothers and sisters and supervising their homework. Only when they were settled to her satis-faction would she come down in the rather chic waiter's outfit we'd picked out and do her stuff. She was a draw: the older clients cooed over her devotion to the kids, the younger men chatting her up for all they were worth. She flirted and chatted, but as soon as the rush was over would disappear once more, this time into the bar to tackle homework while pulling desultory halves of cider for the locals. In fact, I often decreed the rush was over long before it was, to make sure she got decent grades, because if ever a girl was destined for better things than waitressing it was Lucy. My assistant manager? She'd end up running the Ritz, if I had anything to do with it.

I'd got as far as the reception desk when Nick surged in, steaming with fury.

'At my age!' he fulminated, slamming his open hands on the wood. 'With my experience! And I fall for the oldest trick in the book!'

He was too taken up with his problem to notice any damage to me, and I was happy to keep it that way. Asking a few more questions might help. 'Which is?'

'I'm on my way back to the kids' evensong when some bloke shunts me, and when I get out to investigate, his mate jumps in and nicks my briefcase. And my laptop.'

'But not the Honda itself?' I pursued.

'I might be cabbage-looking but I'm not that green. I took my key with me.'

'And this is in *Taunton?* Hardly a hotbed of urban crime!'

'Which is why I fell for it, I suppose.'

178

'What about the Honda?'

'Hardly a scar. Expertly done. Shit!' He slammed his hand on the desk again and let off a stream of invective.

Mindful of my customers' sensibilities, I interrupted. 'Much in the briefcase?'

'Hardly anything. Don't know why I bothered to take it in.'

'You were flourishing it like a flag last night.'

'Only because I'd got a list of chicken processing plants to check out. Hell, they'll have gone. But I've still got them on file on my work computer, so not to worry.'

'Except someone knows you're interested in chicken processing plants.'

'Which I'm entitled to be, given my job.'

So why the anxiety? Well, Nick would even be anxious if he won the Lottery on roll-over night.

'Bell-ringing tonight?' I used a doubtful inflection.

'Hardly.'

'Quite. So why not go and have a shower and then come down here and get some food inside you: it looks like a quiet evening, and I can really recommend the herb-roasted chicken.'

His smile flickered. 'Your special roast potatoes?'

'Is there any other sort?'

'The other thing,' Nick said, as if there hadn't been a half-hour gap between his last words and these, 'is that I've got to go up to Heathrow. I shall be on the road about five and I'll get breakfast en route.'

'Heathrow? That's hardly your patch, is it?'

'Everyone's patch for the next few days. All five of us FSA inspectors, plus Customs and Excise and Trading Standards. There's going to be a purge on people bringing in bush meat.'

I pondered. 'That's dried wild animals from Africa, right? Totally illegal?'

'But on sale all over London. And wherever there's a large African community. A real health risk, not just to humans but to animals, too. We absolutely don't want it getting into the food chain. So I may be spending time in Bristol, Cardiff and even dear old Brum.' He grew almost animated. 'A purge worthy of Stalin, that's what we're having. And it's a three-line whip. All leave cancelled,' he concluded, slumping as if there were no chicken in prospect.

'So how long will you be away?'

'So that you can let my room, and offer my favourite table to someone else!'

'Of course.'

We exchanged companionable grins. 'As long as it takes, I suppose. Probably till Sunday. There's talk of it for the following

180

weekend, too, in the hope we've lulled them into thinking it was all over.'

'Any idea why your lords and masters should want to have their purge now?'

'None.' He looked me straight in the eye. 'Which worries me.'

I nodded soberly. As I made my way to the next table, I pressed his shoulder. Goodness knew why: part of our tacit deal was that we never got remotely physical. But this was a matey gesture, not a mating one, and I was sure he wouldn't take it the wrong way.

He tended not to have a dessert, but once I'd cleared his main course, I returned to his table. 'I can recommend the baked apples. Stuffed with the last of our homemade mincemeat.'

'With thick, gooey yellow custard? With a skin?'

Finger on lips, I whispered, 'It's supposed to be proper organic egg custard here!'

His mouth drooped. 'Oh. Not Bird's?'

'I'll see what I can do.'

Lucy Gay had joined the lads in the kitchen, and smiled when I came in with the private order. 'Looking so much better, isn't he?' she asked, proprietorially. She and her siblings regarded him tolerantly as a sort of uncle. He didn't go much for horseplay, but was great when it came to mending things, and he read aloud – Lucy insisted on a nightly family get-together – with more drama than the whole RSC put together.

'Much.'

'But this church business – it's hit him hard. I hope it won't set him back.'

'He was a policeman, Lucy: they get hardened to sudden death,' Robin threw in, over his shoulder.

'Not always. He'd got something called post-traumatic stress disorder when he first came. Made him really weird, didn't it, Josie? This time, I know they weren't real friends, but you could see he was upset. Poor Nick.'

'He'll tough it out,' Robin said.

He would. And I would too.

The last pan washed, Robin said, 'I suppose she needs a decent father figure – better than the last one, anyway.'

Without blinking, Pix asked, 'What was wrong with the last one? Apart from dying and leaving a family of five orphaned?'

I counted off my fingers. 'Alcoholic. Unemployable. Went totally to pieces when his wife died.'

'And blew himself up preparing a bomb for the White Hart, don't forget, Josie,' Robin concluded. 'They don't talk about it much in the village because of Lucy.'

'I bet they talk about it like buggery behind her back. Sorry, Josie. Can't get the hang of this no swearing rule.'

'So I'd noticed.'

Pix peered at me. 'You're going to have a real shiner tomorrow. Maybe two. What did Nick say about the accident?'

I aimed to look mildly amused and exasperated: it probably came out sheepish. 'He – well, it didn't come up.'

'It bloody well should have done. I was hoping he'd offer to take a few days' leave to keep an eye on you.'

In my heart, so was I. 'There's a crisis on. A national one.'

'Not more carcinogenic food dye!'

'Not this time. But it's dead serious. I couldn't ask him, and even if I did, he'd have to say no. Have to.' Even if I pleaded, which I'd never done yet and wasn't proposing to practise now.

As for Andy, his name never came up. So I had no one to confess to but myself that I was disappointed he hadn't popped in to see why I'd missed the service.

It wasn't, I reflected as I tried to find a halfway comfortable spot in bed, as if I didn't know half a dozen potential minders. Professional minders, that is. Heavies, prepared to use muscle and – well, anything else necessary. I only had to make a phone call.

That's what Tony would have done, would

have wanted me to do now. But that sort of thing was from my past life, the one I'd so firmly put behind me.

Income apart, of course.

Chapter Twelve

True to his word, the next morning Nick slipped out without disturbing anyone. I was awake, of course, having stupidly refused to take the maximum dose of the painkillers the hospital had provided. But I was too muzzy – and in much too much pain – to be able to leap out of bed, don a demure wrap, sprint down the corridor after him and make any selfish suggestions about his staying put to guard me. In any case, after the slowest set of stretches ever and a very leisurely shower, a cursory Internet scan showed me exactly why bush meat should be kept out of the country. Ebola fever, for instance: I wouldn't fancy an epidemic of that. It'd make bird flu look a complete doddle.

It might even make my present state look a complete doddle.

If I hadn't seen all the X-rays for myself, I'd have stormed back and demanded a recount: surely simple bruises couldn't hurt this much? But I was definitely in one piece, and I knew from bitter experience the best way to deal with pain was to work through it.

To be honest, tidying Tim's things wouldn't have been my idea of therapy, but Andy phoned me before I'd got enough caffeine in me to pass for alert. He jumped straight in without mentioning my absence the previous night. 'The police say they've finished with the rectory. They've not made much mess, but then, it doesn't look as if it was very tidy to start with. And the kitchen's a typical bachelor mess.'

'Are we talking thorough spring-clean or a superficial Hoover?' I might just manage the latter.

'Just enough to make it acceptable, I should think. After all, it might just help the parents' healing process to sort through all his belongings.'

'And if they don't want to?'

'Professional house clearers, I'm afraid. The police recommended a couple of firms. But I'd hate that.'

'Me too. So count me in if necessary. Meanwhile, I'll make the place presentable, don't you worry.'

At least I was now awake enough to play down the hit and run when a reporter phoned.

'Just getting clumsy in my old age,' I assured him. 'And how's that lovely little girl of yours? Sara? You know we're having a proper play area in the spring?'

Just in case anyone else might phone, I headed straight for the rectory the moment I'd breakfasted. I overcame the pain every footstep gave me by reminding myself I'd wanted a sniff round the place, hadn't I?

Not literally.

Prisons had a very male smell, which percolated even the visiting area. The same musty smell hit us the moment Andy opened the rectory door. Poor Tim, he'd not had a great sense of housekeeping. The lounge where he had to hold parochial church council and other church business meetings was tidyish, but not even superficially clean. His study – I'd never seen a study before, not a real, live study, which Andy assured me this was – smelt variously of dank old books and sweaty feet. With more than a hint of pot.

Andy's eyebrows disappeared towards his hairline. 'Oh, dear.'

'If we throw the windows open and get one of those powered air-fresheners it'll be OK,' I hazarded.

'It's getting rid of the cannabis, not the smell, I was worried about.'

'First find it. He can't have afforded a great stash, surely. If he did, you've got plenty of options – pop it on a bonfire or flush it down a loo or–'

186

'I was thinking about handing it over to the police.'

'Who will probably smoke it themselves,' I overrode him. For God's sake, what was he thinking of? 'I didn't know that clergymen were allowed to take drugs,' I added more gently.

'Who is? And I know of more clergymen who are full-blown alcoholics than I care to think of: I suppose it's having to polish off the communion wine that pushes them down the slippery slope.'

'Non-alcoholic wine? Or you could tip the spare into a flower arrangement? OK, OK – only joking. But people like me don't understand the ins and outs of church lore. Or do I mean law?' He was not amused, but seemed more anxious than angry. 'Look,' I continued, 'leave any pot you find for me to deal with. Meanwhile I'll nip round to the shop for an air-freshener.' Nip? A slow waddle, more like. It was either that or get back into the car, which had been an ordeal.

It was only when he held the study door open for me – I do like old-fashioned courtesy – that he gasped, 'Are you all right, Josie?'

'Sure. Why not?'

His voice dropped into what I recognised as counselling hush. 'If you and Nick – if there's a problem...'

'Nick? What's he got to do with the price

of coal?'

'Your ... injuries,' he explained, delicately. In general I really liked his voice, deep and mellifluous, as you'd expect. But now he sounded more sickly than honeyed.

I threw my head back and roared with laughter. 'Nick! You think Nick–! Good God, this wasn't domestic violence! Some maniac in a 4x4 and I had a bit of a disagreement.'

'You mean, road rage?'

Still laughing, I told him, 'I mean rank bad driving. It's only pedestrians who are supposed to be on the pavement. Cars – though I hate to dignify the ugly great things with the term – are supposed to be on the road. I got knocked over, right in front of my own pub,' I said flatly. 'That's why I didn't come to your special evensong.'

A flash of the hand dismissed that. 'Are you sure you–? I mean, shouldn't you be resting?' Despite the professional sympathy, he really did sound quite concerned.

'I've been perfectly all right for the past half hour, haven't I?' I probably sounded even more acidulated than I felt.

'I'm so sorry. I really am. Why didn't you tell me?'

'Because there was a job to be done, and someone had to do it. Besides which,' I added soberly, 'I was rather hoping the police might have spoken to you about the cause of death.'

He blinked. 'The fire. No? Nick was talking about smoke inhalation and I assumed... Was I wrong?'

'Why don't we sit down?' There was no point in standing half-in, half-out of the study. 'Here, in this apology for a living room. Andy – surely the diocese could have come up with some money for emulsion and decent carpet and curtains? These were Sue's taste, if such a word can honestly be used.' I found an upright chair and lowered myself carefully.

'We weren't talking about interior decor,' he said, forgetting he was trying to be gentle with an invalid.

'So we weren't. And I won't any more, so long as you promise the place will be tarted up before the next incumbent moves in. Tang and Tim. They may well have died of smoke inhalation, but can you honestly tell me that two fit young men wouldn't have tried to fight any fire and scarpered when they saw they couldn't? The door was only locked on the inside. The lock was beautifully oiled. Work of seconds.'

'If they were asleep?'

'Possibly. But why should they bother to slit the throats of Samson and Delilah? The geese,' I prompted, when he looked blank. 'Someone had sliced their heads off. Does that sound like Tim? I know Tang didn't like chicken, but that's carrying an avian phobia

189

a bit far.'

He sat down heavily. 'You don't think–? Killing someone in a church? Josie – that must be the worst sacrilege!'

I said mildly, 'Wasn't that what Shakespeare thought? When he made Laertes swear his revenge against Hamlet?'

He blinked again. I never liked anything better than taking someone aback like that. I continued smoothly, 'I shall be interested to hear what the post-mortems revealed. If anything. They were talking dental records to identify Tim,' I said. 'As for Tang...'

We shook sad heads in concert.

'Somehow it would help to know who he was,' Andy said at last, surprising me. I suppose I was expecting some platitude about God knowing who he was – but then, in general, Andy wasn't into clichés.

Hands on knees, I pushed myself vertical. 'This won't get the air-freshener.' And I set off before he could argue.

By the time I'd got back from my expedition to the shops, with no fewer than three plug-in fresheners, plus dusters, spray-polish and bleach and no gossip worth repeating, Andy had a load chugging in the washing machine, with another pile – bedclothes – waiting to go through.

'Why not pick some daffodils and pop them in a jam jar or something? There are already some at the end of the garden that managed to avoid Sue's depredations, but I can't find anything like a vase. Andy, it's wrong to catapult a young man or woman in here with no support. Kids these days don't seem to learn housekeeping from their mothers. How are they going to cope living on their own, cooking for themselves and trying to juggle half a dozen churches? And being active in the local community? Can't be done,' I answered for him.

'In the old days someone like Tim would have raised enough money from farming his glebelands to pay for a housekeeper and a gardener and whatever. Now I suppose we expect the parishioners to help a bit.'

'In this village? Talk about a house divided... Half the folk are incomers using the place as a dormitory and forcing up prices beyond the range of locals. The other half are resentful natives. The trouble is, without people like Tim and me, the village has to do without its essentials – no church, no pub – and, without the commuting incomers, no kids for the village school either.'

'But there ought to be enough people willing to rally round in case of need.'

'I'm sure there are. Look how we responded to the crisis at St Jude's. I bet the money-raising efforts to refurbish it will be breathtaking. But that catches the imagination far more than day-to-day support. And I'm as much to blame as anyone.'

'But you have enough on your hands, running a business like yours. What about retired people?'

'I think the consensus is that they've done their share. As for the younger women, either they too work or they devote any space in their lives left over from ferrying their kids around to their fingernails and the gym.'

'You sound very bitter.'

'Realistic. Plus my back is hurting, which always gives a jaundiced view of life. But, emotive language apart–'

'You fascinate me, Josie,' he said, laughter making those blue eyes dangerously attractive. 'One minute you're as down to earth as they come; next you're flashing fancy vocabulary and talking about Shakespeare. I just can't stick a label on you.'

'Good. Why should I want to be labelled? Why should anyone for that matter? You must hate it yourself, everyone watching their p's and q's and creeping round in your presence as if they were at a funeral.' I nodded home my point, and turned to the washing machine, now chuntering its way to a halt. 'So here you have a perfect opportunity to go against stereotype: it can't be everyday a dean gets a chance to hang washing on a line.'

Lest he argue, and I had to remind him that my knees and back were simply not up to such simple tasks, I bustled out into the hall, hoping to locate a vacuum cleaner in the cubby-hole under the stairs. Success! But it wouldn't work because it was completely bunged up, and there was no sign of new bags anywhere. There was nothing for it but to empty the existing one into the bin, fistful by unlovely fistful. I was hard at work when Andy got back from the garden.

'Actually, you do me less than justice,' he complained, peering down the garden to admire the result of his efforts. 'Since Marcia died, I've become pretty self-sufficient. And I find a line of washing flapping on a spring day like this quite inspiring. I suppose it reminds me of when I was a child, when there were rows and rows of brilliant white nappies on all our neighbours' lines. People don't seem to go in for them these days, do they?'

Marcia? I hadn't skipped a beat in my polishing, but did now. 'Don't get me started on landfill and disposable nappies,' I said. 'Right, have you started the sheets yet? Because there's even more washing than we thought: I found a heap of towels under the bed.'

'I dread to think what the loo'll be like.'

'Full of bleach now,' I said dryly.

'I'll load that machine.'

So he was a widower, was he? I found the information oddly reassuring, though why, since I'd no intention of ever making a pass at him, I couldn't say. What did interest me was why he'd never mentioned his wife before. But I could hardly ask.

I was making our third cup of coffee, counting the minutes till I dared pop more pills, and Andy, at his insistence, was on his knees ('I get a lot of practice, after all!') attacking the bathroom floor, when his mobile rang. Grabbing it, I trotted – which was about the best I could manage – to the foot of the stairs, flourishing it. His descent was faster than I can manage on a good day. He showed no signs of wanting privacy, but I left him to it anyway: I had a kitchen to rescue. I had binned any perishable food I couldn't give the birds. No wonder Tim had looked so skeletal – there wasn't much of anything. Now I was attacking the work surfaces and cupboard doors: to my shame I abandoned elbow grease in favour of a virgin bottle of patent cleanser lurking at the back of a cupboard otherwise devoted to crockery.

'If he had eaten in here, he'd have stood a good chance of getting e.coli, salmonella, campylobacter and any other food poisoning bug going,' I told Andy, as he came in, looking particularly sober.

'None of them as lethal as knife thrusts so hard they damaged the surface of the bone. Tang, too. You were right, Josie. Those kids were murdered.' He sat down heavily on a filthy-looking chair. 'And do you know what I said to the policewoman – that DI Lawton? I said, "Who by?" Stupidly, just like that. As if you hadn't warned me, as if I hadn't in my heart known, as if I don't deal with the dying and the dead all the time.' He stared at the coffee mug I'd pressed into his hand as if it were a book in Sanskrit.

Any other man I'd have simply gathered him to me. In similar crises, some of Tony's mates cried their eyes out as if they were babies; one or two ended up in my bed. Is there something about death and bereavement, especially funerals, that brings out the testosterone? Even as I stepped forward to hold him, however, I heard Corbishley's judgement on me. I didn't want to confirm any suspicions Andy might have of its accuracy.

His knuckles were white against the mug, from which he sipped convulsively. An enormous clock over the fridge told me it was after twelve. Time to knock off. I wanted to be at the White Hart, where there was life and live kids.

Leaving him still immobile, I heaved myself upstairs and into the bathroom. He'd finished the floor apart from one corner. Try as I might, I couldn't kneel, so I hoicked the bucket on to the closed loo and fished out the cloth – a pair of Tim's underpants, it transpired – and wringing it out, dropped it. My footwork might not have got me into Manchester United but it did the trick. All I had to do then was scoop the cloth up again – for which the loo brush came in handy – and I was done.

The only indication that Andy had moved was that the coffee mug was empty. I took it from him and rinsed it.

'How can you be so calm?' he screamed, almost making me drop it. 'Washing up as if nothing had happened?'

I stared.

'Don't you feel anything? You don't react when the church burns down. You don't react when Corbishley insults you. You don't react when you're run over. You don't react when you hear murder's been committed. What in God's name does it take to crack that carapace of yours?'

Chapter Thirteen

If there was a sensible reply to Andy's question, I couldn't think of it. Not without going into a long explanation I didn't want to give – and he probably didn't want to hear – about how I coped with Tony's long jail terms. In my head I tried words to describe myself like *stoic* or *phlegmatic*, thinking a touch of quasi-academic vocabulary might appeal. In the end, I gave a stiff shrug: he could make of it and indeed of me what he liked. I said flatly, 'I'm knackered. And the White Hart needs me.' As an afterthought, I added, 'Can I offer you some lunch?' Perhaps it was an apology for my brusqueness.

He opened his mouth, flushed and dropped his eyes. Then he looked vaguely about, as if assessing whether we'd done enough. 'The washing. On the line and in the machine.'

'Not to mention the load I shoved into the hall.' My bloody voice cracked. It must have been the pain and fatigue – so perhaps that was the answer to his question. But I didn't share it with him. 'Tell you what, I'll bundle those dirty towels together and take them back to the White Hart. I'll take the load in the machine to dry too. As for the stuff on the line, I suppose we could fold it loosely and put it on a clothes horse, if he's got one.'

'The airing cupboard,' he said. 'The tank's so poorly insulated it's like a little dryer. Even after we've switched off the immersion heater, it should do the job.'

'Great.'

I felt his eyes on me. 'Tell you what, I put it out so I'll get it in. If you wouldn't mind washing the mugs and finishing in here.'

I nodded – I was too weary to argue. And he'd tried to be tactful without sounding sorry for me. Unfortunately his plan backfired. Whereas gathering the clothes from the line would have meant just stretching, the job he'd given me, picking up the soiled towels, meant bending. I managed. And emptied the machine too.

'I'll set off now,' I said. 'I'll see you in a few minutes.'

'If you just hang on while I shut all the windows, we could drive in convoy.'

'You won't get lost,' I said crisply. 'See you back at the pub.' No point in telling him it might be better if we weren't seen arriving together. No, I wasn't worried about his reputation, or mine, this time. Or even about Corbishley and Malins. Just about the person who'd run me down. There was no point in offering him another potential target.

As I fell through the back door, Pix greeted me with a yell from the kitchen. 'Thank God you're back. Robin's got one of his migraines. He couldn't see to slice an onion so I packed him off to bed.'

'Well done.'

'And we've got twelve heavy-duty walkers wanting mega-meals.'

'Give me three minutes and I'll be with you.'

Shame about the *tête-à-tête* lunch with Andy – but maybe I wasn't sorry at all. For a variety of reasons. Not least of which was that a long stint under pressure in the kitchen would force me to keep moving and forget I couldn't.

'I quite understand,' Andy said, not even in the huffy tone of someone who didn't. 'I take it you'll be tied up all evening, too?'

What else did he have in mind? 'I'm afraid it looks like it. Poor Robin doesn't often get migraines but when he does they blast him. Anyway, can I take your order? If you're in a hurry I'll slip you to the top of the pile.'

After the rush, while the day-time minion was scrubbing down the kitchen, I gave myself a couple of minutes to check my emails and incoming phone messages. Nothing on the chicken front from any of my contacts. No Nick and no Nick's list, of course. I'd have to do a spot of investigating another way. But not today: I was too stiff and Pix needed me. But the next fine day. OK, if my body persisted in being a nuisance, the one after that.

And to my horror I found myself popping a couple of painkillers and lying down on my bed, just for five minutes. Or until a panicking Pix banged so hard on my door it sounded as if he was coming through it: it was after five, and it was time for the evening shift.

Friday had seen me tied to the day (and evening) job. Then the weekend was upon us. And weekends involved work.

However, there was just one thing – and I suppose it showed just how badly I'd been shaken – that someone else ought to do something about. I'd clean forgotten the wreath kindly left where I'd fallen (I was already revising the word *accident*). What was that police constable's name? Hell, did I really need to find the card she'd given me to remember?

I did. Bernie Downs.

A man took the call, though it was to her direct line. 'I phoned PC Downs the other day,' I said, not wishing to suggest I thought she'd been lax in not getting back to me, but letting him think she might have been. 'About a wreath. I was wondering if she'd found anything.'

'She's off sick,' he told me.

'In that case...' I regaled him with an edited version of the accident and the subsequent floral tribute.

'Could be a joke?' he said.

'Of course it could. But not a nice one. Just in case it might help you people, I kept it in one of my outhouses.'

He promised to come round as soon as he had a moment, which I took to mean it was hardly a priority. I drifted back downstairs. There were dozens of more important jobs to do but only one I felt capable of. It was my comfort task: filling the pepper mills. Whether it was the simple folding of a paper cone to funnel the corns into the mills or the soft warm smell of the peppercorns I don't know. But I always felt better when I did it, which was a good thing.

We were fully booked for Saturday evening: we could have filled the room twice over. I was deep into preparation work at about eleven on Saturday morning when PC Downs turned up, apologising for her cold. If I expected a bright red nose and a rasping voice, I was disappointed.

'You mentioned other flowers?' she muttered, through a mug of steaming blackcurrant juice made from my own frozen blackcurrants. If she claimed a cold, a cold I'd treat her for.

'All of them had little notes from people I knew hoping I'd soon be on my feet.' All? Three. 'None of them was anonymous; none wished me to rest, in peace or anywhere else. Which was a good job really. Now, it's getting awfully close to lunch time...' She took my hint and left.

Why it should have taken ten hours and the Saturday evening special starter of hot smoked salmon on crushed baby potatoes, garnished with French beans and home-made basil mayonnaise to remind me, I prefer not to ask. But just as I was serving a particularly picky customer with this delect-able warm salad I remembered I hadn't checked with Downs if the police had found the sack of Tang's clothes. If Tim had tucked it in his garage, it was just the sort of thing to be overlooked. It didn't strike me that DI Lawton would welcome a call from me, however, nor even from Nick – especially from Nick, not if he was implying a criticism – had he happened to be around. If anyone would make her eat out of his hand it would be Andy. I risked a glance at my watch. Nine-thirty on a Saturday evening might not be the best time to phone him, however, if he was sweating over whatever sermon he had to deliver tomorrow. As for our benefice, the first scheduled service was eight o'clock communion at St Faith and St Lawrence.

Presumably the church wardens would manage to find a locum to take it. There should also be some sort of announcement about the rest of the temporary arrangements until a new incumbent could be installed. I might just get up and go.

Meanwhile, should I disturb Andy or not?

Why not? It was quiet enough here for me to take a break, Robin insisting he was now as fit as the proverbial flea and doing wondrous public things with crêpes – a bit seventies, perhaps, but he was such a dramatic genius with the flambé pan no one could complain, and indeed his display could be guaranteed to entertain the whole dining room. So I slid upstairs – OK, hauled myself slowly upstairs – and dialled Andy's number. He answered, third ring, his voice brusque enough to suggest he hadn't enjoyed being interrupted in whatever deans did at that time. But when I announced my name, I could hear a smile arrive.

'Josie! I thought you'd be chained to the stove or the sink.'

'Pix and Robin are at the former, and I've got a work experience sixth-former at the latter. I think he'll prefer psychiatric nursing to catering. And you: are you toiling with a quill pen or a word processor?'

'Tomorrow's sermon? Neither. Done and dusted. I was tossing up between a Macallan or a Bushmills.'

Was he indeed? 'What a tough call. Now, something with a much less lovely nose. Tang's clothes. Remember we had a bin liner full of them? I told Tim not to burn them in case they might provide some evidence of where Tang came from. His job, not China! But I never asked Tim what he'd done with the bin liner. I did mention it to DI Lawton, but she wasn't very pleased with me at the time. So if anyone was going to ask if the clothes had been found...You're entitled to ask, after all,' I wheedled.

'I'll get on to it first thing on Monday,' he said, 'unless you think there'll be someone on duty now?'

'The usual working day never seemed to prevail when they were after Tony,' I said, 'and he never killed anyone. Not personally,' I conceded, in the interests of honesty.

There was a short silence. His voice was totally neutral when he replied, 'This evening, then. Have you any idea where the sack might be? I didn't see it yesterday.'

'It was very noisome: if I'd been in charge of it, it would have been in a garage or shed, preferably well away from the house.'

'Noisome ... noisome,' he repeated, for no apparent reason. Another pause. 'Will you be in church tomorrow? St Faith and St Lawrence? Or one of the others in the benefice?'

'It's eight o'clock communion, isn't it?' The

only problem with attending a communion service was that I didn't take communion. That was reserved for people baptised and then confirmed into the church – or for visitors who were regular communicants in their own churches. But I did like the language of this particular service, since it used the King James Prayer Book, with all its measured archaisms. While the others took communion, I would simply sit at the back and be absorbed into the stillness.

He jumped in very fast. 'I suppose it's very hard for you – since you have to work so late tonight.'

'Better than the usual morning service: I start serving lunches half an hour after the closing hymn, which is a problem if the church is fifteen miles away. Any idea who'll be taking it?'

'Me.' For so short a syllable it seemed to have a lot of nuances. I picked up a lot of embarrassment, a touch of pleading and a smidgen of plain fact.

'I'd better set the alarm, then, hadn't I?' I nearly offered a post-service breakfast, but that seemed to bit sacrilegious.

St Faith and St Lawrence did encourage kneeling, but at least the pews were solid enough for me to be able to heave myself skywards when necessary. The service was held in the Lady Chapel, an altogether grander affair than the St Jude's equivalent.

I'd bargained on slipping in unobtrusively and lurking at the rear. However, Andy was waiting at the chapel entrance in the south transept to greet us all – there were nine in total, plus him. He rewarded us all with a smile, and, in my case at least, a searching look when I flinched at his too-firm hand-shake.

He took the service at a brisk but not rattling pace, delivering a short and moving sermon focused on death and rebirth, all in a voice pitched slightly lower than usual. I had no idea what might constitute a dress code for clergymen, but he was in simple black, head to toe.

Taking his place at the church door, he had a private word for each of us. I should imagine, however, that I was the only one asked for an invitation for coffee.

'When I've changed,' he added.

'You can have breakfast, if you like. I'll leave the back door unlocked.'

'Is that a good idea?'

'OK. *Knock three times and ask for Josie,*' I misquoted, badly. Should I have done? Comparing myself obliquely with a sexually generous character in *Under Milk Wood* wasn't necessarily the wisest thing in the world. It might not put him in the best of lights, either.

'Are you sure about this black sack?' DI

Lawton demanded, unable quite to disdain the coffee and croissant I'd pressed on her. She was here in search not of me but of Andy, in response to the call he'd made last night. Since then she'd obviously been commendably busy, her Sundays clearly being working days too.

'I told you. I know it was left in the church porch. And I'm sure Tim said he would take it home,' I added helplessly.

'Dean?' The hierarchies in her own profession almost brought her hand to the salute.

'I saw it in the porch, I'm sure of that. And I heard people talking about it. Tim promised to deal with it. Whether he did or whether it slipped his mind...' He shrugged elegantly. 'I take it that it really does matter?'

'If it can supply evidence of what Tang seems to have done... I suppose he never drew a picture for that nice woman?'

'Annie,' I replied. 'She'd have told us. As you're aware, there was a great deal of moral doubt whether we could ask him anything without knowing what to do with the information.' Secretly I kicked myself – in the most metaphorical sense, of course. Why, why, why hadn't I got him to draw what he'd done? Answer: because of those little communication difficulties. 'Meanwhile, the bag has gone totally missing?'

'I've checked with all my officers, with the forensic science teams and even the fire service. No trace. Yet. But we'll naturally go on looking.' She stopped abruptly, lips in a pucker she'd later regret.

I added as if it were just dawning on me, 'And their killers might have come from the same place, I suppose?'

'Is the implication then that someone didn't want it found?' Andy asked.

'Or that some over-anxious parishioner thought she ought to take it home to wash it?' I asked, clapping my hand – foolishly – to the side of my head. 'Those who got involved – I know most of their first names, but not their surnames or addresses, of course.'

'Surely someone from the church would?'

'Poor Tim. And, I suspect, the church wardens,' Andy said, as if grudging the information.

'Messrs Corbishley and Malins?'

'They did know about the sack and its contents,' I said. 'So might it be better not to explain why you want to know names?'

'Mrs Welford!' She turned to me as if I were in infant school. 'You really must permit us to get on with our task in our own way. You and Mr Thomas seem to think – where is he, by the way?'

'Working.'

Her eyes shot up in derision: those poor

wrinkles. 'Dead cows?'

'He's working near London.' I stopped, as abruptly as if Tony were pressing a hand on my shoulder.

She clicked her tongue. 'All right for some.'

'If picking through people's luggage for putrefying monkeys' heads is "all right", I'd like to know what constitutes unpleasant.'

That silenced her.

We walked her to her car, then Andy got into his, ready to drive to the next service within Tim's benefice. He looked altogether too grand for his Focus. I was within an inch of throwing him the keys to my Saab, which was altogether more appropriate.

But I didn't.

Sunday lunch passed without so much as a dropped saucer. There's never a moment to rest, but as a team we simply intermeshed, with no cross words, let alone obscene ones. We shared a short group meal afterwards with Lucy Gay and her brothers and sisters.

'Here we are, boys and girls: have a bit of Pix's special turkey,' Robin said.

'I don't like brown meat,' one of them whined, to be hushed by Lucy.

'No probs. This here was a Dolly Parton turkey – silly little legs and great big–'

'Thanks, Pix!' I said. 'And some of these wonderful potatoes.' I didn't bother the kids with their French name.

'How do you make them, Pix?' Lucy asked.

'Slice potatoes about as thick as a pound coin, and watch your fingers on the mandolin. Layer with chopped onion, chopped parsley, salt and pepper. Top with chicken stock. Little pats of butter or paint with oil – depending on whether that dairy allergy bloke is eating.'

'And they go especially well with leeks and carrots and spring greens!' Lucy insisted, doling out portions all round.

At their age, I hadn't thought anything went well with spring greens, but then, I hadn't had Pix and Robin to cook them.

Since we never had a Sunday evening shift – just Lucy with her homework on duty in a virtually moribund snug – I had no excuse not to go for an afternoon walk. The sun was shining: it was spring, and I ought to have some in my step.

But there were springs in my bed, too. A zillion, hadn't I claimed? And they all called, each last one.

Even as I headed upstairs, Tony smacked my head. 'Where's your will power, woman?'

I reached for my boots.

Today's path took me away from the village to the richer farmlands of the valley. Here grazed the organic cattle and sheep that would find their way into my kitchen, the lambs looking like children's toys and far too cuddly ever to eat. That way vegetarianism lay! So I ignored the frantically waggling hindquarters as the lambs demanded to suckle, and turned my attention to the hedgerows. Was this weed in fact a herb? Was that herb deadly if eaten raw?

I stopped to sniff. My feet had released the most glorious smell of garlic. Now, on my Internet rambles I'd seen a recipe for wild garlic soup: I must be stomping on its main ingredient this very moment. Yes! But I could hardly gather armfuls without permission. This might be what made my roast lamb so delicious, not my cooking skills at all. So I carried on down to the farm shop, always stuffed with organic produce. Since I was after a favour, I greeted Abigail Tromans like a long-lost sister. She was always rather cooler to me than her husband Dan, who'd once been known, when I told him he wasn't charging me enough for his prime beef, to swing me off my feet to celebrate the deal. He'd have difficulty swinging Abigail anywhere at the moment, since she was seven months' pregnant with twins. Her blonde hair hung in rat's tails, and she'd applied what little make-up she wore by touch, it seemed. Even I could see that her ankles were swollen; she'd had to remove her wedding ring, too.

'And why aren't you sitting down with your feet up?' I asked, forgetting all about the garlic.

'Sitting, standing, walking – they're all the same,' she said, so pale and drawn I almost believed her.

'Here: give me those,' I said, seizing a cardboard box of Easter eggs – Green and Black's organic and deeply wonderful. 'Stacked or sort of popped in artistically between other things? A couple here, maybe. And a few – have you got a spare display basket behind the counter? Yes, excellent. No, I'll get it. How's your blood pressure?'

She made a so-so gesture.

'Able to relax at all?'

She snorted. 'Cream teas just picking up nicely and I'm not supposed to bake and that.'

I loaded the basket with a jumble of eggs. 'You give me the ingredients and I'll look after scones for you: how many do you need a day?'

She opened her mouth to argue, but a yawn came out instead. Shrugging, she worked it out and I jotted. If they were Robin's scones, not mine, she needn't know.

'But Josie–'

'Abigail: I simply couldn't manage without your farm and your organic produce. Helping out's the least I can do. So long as you promise me one thing: this is absolutely our secret.'

'It's going to be even worse when the twins arrive.' Her face puckered, and sobs, painful to listen to let alone make, racked her bulk. 'We need every penny, Josie: we're this close to the edge.'

I'd seen Dan's books so I couldn't argue. The only thing to do was to abandon the Easter eggs and hold her.

'The bank won't give us any more. One baby would have been bad enough but two!'

'As a matter of fact,' I said slowly, remembering that garlic, 'maybe I can help.'

'We don't want charity!' But her head still rested against my shoulder.

'Of course you don't. But you've got something extremely valuable growing on your farm, apart from those lovely beasts of yours. It'd bring in–' I clawed desperately at figures that would sound just on the upper side of sensible, '–about £10 a kilo. Cash, of course.'

'£10 a kilo!'

'And I'd need a kilo a day. Weekends, two. Why don't we go and have a cuppa and talk about it?'

She was looking well enough by the time I took my leave, the remaining Easter eggs in a pyramid by the till, for me to mention the topic currently nearest my heart – chicken.

'Have you heard anything on the grapevine about cheap chooks?' I asked.

'I thought you stuck to organic.' She was prepared to be affronted.

'I do. But you know me,' I said ambiguously.

'For yourself, would this be?' she asked doubtingly.

'A friend,' I said. 'Look, if I start asking, people might start doubting my quality. This – it's a different market altogether. Organic's getting fashionable, but producing the best quality birds can never be cheap. So if someone comes along offering them at a couple of quid less a kilo, there must be people whose noses have been put out of joint–'

'Beaks, rather,' she put in, with a still wettish smile, which took some ten years off her and returned her to the doll-like prettiness that might have attracted Dan to her in the first place.

'Exactly. If you get genuine producers with minimal profit margins getting viciously undercut people must talk about it. Next time you go to a market, better still a farmers' market, you couldn't sniff around a bit for me? You or Dan?'

'For ten pounds for a kilo of old weeds, I'm sure he'd sniff anything,' she said. 'Even a slaughterman's armpit.'

Chapter Fourteen

I don't do loneliness. Never have. All those years Tony and I were apart, I didn't do loneliness. So why should I start tonight? I'd better stop, PDQ.

The obvious thing was to be busy. I replaced Lucy behind the bar in the snug. In the privacy of her room she could work uninterrupted. Or watch TV if the spirit moved her, since even she didn't demand the little ones do homework on Sunday evenings. While I was waiting for the action – any action – I phoned Nick.

'Hell, Josie, the stuff some people try to bring in. I've had rotting zebra and dried impala. You wouldn't believe– Ah, there's a plane just landing: I'd better go.'

'When will you be back?' I heard myself asking – me, who never asked such personal questions.

'I thought I might come via Brum. Elly's got some tickets for a midweeker.'

'Great. Enjoy yourself. And take care.' I cut the call.

Enjoy indeed: trotting round the country-side watching bloody soccer while I was trying to sort out the wrongs of the world.

And then I remembered the rotting zebra and hoped the match produced a lot of compensatory goals.

As for Andy, presumably his busiest working day was drawing to a close. He'd conducted four services to Tim's five, St Jude's being out of action, but he must be reasonably tired, and I didn't know him well enough to phone just for a natter. I wondered idly who had taken the services in his own church; presumably he was grand enough to warrant a curate for just such an event.

'Josie, my love! Did that terrible accident of yours deprive you of your senses? I've been standing here ten minutes panting for a glass of ale, and I don't think you even knew I'd come in.'

I hoped I hadn't visibly jumped. 'Ten minutes my Aunt Fanny, Aidan Carr. I'd have leapt to the pumps only you'd got your nose sucked into that scandal-sheet old Archie left behind! Funny, I never had you down as a tits and bum man.'

'My sweet, the day you do, you can sign me up for the SAS. Guilty as charged. I was peeping to see what people read these days. Only I fancy read is the wrong verb. "Look at" would be more accurate. You'd got a very long face, Josie, when you thought no one was looking.'

'Maybe the accident knocked me about

more than I realised.'

He switched on his solemn face, never easy when the natural lines on his face tended upwards, not down. 'The word on the street, Josie, is that it wasn't an accident.'

'No?' Impassive as possible, I pulled the half of real ale he always had if he thought no one was looking. In a crowd, he took a delight in finicking around with gin and tonic with crushed ice and the thinnest slices of lime. 'Does the street identify the malefactor?'

He raised his glass in a toast. 'Blessings upon your brewer and perdition to your malefactor. Such a lovely term. But not a lovely man.'

'A man. We're getting somewhere. Do I know him? Does his name begin with C?'

'Good God, no!' Aidan was genuinely shocked. Then he donned his puzzled expression. 'Why should you think that?'

'No matter. So does the name begin with M?'

'Darling girl, we don't know what letter it begins with. But they do say someone in a big blue 4x4 stopped someone in Taunton and asked his way here.'

I spread my hands. 'And do they say whether someone took this information to the police?'

'You know this part of the world and us grockles, sweetie. We're fair game and there's no closed season. And if another grockle takes arms against us – so be it.'

'I suppose they might just talk to Ian Strand. I know he's a cop, but cut him across and you'd find Devon all the way through.'

'Get Lucy on to it. And then she'd have a reason to talk to poor Ian. Come on, Josie, when are you going to set up as match-maker?'

'When she's finished her exams. But I wouldn't want to get involved. The village only forgave her for moving in here because her dad's bomb was intended for me.'

'A perverse form of logic, but I take your point. So I'd better have the undeniable pleasure of talking to young Ian myself.'

I could imagine the lustre of Aidan's eyes as he approached the young man. At least he'd always said he knew looking in shop windows wasn't the same as buying. I agreed with a twinkle. 'What burdens life thrusts upon us!'

Aidan's stomach rumbled. He patted it: 'Down, boy. It's this GI diet, Josie. I don't seem to have the right sort of food in the house, and–' He cocked his head win-somely. 'I don't suppose? For an old mate? A bit of cold roast and salad?'

'You know my rule, Aidan. No food on Sunday evenings. Ever. But since there's no one to see, I might just run to earth some cold beef.'

'Josie! I adore you! Marry me, my sweet!'

'I thought you'd never ask!' I seized his hand and dragged him into the most smacking of kisses, only releasing him when I realised we were no longer alone. The door of the snug – beautifully oiled these days, thanks to Nick – stood ajar to reveal Andy Braithwaite. Rather too clearly, he was not amused.

'I do apologise,' he said, in the huffy tone this time of someone not apologising at all.

'Not at all, Dean,' Aidan said, recovering much more quickly than I. 'It's not every day I have a proposal of marriage accepted. You must wish me well, you know. Or congratulate me. Not being versed in these matters, I'm not at all sure what etiquette requires. Are you? No? Alas, I thought I could rely on you.' Turning back to me, he kissed my hand. 'Josie, my love, maybe the dean would like a plate of the excellent cold beef which prompted my declaration of love. She does a wonderful salad to go with it, or the most scrumptious homemade pickles. And bread to die for.'

I let him rabbit on, at his campest, digging me out of any possible hole far quicker than self-justification from me. Until he paused for breath.

Time to clasp my hands to my bosom. 'So you only wanted me for my cold meat!' I declared. 'Alack, sir, then I am undone.' In my normal, twenty-first-century voice, I continued, 'And would you like some beef, Andy? There's plenty, so long as you promise utmost secrecy. Only my friends eat out of hours, you see.'

'Friends and fiancés,' Aidan amended smugly. 'Ooh, I never thought I'd get engaged! Not to a woman!'

So why, I asked myself as I sliced beef, had it mattered so much to Andy to see me locked in someone's embrace? He'd laughed heartily enough at Aidan's subsequent posturings, but only after a time lag, as it were. Hell! That might have been a finger gone. That would have taught me to let my mind wander with a knife like that in my hand. I slapped on a blue plaster and got on with my job. With absolutely no more speculating.

'You see,' Aidan crowed as I carried their plates through, 'the woman's an arrant temptress. There's me on the latest song in diets, and she offers me bread. I ask you! But what's a boy to do?'

'Leave the bread for Andy of course. There wasn't much salad left, so here are some pickles and chutneys if you want them.'

By now Andy's grin seemed genuinely relaxed. 'There's only one thing I can't resist,' he said, with as much panache as if the idea were original, 'and that's temptation.'

But when Aidan, replete and relaxed, announced he needed his beauty sleep, Andy made a similar discovery, and they left together.

No one else joined me in the snug, either for food or for a quiet pint, so I had plenty of time to ponder the question that was vexing me: was Andy shocked to see Aidan kissing me, or to see me kissing Aidan?

There was something enormously satisfying about getting up early to make the scones I'd promised Abigail Tromans, turning the incredibly sticky mixture into proudly lopsided moist cakes, good enough in my book to eat without cream and jam. In fact that was how I ate the only taster I permitted myself. Yes, it was fine. The dried fruit Abigail's recipe demanded had plumped up nicely. What else could you use scone mixture for? I'd seen both savoury and dessert recipes and now I remembered how easy it was to get excellent results, I was dying to try again.

Dying! I'd have to stop using the word so loosely. Especially when Tim's parents appeared. I'd scarcely had time to speculate what they might be like. Tim had said I reminded him of his godmother. Abrasive, aggressive, domineering, then. But what about his parents? And what about Tim's refusal to have them contacted?

Andy should be calling to let me know when to expect them. Perhaps he'd accompany them to ease their path.

Meanwhile, unobtrusively, I had to get the scones down to Abigail. It was highly unlikely that anyone would be miffed by our arrangement, but one thing I'd learned living in Kings Duncombe was that you couldn't predict how country people might react.

The problem was solved at our morning meeting. On Mondays these were perfunctory, to say the least, as I wanted to make sure the lads could maximise their free time. Pix turned up in an embarrassing Lycra cycling outfit, which showed precisely why he needed more exercise.

'No probs. But,' he added, filching at least another ten miles' worth of calories, 'just why are we taking coals to Newcastle?'

'Hush-hush coals, moreover,' Robin added, still in the cut off tracksuit bottoms that constituted his jimmies.

'I'm worried about Abigail. Blood pressure.' I mimed her bulge.

'Yuck: women's talk.'

'Quite. No one needs to know why the scones aren't up to her usual standard. Not that anyone'll know anything about them at all if you keep on pigging, young Pix.'

For answer he passed the plastic box across to Robin.

He assumed a blissful expression. 'Not bad, gaffer. So you do this every morning and one of us bikes them down?'

'Not exactly. Whoever's duty pastry cook can do them, if that's OK with you two? Some mornings Dan'll be able to collect them when he drops off our wild garlic. Executive decision time, lads. We're going native.'

I was laying up for lunch – only rolls and salads, remember – thinking about Abigail and her problems, when something she said struck me so smartly I nearly dropped the cutlery box. She said that in exchange for the wild garlic business, Dan wouldn't mind sniffing a slaughterman's armpit. As if that was the worst smell in the world. Tang's smell: could he have been a slaughterman somewhere? Why hadn't I thought of that before? I'd had an intimate acquaintance with a slaughterhouse only a few months back, after all. Or had my memory done as Nick's had done – shut down on the experience. But it wasn't meat he'd reacted to, but chicken. No. I must be right. If only Nick hadn't lost his files. If only he hadn't been called away. And if only he were making a speedy return to get at the information.

Perhaps that was deliberate. He didn't want me flying solo on this, did he?

Tough.

Because that was exactly what I was going to do.

Chapter Fifteen

'Oh, Josie! I'd no idea it could be so exhilarating! It's wonderful! I never want it to stop!' Unfortunately Andy was yelling all this into his mike, not my ear.

But I mustn't let him disturb my concentration. For flying I was, if not, in the event, solo. Flying literally, too.

'Josie, why have I never tried this before? It's so beautiful! Wow!'

I started to laugh. With pleasure, as much as anything. And at myself, too.

'Oh, Josie, thank you, thank you!'

'Don't mention it.'

'Look at it: all spread out like a living map,' he continued.

Wet blanket I might be, but eventually I had to point downwards. We weren't flying for fun, not really, but to do the sort of thing I'd rather hoped the police might have done: to scan for buildings, outhouses, whatever, where people might slaughter or process chickens. My job was to fly the helicopter: Andy's was to photograph possible sites and record them on the map.

So far, it had to be said, we'd had little success. I might be a qualified pilot, but I was relatively inexperienced, and I was far too respectful of the machine to risk violating any of the flying height regulations. Besides which, as I'd told Andy, we didn't want to draw attention to ourselves. That was why he had my biggest and best telephoto lens to shoot through. I just hoped I could trust him with it.

'There! Down there!' I shouted.

'It looks more like a scrap metal yard, with those tarpaulins covering spare parts.'

'Make a note anyway,' I said, as I had on several other occasions. 'It's time we headed back.' I only hired this thing by the hour, and even that cost an arm and a leg.

'And there! Yes, there!'

Possibly.

I returned us neatly to Exeter Airport, with Andy still as joyous as a kid. I let him stand me a cup of tea, and together we peered at the circles he'd scrawled on the maps.

He pointed. 'What about this one?'

'It looked too well organised and public to be anything other than legitimate. I'd bet a weekend's takings it was a bona fide battery farm.'

'But then, how many times does a genuine business front a dodgy one?' He flushed crimson. 'I mean– I do apologise!'

'For implying that the White Hart's an extension of Tony's empire? So you should. The cleanliness of my books shocks my accountant.'

His voice sounded hopeful to the point of pleading. 'So you never profited from your late husband's criminal activities?'

Was he mad? 'Of course I did! How do you think I survived all those years when Tony was in the nick? He wouldn't let me work, objected to my thinking of studying formally–'

'Despite the books you shared?'

'Possibly because of them. I was much younger than he. He thought I'd get shacked up with hairy students and forget about him. Just to make sure, if I started getting close to anyone, anyone at all, he'd get them warned off. And I must never ask where my weekly allowance was coming from.' Was it Andy's fault he'd caught me on the raw? I controlled my voice, continuing more reflectively, 'To all intents and purposes I was just a con's wife, living on benefit in a not very nice council estate in Birmingham. He made sure I had just enough money for a few extras without attracting anyone's attention. And by anyone I mean the police, the taxman, the nosy neighbours on whom I depended for support and friendship and a set of in-laws that would have given Lucretia Borgia the willies.'

His efforts to pour tea from the empty pot were probably just to give himself time to frame the next question as inoffensively as possible. 'So all your income now derives from the White Hart?'

'No. And if that's a problem, you'd better take a taxi back.' Getting to my feet, I flipped a twenty-pound note on his plate. I'd gone from confiding to incandescent in one breath.

He left it there but stood to meet me eyeball to eyeball. 'It depends what you do with the rest.'

I held his gaze. 'That's between my conscience and me, Andy. One day you may find out. But you don't tell a single soul. Understand?' I jabbed towards his chest.

To my amazement a slight smile flitted across his face, not eliminating his fury but irretrievably softening it. Pompous ass or frail human? He opted for the latter, succumbing at last to a laugh. 'Tim warned me you were formidable.' His face softened still more. 'He was very fond of you, you know. And very grateful for the pavilion. He loved his cricket.'

'They say it's like human chess,' I said, falling into step with him after I'd picked up the note, which, to make some point, though I wasn't sure which, I popped into a charity box. 'But it's never grabbed me. It's quite sexy when they play in white, but those garish pyjamas leave me cold.'

'So you prefer football?'

'Not since someone tried to explain the offside rule to me. And rugby's a closed book. I'm not a team player, that's the answer.' I irritated the automatic doors by standing still. 'Andy, you may have found out about my donations, but I'll thank you to keep your mouth shut. The villagers would only see it as trying to buy my way into their affections.'

'Is that the only reason?' He set us in motion again: the doors closed behind us with a sigh. 'It isn't, is it?'

It's so hard to have an argument when you can't stand still.

'Oh, surely you've heard the advice, *Do good by stealth,*' I said, deciding to end the discussion by setting off at my briskest towards the car park. I should have remembered that it was my briskest minus quite a lot for bruises. He easily fell into step with me and seemed about to pursue the matter further. I'd better sidestep him.

'What else did Tim tell you about me?'

He produced a reminiscent smile. 'He said he thanked God you were on his side, because he'd hate you as an enemy. You'd be implacable, he said.'

'Sounds OK to me.'

'Not forgiving?'

'Depends on who's done what to whom, doesn't it? I can forgive on my own behalf, but not on others'. That's why I can tolerate Corbishley being rude to me, but if he's in any way connected with those lads' deaths I'll hound him till one of us drops.'

'Why Corbishley? I can see you might have a personal grudge against him – who wouldn't, in your position?' He swallowed whatever he'd meant to say.

'Whichever position that happens to be,' I agreed, affably enough to make him blush.

'But I get the feeling you think he's some-how connected with the – the outrage.'

I zapped the Saab's central locking and we both got in. 'Everyone tells me he's got fingers in a lot of pies. Don't you think I'm qualified to say that that sounds suspicious? And when I tried to find out how he'd made his loot he clammed – even more than I do!' Would a grin help?

'Tim thought he was a God-fearing man.'

'Who obviously hadn't been listening to Tim's sermon about the Good Samaritan. Not that I had, mind you. Tim's sermons weren't great, poor kid. There were times I wanted to say to him, "Tell me what you want to say and give me half an hour and I'll knock up a decent piece for you." All those college essays,' I added by way of explanation or apology. 'Now, I know Corbishley put time and money into the church, lots of both. But isn't there some argument about faith or good works? Why don't you talk to him again? You've got the excuse of the funerals, which never really got resolved. Malins, too. Just a quiet ordinary civil servant, I hear. But very quickly promoted in the hierarchy here. A decent man, then. Maybe.' I hadn't meant the last word to sound quite so doubting, but I couldn't rewind it now.

'I meant to involve them anyway, but thank you for a timely reminder,' he said, stiffly enough to knock about a week off our acquaintance.

Having no idea why he'd put his formal hat on again – or maybe I mean dog-collar, since he'd been notably open-necked on our flight – I started the car and turned for the M5, a nasty enough road in its way, but nothing like as grim as the A30 or its friend the A303; despite its splendid new improvements in this section, I couldn't forgive it its tedious single-carriageway, no-overtaking expanses with no decent loos for miles.

Andy had left his car at the White Hart, so there was no need for discussion about where we were heading. And I simply drove. Let him talk when he wanted to.

In fact we were near the Wellington junction when he said, audibly relaxed, 'You've no idea what a luxury it is to be driven. And in such a nice car, too.'

'Bought out of White Hart profits, just so you can carry on enjoying it!'

'I deserved that. Usually I seem to bum lifts with middle-aged curates with beat-up Metros and long tales of woe. Your silence is so restful.'

'It would be, after my mouthful earlier.' We exchanged a sideways glance. Somehow I didn't think my past would arise for quite some time.

'I was wondering if we might stop off at the rectory. Just to make sure it's all right for his parents.'

'That's a very womanly worry.'

'Marcia must have bequeathed it to me. She was house-proud to a fault. If we went away, she'd clean the bathroom before we left, so the chambermaid didn't have to wipe her toothpaste out of the basin. And strip the bed. A good woman,' he summed up.

'How long have you been on your own?' He wasn't the only one used to phrasing questions tactfully.

'Five years now.' He reflected, no doubt wanting to tell me about her last illness. 'A good woman but one very hard to live with.'

I was so surprised I nearly missed the junction. But I hadn't worked behind a bar all those years to know that to be a good listener you needed to do more than nod and incline a listening ear.

'She should have been a martyr. Was one, to her various illnesses, all unexplained. I sometimes wonder if she'd made less fuss we'd have – I'd have – taken more notice when she got something serious. You see, she'd complain of this ache or that, and then insist on spring-cleaning a room or making new curtains, all to the accompaniment of pained sighs and sniffs. The end result was a wonderfully spruce home, but a very frayed marriage. Had it not been for my position – more, hers, since she rated any spurious status far more highly than I – I'm sure we'd have ended up apart. There was nothing to keep us together. Apart from the wedding vows we made when we were hardly out of our teens.'

'No children?' Lest the question seemed intrusive, I made a great show of checking the road as I took the island for our B road. How long had that black BMW been behind me?

'One son. He emigrated post-haste to Australia, where he married immediately and started a family. The message was crystal clear, believe me. And he was right. There was no way my wife could have let his family alone. It would have ended in matricide.'

I smothered a laugh at the precision of the term.

'Anyway, one day she insisted that a letter had to go in the post, though it was tipping down with rain and she had a vicious cold. The next day she had bronchitis, I thought, and when she wouldn't let me call the doctor I made her an appointment at the surgery. That morning. An emergency one, with a locum. I did, Josie. I did everything I could. I even got the car out. But she insisted I was just making a fuss. When I brought the doctor in that evening, she had pneumonia and she died two days later.' He dropped his voice but the words were clear. 'And I was so relieved.'

I was near to panic. This conversation should surely have taken place with his boss. Or even his Boss. Not with me, on whom half the villagers would have pinned a nice big scarlet letter A. Not unless he was about to make a pass at me, and then I could have told him straight out that I didn't do clergymen. Not no-how. They came with consciences and guilt and a life already pledged so someone rather more important.

Having nothing useful to say, I stayed silent; he sat staring at his nails. The BMW had dropped to a discreet distance, but was still there. Paranoia or years of Tony's training? I slowed down long enough to clock the number, which I made Andy write down, and then accelerated hard.

Three miles later, it was still there. Without signalling I took a right, taking us back on our tracks, then nipped straight across the main road into the back lane into the village – one that conveniently passed the rectory.

'What was all that about?' Andy asked, as if only now having enough breath to speak.

'Precautions. Look, open the garage doors, will you? Quickly!'

I reversed in as swiftly as Reg – or it might have been Don – had shown me years ago. When Andy joined me, I shut the doors again, and opened the back one, which led on to the garden. We could make a quick exit if only on foot.

If there had been a black sack in Tim's garage, there was no sign of it now. Nor, as I sniffed the air, any indication of it ever having been there. He'd made a rather pathetic attempt to overwinter some geraniums and what might once have been fuchsias: now everything was a dried out mess, home to woodlice and a colony of spiders.

'Compost heap?' Andy asked, picking up a couple of terracotta pots.

'Only place.'

To my amazement, there was a pair of new green plastic compost converters in the garden: quite out of character with the rest of the place, which, lawn apart, was both undernourished and overgrown. He'd obviously come with good intentions. One converter was quite empty. The other smelt unpleasant, not the sweet rotting moistness of my converter but of unwashed male.

I pointed.

Andy gaped. 'He thought it important enough to hide it here!'

'And I think it's important enough to take it hotfoot into Taunton nick.' I bit my lip.

'Can you trust me to do it?' His humility sounded genuine. 'I mean, you've got responsibilities.'

'Trust? I was about to beg and implore! I know there are no meals tonight, and the lads are more than capable of running the whole place without me... All the same.' I thought of the black Beamer. 'And, while you're about it, could you drop the film in for overnight development? Two sets of prints. No, three. Stick one set in your church strong box, with the negatives. One set of prints for me; the other for the police.'

'You're really worried about that car, aren't you?'

'Once run over, twice shy. All the same... Look, how good an actor are you?'

He goggled. 'I blacked up for Othello at school once, in the days a white kid could. Why?'

'Tony always told me to trust my instincts, however oddly they might make me behave. So I'm going to. And my instinct tells me something's wrong. I want to protect you– No, listen to me. This is self-interest on my part, pure self-interest.'

'Self-interest? Protecting me?' He shook his head.

'When I stop at the White Hart, you and I are going to have a very public row. You're not going to come in. You're going to bellow and shout and I'm going to tell you to give me back my camera. And you're going to drive off in a huff. Real spurt of gravel stuff.'

'I don't know whether modern cars run to spurts of gravel.'

'If you try hard enough they will. Then I shall slam inside with the passion of a teenager.'

'So we're not part of a team any longer.'

Were we before? 'Quite. But – this may sound...'

'It doesn't matter how it sounds. Just tell me.' He raised his hand, but then let it fall.

'I want you to phone me, every few minutes. Say every twenty. If I don't reply in person, call back a minute later. If I don't reply then, get the police in. I know it's all very *Boy's Own*,' I pleaded, 'but just in case.'

The BMW lurked in a lay-by fifty yards down the road. The driver made no effort to tail me this time: why should he? He knew where I lived, after all. He and his passenger.

'You're hysterical! You're off your head.' Andy gave my face a remarkably convincing stage-slap.

I reeled but recovered. 'Listen to you.

You're so full of it. Just give me my stuff and get out of my life. Now!'

And so on and so on. I was better at it than he, of course, and to a large extent reprised a performance I once gave in the middle of Birmingham when Nick had had Tony sent down for the last time. On that occasion, when I'd slung my shoe at the offender – a very high stiletto, as I recall – he'd returned it with a courtly bow you wouldn't credit from the present all-grey Nick. This time I was wearing soft casuals – all I could bear with the bruises – and I slung first one, then the other, at the retreating Ford. They could lie there in the road for all I cared.

Later on I'd creep back and get them. Ignominiously.

Ignominiously?

Like hell I'd do anything ignominiously. Especially with that pair in the black BMW now watching me from the bus stop lay-by. Barefoot I strode towards them, arms akimbo.

'And what might you be looking at? You! With that silly grin! Eh? What are you smiling at? My life's something to do with you, is it? I don't think so. So let's have a bit of respect. That's better.'

They both dropped their eyes. I'd won. This round at least.

'I've seen you round here before, haven't I? Well, I don't want to see you here again.

You or your little mate. Get that?'

They nodded in unison. It was hard not to laugh. Or it would have been if one of them hadn't run me over. It must have been him, surely, in the 4x4.

I started again. 'Lowlifes like you don't trail round the sticks like this just because you like a bit of fresh air. You're under orders. So tell your boss you've got to try the air somewhere else.' I leaned much closer. 'Understand? No one messes with Tony Welford's widow. No one. Now, get out of my face. And stay out.' I nodded home my point and stepped back, arms now folded implacably, to watch them on their way.

If cars had tails, this one's would have been between its legs. I watched it out of sight. No way was I going to spoil my act by ferreting stiffly for my footwear.

Chapter Sixteen

I settled more comfortably on the barstool, transferring the phone to the ear that wasn't getting irritatingly deaf. 'The trouble is, Andy, they didn't recognise Tony's name. Either they're not high enough in the pecking order or his reputation no longer strikes fear. I suspect the latter,' I confessed, knowing he'd appreciate the swing to formal speech. 'All the same, I reckon you can cancel the twenty minute phone calls. They'll have to decide what to tell their boss – never nice if you have to admit you messed up – and he'll need to work out his next move.'

'I shan't cancel the phone calls. If you're in danger, you're not facing it alone. Especially as it involves the Church. Indeed, the Church involved you.'

'It was my nosiness that involved me. I could simply have done the sensible thing and nagged the fuzz a bit harder and more often. They've got the resources and the manpower.'

'I'm not sure about their commitment. And the tension between Lawton and Nick seemed to be bringing out the worst, in Lawton, not the best.'

'Funny thing about sex,' I agreed, 'you can never predict how it'll make people react.' There was a long silence. 'I'll give them another call. That nice kid Bernie Downs'll take some notice, surely.'

A couple of villagers mooched in, two middle-aged men who could, probably would, make a pint last a whole night. I might not get much custom from them but they could offer something far more valuable: protection. Smiling, I gestured one minute.

'The bar's filling up,' I told the still silent Andy. 'I must go. Talk to you later.' So why had I stooped to the current cliché, as if acquiescing in his repeat calls, and not merely said goodbye?

The regulars notwithstanding, I was reluctant to risk Lucy's taking my place in the bar – just in case. So when she appeared, beaming with apparent pleasure at the prospect of spending an evening writing an essay between demands for booze, I shook my head.

'What I really need you to do, love, is something my back won't let me. Not at the moment. Would you mind making up the beds in the staff accommodation – the ones Father Martin's parents will be using?' That'd take her ten minutes, that was all. 'After that, you just get on with your assignment, eh? I can fend off the rush down here.'

'But–'

'Look, Lucy, this barstool may look hard and unyielding to you, but it's the most comfortable chair I've found since my accident. And I'm giving it up to no one!'

The two drinkers were soon joined by a couple of men from the St Faith and St Lawrence choir. They'd been putting in an extra practice just in case Father Martin's family wanted their service, they said. Four or five others trickled in minutes later. Suddenly the snug was living up to its name.

'Tell you what, Josie,' one said gruffly,

'you're doing right by that young man and no mistake. Both of them, truth to tell.'

'So are you people,' I said, nodding at his colleagues. 'Going the extra mile.'

'Only right, isn't it?' He leaned closer. 'Not like some you could mention.'

I knew better than to ask outright. 'Surely we're all...'

'Oh, no. There's those who don't want to get involved.' He mimicked – badly – a refined accent.

I fished. In the name of conversation of course. 'You mean Mr Malins and Mr Corbishley? Why wouldn't they want to be involved? Come on, I bet you can't name me a single person in this village who won't do everything they can to give Tim a decent funeral.'

'Well, you just named them. Keep themselves to themselves. That's fine, that's folk for you. But I say Christian is as Christian does: it's all well and good pouring money into a church that's got burned down, but what about one that's still intact, that's what I want to know? We've still got subsidence and dry rot and leaking gutters. A bit of their cash wouldn't have come amiss. After all, we've still got a congregation – I know some of them women can backbite, Josie, and don't blame you for moving on. But you must have seen how few were going to St Jude's. Why not pool our resources, that's what I've always said.'

Another nodded. 'It's a sad fact we can't keep all the churches going. But some are more important than others. St Faith and St Lawrence is big enough to hold all the congregations, and room over.'

Special pleading? But this was getting me nowhere. 'So why do you think they're so wedded to St Jude's? If they had a different vicar it would make sense, I suppose. But the five churches have been sharing the same one for years, haven't they?'

'Maybe it goes back to the time when they didn't,' the first – Mike? – mused. 'Before my time, of course – twenty-five years ago, I should think. Maybe more.' Just yesterday, then, in the eyes of the average villager. 'Tell you what, I'll ask around, shall I? Discreet, like – don't want to tread on any toes, do I?'

'Not with the funeral coming up,' I said.

'If they let us hold it here,' he observed, glumly.

'Who'd stop us?' I asked, neatly returning myself, or so I hoped, to the village fold.

'Well, there's talk of cathedrals and such. We want the service here: he was our parson after all.'

I wouldn't talk about my hotline to the ecclesiastical bigwigs. 'I'm sure if you talk to the church wardens, they'll take your case right up to the bishop, if necessary.'

'That smarmy old git? 'Twas he who

confirmed our three. Didn't like seeing him lay his greasy paws on their little heads, I can tell you.'

I couldn't stop myself nodding – in any case, nodding was something landladies had to do, I told myself, whether they were in agreement or not. 'But everyone at St Faith and St Lawrence is united,' I prompted.

'Ah.'

But that was all I got from him. And at that point my phone rang.

'I said I'd check if you were all right.'

'Perfectly safe, thanks Andy. I've pretty well got a football team in here: better than the Household Cavalry!'

'And have you phoned the police?'

'Next thing on my agenda,' I declared gaily. And cut the call. Since everyone had stopped talking and all eyes were on me, I said, 'Just a friend. I had a spot of bother with a couple of lads earlier.'

'They two in the big black car? Nasty pieces of knitting, they looked. Been around the village quite a bit.' You could see Mike's shoulders bracing for action. Major action. Before he became a central heating engineer Mike had played rugby for Cornwall. 'Not giving you any trouble, are they?'

The people of Kings Duncombe might not like me, but as a resident at least I had the edge on invaders from outside.

'Not after the mouthful she give 'em

earlier,' his mate declared. 'She's a tough old bird, our Josie.'

Yes, in one breath I'd become one of them. I nearly wept. Worse, I nearly stood drinks for everyone on the house.

'What I can't understand,' said DI Lawton, the next morning, her mouth turning down disapprovingly, 'is why it took you so long to tell us you'd been tailed. Twelve hours. More. Fighting crime isn't a nine till five job, you know.'

'Indeed, my late husband often used to lament the fact,' I beamed, pouring her more morning coffee and pushing forward the pastries plate. 'From inside his prison cell. Come on, don't tell me you didn't check me out. Anyway, I gave them an earful. The chief reason was to detain them long enough for Mr Braithwaite to deliver the bag of Tang's garments we'd found. I take it it arrived safely? And will be extremely useful?' I prompted. 'No, we didn't open it, so it shouldn't be contaminated, should it?' I added, having received singularly little response.

'It did arrive safely, and it's already at the forensic science lab,' she said stolidly. 'But I really must insist, Mrs Welford, that there's no need for all these mock heroics. This is work for the police.'

'Of course. Any idea why the young men

should have tailed me back from Junction 26? And have hovered outside the rectory? And then tailed me here?'

'I would have thought you were the one to tell me that. They're presumably to do with your husband's past.'

'Why?'

She flushed an unendearing pink.

I spared her the further embarrassment of a blustering reply. 'When Tony died I severed all my links with his past. He'd always made sure I had the barest minimum of contact with the criminal world anyway.'

'Why do I have such difficulty believing you, Josie?'

'Mrs Welford. I don't know. You can see the White Hart's books whenever you want. My bank statements. Whatever. Which is why I repeat, why should they be following me?' I stepped up a gear. 'If I came and made a formal complaint of harassment, would I have to explain why they were doing it? I should have thought I had enough reason to make a complaint,' I added, rolling up my sleeves to display my bruises. 'And your colleague never implied I'd brought this upon myself by being Tony's widow. Nor did A and E ask if it was self-inflicted.'

Digesting this diatribe, she nodded gravely, but not, I thought, apologetically. 'So why didn't you simply phone the police from the rectory and ask them to take charge of the black sack?'

'We'd no idea what the BMW people intended. Did they want us or what we'd found? It was in the compost heap, by the way, in case you want to tell your search team.' I paused but she made no note. All the same, I thought she would do an excellent job of bollocking her colleagues. 'You wanted us to barricade ourselves in and wait for your people to come storming over? This isn't a city with rapid response vehicles waiting in every cul-de-sac. It's rural Somerset. How long would it have taken? Mr Braithwaite and I thought it was more prudent for him to take the sack, but for that I had to return him to his car.' I edited the spurious row. Actually, I'd edited quite a lot, come to think of it. But I wasn't under arrest, so didn't think it could count against me, legally. 'I dare say I'd be able to pick them out from photos for you. And I already told you the car number.'

'False.' It was as much a dismissal of me as an accusation against the driver.

'Only to be expected, I suppose. But I could ID the faces,' I repeated. 'Never forget a face in my profession. Actually,' I pointed out, 'half the village could too. The incident did not pass unnoticed.'

Completely impassive she made an un-enthusiastic note. But she gave herself away.

'And what does ex-DI Thomas have to say about it all?'

'You've got his number,' I said, relishing the ambiguity. 'Why don't you call him yourself?' But perhaps I should let her off the hook. 'He knows nothing about it. He's still working away from base, remember, and I didn't think he needed to know. It would worry him. He might think he ought to come hotfoot back here. Now, if you don't want me to look at mug shots, I'd best get on. Mr and Mrs Martin are coming down.'

'They're staying here? I thought you'd cleaned out the vicarage.' It sounded like an accusation.

'Rectory. Yes, I did, because I didn't want their memory of their son's home to be of a pigsty. I know I'd hate it. Scruffy, yes, because you can blame that on the church not decorating it properly before he moved in, but not a mess of dirty underwear and s – socks,' I corrected myself smoothly. No need for her to know he'd smoked spliffs.

I didn't think she clocked the hesitation.

'Very kind of you,' she admitted, huffily. 'So why are they staying here, if you're being harassed?'

'I didn't know I was when I issued the invitation. Look,' I said, deciding almost to make a clean breast of it all, 'it all started when I started asking about–'

247

Her mobile rang. She didn't even check the caller before taking the call. Neither did she excuse herself or even turn away.

Bother her. I got up and ostentatiously reviewed the lunch and evening bookings. In our morning's mini-meeting, the lads and I had agreed to offer as an on-the-house extra vegetable the freshly delivered wild garlic, gently braised in butter. (We'd marked up the specials' prices enough to cover it. No such thing as a free portion, remember, especially at £10 the kilo.) Dan had gone away with a batch of scones, grumbling slightly in the way some men do when you spare their partners work.

Robin had forgotten to reserve a table for the Martins. I pencilled it in. They might of course prefer to eat in their quarters, or even in my flat, if I felt sufficiently well-disposed. We didn't have a full house by any means, but then, who did on Tuesdays? So long as we had enough clients to justify a chef, that was all I asked. Most Tuesday evenings I hopped into Taunton for Weight Watchers, but, though I was eternally grateful to them, I no longer depended on them. Sooner or later our relationship would draw to an end.

Which is what Lawton's call was doing now.

'Tell you what,' she said, eyeing the last remaining pastry, 'you could come in and have a go at IDing the BMW pair, if you like.'

'Or, better still, you could send a minion down here with a laptop full of images,' I said, getting to my feet. 'A plainclothes minion, preferably. I don't want to worry my clients. Now, I have food to prepare: wild garlic.' I rubbed my hands, and smiled as if she shared my pleasure.

She merely registered my request with an elevation of a cold eyebrow – more wrinkles in the bud – and stood up. Her eyes were drawn to the pastry as if by a magnet. Tough.

This time the BMW was silver, and a Five, not a Three Series. And the couple inside were not a pair of lads but a sleek man and his expensive-looking wife. The White Hart's gastronomic reputation was such that by now I no longer expected them simply to be asking for directions, but to be badgering me to let them book a table for an overfull Saturday night. They themselves seemed to be checking something on a piece of paper with the newly-painted inn sign.

I made it my business to open the front door to water the tubs of polyanthus and pansies with which I greeted my guests, and happened to follow their gaze.

'It's rather nice, isn't it?' I said. 'There's a lad round here trying to revive the craft, so

I gave him a commission.' The fact he was a recidivist trying to go straight entered into the equation, but there was no need to tell them that.

'So this is really the White Hart?' Disappointment oozed from his voice.

'Yes.' I made it a flat affirmative, keeping any challenge from my reply.

'Oh,' she said. They looked at each other. 'I was expecting something–'

'Bigger,' I supplied, to save her from herself. 'I don't suppose you're Mr and Mrs Martin, by any chance?'

'Dr and Dr Martin.'

Since I'd not long since corrected DI Lawton in the same tone, I suppose I couldn't argue, but I found it hard to smile as hospitably as I should. However, transferring my watering can to my left hand, I stuck out my right. 'Welcome to the White Hart. I'm Josie Welford. I was so fond of your son – I can't tell you how sorry I am.'

He put forward a reluctant hand in response.

'So awful for you – having been so far away when the news came through.'

Nil response. What on earth was Andy doing to let this couple come unannounced and unattended? It didn't square with his usual solicitous behaviour. I smiled warmly at the chilly female Dr Martin, suppressing a guffaw as I realised I had acquired a pair of famous boots. Wouldn't Tony have loved it?

The male one hadn't parked very considerately for a city street, and very badly for what was little more than a country lane, frequented by the sort of monster tractor currently approaching – the sort with bigger wheels and more spikes and other lethal looking pieces of metal than you can imagine off the set of a futuristic film.

'Would you care to pull your car round to the back?'

He cast an eye at the Behemoth and at his paintwork. He did as I suggested, briskly.

Which left me and his other half. 'Andrew Braithwaite must have told you that although this is officially an inn, with sleeping accommodation, the bedrooms are currently occupied by a homeless family.'

As I'd expected, all her prejudices flitted before her wide-open eyes.

'Since I've already upgraded staff accommodation, which is in a separate building, I thought you might be more comfortable there. It's designed for communal living, with a sitting-room, kitchen and so on, but my chefs have moved back into the main building for as long as you wish to stay.' The Gay children had had to double up, something their eldest sister assured them would be good for them. Like spring greens, I suppose. 'Would you care to see it? It's

251

more direct if we simply follow your husband into the car park.' I closed the front door behind me. I didn't want any surprise visitors awaiting me when I returned.

Since the rooms were meant for permanent occupation, they were both spacious and very well appointed. But clearly there was something missing – olde-worlde charm? And rather too clearly they were disappointed. How such a pair could have bred sweet unassuming Tim I'd never know. There was a physical resemblance to his mother, who I rather suspected of having been under the knife, but none to his father.

Ah! No tea trays. A peep into the kitchen, however, showed Lucy hadn't let me down. Everything was laid up beautifully, with an assortment of teas and coffees, and fresh milk in the fridge, along with bottled Exmoor water, sparkling and still – a total extravagance since the same liquid issued *ad lib* from the tap. A biscuit barrel contained some of Pix's finest. Lucy had even popped budding wild daffodils in one of my better vases.

'Please make yourselves at home. Use whichever rooms you please.' I explained how to use the coffee-maker.

Their polite interest told me they wanted only one thing: my absence. So I speedily obliged.

'You'd better hop back to your deanery and change,' I greeted Andy. 'They'll expect gaiters at very least.' Not the shoes he sported with a dark charcoal suit. If he looked good in something so obviously not top-of-the-range, what would he be like in the efforts of Tony's tailor? And bespoke shoes, too?

Today his shirt was a consciously deanish black.

To my surprise, he slung an arm round my shoulders as I led him round to the staff quarters. Briefly, true, but very friendly, with a little squeeze that indicated as clearly as if he'd said out loud that he'd got my measure. The whole thing was so natural I wouldn't have been surprised if he'd given my bum a valedictory pat. Or, of course, I his.

As it was, I made formal introductions, an emphasis I was sure he would notice on their titles, and bowed out.

My emails included a request from the wife of a disgraced African finance minister to help her retrieve millions, only needing complete details of my bank account in return for a fifty percent cut of her profits. And there were still people who got sucked in by such scams. No, I didn't need Viagra, and I didn't need an improved mortgage. Waste of bloody money my spam-block was proving. But there were some genuine messages, notably from Nick, telling me he'd be back

253

on Friday and he'd like to be fed royally – from the vegetarian menu. No need for details about what he'd been up to, then. Then there were a couple headed CHICKEN, one from an old mate in Topsham, an oasis of good eateries, and another from someone I'd never heard of. The first told me she'd been offered heavily discounted chicken breast fillets by her usually reputable supplier; the other, who'd come via my website, was offering meat at amazingly low prices, provided I paid in cash. A month ago and my response would have been that my meat had to have come with all the certification going and to go away and do unnatural things. And perhaps it should still be: I know I was supposed to be scouring the West for dodgy poultry, but that was me going to them, on my own terms. Perhaps DI Lawton was right: perhaps I should leave things to the pros. Except the pro wasn't going to be back till Friday, damn him. All the same, he ought to know, so I forwarded the message to him, with a couple of covering question marks. It was the nearest I could get to asking advice. As for the message itself, I sent an automatic, out-of-the-office reply, saying I'd get back after a (mythical) week's break.

As for my other email respondent, the obvious questions were had she tried it and was it any good?

Then – and I embraced it almost as a

refuge – it was back to the kitchen to see the results of Pix's marketing and to see if we needed to revise the specials board. With rhubarb as pink and sweet as the bunch he waved in triumph, we certainly did. Bearing my dairy-free clients in mind, I wanted individual little jellies, possibly made with champagne; Pix was asserting his inalienable right to produce an old-fashioned fool when the back-door bell pinged.

Andy and the Doc Martens. OK. Fool it was. In a whisk of the apron I was mine hostess again.

The Martins' eyes widened appreciably – and possibly appreciatively – when Andy ushered them into my flat. I wasn't at all sure of the etiquette of offering bereaved parents a pre-lunch drink. If I drank at midday it was only ever champagne, but that was altogether too frivolous. Had I not known Andy better I'd have thought sherry a more ecclesiastical choice. And somehow being the licensee made matters worse: they'd expect some sort of expertise, even if, since I'd promised Andy that all this was gratis, they wouldn't be paying for it.

Gratis. When I made the offer, I'd expected the pair to be down-trodden, possibly slightly down at heel, in the manner of schoolteachers in my youth. I was aware that things had rightly changed in education – apart from anything else, you'd need danger-money to face today's kids, high on all those vicious additives. But these two were not just well off, they were rich. They oozed the sort of money you didn't get working for other people. The sort of money that didn't need subsidies from hard-working people like me.

I told them the possibilities of where they might eat while they were here, adding the proviso that I really would need to pencil in a time if they wanted to eat in the dining room, even at lunchtime. They seemed to approve rather than otherwise my business-like approach, saying they'd lunch down-stairs now with Andy, but would rather visit the rectory on their own.

Urbanely, Andy asked if I had time to join them at their table: clearly they hadn't thought of that, so I declined – I was on duty, I lied. They polished off the very good white burgundy they'd accepted and toddled downstairs to the dining room, where I commended them to the care of a work ex-perience kid, this one adept and con-scientious. One kind word to me and they'd have had my full attention, but I didn't skivvy for people who ignored me. And whose son had not wanted them contacted when he was under siege, and who had lied about their occupation.

Chapter Seventeen

Although I was sure Andy would have repeated his offer to accompany them, the Martins still insisted on going to the rectory alone. Sighing, Andy got up as if to leave.

'I need a cup of tea if you don't,' I breathed into his ear, a restraining hand on his shoulder. 'Upstairs.' Strange, it sounded more like a threat – *Boy, see me in my study after school* – than an invitation to my boudoir. I hadn't meant it as the latter, true, but I certainly hadn't meant it as the former.

Nonetheless, he trotted quite guiltily to my quarters. 'I know, I know,' he protested. 'What miracle produced Tim from such unpromising parents?'

'Quite a big one. You can understand his desire to keep them at a distance. And they seem to be keeping their grief remarkably well under control.'

He looked at me quizzically. 'They certainly got up your nose. I've never seen you so polite to anyone. Except perhaps to Bishop Jonathan. At first I thought it was because you were intimidated by him – people often are, by bishops. But now I've changed my mind. No one would intimidate you, would they?'

He sounded amused rather than amorous, so I grinned back.

'So what do they do, these not teachers?' I prompted. 'They own–? They run–?'

'They play their cards even closer to their chests than you do. But they're bright, Josie – very, very bright.'

I twitched an eyebrow. Too many people like Andy seemed to regard being bright as a virtue in itself.

'Unpleasantly so,' he continued, apparently without a pause. 'Intellect untempered by wisdom.'

'Or their blood by the milk of human kindness.' I held up my tea caddy. 'Green?'

He nodded.

As the kettle boiled, I said slowly, 'I hate to introduce a red herring, but you don't suppose – no, it doesn't make sense.'

'Left-brain stuff often doesn't. Try me. I'm up for it.'

If only he'd been referring to something other than weird ideas. I was often at my most creative after a good bonk, but perhaps between the unmarried that, in ecclesiastical terms, was an oxymoron. In any case, he'd heard all too clearly that the locals regarded me as the village bike. I didn't want to be bedded on the assumption that I was easy. I wanted– I wasn't at all sure what I wanted, a rare and unpleasant state I could only blame on the recent upheavals.

'Could there ... could there be any possible reason why... No. Crazy.'

'Why someone should want to take out their own son? It's not an idea I'd care to put to DI Lawton, but... No, surely it's got to have been Tang the murderers were after. The snakeheads who brought him here. His employers. People avenging something he'd done. No one could have anything against poor Tim. Who, in God's name, could be more innocent?' He mixed exasperation with despair.

I busied myself with the tea. Any more emotion and I'd cry, not a good option. Once I cry, I never know when to stop, which was why I had kept myself so stern and busy since the boys' deaths.

He sat on the sofa, sighing again but soon looking around him. 'This is one of the most restful rooms I've ever encountered.'

'It certainly had the docs pricing it by the item,' I agreed. 'And unsettling them.'

'Which is something you like to do,' he said. He sipped his too hot tea. 'Am I prejudiced against them simply because of their money?'

I hoped not. Some response was called for. I cocked my head inquiringly.

'You know, green eyes? I don't want riches, Josie, and it's certainly wrong to envy people with them. But am I quicker to judge the rich than the poor? None of whom I should be judging in any case!' He pressed his hands to his face, but compromised by rubbing it vigorously as if he were trying to wake up.

'Grief. It's unsettling. But I don't think you took agin' them because they're loaded. It's just that they didn't seem very nice people. Or – let's be charitable to them too! – perhaps grief and shock have closed them down.' I sat in the easy chair at right angles to him. 'Did they say anything about what sort of funeral they wanted? And where?'

'To take your line, perhaps they were too shocked to have made any real decisions. Quiet. They wanted it to be very quiet. Which rather rules out the cathedral.'

'It would be more ... more seemly here,' I said. 'And the villagers would much prefer it on home territory. The choir's already putting in extra practice, they tell me. But what about Tang? A shared or a separate service?'

'The Martins aren't exactly paid up members of the Tang fan club. In any case, I've got one of my colleagues on to the Chinese Embassy for advice.'

'Whatever they say, there's nothing wrong with holding a memorial service, surely? For him and Tim?'

'At St Faith and St Lawrence? Or maybe in the St Jude's graveyard?'

'A bit symbolic, all those ashes and the smell of burning?' I asked doubtfully.

'Exactly. Yes, I'd quite like it there. I wonder what the St Jude's people would say. I suppose you haven't had a chance to talk to them?'

My turn to cover my face – with shame. 'I've not even been in touch with Annie!'

'Who hasn't been in touch with you, either. Don't take all this on yourself, Josie. You've been rocketing round doing your thing. Other people have their own lives too. Sure, Tang touched Annie's, but she was going on holiday anyway, and didn't see any need to change her arrangements. Corbishley and Malins seem to have gone to ground. No one can do more than their best. And how–' he looked pointedly at the bruises clearly visible now I was wearing a skirt '–you managed to clean the rectory when you must have been in real pain, you and God know.'

'And He's not letting on either,' I confirmed. 'Andy, why did they want to go to the rectory alone?'

He looked at me as if I were three. 'It was his home, Josie – personal things, family things...'

'Did you see any personal or family things? When you were cleaning up? Quite. It was more like a hotel – a very tatty motel, then – than a home.'

'All the same...'

'And have they asked to see St Faith and St Lawrence, which he really loved? Or any of his other churches? Especially the one where he died?'

'I think you may be reading too much into the situation,' he said gently. 'There again,' and he was on his feet as swiftly as a man half his age, 'you may not. What if I just drop in on them? Offer to pray with them.'

'And report back to me?'

'Would I dare not?'

Any other man I'd have twisted my head so that his kiss landed not lightly on my cheek, but full on my lips. And there'd have been nothing light about it by the time I'd finished. As it was, I made sure my smile was as conspiratorial as his as he turned to leave, his tea only half-drunk.

Though I really should have had a long hard walk, not just the ambulatory equivalent of a cold bath, but a means of keeping the scales on my side, I was lured to the computer, ready to Google their names as fast as my fingers would tap them. Except, of course, I didn't know their first names. Either of them. Because they weren't technically paying guests, not staying as customers, I hadn't made them sign the White Hart register. Big mistake. I'd shove it under their doctored noses the moment they returned.

Meanwhile, the excuse for not taking a walk had dwindled, and, camera as always to hand, I set off in the opposite direction from the rectory. OK, not at my usual speed, nor anything like. But at least I was moving: I'd keep at it for ten minutes.

I never carried the camera for any special purpose, not unless I was on a jaunt like yesterday's. Which reminded me: I hadn't asked Andy for the photos. At least he'd had the sense not to flash them round in front of other people, as if they were holiday snaps. And he would have stowed the sets of copies where I'd asked.

It was nice being able to trust someone.

Touch wood.

'Health and Safety regulations,' I said blithely, having a nasty feeling the Drs T H and C M Martin knew I was lying. Did they also know I'd wanted to check them out? 'If there were a fire I'd need to account for every one.' Hell, that hadn't been very tactful. 'Name and address there. And car reg. too. Just in case. Thanks.'

I'd laid the register on the table in their quarters – a very official-looking one it was too, thanks to Lucy, who'd once had to improvise with a school folder and had subsequently given me this handsome specimen her family's first Christmas here. All the kids had given me Christmas presents too, which would have reduced me to a quivering pulp of tears, had not turkeys demanded to be basted. But before I disappeared to the kitchen I made sure I saw their faces, as they opened not just the sensible presents of clothes Lucy had suggested but silly extravagances. They'd never be my blood family, but at least I could pretend to be a favourite aunt.

Since no comment was forthcoming, I asked what time the Martins wanted to dine. Or, when that elicited no immediate response, if they would prefer me to phone ahead to one of Taunton's excellent brasseries.

'We'll let you know, shall we?' she said dismissively. When I didn't dismiss, she added, 'Is that a problem?'

'Only for you,' I said, definitely not servile, 'if they happen to be full.' But I wouldn't give even the appearance of soliciting custom, and retreated to my own sanctum.

Where Andy was waiting, kettle poised over a couple of mugs. 'They were looking through his theological textbooks,' he reported without preamble. 'They declined my offer of tea – I'd taken the sort of precaution I associate with you, Josie, of buying supplies at the village shop – and accepted my invitation to go to St Faith and St Lawrence.' He sounded disappointed.

'Which they looked at as emotionally as if

they were Japanese tourists,' I suggested.

'At least they didn't see it only through the lens of a posh camera! The flower ladies had done a wonderful job: they'd blown up a photo of Tim taken at someone's christening, framed it in black, and surrounded it with spring flowers. It was in the porch, of course,' he added, eyes twinkling.

'Of course,' I echoed. 'It being Lent! Did they want to see the other churches in the benefice?'

'Only St Jude's. I expected them to fish some flowers out of the boot and add them to that lovely bank of offerings. No. They talked to the constables on guard, but that was all. They were so cold, Josie, so controlled.'

'I could tip a nice big bowl of rhubarb fool into their laps tonight.'

'If I know your food it would be a total waste.'

'It'll be Pix's. And a dream. You'll be able to try it, anyway.'

'They very clearly didn't invite me.' There was a note in his voice I couldn't identify when he added, 'So I shall spend an evening in front of the computer trying to draft some sort of order for his service: they don't want any input.'

'Spend it in front of mine and I'll slip you some rhubarb fool.'

'Maybe I ought to be getting back... I wish

you did takeouts, Josie.'

'For you, Andy, even that can be arranged. Come and check my emergency freezer – so long as you promise to reheat everything thoroughly.'

He nodded absently.

I repeated the instruction. 'Bacteria, Andy. You need to kill them. Which reminds me, what about our photos?'

'So clear you could have them blown up and sold as mementoes to the owners. All safe and sound. I thought– I was afraid you'd skin me alive if I brought them over here without permission.'

'So I would. Twice. So when am I going to see them? I want to check them against the map, and then on the ground.'

His face fell. I'd used the wrong pronoun, hadn't I? He wanted it to be 'we'.

'So when are you free to come over?' I asked.

Mouth corners up again. 'Let's think... Early communion tomorrow plus a diocese meeting: Bishop Jonathan wants to be apprised of latest developments.' *Apprised:* just the sort of word I'd expect the bishop to employ. 'But I could be here by one?'

I shook my head. 'I shall be tied up till two, at the earliest. And I'd have to be back at five at the latest.'

'We could knock off a couple?' he pleaded.

Was it enthusiasm for detecting or for

266

something else? 'Are you better at driving or navigating?' I asked, by way of agreement.

'You know, once or twice I navigated on rallies. Only student things. But I can read maps quite well. And your car's nicer than mine.' He produced a smile to die for.

It took me about three minutes to establish that it would take more time and patience than I had at my disposal to check all the responses Google and Jeeves and the rest gave to my inquiry. So I'd do something else. I'd ask the Martins themselves.

When you're in my line of business, you can flex your people skills to fulfil the needs of the moment. You can do sycophantic, impassive, helpful, surly – it comes not with mother's milk but with years of training. Tonight I'd do ditzy inquisitive, thickly disguising ruthlessly inquisitorial. It'd help if they were going to eat in, of course – which required other places to be booked out. If I were the one doing the booking, I could more or less guarantee that, either, if I knew the maitre d', by telling him he was full, wasn't he, or simply by lying to the Martins.

In fact the weather came to my assistance, so subterfuge wasn't needed. If the mist rolled in, filling the valleys or topping the hills, whichever its preferred mode of endangering the motorist, then visibility rapidly dropped to zero. It chose to arrive this evening. Unable to see to the end of the village street, I braced myself for a load of cancellations, only two of which materialised as it happens, and looked solemn when the male Dr Martin presented himself at reception and asked for my advice.

'There's no telling, I'm afraid. They could still have brilliant sunshine in Taunton. That's why we get such terrible pile-ups on the M5: people are bundling along minding their own business and suddenly they need radar to see the car in front.'

'We'd better eat here, then.' It didn't sound like a request.

'Would you prefer seven o'clock or nine?'

He could have had any time between those, had I really wanted to be accommodating. When he hesitated, I added, tapping the page, 'There is a table free at eight, as it happens, but there's a big party arriving at the same time, so service might be slow.' Which, I added, under my breath, wouldn't matter since they weren't exactly going anywhere afterwards.

With aperitifs, a particularly strong Australian red to go through the meal, and an enchanting Beaume de Venise to accompany the rhubarb fool, I reckoned liqueurs with their coffees would pretty well have the Martins eating out of my hand.

'But surely you have a police family liaison officer supporting you!' I said, settling myself at their table as they told me curtly they didn't know what progress was being made in the case. 'He or she should practically live with you.'

'Not if they were not invited to do so,' she was still sober enough to riposte, looking meaningfully at me.

'Not literally: I didn't mean that. But they should keep you abreast of every train of enquiry, every development, no matter how small. That's what we pay our taxes for, after all. I mean, with your background you'd be entitled to discuss the post-mortem findings, wouldn't you? As medics?'

'Our expertise doesn't lie in that area,' he conceded.

'Two doctors in the house: I bet you've had so many phone calls saying the baby's on its way. A friend of mine – he had a PhD in nutrition – actually helped deliver twins, would you believe? Now – I'm sorry, I don't know your first names: I'm Josie and you're–?'

I became the holiday nightmare. But by the end of ten minutes I'd established that they were Thomas and Celine, they lived in what I deduced by their scathing references to the footballers who'd become near neighbours in a very chic area of Surrey, that Tim had been to one of the most expensive public schools (how on earth had he shed his accent?) and to Durham University, a terrible disappointment as they'd paid sufficient fees, one would have thought, to guarantee an Oxbridge place, and that he'd caught his religious bug during a tour of Durham Cathedral.

'We hoped he'd grow out of it, but when he didn't, we assumed that with our background and his brains he'd rise rapidly in the hierarchy.' She sighed with regret.

'Becoming a rector before you're thirty can't be seen as failure, surely,' I said, wishing that Andy were here.

'It's hardly the eye of the storm, is it? You're never going to hit the headlines...' He realised what he was saying.

'Except in these most tragic of circumstances,' I concluded for him.

'Mired in controversy,' she added.

'Martyrs tend to be, I suspect. Tim was a very brave, loving, kind, honourable young man,' I declared. I'd said more than enough, and in any case another syllable would have had me in tears.

'And foolhardy to the point of irresponsibility, according to DI – what was the woman's name?'

'Lawton, Thomas,' Celine told her husband.

'Were there any signs – when he was a boy – that he was going to be so altruistic?' I asked, regretting my outburst and hoping my cooler language would obliterate it.

'He did his work experience with some charity organisation,' he said. 'Despite the school finding something altogether more appropriate.'

How could they still be so formal, so distant? I wanted, in the emptying dining room, to shake them into some sort of profession of love. But regular customers wanted to say goodbye, newcomers needed a proprietor's schmooze, and it was none of my business anyway. At least I now had the name of his school to go on, and his university, of course. To go on! What did I think I was doing? As I smiled and shook hands, and diverted praise to my wonderful chefs, I cursed for being so stupid. I might have their names, but I still had no idea what they did and what made them tick, money and conventionality apart.

Many, many years ago I'd been a reasonably adept pickpocket: that was how Tony, much too fly to let me get away with it, had come into my life. Was I nippy enough to dip her bag now? It hung enticingly open on the back of her chair.

I left it a good fifteen minutes before I knocked on their door.

'Dr Martin? Celine? Might I have a word?'

There were a few seconds' scuffling before

I was admitted.

Stepping firmly inside, I smiled. 'One of my staff has just handed this in.' I produced her wallet, a very slim elegant affair with a designer label. 'I wonder if you'd mind just checking it is yours and that the contents are intact.'

They were, of course. But that didn't mean I hadn't searched it thoroughly – every card a platinum one, of course, and, more interestingly, an ID for Danemans, a firm supplying most of the major food manufacturers in Europe, let alone the UK. It didn't say what post she held, but I didn't somehow see her as a minion scraping bits off chicken bones to make them into pâté.

Their laptop computer was still on, the screen saver in place. Nothing as ordinary as blue skies and a palm tree or two. A company logo. It was one I didn't happen to recognise, but I'd soon find out who it belonged to. Did I feel sorry for them working when they might have felt too stunned to pick up so much as a phone, or empathise with them? I always reckoned work was the best way of dealing with disagreeable feelings.

To my amazement, having indeed checked the wallet, she flipped out a twenty-pound note. 'For whoever handed it in.'

I wasn't about to make any confessions, was I?

'Thank you. It's unnecessary, but I'll see she gets it.' And with that I decided to embrace discretion and said my goodnights.

Chapter Eighteen

'I'm just waiting to meet the bishop,' Andy said, his phone voice as discreet as if he were running a betting syndicate in the baptistry. 'But I thought you'd want to hear the latest news. Apparently the coroner doesn't want to release the bodies for burial yet, and I've promised to be there when the police break the news to the parents.'

'*Tim's* parents,' I corrected him. 'Some poor couple back in China will never know what happened to their son...' I pushed away the pile of invoices I was working on to the far side of my desk.

'Perhaps for the best? They'll think he's too busy enjoying himself to think of them?'

'Or wonder why the snakeheads are beating up their other kids because Tang's defaulted on his payments?' I asked, as grim as Nick on a bad day. It was, after all, well before nine in the morning.

'I'm afraid you could be right.' There was a moment's hesitation before he continued, 'Anyway, we're all meeting for lunch – *chez vous* if that's OK.'

'Which you want served where?'

'The restaurant, I think. Because they're not going to like Lawton's news, and I think being with other people may protect her from their acid tongues.'

'Protect? She strikes me as having a thick enough hide.'

'I don't think the devil himself has a hide so thick he'd risk the Martins' ire. Cold, penetrating ire.'

'Executive ire,' I agreed, 'honed on myriad minions. I Googled them,' I explained. 'She worked in the food processing industry – she's a major player – and he's in an international biochemistry firm. Which once belonged to his family, but then got floated on the stock market, resulting in a personal profit of millions. And he's still in place as a director.'

'So – ah, here's Bishop Jonathan.' He cut the call immediately.

I returned to the real world of paying bills. The sun shone so brightly into my office I had half a mind simply to take the map and drive round looking for the sites Andy had marked. Then I imagined the disappointment on his face if I deprived him of what he seemed to consider as a treat. And the anger on Nick's if I did anything foolhardy. So I adjusted the blinds and got on with the day job.

Any plans I had to listen in to the Martins' reaction to Lawton's news were thwarted by an inrush of friendly but vocal elderly walkers and the Martins' consequent decision to demand room service. Fuming that I only had myself to blame for offering such privacy when they'd first arrived, I ferried through to their quarters plates of ploughman's and chilled water. But I returned the instant I could to my rightful role of making money rather than squandering it on people who neither needed nor deserved it.

And enjoyed myself, as usual, by being able to surprise folk. Two men were chuntering about their gluten-free diets, and I was able to provide them with wheat-free pizzas (OK, I'd bought the bases, but the toppings were my own, and the delight very much shared); then I reassured a woman that today's soup was dairy-free.

'Someday someone ought to set up a funny diet restaurant,' I joked as I took her order. 'They have vegetarian ones: why not lactose-free or gluten-free?'

'So long as they're *fun*,' she responded. 'Have you seen some of the recipe books? You don't want to be done good to all the time. You just want to enjoy the wonderful food you once ate. What I want more than anything else is a cheese sandwich! And try getting that dairy-free.'

'I will,' I declared. And meant it.

'What do you mean, they've left?' I demanded, putting down the tray of coffee with extreme care.

'Exactly what I said,' DI Lawton said, her face an interesting mixture of amusement and embarrassment. 'They were so furious that they couldn't make arrangements for the funeral they simply packed their bags and went.'

It takes a lot to stun me. At very least, I was taken aback. I sat heavily on the sofa to catch my breath.

'Without – without paying,' she added, as if braced for my reaction.

Andy returned from the bathroom, eyes widening when he saw me. 'Er–'

'My fault,' I sighed. 'I did offer a freebie.'

Time for Lawton to stare. 'Them? A freebie? But they're loaded! Stinking!'

Suddenly I warmed to her.

'Tim had them on record as school teachers,' Andy explained. 'So Josie most charitably–'

'And stupidly!' I inserted.

'–offered them accommodation here. I don't suppose they paid for last night's meal either, did they?'

'I didn't ask them,' I confessed. 'Having made the offer, I felt honour bound to stick to it, even when I saw the car and the clothes.

And even when I was on the receiving end of their attitude. All that good food, all that wonderful wine!' I lamented. Then I perked up: I'd had an idea. 'Tell you what, if they go round behaving like that in their business as well as their private lives, they must have made a lot of enemies. I wonder if it was one of them who killed the boys. And if that was why the Martins were so deadpan. Damn it, they made Tang look positively effusive!'

'I don't follow,' Lawton protested.

'Nor me.' Andy seated himself beside me.

'Sorry. I'll try to slow down. I wondered if someone had threatened them or Tim if they dealt badly again. Or to stop them dealing badly. I don't know. It's not so much left-brain as off the wall. I did print some stuff off about their companies,' I admitted to Lawton. 'Would you be interested?'

'Might save one of my team a moment... I suppose,' she continued, more slowly, 'that they were who they said they were? Not just con-artists?'

'Just to check out the rectory and to blag a free stay in a country pub? I'm not knocking the idea *per se*, Inspector, but they'd want a good reason.'

She looked agreeably surprised by my venture into Latin. I didn't tell her getting Latin GCSE was another of the ways Tony had passed his time. 'I'll risk life and career by getting them checked out,' she said. 'A car number would be a good start.'

'In my register. It's on the reception desk. I'll nip and get it.' I had a sudden vision of the page torn out, with Boy Scoutery needed to lift the details left on the page beneath, but no, it was all intact. I fetched the printouts at the same time, passing them over with a sunny smile.

She phoned, waited and produced a rueful, wrinkle-full grin. 'Unless they nicked the Martins' car, they are who they say they are. But I will double check. What a pair! You know,' she continued, 'this coffee is wonderful.'

'That isn't what you were going to say,' Andy observed.

She had the grace to blush. 'I was going to say, how nice it is to have you cooperating with us, Mrs Welford. You seemed very hands off before.'

'On the contrary, I wanted to take over the investigation myself. If I had, I might have got someone round with mug shots before now! My assault: remember? Not to mention the two little runts in the black BMW that tailed me.'

She muttered and made an irate note.

My facial expression certainly said something about getting a move on. I added, 'And also I'd know everything you've done and everything you've found out.'

In the circumstances, it wasn't surprising

she sighed, 'Shall we swap information, then? What have you got so far?'

'Uh, uh. You talk while I drink this coffee. I give free lunches – no, I can't possibly charge just you – you give free updates. Only what you'd have told the Martins had they stayed.'

She shrugged. 'What we have is very little. The throats of the geese were cut by a sharp implement we've not found yet, possibly a kitchen knife – I don't suppose any have gone missing from here recently?'

'If they had, I'd be on the phone before you could say – well, knife. Dangerous weapons: I keep them locked up.'

'OK. The wounds suggest their assailant was left-handed. Pathologist stuff – don't ask. The same is true of the two victims. They were definitely dead before the fire. We have reason to believe that this was caused deliberately: the fire service forensic team–'

'In other words, that dog with the bootees?'

'Exactly. But dogs' noses are supposed to be good enough to sniff out cancer, aren't they? They found traces of an accelerant. Petrol to you and me. We have no reason to believe that anyone wanted Father Martin killed, though we have not officially ruled this out.' She cast a sideways glance at Andy.

'I'm sure it was Inspector Lawton's questions on this subject that offended the

279

Martins and led to their unseemly depart-ure,' he said.

She nodded in acknowledgement. 'But we are fairly sure, as I think you are, that it was Tang who was the target. The only question is, whose?'

'Hang on.' I raised a hand. 'You've just said talking about Tim made the Martins bolt. Does this mean you've come round to my weird theory?'

She put down her cup and stared. 'No. But I'll tell you what: I'm going to check. Just on the off chance. Now.' She got to her feet.

'I suppose you couldn't somehow *impose* a family liaison officer on them? To see what he or she can pick up on them?'

'That's absolutely not why we offer a liaison officer!'

'Of course not,' I said, meek as if I absolutely believed her.

She snorted. 'And, more to the point, I think they've turned one down once. How-ever, there's no reason why we shouldn't have another go. Right. I'll be off. Mrs Welford—'

'Josie,' I corrected her expansively.

'If you want to bill me for their lunches, I can run them through expenses.'

'You're on. I suppose you wouldn't want to pick up the tab for the rest of their jolly? No? Well, it was worth a try,' I said amicably. 'While I write out the bill, you may want to look at some photos Andy and I took the other day. They're meant for Nick, as part of his job, you understand, but you never know if they'll ring any bells.'

Andy looked at me in disbelief. But he burrowed in his briefcase, at first with confidence, and then with increasing desperation. 'They've gone! I know I put them there this morning. I know I did. I checked. Like you check the front door – twice, three times.'

'Did you check while the Martins were there?'

'Surely not. I can't even remember their being on their own.'

I chimed in. 'Where did you put the case when you left the bishop?'

'In the back of my car. You know, never leave anything in the passenger seat, in case you get "taxed". Years of working in an inner city,' he explained.

The more the conversation circled, the more obvious it became that the Martins must have seized an opportunity to rifle it.

'It's something you might want your family liaison officer to talk about,' I said. 'Not an accusation, of course. After all, the briefcase could have tipped over, the bishop might have picked them up – there might be all sorts of innocent explanations. Anyway, why should they want aerial views of food-processing plants?' As a Parthian shot I added, 'And get your minion to fix a time for me to check those mug shots, eh?'

It wasn't until she'd gone that I 'found' the packet of photos – down the side of the sofa on which I'd been sitting.

Andy goggled. 'How on earth did that get there?'

I shook my head in disbelief. 'Who knows?' And then I felt Tony's hand on my shoulder, telling me not to press my luck. And congratulating me on not losing my unpractised skills.

Andy gathered coffee cups, not meeting my eye. Then he started on the ploughman's plates. 'All this food wasted. My mother told me to eat every scrap, but no one except me seems to do that, these days.'

I nodded. 'Didn't I read that we throw about forty per cent of our food away? That we've got the best fed rats in Europe?' Had he twigged what I'd done? There was a real tension between us.

I waited while he opened the kitchen door. 'Thanks.'

The kitchen was pristine, as if no one had ever so much as peeled an apple in it. Excellent. I could hardly let my standards slip below those of my staff, so I attended to all the scraps, and, the dishwashers already in action, washed up by hand. All the time Andy was mooning round, looking at lists and first aid notices and fire blankets without feigning a satisfactory interest in any of them.

'I thought,' he said at last, in the tone of a little boy late for his trip to the park, 'we were going on a hunting expedition.'

'So we are. But being meticulous in a restaurant kitchen isn't a matter of choice, Andy, or responding to a psychological compulsion or whatever. It's obeying the law. Heavens, I can't believe I said that! Put it another way, it's preventing people contracting all sorts of nasty food-poisoning bugs. I'll be with you in five minutes. And I mean five. Promise.'

It was probably seven, but he didn't complain. He'd used the interval while I changed to appropriate one of the round tables in the restaurant and lay the photos of the possible sites on the map. 'We'd have done better with pins and coloured string,' he greeted me. 'But this isn't bad, considering the Martins are supposed to have nicked the photos. What's going on, Josie? All that business when you'd put them down the sofa yourself?'

'You didn't see, did you? Must have lost my touch.' *Never apologise, never explain*, as the man said.

'No, of course I didn't. Or I'd have said something there and then. No, probably I wouldn't. At least it galvanised Lawton into action. And she'd been very remiss not to follow up the ID business. But it – let's say, it totally disconcerted me.'

'And is that a good or a bad thing?'

He sighed heavily. 'I really don't know.' And then he did surprise me. He looked me straight in the eye. 'Do you?'

Are phones primed to ring at the wrong moment? Mine at least? I grimaced. 'Sorry. But it says here it's Bernie Downs. The galvanisation seems to have worked.' I took the call. 'Half an hour would be fine,' I confirmed without thinking. 'And by the way, tell your DI we've found the photos.' I turned to Andy. 'All the same, I'd rather we didn't have this lot lying around in full view. Hey, what are you doing?'

'Just putting the map reference on the back of each photo. See? Using the coordinates?'

'All Chinese to me,' I quipped. And then, to my absolute horror, I started to cry. 'No. Don't dare be nice to me. Don't even think about it. Get on with what you're doing and leave me to sort myself out.' Which I did with a viciously cold shower and meticulous make-up.

I returned to the restaurant to find a pot of tea waiting for me. But no Andy. And no map or photos either.

The idiot! The absolute stupid idiot! With no more idea of how to look after himself than a babe in arms! Except, of course, he'd got enough nous to switch off his mobile. If

I'd allowed myself to cry, this time my tears would have been pure frustration.

Or was that an oxymoron too?

Chapter Nineteen

'You're positive you don't recognise any of these faces? Absolutely positive?' Poor Bernie Downs took it as a matter of personal failure on her part.

Hard-hearted in the face of her pleading, I shook my head firmly.

'Tell you what, I'll ask the villagers who said they'd witnessed it. After all,' she added as kindly as if I were ninety, 'you'd have been very upset, very shocked.'

I suppressed a fierce desire to snarl, not least because they should have been questioned the day I was run down. 'OK: let's go through one more time.' Once or twice I caught myself with a false memory, I wanted so much to get an ID. And then: 'Yes! Yes, I'm sure that's him!'

Downs made a note, but didn't overwhelm me with her enthusiasm. 'I thought you said you hardly saw the BMW driver.'

'I eyeballed him! I yelled at him!'

'I thought you said he was clean shaven.'

'Easy enough to shave a bit of facial

fungus, for goodness' sake!'

'But–'

'Look at that expression: look how knowing it is. My assailant had exactly that look.'

'So, unfortunately, have a lot of young scrotes. But we'll follow him up.'

'I have a pretty good memory for faces. Especially the faces of people who try to run me over.'

She nodded. 'Just to make sure, let's try the national database.'

'But–' On the other hand, if I'd been indignant about Lawton's laxity, how could I complain when someone was trying?

So we clicked away, Bernie prompting me as if her life depended on my finding someone. We must have been at it half an hour, bless her. At last, hardly remembering who I'd said it was in the first place, I pointed to my watch: 'Afternoon tea?'

I was well into preparation for the evening, when a phone rang. My mobile. So it wasn't a late booking or a cancellation, for which I was grateful. A bit of stability was called for, in my professional as much as my personal doings. Which was why I didn't respond immediately to the call, which was from Andy: if he left a message, I could judge better how to react.

It sounded as if he might have written it down or even rehearsed it. Either that, or he was better at leaving phone messages than most. 'Nil returns, so far, I'm afraid. Both places I checked out on the way home had proper signs outside, labelled vans coming and going: everything looked eminently respectable. I'll speak to you soon, I hope.'

At least he hadn't been torn apart by a dozen slavering guard dogs or got himself kidnapped and beaten up. I returned to my onion peeling – yes, we all mucked in together, which is why we made such a good team. So the tears pouring down my face were purely chemical in origin when, suddenly panicking that his call was a sop to kidnappers to put me off the scent, I returned his call.

'Sorry: I'm just off to the cathedral for a confirmation service,' he said. 'Literally getting in the car now.'

'Is there some sort of ceremonial booze up afterwards? No? Suppose you call me then.' But I had a feeling he was as angry as I was, him because of the photograph trick I'd pulled and I – well, because I was. So I certainly wouldn't hold my breath. I cut the call without waiting for his response. After all, if my appointment was with fifty or so diners, his was with God.

I was just tarting myself up for my evening front of house role when my phone rang. This time it was Abigail Tromans, the farmer's wife. 'Cheap chickens,' she said.

'And chickens cheep,' I responded, foolishly, given that while Abigail is a shrewd businesswoman – compared with her husband, anyway – her sense of humour isn't in the premier league.

'Sorry?'

'Nothing. Sorry. Cheap chickens?'

'Dan says there were a couple of free-range chicken farmers at the market this morning who supply one of the big places in Exeter. They've been asked to cut their prices. Halve them. Some other supplier's come along, see, and is offering dressed meat at silly prices. Breast meat, it is, too.'

'So it's delivered to the restaurant without skin or bones?'

'That's right.'

'I wonder what happens to the rest of the bird,' I pondered aloud.

'That's the supplier's problem, see. All these legs. What do you do with them? I mean, even you want extra breasts, don't you?'

Not personally I didn't, but I could hardly say that. 'Of course. One of the slips in God's design plan, chickens with only two supremes. He's obviously not a chef. How are you keeping, by the way, Abigail?'

'So so. Thanks to you I can put my feet up a bit longer. And you've got a good hand with scone dough, no doubt about that.'

'It isn't always me, Abigail: it's whoever's on the early turn. So long as they're OK, though, that's all that matters. And the wild garlic's going down a treat, tell Dan. I suppose,' I added, as casually as I could, 'that your Dan didn't get the name of the restaurant offered cheap chooks?' Because that was something I could get on to, if it was one of my contacts. Or Nick, if it wasn't.

'I'll ask him, shall I?'

'That'd be great. But it's not urgent. Nothing to raise your blood pressure over.'

But it seemed something was, and I heard all her symptoms, with as much sympathy as I could, for the next five minutes, until I managed to end the call. Her working day might be over, but mine certainly wasn't.

In fact, we became busy – a party booked for eight-thirty didn't appear till after nine – so that, having neither time nor energy for an encounter with Andy, I switched off my mobile phone, though I kept it as always clipped to my waist band. I left clear instructions with Lucy that she mustn't disturb me but just take a message if he came through on the restaurant line. And I wouldn't, at this rate, be heading upstairs to my sanctum till too late to respond to any messages left on the answerphone there.

Everything was going very well, and I was giving my laurels a polish, when one of the guests waved me over.

'Oi! Waitress! This here dessert menu: it looks a bit fancy to me,' he said. His shirt was just a bit too snappy, the tie too wide. And his trousers were definitely too tight for his belly, so he wore it over his waistband, in the best manner of potential heart attacks. So perhaps he was telling the truth.

'I can always offer fresh fruit,' I said limpidly. 'In fact, give me five minutes and it can be a nice alcoholic fruit salad.'

He looked at his companion, the sort of man in the old days I'd have been able to judge to the pound how much he made from crime. Don't ask how: it's to do with the prison skin and cockiness and – like the first man – dress style and posture and a damned great ring. Even without Tony's whisper in my ear, I was on my guard.

'I don't much go for fruit,' he said, 'unless it's made into a nice drop of cider or wine. I was thinking more like – more like a nice scone. The sort you make for other people I'm sure you'd not want any harm to come to.'

Tony pressed my shoulder. I must keep calm. Buy thinking time.

I looked at my watch and shook my head sadly. 'I'm sorry, at this hour I couldn't ask Chef to knock up anything special like that.'

'We thought you might have some in, like. Suppose we just go into that kitchen of yours and have a look.' Both men rose to their feet. One swept his tablecloth off, with all the glass and china smashing to the ground. The other grabbed a wine bottle from an adjoining table and smashed it. So now he had a nasty weapon.

The first shouldered me out of the way, and I fell heavily against another diner. It might reactivate a lot of my old bruises, but I was actually glad to have an excuse for a firm response.

As I scrabbled to my feet, I grabbed the mobile and pressed the pager button. Kitchens were such noisy places they might not hear the racket outside. So I had to let everyone know there was trouble, so that they could prepare accordingly. In these days of binge drinking and drunken yobbishness there probably wasn't a restaurant in the land whose staff weren't trained in defusing situations. Or acting fast if they couldn't.

But not as fast as one of my regulars. I knew him merely as Mr Jenkins, a mildmannered, middle-aged A and E consultant based in Plymouth, with an educated taste for English wines. What I didn't know was that he could arm-lock someone from a standing start, his grip so fierce the bottle fell uselessly – and noisily – to the floor, and use his captive to shunt the other man to his knees.

'This is on the house,' I assured Mr Jenkins ten minutes later as we all metaphorically dusted our hands and I presented him with a bottle of champagne. 'With my gratitude.'

Despite our superior numbers – and several other diners suddenly discovered how brave they were – we'd had to let the offenders go. Much as I'd have liked to lock them in the boiler house till the police came, I was terrified a customer might get hurt. Neither man would submit tamely to detention, and Mr Jenkins had already rather preempted me by frogmarching his captive outside and slinging him on to the road. The other crawled swiftly after him, taking lunges and swings at anyone foolhardy enough to get in his way.

There was, however, nothing in the world to stop us taking their number as they drove off. The plate was as dirty as the filthy beat-up Mazda bearing it, so it might even be genuine. To my irritation my fingers shook as I put in a call to the police, mentioning to the duty officer I got through to that the incident might well be connected with a murder case DI Lawton was working on. This time I could even promise photos: it transpired that two of my customers had taken nice mug shots with their clever phones. My top of the range security cameras should have something too. DI Lawton would be round first thing, the officer said.

She better had be. I'd jotted down the man's name as he first barked it down the phone. Tony had slithered free a couple of times because of police inefficiency and I'd make damned sure anyone who neglected to pass on messages wouldn't ever forget again.

We were in the thank you and goodnight ritual when it dawned on me that I'd been the one to forget. Something. Something pretty vital. Life and death vital.

'Sergeant Parsons: I'm glad you're taking this so seriously. Because now I'm asking you to take something else even more seriously. There's no time to explain now, but I'm afraid Dan and Abigail Tromans at Whitemay Farm may be the assailants' target. Could you get someone out there urgently? Please?'

I must have made some sort of impression on him because he said ruefully, 'Out of the way places aren't easy to reach quickly, Mrs Welford. But I'll do my best, I promise.'

What if their best wasn't good enough?

I only had the Tromans' officer number, and there was little point in leaving a warning that they wouldn't look at till the next morning. Telling myself they had security fences and spotlights that might have dazzled the Luftwaffe didn't work. All the time I was beaming my thanks at my more peaceable customers, my mental hamster was whizzing round working out how to reach the Tromans in person. Again I risked honesty: 'Mr Jenkins, it occurs to me that our friends may have gone on somewhere else. Will you excuse me? Take your time over your coffee, please – but I must shoot off.'

The Saab was boxed in, of course.

I dived back into the kitchen. 'Robin? Can you do me the most enormous favour? Get me to Whitemay Farm, soonest?'

His face lit up. 'You mean soonest as in motorbike on unmade road? Do bears need Portaloos? OK, gaffer, let's go.'

It had always looked such fun, and I supposed it was grimly exhilarating. I'd have enjoyed it far more if I'd known that the only thing awaiting me at the end of the so-called lane was a warm if surprised welcome. Anyway, the least said about Robin's nocturnal adventure, which is all it was to him, the better.

That seemed to be the sentiment of the Tromans, wakened from their slumber by the 1000cc roar of our approach. In fact, Dan greeted me with the suggestion that I go away promptly – in slightly different words, at least. Despite the chill of the night, he was wearing nothing except an England rugby shirt, some very brief shorts and flip-flops.

'Something wrong with my ewes?' he demanded.

Of course: lambing season. Any day now and he wouldn't know the meaning of a full night's sleep. And then there'd be the babies.

When I explained in breathless detail why I was there, he became grimmer than ever. 'I might have known getting into bed with you wouldn't do my business any good.'

'I think it's more a case of careless talk costing lives,' I snapped, forgetting, as my bum recovered from the indignities of that saddle, to be sympathetic. 'Someone told someone else of my connection with the enquiries into dodgy chicken. Just to make sure, the second someone wants to talk to me – I use the word loosely – about scones. Information about which could only have come from you or Abigail...' I tailed off, leaving him to work out the sums. 'Abigail and I had agreed it was top secret, remember – to protect her business, rather than mine. Anyway, if all is well, I shall disappear into the night whence I came.' I grinned at Robin. 'Only by a slightly smoother route.'

'She talked you into this caper, did she?' Dan demanded. 'You must be off your head, man.' He turned on his flip-flop – hard to do that with any dignity – and prepared to stride off.

As Robin turned the bike, his headlight

powered over the farmyard. And dwelt on a bottle. A bottle with a rag sticking out.

Furious that Robin had apparently turned a spotlight on him, Dan turned again, finger upraised. But it and he crumpled. He scurried over to the bottle.

I probably screamed, 'Don't touch it.' Maybe it didn't matter, because he'd fished the rag out and shaken it open. Paper, not a rag. And there was no smell of petrol. He put the bottle down and opened the paper, reading its message in the light from the bike. Pulling a face, he slopped over to us.

YOU WANT TO BE CAREFULL WHO YOU DO BUISNESS WITH, DON'T YOU NEXT TIME YOU'LL SEA WHY

'The police are supposed to be on their way. You'd best show it to them. But for God's sake, don't alarm Abigail. Not with her blood pressure. They'll have her in hospital before you can blink if it goes up any further.'

He gaped. 'What business do you suppose they mean?'

'Scones? Meat? Wild garlic? Or is it just the questions you asked? Here are the police now, by the look of it.' The blue light touched the treetops and hedges weirdly. Blues but not twos – this was the country-side, after all. 'I'll leave you to it, shall I?' It was cold and I was tired and I was furious.

Who with, I wasn't quite sure. OK, Tony – with whom.

Although it was very late, or even fairly early, when we got back, I was so pulsing with adrenaline that I could have cleaned the kitchen twice over, defrosting the fridge for good measure. But the scullions had done their usual brilliant job. To my surprise Pix presented me with a glass of my own brandy – the sort I have seen charged at a hundred pounds a glass.

You couldn't drink stuff that good standing up, so I found a stool and gestured to them to help themselves too.

'Wasted on me,' Robin said, helping himself to a Beck's, while Pix tasted an eye-dropperful. 'Thing is, Josie, we're a bit worried about you, especially after tonight. Well, the farm business, too. It isn't all that long ago that people dropped all sorts of nastiness on your doorstep – and not to mention trying to blow the place up,' he added, dropping his voice although Lucy had been despatched to bed ages ago.

'If anyone tries anything nasty, they'll have to smile while they're doing it.'

'It's all very well having security cameras and alarms and the rest of it. But what if they took a pot shot at you out of camera-range?'

'They'd have to be damned good shots. I paid extra for the cameras to track, remember. But I take your point. And I'll raise it with the police tomorrow, first thing.' I looked at my watch. 'Which can't be many hours away now.'

They took the hint, but with obvious reluctance. Pix turned. 'What with one thing and another, I shall be glad when Nick's back. You listen to him.'

'Sometimes,' Robin grunted.

The mobile phone photographers had sent me their snaps via my computer, and I duly printed them off. I also circulated them to all the restaurateurs in our organisation. But I didn't think many of them would be similarly bothered. Not unless they were asking awkward questions about chicken suppliers and baking scones for their neighbours. There was no email address on Bernie's card or on Lawton's, so they'd have to make a personal appearance for me to pass them on.

Thence to my phone. No, no message from Andy. Nor one on the answerphone. Was I relieved or miffed? But by then the brandy was kicking in, and I discovered I didn't care either way, so long as I could tumble into my bed.

Chapter Twenty

Dim I might have been after all my nocturnal activities, but even before nine in the morning I could tell a detective chief inspector in his later forties from a detective inspector in her thirties. Especially when the male officer spent a possibly narcissistic amount of time on his physique and his appearance.

Thank goodness I always started the day with stretches and a shower; thank goodness for my diet and my daily walks; thank goodness for a job that demanded chic at a time I'd much rather have been in bed.

No, it wasn't because I wanted to pull him. A couple of years ago it might have been. And I had to admit he was terribly personable, with a smile that positively caressed and the sort of suit and shoes I'd have loved to kit Andy out in. If he hadn't been a dog-collar man, I'd certainly have bought him a tie like that too. Silk, the sort of quality you could only get in one shop in Exeter.

It was because in my experience men like that disregarded women who weren't equally spruce and elegant. Looked straight through them. I'd been there, remember, the tub of lard. The thinner I got, the better clothes I bought; when I didn't have to pretend to be just another woman from a sink estate, the more attention I got. Polite attention, mind, not just the appraising sort.

DCI Burford cast the same sort of eye around my apartment as the Martins had. 'Left you well off, did he, Mrs Welford?'

'A lot of hard work and wise investments,' I countered. 'Mine. I've been all through this with so many people, Mr Burford, you'll excuse me if I don't rehearse it again with you?'

'Not my case. But I'm always open to spontaneous confessions,' he added, with a smile to die for.

'A cup of coffee is more likely.'

He shook his head seriously. 'I'd rather have water, please. Out of the tap.'

A body as temple man, perhaps. Who was I to argue? I joined him, adding lime and ice-cubes to Adam's ale in fine crystal tumblers. Fine, but not my finest. Since I hadn't yet breakfasted, I laid out the pastries Pix had produced when he'd done today's batch of scones. Robin had couriered them down: I expected a detailed report when he re-turned.

'So why do I no longer merit a bright and hard-working DI?'

'You merit an equally bright and equally

300

hard-working DCI. I'm part of an MIT that has taken over the St Jude's murders case. And I gather you've been having what may or may not be problems associated with my case.'

My case: a tad possessive, since it had taken over a week for him to take it on. How did Lawton feel about the move?

'Certain problems, yes. Which may or may not simply be associated with my business. I've been trying to source cheaper poultry, Mr Burford, and my enquiries have produced no chicken but a lot of interest. And it's not a figment of my imagination: your colleagues will have no doubt reported on the threat in a bottle one of my neighbours received, presumably from the same source.'

'Heinz or HP?'

Oh, we were a wit, were we? I granted him a token smile.

'So why should people object to your wanting cheaper chicken?'

'Because I think – and you may have the evidence to support or contradict this – that Tang–'

'That's the dead Chinese lad, right?'

A token nod, this time. Even newcomers – especially newcomers? – should be up to speed. Despite his shapely ankles, clad in the sort of socks I used to buy Tony as a welcome home present, I got less impressed by the moment. At least, most of the time,

Lawton had seemed interested, if ultimately out of her depth. OK, and antagonistic – or attracted – to Nick. 'Have his clothes shown anything interesting?' I asked. 'I found them in the compost maker at the rectory.'

His eyes widened, then narrowed with something like hostility. 'And why would you look for them there?'

'More to the point, why didn't your colleagues find them there?' My eyes and voice went into senior management mode. 'All trained officers, presumably – you'd expect them to explore every nook and cranny. I found them when I was throwing out dead geraniums,' I added blazing all my charm guns at him, just when he wasn't expecting it.

He responded with an A grade smile. 'As far as I know, the bag's still with the forensic science people. But you're expecting it to have–?'

'The clothes stank. Something foetid. Rotting flesh. Maybe human, if he killed someone, but maybe – and this would be my theory – dead animal or chicken. Chicken because he wouldn't touch cooked chicken.'

'So you weren't really trying to source chicken? Not for use in your restaurant? You were trying to get some handle on – what? Somewhere Tang might have worked? Forgive me, Mrs Welford, but I don't see chickens turning up with "killed by Tang" stamped all over them.'

My nod suggested that he, as an Alpha male, was of course right, and I was a Silly Billy.

'Why do you think Tang and Tim were killed, then?' I asked. Gotcha!

'This is why the MIT has been brought in, Mrs Welford. And we shall certainly look into the chicken connection. Thank you very much.' He stood, eyeing the spare pastries.

As if absent-mindedly I passed the plate. Equally absent-mindedly he took another.

'And of course,' I added, 'there's always the problem of whatever crime Tang sought sanctuary for. Isn't there? A problem which has been systematically ignored by everyone.' Including myself, but I didn't add that.

'Hospital?' I echoed. 'And they're keeping her in?' I sat heavily on a kitchen stool.

Robin nodded. 'Apparently they wanted Abby to stay in last check up, but she said Dan couldn't spare her. Well, he's got to now. Till she pods, I should think. And now he's wringing his hands saying he doesn't know how to manage. I guess it'd be financially as much as anything else. I don't suppose that tea and scones venture brings in more than fifty quid a week, maybe more if they have a fine weekend, but it seems to me that's what they live on. That,' he added, looking hard at me, 'and the wild garlic.'

'Which is vital for your wild garlic risotto, wild garlic soup and butter-braised wild garlic,' I said, smiling innocently.

'Absolutely, gaffer,' he responded. 'Even at £10 a kilo. So how are we going to keep them afloat, eh?'

My shock was genuine. 'We? Are you off your head, Robin? We're fully stretched here – more, with me gadding around hither and there.'

'The cooking's no problem. It's just finding someone to serve the teas.'

'"Just" finding someone. The age of miracles is past, kid.' But when his face fell like that, what else could I do? 'Or maybe, just maybe, it isn't. Leave it with me. And by the way,' I added, patting his arm before I headed back upstairs, 'you're a nice lad – you know that?'

'I'm sorry everything's such a mess,' Annie apologised.

All her cottage showed was that she was just back from her holiday, with a pile of unopened mail on the hall table and the sound of a washing-machine already in action.

'Doesn't look messy to me. And I'm sorry I came at an inconvenient time. Only I needed some help and thought of you.'

'Why don't you sit down and tell me about it? And you can fill me in on what the police have found so far.'

I sat. The Regency day bed she used as a sofa was as excruciating as it was elegant. I kept the narrative brief. It could have been briefer but I wasn't sure how she'd respond to a single four-letter word before 'all'. And in any case, Tony never liked to hear me use the word, except in an appropriate context.

'No wonder they've handed it over to a specialist team,' she summed up for me. 'And those poor boys denied a burial. Dear me. I almost wish I'd stayed away a bit longer, but I could hear the garden calling me. You know how it is. You plan a low-maintenance life, and need to add a bit more spice to it because it's so bland, and next thing you know you've got a water feature and fish to worry about. And still have time round the edges.'

'That's music to my ears! Annie, I know you've got your CAB commitment – but could you take something else on? Maybe just for a few days – maybe for a good deal longer?' I explained. 'But before you say anything, I ought to warn you: someone disapproved of my connections with the place – they sent a warning message in a bottle last night.'

Her chin went up. 'All the more reason to get involved, then. Count me in, Josie. I bet there are a couple of other ladies from St Jude's we could involve, too.'

'They'd have to know the risk.'

'That's about the only advantage of growing old I can think of: even thugs tend to treat you more gently.'

I would have argued, but she embarked on a reminiscence of her teaching days, and I didn't want to interrupt.

As I stood, eventually, to go – my bum announcing that it simply would not countenance another minute on the unyielding springs – she asked, 'Was this Andrew Braithwaite's idea?'

I nearly sat down again. 'No. Why should it be?'

'I just wondered. He seems such an imaginative man. Very attractive too,' she added, shooting a look from beneath her eyebrows.

'Very,' I said.

'But already spoken for, I'd say.'

'He has a lady friend?' I was quite pleased by my choice of term, given the shock.

'Not that I know of.'

'By whom, then?'

'By God.'

I popped the portable CD player, with a supply of batteries and a selection of discs, on Abigail's bedside cabinet, plus a pile of glossy mags she might just care to leaf through. 'You're looking better already,' I told her, almost truthfully.

'Don't tell Dan, or he'll want me straight

back again.'

I didn't think she was joking. 'Of course he misses you.'

She dismissed the platitude with the sniff it deserved. 'Misses the work I do, more like.'

'Well, he won't be missing that, not if the ladies of St Jude's have anything to do with it. The afternoon teas, at least. And one of them swears she enjoys cleaning. Truly!'

'You're having me on.'

'Why should I do that? It gives them some-thing to do, Abigail – they can't lovingly polish the church or tend the graveyard, not till the police say they can. Their families have moved away. They'll be operating in pairs so they'll have a bit of company. It'll work, I promise you. Because Annie Bryant's running it.'

'Not you?'

I shook my head. 'I'm sorry: I truly don't have the time. Which is why I have to dash. I'm so sorry.'

To the shops. If that nightie was the best she could manage, I'd better hit Taunton fast. A couple of places on my own behalf. Marks and Sparks for Abby's nighties and some flowers. I couldn't trust Dan to take either, though I didn't say so to his face as I handed them over at the farm gate.

'Don't you dare let on who they came from!'

'I don't want your charity.'

'How about they're an apology for disturbing your sleep last night? Come on, man, you don't have time to shop, but it'll do her heart good to think you did. Won't it? How did Annie get on, by the way?'

He looked at me hard. 'Like you. Like a bloody whirlwind.'

Whirlwind? All I wanted to do was sleep when at last I got back to the White Hart. That, and pop aspirin for a vicious headache. But I had scarcely ten minutes before I had to be on duty. The bookings file showed we were pretty full again, and this only a Thursday. Friday and Saturday evenings were already booked out, and not even Jamie Oliver would get a table for the next three Sunday lunches. We'd have to get more staff. No argument. At very least someone we could call on for emergencies. It wasn't fair to put pressure on Lucy, not when she had exams to worry about.

There were a couple of messages on the answerphone, and my mobile had a couple of calls I hadn't taken. Damn it, they could wait till I'd had a cup of tea.

Better still, a stiff gin and tonic. A very stiff gin and tonic.

Crazy. You start drinking on your own in this business and you might as well book in for the next session of AA.

Green tea, then, and the quickest shower going.

Just as I'd undressed, the phone rang. Nick.

I never thought I'd say it, albeit strictly under my breath: 'Thank goodness you're coming back!'

But he wasn't. He was ringing to say he'd picked up some bug. He was sure it was flu, but since he'd been in contact with all that vile meat, Elly had insisted he stay put. I never argued with Elly and this wasn't the time to begin.

'Everything's absolutely fine down here,' I insisted. 'And Elly's right: if you're not better in the morning, you get into A and E and insist you have the proper tests.'

'OK. I will.'

His docility worried me: he must really be ill. Ebola Fever! All those zoonoses – animal diseases that could attack humans – I'd read about on the Internet! What if he didn't make it through the night? If only Andy and I were on speaking terms, and I could ask him to have a quiet word with his Boss.

Chapter Twenty-One

Andy smiled. 'So we're on our own, then?'

I took it that he referred to our amateur sleuthing, rather than the absence of a third party from my flat. Having Friday breakfast together we might be, but that was because he wanted to make an early start to our combined hunt for the chicken plant, not because of any joint nocturnal activity.

Despite the seriousness of it all, the weather was glorious enough to impart a holiday air; had I not been on duty for lunch, I'd even have suggested we take a picnic and do the thing properly.

'How ill is Nick?' he pursued.

'He's never one to underestimate his illnesses,' I said. 'Except when they're truly serious, like a stomach ulcer he insisted on neglecting. Like most men, I suppose. Tony would worry about gangrene when the tiniest splinter punctured his skin, but he was stoicism itself when confronted by cancer.' And then I remembered Andy's wife and her illness, and stopped short.

He was too preoccupied with his full English breakfast to argue. I treated myself occasionally, especially when, as today, I wanted to try a new type of sausage. I loved extra-meaty sausages for the dinner menu, but worried that they'd be overpowering at any other time. They weren't. And they were gluten-free, a real bonus for my poor allergy sufferers. As for the bacon, that was organic, traditionally dry-cured – none of that white gloop in the pan, and a piece of shrunken something or other on your plate that tasted of nothing but salt. Organic eggs from my neighbour. Bread baked in my own kitchen. A feast.

'First of all,' I continued, 'we'll pick up a hire car in Taunton. It's booked – won't take a minute.'

'A hire car?'

I wilfully misunderstood. 'All the choppers are booked on Fridays.'

He shook his head dismissively. 'But we've got two perfectly good vehicles outside.'

'There aren't a lot like mine round here – look how easy it was for our two friends to pick up our trail the other day. And they may have noted yours when I dropped you off. So we'll go incognito. I wonder if it's too warm to wear my party wig? And if you don't mind my saying so, I know your shirt's a nice blue, but the dog-collar gives the game away. So you could try this.' It wasn't just nighties I'd found in Taunton the previous day. I'd had to guess at the size, of course, but any taking back was my job: there was no way he'd discover the price. Before he could argue, I continued. 'If it fits, you might want to iron out the creases. The ironing board's in the kitchen. Now, give me five minutes to brief the lads, and we'll be off.'

'A nice anonymous silver Fiesta,' I said, patting it affectionately. 'The only trouble is, it's towards the bottom of the range, so it won't have as much poke as I like. Still, I can use the gear box to get us out of trouble.' He was looking at me sideways. 'Well, you've got the navigating skills.'

'Dare I ask how you learned to drive?'

'I don't see why not. One of my husband's getaway drivers. He'd learned in the Met. Now that's one thing I don't like – a bent policeman.'

Our eyes met.

'You don't suppose–' He coughed. 'Didn't Nick say these people smugglers might have infiltrated the law enforcement agencies? That could explain the police's singular lack of obvious progress.'

'I wonder... They've changed the investigating team. Which may or may not be a good thing.' He didn't need to know about the mild flirtation Burford seemed to be initiating. But Andy, chic in that new shirt, which he'd ironed, to do him justice, very well, was still distinctly more intriguing. Largely, I suppose, because he wasn't attempting to intrigue. 'Have they updated you regularly?' I pursued.

'No. But I don't really have any rights.'

'More than I do. His parents?'

'As you know, they refused to have a family liaison officer. If they have had any information from the police, I can't imagine either of us being *persona grata* – popular enough–'

'It's OK. Tony had GCSE Latin, although I never quite got round to it.' I might have added that I didn't take the exam because he'd had to put the frighteners on me for embarking on an unsuitable affair.

He flushed. 'Sorry. I didn't mean to patronise you. My parishioners were always telling me they didn't understand the Latin and Greek tags I kept using.'

'You can use Greek if you want to baffle me. As one of the hoi polloi,' I added, with a twinkle. Dear me, he could be so uptight. I knew of only one cure for the condition, but I'd probably ruled that out even before Annie dropped her hint, hadn't I? 'Anyway, let's return to our *moutons.*' Thank you, Tony's A level French. Which site do you want to check out first?' I'd better let him think he was in charge, hadn't I?

'As I said when I went hunting on my own, if a business looks legitimate, it probably is. You aren't going to go round in a van blazoned with the firm's phone number and address, are you?'

'So it's white van territory we're searching for, those anonymous bullies of the road. OK. Hang on: just in case.' I donned sunglasses, and silently passed him a pair. And then I pulled on my wig. Patting the white blonde bubble curls, I asked, pouting my lips and slapping on cerise gloss, 'How do I look?'

This time his flush must have hurt, and he dropped his eyes. I adjusted the mirror. 'Hell's bells, I look like a tart! Well, thank goodness you don't look like a vicar!'

We'd parked in a lay-by on a gently winding B road, the trees greening nicely and the verges already plumping up. It carried so little traffic that in any other part of the country it would never have been classified. Off it to our right, about a mile away, we thought, lay our first yard. What I saw in my rear-view mirror made me fling myself at him as if in a passionate snog. Repeat: *as if.* Bowling merrily up behind us was a van bearing a name I recognised: that of my samphire-pickling colleague Michael Rousdon, from Starcross. Now what was he doing so far from home? Before Andy could gasp, 'Goodness, I didn't know you had feelings for me,' or words to that effect, I had the car in gear and pulled out, ready to tail him at a discreet distance.

'Shouldn't you be a bit closer? Following him, I mean? You might lose him.' Top marks for realising what I was up to.

'Think ex-Met instructor,' I said. 'And trust me.'

Andy snorted with laughter. 'I think that's asking a bit too much of me! Look, he's turning. Into that farmyard.'

'I'm going to drive past slowly. Mark it on the map. I'm not going to risk getting in close. I know him, you see. A fellow restaurateur.' One who still appeared to carry a torch for me, and I'd briefly fancied enough to contemplate sex with. Did I regret not indulging? No: I really hoped my taste hadn't been bad enough for me to fancy a possible criminal. And then I thought of Tony, and it was my turn to blush. Painfully.

I pulled into a gate.

'What do you think you're doing?' Andy demanded.

'Going for a quick shuftie.'

'Uh, uh. You say he knows you. You may have – considerably! – changed your appearance, but you still walk and talk the same.'

In spite of myself, my chin went up. 'You want a bet?'

'No. This one's my call. I shan't take any risks. And my camera's less obtrusive than that huge phallic symbol of yours.' He flourished a snazzy mobile phone. 'Why, I could just be trying to get a signal in this benighted place. And if necessary, I can take a pee in the hedge.'

I didn't argue. Instead, as soon as he was out of the car, I edged it nearer the road and prepared for a rapid exit. Had the road been wide and straight I wouldn't have stood a chance of outrunning anyone; in fact, I'd increase the odds by taking to the real lanes. The OS map showed a satisfactorily winding, narrow track first left: I'd plunge into that. Of course, that risked our being entirely scuppered should a heavy vehicle or a flock of sheep be heading our way.

Through the mirror I could see Andy returning at a leisurely pace, apparently doing up his flies. Once out of sight of the farm, however, he broke into a canter and flung himself breathlessly into the car.

'They may have seen me. But I don't think there was anything to worry about. It all looked legit. Want to see the photos on my new toy?'

'Only when we're well clear. Just in case.'

For no reason but that it seemed attractive, I took the lane I'd planned, pulling at last under a tree. 'Let's see.'

'I only hope I've got it right. The guy at the shop said it was foolproof, but that might mean foolproof if you're under twenty. Wow. Look!'

'Well done. Next?'

He thumbed his way through a pretty

series of shots, all including cars with nice clear plates and people's faces.

'That one there – could you bring it up a bit?'

He ostentatiously crossed his fingers before applying a thumb to the pads. 'So long as I don't lose it – no, there we are.'

'Nope. Sorry to raise your hopes, but it doesn't ring any bells. I hoped for a minute it might be one of the other night's visitors, but he's much younger. But maybe you should send it through to my computer anyway?' I paused while, breathing heavily, he pressed buttons. 'Is there another place within range?'

For reply he checked his watch. 'What time do you have to be back?'

'Twelve fifteen latest.'

He refolded the map and traced a route with his index finger. 'The next place is over here – see? Half an hour on these roads. So it'd be cutting it a little fine. Tell you what, there's the most marvellous little church in the next hamlet. I'd love you to see it.'

Well, he had a day job, too.

He opened the door as shyly as if he were a lad bringing home a girlfriend. Now wasn't the time for brash remarks. Nor indeed was it the place. The graveyard was one side of a deep lane, the church the other. Even smaller than St Jude's, St Peter's in the Combe was

317

so dark inside it took long moments for the eyes to get accustomed.

'No, no electricity,' Andy said, in an ordinary unhushed voice. 'I could light an oil-lamp? But it'd ruin the effect of the sun on the stained glass. Very early medieval.'

By now I could move forward. 'That screen!' I breathed. It was carved wood, black with age. 'Look at those little figures! It must be – what? Fourteenth or fifteenth century?'

'Exactly. Have you ever seen anything like it?'

'I think you're about to tell me I couldn't have.'

He laughed, the sound ringing through the tiny space. 'I am. There's a better known one of a similar age at Buckland in the Moor – Dartmoor, that is. But nothing quite like this. There, you can see the pike marks in the wood – here and here – where the Round-heads tried to chop it down, but for some reason they just stopped in mid-attack. And the glass, apart from that corner there. A miracle. And though they hacked at several of the statues, the locals repaired them – see? The trouble is,' he continued, setting us gently in motion to look at aged monu-ments, 'the present parishioners simply can't afford to maintain it. Look at that damp.'

An ominous stain spread across the roof. Come to think of it, there was a sickly sweet smell that wasn't incense. It wasn't a corpse either, but dry rot. Worse than death.

'English Heritage? A Lottery grant? Even that lovely Restoration programme on TV?'

'I couldn't coopt you on to the fundraising committee, could I?' he laughed. But he waved his hands as if cutting a camera shot. 'No! Please don't think I brought you here with that in mind. I didn't. I promise you, I just wanted you to see it.'

'Before it falls down,' I concluded for him. Actually I believed him. 'I don't usually do committees, Andy. But I'd stop this place collapsing if I had to take a course in masonry myself.'

Afraid for a moment he might want to seal our ambiguous bargain with a kiss, or – more, to the point, that I might – I busied myself translating the Latin valediction on a seventeenth-century memorial tablet. No, it was no good: I could only manage about one word in five.

At last, thinking he'd want to have a word with his Employer, I withdrew quietly to the back pew to wait. There was enough to feast my eyes on, for goodness' sake. To my amazement, he sat quietly beside me, simply bowing his head. No genuflecting, no breast crossing, no nothing. Tim would have been disconcerted, maybe even outraged by the lack of display.

When he was ready, we left as quietly as

we had come in.

'I noticed,' he said, replacing the key under the fallen headstone where he'd found it, 'that you didn't take Communion the other day.'

Why had it taken him so long to raise that? 'I don't. Not christened.'

'You could be – only we'd call it adult baptism.'

My normal response was to tell anyone talking religion that mine was my own business and something I never talked about. You couldn't say that to anyone who'd just shown you St Peter's in the Combe, could you?

He took my silence as my reply. 'Well, if ever you change your mind, I'd ... I'd... Nothing would give me more pleasure.'

'There's only one problem.' I fended him off. 'Getting confirmed afterwards and having that creep Bishop Jonathan lay his greasy mitts on my head.'

To my surprise Malins and his wife were some of the first lunchtime customers. I greeted them as if we were simply fellow churchgoers with no history; he responded in much the same way. Clean consciences all round then.

At least until I brought them their bill.

'Actually, I was expecting to see the rural dean here,' he said, looking ostentatiously around the room.

'He might be in the snug,' I said, off-hand but seething. In fact I had offered Andy lunch, but he'd had a call from a sick parishioner – it seemed he did his deaning as an unpaid extra to being an ordinary parish priest, the Church's coffers being so empty.

'He's around here a lot,' he pursued, to a casual listener not quite insolently.

'He spent a lot of time with Tim's parents.' Anyone knowing me better would have been worried by the quietness of my voice.

'Whom you accommodated here.'

I personified reasonableness. 'Where else could they have stayed? The rectory isn't just as cold as charity, it's as miserable as sin.'

'You wonder how poor schoolteachers could afford to stay in a place like this. En suite and full board, I hear.'

Should I tip the contents of the water jug over his head? 'I'm sure you'll have heard exactly how much they paid, then. Now, if you'll excuse me, I see I'm needed by some other guests.'

'Ten pounds a kilo! It's highway robbery, that's what it is!'

Pix had summoned me to the office to deal with a furious Dan Tromans. To say I was taken aback by his attitude would be a

321

major understatement. He was waving a page torn from a weekend colour supplement about six inches from my nose, where, these days, I found it impossible to read.

I pulled my head back and squinted.

'It's all about people like you buying stuff people like me pick in the hedgerows, right? Foraging, they call it. You come swanning in to my farm and offer to buy it at ten pounds a go. Look what it says here: "a flat rate of fifteen pounds a kilo" – see?'

My eyes felt as if they were rotating in their sockets as they tried to scan the article. They found a couple of distinguished London restaurants. 'OK. So what's the problem?'

'You're doing me down by a fiver a kilo, that's what.'

Neither Pix nor Robin would shed a tear if I told him to put his wild garlic where it would no longer be bothered by sunshine. To be honest, neither would I. It had been accepted with equanimity rather than enthusiasm by my customers, and I knew it would take a long build to make it into an attraction at the White Hart or wherever. But I hadn't asked him to gather it so much for my benefit as for his wife's – well, his too, come to think of it: it was a way of guaranteeing them more cash, remember. It was for that reason the White Hart team were baking scones every morning, and why

I'd organised the ladies of St Jude's. And now Abigail was in hospital with pre-eclampsia, probably made worse by worrying about money all the time.

'Does Abigail know you're here?'

'What's that got to do with anything?'

Only a set of expensive nighties she thought he'd bought. And he now seemed to think he'd bought.

'It was she and I who made the deal. But I don't want anything to bother her in her present state. So as far as she knows everything's hunky-dory – right?'

'But it's not, is it?'

I didn't have time for such stupidity. 'Tell you what, you tell me what you charge your other customers and I'll match it immediately.' Would he find another Ivy or J Sheekey down here? I rather doubted it.

He fidgeted like a naughty schoolboy.

'Perhaps you've forgotten who they are. No matter. You know where I live: I'll settle my arrears.' And thus I let the silly sod off the hook. Nearly. All he had to do was find another buyer. All!

While he was still letting his features sink into smug mode, I asked, 'Whom did you tell about the scone deal? When you were asking about cheap chickens?' I cranked up the anger. 'It was part of the deal you kept it quiet, remember. But I had these two guys come in to try and trash my kitchen. You and Abby are the only ones who knew about the scones. Correction – were. Because somehow you gave the game away when you were asking about chickens. Who was it, Dan?'

'Why are you so sure it was me? Could have been Abby.'

I surveyed the sky for flying pigs. 'Oink, oink? No, I don't see any either. You go to market, just like the little pigs, come to think of it: Abby stays at home serving wonderful cream teas. Come on, who did you talk to?'

'Well, like you wanted, I asked around for you. Said you'd got it into your head to find a cheaper supplier.'

'Did you mention me by name?'

He scratched his head. 'I just said it was someone I owed a favour.'

'And they asked why?'

'Just said someone was helping out while Abby was too tired to cook.'

So someone was bright enough to do a lot of sums. 'You wouldn't remember who it was? Tell you what: I've some got pictures for you to check out – OK?'

'Haven't got time to hang about,' he grumbled, heading for the door.

If he'd been a dog, I'd have raised a minatory finger and told him to stay. As it was, I simply spread the photos from my clients' phones in front of him and said, 'Here they are. Recognise either of them?

Or how about these?' The results of Andy's little expedition.

He didn't want to acknowledge them, that's for sure, but his eyes gave him away.

'Which one? These or these?'

He squirmed: I almost felt sorry for him. 'Like this man. The one in the armlock. Only younger. Young enough,' he added slowly, 'to have been his son.'

I'd always known there must have been something in him to attract Abby. 'You're my hero! And a name,' I prompted, my hand making little pulling movements as if to tug it out of him.

He shook his head, with such conviction I probably believed him. 'Only know him as the guy from up Duncombe Trinity way. Do you want me to ask? Only I wouldn't want to get you into even more trouble.'

'Quite right. Just keep out of it. Because I'd hate you to get into trouble, too. Any more messages in bottles?'

This time I absolutely believed him when he shook his head. 'Not with my brother's Alsatians to keep me company.'

Chapter Twenty-Two

'Work is the curse of the drinking classes,' someone or other once said. Was it Wilde? It certainly wasn't one of the wits in the bar, though most of them had probably thought as much without exactly putting it into words. Work, which meant satisfying others' need to drink, was certainly the curse of the would-be investigator.

As Andy observed over the phone, at round about five on Friday afternoon, we were both coming up to the busiest parts of our weeks. Naturally they didn't quite coincide. Friday evenings were his time for polishing sermons, and Saturdays slack, unless he was burdened with weddings. He weighed in on Sundays, of course, at a time when, lunch apart, I could run down.

I was afraid he would try to do a little solo sleuthing, putting himself at risk. He obviously feared I might do the same: he had phoned, ostensibly to make sure his photos had got through, but in reality I suspected to check on me.

'You won't spend the rest of Sunday hurtling from site to site, will you?' he pressed.

'What's the problem? You want to be in on

the discovery? Honestly, I'll be so knackered all I shall want to do is put my feet up.'

But he was too bright for that. 'Want, but not necessarily do. I know you, Josie Welford!'

We shared a laugh, but I added 'And what about you?'

'Wall to wall weddings. And it doesn't do for the parson to turn up with missing limbs or black eyes – any more,' he added with mock severity, 'than for you to present yourself thus to your guests.'

I was so disconcerted that a man could shove a 'thus' into the conversation like that, that I didn't point out I'd appeared *thus* for the last week.

'As a matter of fact–' he was decidedly hesitant, after his earlier ease, 'I'm taking evensong in St Peter's in the Combe on Sunday. They only get one service a month, and the incumbent has flu.'

'Time?'

'Six.'

'See you Sunday, then,' I said, preparing to ring off.

But suddenly another thread of conversation started to unravel itself, and before I knew it it was time to change for the evening rush. All hands to the plough time. And absolutely no time to wonder why Andy wanted my presence at St Peter's.

Was it to save my soul? Or to save his church?

Or was it for an altogether more personal reason?

No, no time at all. Not if I were going to check my emails before helping prepare for the evening, in case there were any developments in the great cheap chicken chase.

I was greeted by a little flurry of responses from my catering colleagues. Several had now been approached, but descriptions of the vendor differed widely and no one linked anyone to the photos I'd circulated. There was one I read more carefully than most, from Nigel Ho, now back on these shores and interesting himself once more in the day-to-day running of his little empire. Nigel's restaurants bore no more relation to the average flock and surly-serviced high street Chinese than the White Hart did to a spit and sawdust pub. His were chic, minimalist affairs – OK, with surly waiters, but I told myself that they added to the authenticity. The food was wonderfully varied: it was possible to work your way through his wonderful *dégustation* menu without coming across a single Peking or Cantonese standard.

After a tedious preamble suggesting he'd like another non-professional encounter – his place or mine – he started on the interesting stuff. An individual offering chicken at very reasonable prices but with no certification, he said, had approached his

Plymouth head chef. He thought I'd like to know. Unfortunately he hadn't got much of a description because to the chef all white Europeans looked the same. In any case, he pursued, wasn't it time I gave up my Miss Marple activities, lest they attract the attention of the miscreants who had killed the young vicar and his Chinese refugee?

'Who, me?' I fired back ambiguously, hoping the response covered both his carnal invitation and his detective suggestion. He was right, of course: had we been able to persuade Tang to accept protective custody, he and Tim would still be alive now. I continued, 'I'm too busy trying to locate wood sorrel to go with my braised wood-pigeons.' But I pressed him, all the same, for more information about the chicken dealer so I could pass it on to the police. He was welcome to do it himself, of course, but I seemed to have the ear of a senior police-man.

Who should be dining with a small party at eight, but Mr Corbishley. The table wasn't booked in his name: don't think I'd not have noticed something like that. Lorna, Lucy's younger sister, was doing her best, which was usually very good – possibly better in these circumstances than Lucy, who of course was covering the snug. But they were giving her a rough time, changing orders, calling her back, that sort of thing. Although I was running in a new couple of kids, I thought it behoved me – wasn't that a word Andy would have been proud of? Or did I mean Tony? – to keep an eye on things. I slipped into the kitchen after her.

'Problems with table 7?'

'And how! I mean, yes, Mrs Welford.' Bless her, she almost curtsied.

'Why don't you write it all out again, just to make sure it's correct? And if you like, I'll go back to double check. I don't know what their game is, Lorna, but you don't have to be part of it. Right: now that's five starters and six mains. Did someone not want a starter?'

'The thin man – by the window. I don't think he – but he might.' Her lip trembled.

'Leave it to me, love. Take extra bread but only margarine to table 2: dairy allergy, remember.'

Pix looked up from the tomato, basil and mozzarella salads he was already assembling. 'Trouble at t'mill, gaffer?'

'Not if I can help it. I'm not having them sending back well cooked fillet steak because they've changed their minds and want it rare.'

Nor was I. Sailing back with a sunny beam strapped tightly to my face, I gave the impression of an officious maitre d' elbowing out a junior. Which, in a sense, I was.

But I could greet Mr Corbishley with every appearance of pleasure, and by so doing let him know, I hoped, that I was on to him, telling him, affably of course, that Malins had been in for lunch. I'd have loved to add, 'but he didn't find out anything either', but didn't have time to play games – not with another party due any moment. The thin man by the window changed his mind yet again while I was checking on the steak orders. Now we definitely did have six starters, so all credit to Lorna for getting it right. And to me, for what should happen but one of the women suddenly decide against her oriental seafood salad starter in favour of mackerel pâté. Never once did my smile waver. Even if the seafood was already waiting.

It was odds on someone else would order it, after all.

Corbishley made no attempt to speak to me for the rest of the meal, rightly judging, perhaps, that I was simply too busy to engage in light banter or anything else. They were ready to baulk at the dreamy braised wild garlic, and sniffed audibly when they realised the delicate, crisp garnish to their steaks was early chickweed I'd found – unarguably – in my own herb garden. But not a scrap burdened any plate, and I let Lorna loose with the dessert menu.

No problems.

No problems with the coffee and liqueurs.

Were they going to argue over the bill? Refuse a tip?

None of those things, it seemed. And if it had been Corbishley's intention to engage me in further conversation, perhaps as provocatively as Malins at lunchtime, then he found me otherwise engaged. Every other table had my assiduous attention, and it was Lorna who took them their bill. To do them justice, though they paid by card, they left a cash tip, thus (how about that, Andy?) making it clear whom the money was to go to. I always did the same myself, after I'd discovered that some establishments used the plastic-paid tips not as a well-earned bonus but simply to raise the staff's wages to the national minimum wage, rather than pay properly themselves. We bowed stately goodnights across the room and that was it.

Was I seeing trouble where none existed? Had Corbishley chosen to eat at the White Hart for pure pleasure's sake, or to stir up trouble? All I knew was that I was vaguely unsettled, and irritated because I suspected that that had been his precise intention.

Saturday morning brought no response from Nigel, but the ear of the policeman I'd referred to, DCI Burford. I'd had rather more than the ear of a detective chief inspector I'd dealt with before, of course, before he was promoted up north. But, sexy though Burford thought himself, we weren't about to have anything more than a strictly professional relationship. Burford, as if on cue, was now to be seen, shirt-sleeved, emerging from an innocent-looking Vauxhall. What was it that policemen put in their tea that enabled them to appear, like Saturday night kids at a disco, without decent warm clothes? It might have been bright today, but there was a lazy wind, cutting straight through you, as I'd discovered on my early morning dash for the paper: yes, at long last my limbs were beginning to feel as if they were mine once more. I could hardly wait to embark on the sort of vigorous exercise that I had come to enjoy so much. Walking. What else?

He shrugged on a jacket – Armani, by the look of it – and headed my way. It would have been nice to wait for my staff to announce him. But it was lie-in day for Pix, and Robin was at farmers' markets, running down the best ingredients. So I was my own staff. I thought it best to let him knock. I didn't want to look too eager, lest he misinterpret it. Nonetheless, I showed him up into my apartment.

Providing water and a couple of redundant scones, with enough clotted cream to send his cholesterol levels skywards and great gouts of homemade strawberry jam, I

333

smiled expectantly. At least this guy was doing his duty and keeping us informed, though I did think a junior officer would have done just as well as a senior one.

If he was doing his duty, I was prepared to do mine. I gathered the sheaf of colleagues' emails I'd printed off. For some reason I kept back Nigel's: I hadn't told him I'd be making it public knowledge, after all. Nor had I deleted the personal references.

'So where are you now?' I asked, as if entitled to: such a brazen approach often seemed to work.

'This is a murder investigation, Mrs Welford: all my information is confidential.' His serious expression was rather undercut by a dab of cream at the corner of his mouth.

'Of course. I was just wondering if any of these emails might be useful. But I wouldn't want to hand over personal communications if they were irrelevant.'

'Why don't you let me be the judge of that? Mrs Welford, we don't take kindly to members of the public withholding information. In fact, obstructing the police is – as I'm sure you're well aware – an offence.'

My eyes were open to their widest extent. 'DCI Burford, surely you misunderstand me deliberately.'

'On the contrary, I understand you all too well. What's your game, Josie?'

'Mrs Welford. I do not have a game. I have

lost a very dear friend and another young man has died too. Don't friends have rights? If not as many as uncaring parents, enough to be told if you have a killer in your sights?' My voice broke with passion. Tony gave a silent round of applause. For good measure I flung down the emails. 'All I ask is that you respect my correspondents' confidentiality – and that means, DCI Burford,' I continued, my voice turning steely, 'that you don't send to interview them stupid plods in clearly marked cars. Not unless you want a re-run of the warning goings on at the Tromans' farm. *Careless talk costs lives*, remember – and so do careless actions.'

'We have instituted regular patrols in the vicinity,' he said stiffly.

'Gee, how reassuring. And round this place too? I can sleep soundly at nights.'

'No need for sarcasm.'

'As I told DI Lawton, this is the country, not a town. If I dialled 999, how long would it take for help to reach me? Quite.' Without warning, I changed direction. 'What did *you* make of Father Martin's parents? Weird, or what? You don't suppose he was killed to get at them in some way?'

In his confusion he embarked on the scone he'd left half-eaten. 'Why should you think that?'

'Have you met them? No? You should. In fact, I'd prioritise it. Seriously, Mr Burford,

335

they are weird. Either in complete denial or deliberately concealing something.'

'Or simply weird?'

'Whatever. Don't just rely on DI Lawton's notes. Check them out. Better still, ask them to come down here again: I'll happily offer accommodation but they'll bloody well pay this time.'

'They didn't last time?' He jotted.

I explained, delivering my account in a self-mocking tone that had him roaring with laughter.

'The biter bit, eh?' he asked.

I frowned. 'All I did was offer charity to those I thought needed it – profit didn't enter my mind.'

'I'm sorry. I meant the opposite, that it was your turn for revenge. But you may not get it: it'd be cheaper for me to go to them.'

'And very revealing, I hope. There's nothing like seeing someone in their own territory, is there? I suppose I couldn't go along as your navigator?'

'Absolutely not. But I know what you mean. What do you imagine we'll find?'

'Stockbroker Tudor, phenomenally ugly. And inside – either total ostentation or minimalist chic of the most expensive order. Even money. But I do know they priced this room item by item.'

'So they know their antiques. OK, do you want a fiver on it?'

'Boring. No, I never bet for money anyway: I've seen too many lives ruined.'

'How about something more interesting? If I'm right, you give me all your information, not just selected snippets?' He rose to go. But then changed his mind. 'Just how well do you know this Nigel Ho guy?'

Nigel Ho? Why him specifically? I could hardly say I knew Nigel just well enough to have sex with him; even the less circumspect, younger me would have drawn the line at such honesty. So I said, fairly, 'We're the sort of casual mates who could become friends, circumstances permitting. I trusted him enough to want his help providing a translator so we could communicate with poor Tang, and to act on his advice when he said Tang was in imminent danger.'

He nodded, as if that wasn't quite the response he'd hoped for. 'He's got quite an empire, hasn't he?'

'You know these Chinese businessmen,' I said. 'At least, the stereotype! Incredibly hardworking, driving others hard – and being, above all, totally inscrutable.'

'Is he any of those things?' He sat down again.

'He's a very suave restaurateur – that's all I know. And he was concerned enough to contact me from New York in an effort to help Tang.' I tossed a mental coin, which came down on the side of being frank with

Burford. 'One email I didn't give you was one from him. I was waiting for permission to: he's that sort of person.'

'Dominant? Controlling? I wouldn't have thought either of those qualities would wash with you, Mrs Welford.'

Head on one side, I reflected. 'No, neither would I. Tell you what, I'll forward it to you if you give me your email address.' I was half-tempted to reward his percipience by an invitation to lunch, but decided I had too much work to do. However, just as I was showing him out, I decided that there was one more name I might give him: Michael Rousdon's. Just in case. There were chicken connections, after all.

Burford's eyes asked uncomfortably clearly whether there'd been other connections – and I didn't think he meant the samphire one.

As he drove away I realised it was time I checked on Nick. I couldn't believe there was anything seriously wrong, but you never knew. He was a mate, after all, and the least I could do was express decent interest.

His voice told me: he had a stinking cold. 'Just dripping. Couldn't drive for sneezing,' he said, demonstrating.

'You just look after yourself,' I said, assuring him that everything was fine, even though he hadn't actually got round to asking.

For the next twenty-six hours all I had time for was work: we were fully booked for dinner on Saturday and for Sunday lunch, and already people were pouring into the place for a Saturday lunchtime snack before going on their walks. I didn't even have time to envy them.

Sunday lunch over, half of me wanted a snooze. However, a quick cup of green tea convinced me I could stick to my resolve to walk to St Peter's in the Combe for Evensong. It was only about seven miles, after all. Andy could give me a lift home, in return, perhaps, for a cold supper. I could stow gear more appropriate for church in my light-weight rucksack – probably an extra-heavy fleece, given the obvious lack of central heating.

Although I made no claim to be as good a navigator as Andy, I could read maps well enough – and better than most, given the amount of walking I'd packed in since I'd discovered exercise as an essential adjunct to my diet. At first I'd panicked, because the weight not only remained stationary it actually went up. But then I read about the difference in weight between muscle and fat and got on with it. At first it was deeply unpleasant, my inner-thighs chafing as I strode. I even needed a sports bra. Giving up, however, wasn't an option. Joints creaked, muscles screamed, and lungs announced flatly that up that hill they would not go. And I ignored the lot. Thank goodness, all that pain was in the past now, and I swore a good walk was better than sex. Well, better than bad sex. It was so long since I had any of the other sort I could hardly judge. Purely in the interests of research, I wouldn't have minded experimenting. Until I'd heard Corbishley's comments, of course.

There were two alternative routes to St Peter's. One was longer, but flatter; the other was markedly shorter, but had several steep gradients. I flipped a coin. The latter, then. So a stout walking stick was called for, and boots, rather than shoes. The plastic map cover; fleece; cagoule. Drat! What about the camera? I ran back upstairs for it. And realised I'd chosen the wrong route. If I followed the other, I passed reasonably close to one of the sites Andy had circled.

It wouldn't do any harm just to walk past, would it?

So why would a scrapyard pong? Cars and broken washing machines might be an affront to the eye, but they shouldn't smell like the worst butcher's you've ever passed. I drifted closer. Yes, definitely something rotten in the place. Flies, too. And a couple of white vans, anonymous, by the look of them. Everything to attract a perambulating

Miss Marple.

But I had given a tacit promise not to take risks, and with the destination I was heading for I felt uneasy about breaking it.

I hadn't promised not to take photos, though. And, with the lens that Andy so derided, I could do it from a safe distance.

Or could I? That strolling figure, dressed like me, with an innocent dog on a retractable lead – he was just a walker, wasn't he? He was certainly heading purposefully towards me. But instead of the neutral smile most walkers exchange, he offered me a penetrating scowl. Getting no response, he slowed to a halt. I was clearly being seen off. Ostentatiously, I reached for my map, as if all I'd been doing was getting my bearings. The camera stayed put. But since I had six inches of serious optical equipment sticking out from my chest, I had to look very lost indeed to look convincing. Thank goodness there was a path about three hundred metres back. To retrace my steps to it meant passing the hound of the Baskervilles, but I spread my hands helplessly.

'I should have turned west up there. Your dog's all right with strangers, is he?'

The man gave a curt nod at variance with the rumble coming from deep in the Alsatian's chest. 'Just keep walking with your eyes down. You should be all right.'

It took me all my will power not to break

into a run once I was past it. All. Dogs can smell fear, can't they? This one certainly had plenty to sniff. But I did as I'd been told, head down, eyes averted, and I made it. Then the bugger let out some of the slack in the lead. The dog's jaws snapped perhaps an inch from my heels. And again. And again.

At last he judged I'd gone far enough, and I was left alone. Half way up a hill I didn't know, with a footpath little more than a sheep track to follow, and evensong in less than an hour.

Well, I told myself with a brightness belied by my shaking and sweating hands, weak knees and pounding heart, if God wanted me there, He'd get me there.

Chapter Twenty-Three

The St Peter's congregation were well into the first hymn before my pulse settled to anything approaching a normal pace. My route had taken me nearly a mile out of my way, and what should have been a pleasant stroll down into the hamlet had degenerated into an ungainly scramble. I always walked very fast, but running used a different set of muscles altogether, ones that would far rather have remained dormant. Scarlet in the face, chest heaving asthmatically, I'd managed to collapse into the back pew just as the hand-pumped organ wheezed into action. It and me both, eh? The light was so dim I might just have escaped Andy's scrutiny, especially as his mind was on more important things.

Eventually I could look at the rest of the congregation – the backs of their heads, at least. There must have been about thirty, mostly elderly people but a couple or so in their twenties, plus a choir led by a really good tenor, who didn't quite make up for the others' deficiencies: decidedly evensong had been a poor choice of service. Something with only the spoken word would have been kinder all round. It even threw up Andy's only perceptible fault so far – he led the responses with a very uncertain baritone, his pitch wandering round all over the place. I'd never been any good with sung psalms, not knowing when to go up or down or what, so I just mouthed hopefully.

The sermon was short. One of the readings had been from Corinthians, Paul telling us not to be childish: it was good to be as innocent as babes, but essential to be grown-up in our thinking. Andy soberly developed the idea, drawing, he freely admitted, on a piece on choices from the previous day's *Guardian*. It had me metaphorically punching the air in agreement in a way poor

Tim's had never managed. Of course, the comparison was unfair, as if our local soccer team were judged against Chelsea's standards. It would be good to talk about the points he'd raised over supper.

I joined the rest of the congregation trailing out for the formal handshake with him to end the service. Perhaps his eyes didn't light up because I hadn't had time to spruce myself up properly? No, it was more as if something had been switched off. He'd definitely dropped them in something horribly like embarrassment.

Although I was alarmed and puzzled, I could hardly ask there and then what the problem was. Instead I asked, polite as if we were no more than priest and parishioner, 'I wonder if you'd be kind enough to give me a lift back to Kings Duncombe?'

He checked his watch with a very strange expression. 'I suppose ... is there a problem with your car?'

'Not that I know of. I walked, that's all.' As a quick glance at me would have confirmed.

Another glance at his watch. 'OK. I'll finish up here in – what? Five minutes? Don't keep me waiting, please.'

When someone speaks to me like that my immediate response would normally be to tell them to cancel the request. Perhaps not in those terms. But my limbs informed me that walking back to the White Hart was a pretty poor option. In any case, the road route was far longer than the cross-country one. It was already dark, and the country-side doesn't go in for streetlights. The torch in my rucksack was an emergency affair, and might not hold out for a solid two hours' walking. As for simply retracing my steps, that wasn't an option. There was too much of the city-dweller in me ever to be happy in the open on my own after dark. I saw rapists behind every tree. Not to mention that slavering dog...

'I wouldn't dream of putting you out,' I snapped.

Members of the congregation were notice-ably warmer. They saw me only as a lone walker, a woman without history, hoping I'd pass this way again to enjoy their lovely church.

'Not that we usually get a sermon like that – what an honour, to have the rural dean addressing us. Such a lovely man. Such a tragedy the way he lost his wife. They say they were devoted – that's why he moved down here, to get away from sad memories...'

I nodded, expressed decent interest and gratitude for their kindness, and set off towards Kings Duncombe without a back-ward glance. Eight miles wasn't far. It was a wonderful starlit night, and if someone didn't wish to favour me with his company I wouldn't impose it on him.

A blaze of light announced the approach of a large vehicle from behind me, so I pressed myself into the bank, nuzzling the spring flowers and being embraced by brambles. It was a good job there was so much less of me than there used be, or there might not have been room for the two of us, especially as the other one was a Mercedes van, the sort that tailgates you apparently by instinct. It passed with inches to spare: the driver might not even have registered my presence had not the door mirror caught me a glancing blow on the rucksack. Better the rucksack than me, at least.

The driver of the next certainly did. This time it was a car that came up beside me, the driver yelling furiously through the half-open window, 'What on earth are you doing?'

'What does it look like? Walking home.'

'I said I'd give you a lift.'

'You were ashamed of me. Either of my gear or me myself. That's why I chose to walk.'

'Just get in.'

'No thanks.'

'You – for goodness' sake, I'm blocking the road here.'

'And there must be fifty cars stacked up behind you,' I agreed affably.

'Just get in. Please. I have an – a – there's

something I have– I–'

Through his gibberish, I picked up the sound of another van. 'OK. Just as far as the next crossroads. Then you can drop me, turn right and head for home.'

True to form, the van – another big white one – virtually pushed us for the next two miles. Had there been any proper passing places, Andy could have pulled over – would have, I'm sure. But there was simply no room, even if he'd pulled right into the banks, towering ten feet high along here. Perhaps he didn't speak because he was concentrating on his driving. Perhaps I didn't because I didn't want to disturb him.

The crossroads at last. Andy signalled right, and the van sped past us towards my village.

'You can pull in over there. Carry straight on for about five hundred yards, then turn left and immediately right. Someone's removed the fingerposts. Just there, please.'

And he did! No arguments about not letting me walk. He stopped: just like that.

'Thanks.' I released the seatbelt and opened the door.

The interior light showed him shaking his head, as if to clear cobwebs. Perhaps the sharp click of the door helped – no, I very definitely did not slam it.

He wasn't a good enough driver to go sharply into reverse. He got out slowly, and stood helplessly in the road – I presume, because although I heard his door slam, I didn't turn round, but kept walking. By this time I wasn't sure what was happening in either of our heads. I was being foolish in the extreme, a middle-aged woman walking with a dodgy torch through lanes so deep even the growing moonlight couldn't penetrate. As for him, I presume he really did have some appointment he'd forgotten to tell me about, but there was no doubting something had happened to dent our friendship. Maybe St Paul had intervened, the old misogynist. All that stuff about marriage and fornication and burning.

At last I heard running feet and turned: there was no point in inflicting a heart attack on him.

'Please – just get in the car and let me run you safely home. I'm sorry if I gave–'

I obeyed. 'Just drive. Then you can go wherever you have to. OK? So carry on down here, turn left, and instead of turning immediate right, keep going up the hill.'

He drove in silence. I didn't speak except to give further instructions. What a pair of fools.

Scones are satisfactorily sticky, but there's nothing like making bread to vent emotions you'd rather not have. Pummelling and pulling are wonderful therapy, plus good exercise for the poor old neglected triceps.

When this was all over I might just enrol in a gym.

So what was the *this* I wanted to be over? The damned murder investigation, so we could literally lay Tim and Tang to rest? Or my stupid, stupid entanglement with Andy? How crazy could I be, to be falling in love with a priest, for God's sake? Wrong expletive, Josie. I managed a dry laugh. The driest thing I'd done for about nine hours, come to think of it. That was why I never cried, of course: now I'd started I didn't know how to stop. The prospect of the lads seeing me was the best cure. Sympathy, kind questions, or, worse, tactful avoidance of tricky areas were not about to appear on the menu.

There! Bread proving and scones ready to be fished out of the oven. They'd better be up to Pix's standards. And I could walk them down to the Tromans' farm, just to blow away the last of the self-pity.

Dan was busy in the yards, calling his baying security guards to heel and quickly muzzling them, an encouraging sight should I ever want to pay a chance visit.

'Early bird, aren't you?' he greeted me.

'Early to bed, early to rise…' I said, offhand. No point in saying I'd not actually got between the sheets. 'How's Abby?'

'Still lying round in bed all day like a beached whale. Looks fine, mind you. Anyway, those friends of yours are seeing me all right: casseroles here, cold joints there. And that little tea shop's not doing so bad, either.' He seemed to be having difficulty framing the word *thanks*.

So I smiled helpfully.

'This chicken business. I do recall something, Josie – can't think why it slipped my mind.'

I wouldn't ever have placed any bets on the adhesive qualities of that organ. True, he was a genius with animals. But – no, perhaps genius in one area was all you could ask. I don't suppose Einstein would have been too good in the lambing shed.

'Anyway, this bloke with the chicken. The one at market. He drove one of those great white van things.'

What a surprise.

'And the funny thing is, though he didn't have any writing on the side, his number-plate made a word. You know how they muck around with the letters and that. Anyways, his said FOWL, or something like it. How about that?'

'Dan, that's brilliant. Wonderful. I could kiss you.'

He went a cheery rose pink under his all-weather tan. 'What, you *and* them ladies of yours?'

I thought it time to make a tactical withdrawal, but he was scratching his chin again. 'This wild garlic stuff. I'm running a bit low.

What do you think about fat hen?'

Wasn't it that beer with the fox adverts? 'What should I think?'

'Well, I got plenty of that. It'd be a shame not to see if you could cook it, like.'

It would indeed. Funnily enough, a price was not mentioned.

It was a good job the bread was ready for the oven when I got back or I might simply have allowed myself to go to bed. As it was, I had a wonderful time: I hadn't come top of my breadmaking classes for nothing. Much might have to be frozen: after the brilliant dawn and early morning, mist was now rolling purposefully in, as if literally to dampen our spirits.

So I would make soup as the lunch special. My college tutor always reckoned I could have made soup from gravel chippings. This time I didn't have to raid the car park, but I did use what I happened to have handy, and a damned good Italian peasant soup I made too: unfortunately ribollita is thickened with bread so my coeliac customers would have to give it a miss. So I turned to and produced curried parsnip and apple, just for them.

'So who's got up your nose?' Robin demanded, coming down for the morning meeting half an hour later. 'Come on, Josie, you never clean out cupboards unless you're furious.'

351

'Just a hangover from being ripped off by the good doctors Martin last week,' I said. 'That new policeman thinks he needs to talk to them, and I was hoping to have them back here and charge them appropriately.'

'By which you mean enough for last week as well?'

'I do indeed. But alas, the police Mohammed has gone to the Martin mountain, so I shan't get the chance.'

'And what really pees you off is that you can't go too and have a good poke round their house. I know you, gaffer: don't try to deny it.'

I didn't. Instead I reached out the best bacon, patted one of my new loaves, and suggested a breakfast meeting.

At least my lads... I nearly used the L word! But they were like sons to me, and their very joshing and mockery were balm to my heart.

A new email from a contact saying she'd had some chicken that tasted vaguely perfumed prompted me to phone Burford; I'd also give him Dan's information about the van. The underling I reached – and I knew that now an MIT was involved there would be many beavering away – was not impressed, so I suggested in my frostiest voice that since his boss had thought my inside knowledge important enough to glean in person he ought to make sure it was properly logged.

There was a muttering the far end: he'd obviously half covered the phone to make a quip to a mate. All I managed to pick up was, 'That bird that Burford's got the hots for.' Or rather more vulgar words to that effect.

I managed not to laugh out loud till I'd ended the call. In vain did I remind myself that Burford had a funny way of showing his interest, and that I didn't fancy him anyway – my ego was suddenly as plump as a goose-down pillow. Why not settle for a sociable shag?

Because. Nothing more. Just because. In weather like this, the clouds swirling great gusts of rain across the windows, there was no way I'd finish that sentence.

It was my turn to do the basic weekly shop – the staples, as opposed to fresh produce. When I changed for the errand I noticed for the first time the bruises on my back and round my shoulder. For a moment I'd no idea how they'd got there. Then it dawned that the white van's mirror must be the culprit. It would give me a great deal of pleasure to know that I'd broken it. And what if – very big if – what if the white van were the white van Dan had mentioned? It wasn't so very long a walk, not compared with the other route marches I'd recently undertaken: I could do it after lunch.

Once the shopping was done, it was time to return the hire car and get a substitute. The one they offered was a Focus, just the same as all the other Focuses (or should it be Foci?) on the road. I signed on the dotted line. Yes, limited business use, no racing, no rallying – you know the system.

And got outside to find I'd only hired a silver one. Yes, a silver Focus, just the same as Andy's. After all that trouble I'd gone to the other day to get something quite different from either of our cars!

I was back in the office like a shot. And came out again, frustrated. It seemed all the alternatives were either underpowered or rented out or being serviced, and no amount of crisp fivers could change the situation, not till tomorrow. OK. Needs must, but it wouldn't be the Devil but Josie driving.

Coming back down the lane where I'd been bashed by the white van, I slowed to a walking pace at the site of the encounter. Yes, there was one big sliver of mirror-glass. Just for the say-so, I retrieved it, wrapped it in a tissue, and stowed it in the boot. If nothing more, it would prevent some innocent animal's feet being cut.

By the time I got back to the White Hart, my energy levels were so low I'd have to do something. I must have either a huge wodge of chocolate, which might contain enough anticoagulants to prevent DVT on a long-haul flight but certainly had enough calories to fly the damned plane, or a zizz. A zizz was certainly less fattening. The lads could stow the food, and then give me a call: no matter how little sleep I had, I never allowed myself more then half an hour during the day. Then, and only then, would I check the post and the answerphone. It was one thing to think there might be bad news, another to know.

I didn't specify even to myself, what that bad news might be.

The news was that there was no news. Monday was a day for circulars and junk. No phone messages. All right, then, I'd get on with the lunch trade. I even lit the fires in both the snug and the dining room, thinking the sight of a few flames and the smell of apple wood would cheer everyone up. Guess who I meant by everyone. But a nap had improved the world, there was no doubt about it, and when both soups disappeared as if by evaporation, I was ready for my walk. We were all free agents on Monday, with Lucy coping in the snug bar. In fact, walk be damned, I'd go and have a bit of retail therapy. The road conditions were still foul, of course, but I'd picked my way through mist worse than this before and I deserved a new outfit. A phone call established my hairdresser could fit me in, and I was made.

Or I would have been, had I not developed this paranoia about white vans. Every time I saw one I wanted to check the number-plate or the side mirror. Fortunately for the safety of all concerned most seemed to have been wiped from the road, and I arrived in Exeter with time to spare. With its main street a clone of every other main street, Exeter's not the best place in the world for shopping. But there are individual shops tucked away, for those in the know. Within half an hour of my parking, I'd acquired a trouser suit, a top to die for and two pairs of shoes. While my hair colour took, I had a pedicure – vital in a job like mine – and a manicure.

There: I was ready to face the world again. Even a world – I had to confront the possibility – with no Andy.

Chapter Twenty-Four

Once when I wasn't at my best – I'd actually been tempted to end it all, to be honest, only deterred by the thought I wouldn't know the rest of the story – someone passed on a tip they'd learnt to keep their mind off their problems. It was a rubber band around the wrist. No, not the fashionable wristbands all the kids were wearing these days, declaring their support for some charity or another. Just the sort of simple rubber band the postie uses to hold a bundle of mail. You could twang when your thoughts strayed in negative directions. Despite my retail therapy – possibly because of it – I slipped a band on before I even tried my new outfit. I couldn't imagine Andy ever approving of spending a small fortune on such non-essentials. Twang. The clothes looked as good at home as in the shop. The shoes were bliss. It probably meant they'd stretch, in which case the nearest charity shop would end up with designer shoes, but at least they gave me pleasure at a time when – twang!

As for the rest of the evening, I did something guaranteed to make you concentrate, the VAT figures. Until I got restless. I peered out of the window: the mist had cleared to give a perfect moonlit night. Even I admitted it was too late to go for a walk, and I'd much rather not have put on my oldest clothes, but I had to have another look at the yard at which I'd patently been so unwelcome yesterday. It might be that they maintained a night patrol: more likely they'd simply let the dogs run loose inside the – preferably stout – fence.

I longed for a phone like Andy's that would have enabled me to take discreet photos. Why hadn't I used the sense I was born with and bought one this afternoon? What a fool, to waste time and money on fripperies – twang! Come on: my old war-horse was familiar in my hands, and I could use film fast enough to accommodate poor light. Assuming there was light.

There was.

It hadn't taken me long to drive to the suspect yard, even in the still relatively un-familiar Focus. I parked well away from a casual observer's eyes.

Curiously they'd not installed security lights; there was just a pallid and inadequate affair over the office door. But the moon-light was bright enough for me to pick out piles of wheels and bumpers and other genuine-looking spare parts. I took photos galore. So why the secrecy? And why weren't the dogs loose? And why was there such a stench?

The gates were fastened with both a serious padlock and a motorbike-quality chain, and my gate-scaling days were in the past. And I was on my own.

It would be hard simply to drive away, but at least I'd have something to report to Burford or even to Nick, when he was well enough to return. A cold? I still feared it might be something more serious. I'd give him a call when I got back home.

Where I didn't especially want to be. So, twanging the band sharply, I checked the

OS map and set the car in motion, heading in a generally uphill direction. I'd never seen the view from the Quantocks in moonlight and tonight seemed as good as any.

I was bowling merrily along when I ran into mist. Good, thick stuff. And of course, unlike my Saab, the bottom of the range Focus wasn't equipped with fog-lights. I was trying to work out whether I was better on main beam or dipped when I realised I wasn't alone. Someone was following me, their speed not dropping even though they could surely see that there was nowhere to overtake and that I was going as fast as I could.

Using a short, sharp expletive banned in my kitchen, I accelerated as hard as I dared, which wasn't much. My tail kept up. Was there a turning? I forced myself to visualise the OS map. My ex-Met instructor had been more concerned with cul-de-sacs and rat-runs. I needed a farm gate or – yes, a left here. I plunged on to Forestry Commission land, with the sort of tracks beloved of rally drivers, not mature ladies in hire cars with inadequate lights. But at least I had skills, and the Focus was manoeuvrable in a way that a white van probably wasn't. Yes! He'd dropped back a bit.

If only Andy had been here, he could have offered up a prayer.

No time to twang now.

For an instant, the mist cleared. The track forked at the bottom of the hill. Left took me back into mist, the right into moonlight. My mist-vision or his? The clear track it must be, the car drifting faster into corners than a van would dare. Tony patted me on my shoulder. The longer I kept going, the more opportunities for the other guy to make a mistake.

We weren't so far from the main road when I lost him. Just like that. Had he turned off a track I didn't register, ready to ambush me on the main road? It's what I'd do in his situation. Which rather limited the left or right options. So I plunged across what looked as good as a B road into a definite lane. Soon a scattering of cottages appeared either side. I slowed for a man walking his elderly spaniel. Heavens above: streetlights! Something Kings Duncombe didn't run to. A thirty sign – rather superfluous, since I'd had my heart in my mouth doing twenty-five. A church large and solid enough to be spotlit: St Mark's, the clean bright notice board said. A pub! Oh, a cheery, welcoming pub, the Queen's Head, maybe run by some-one I knew! And, nestling between the two, the vicarage, a silver Focus with a familiar number-plate on the drive.

Without trying, I'd only fetched up in Langworthy, Andy's home village.

I do stubborn very well. I always have. So

though I had an ideal opportunity to knock on his front door and beg – quite legitimately – for succour and a loo, not necessarily in that order, I pulled into the pub car park instead, right round the back, where no one could see me.

However, I had something other people might want. Bother the car. Insurance would cover it. What had provoked my tailgaters was presumably the contents of the camera. So, just in case we had a second encounter, and for no other reason, I slipped the film through Andy's letterbox. And scuttled, like a naughty child who'd rung an old lady's bell. He'd have the nous to know who was responsible, and his loyalty to Tim's memory would probably make him get the film developed and copied. He could return the prints to me, as anonymously as I'd dropped off the film, if he wanted to. Or did I mean impersonally? Maybe a stiff diet tonic water would sort me out.

It was sparkling on the table in front of me, ready to be lifted to my deserving lips, when, in the middle of all my self-congratulation, ideas popped into my head – just like the bubbles in the glass. I had been driving a silver Focus. The white van driver wanted me enough to give chase over dangerous terrain. It was all very well my out-driving him and having time to conceal my vehicle. He'd see a car like the one he was looking for just waiting for him on Andy's drive. It wouldn't be hard for him to assume that I might be in the vicarage.

Greyhounds out of slips had nothing on me. It took seconds to reach Andy's front door. Someone had taped over the bell-push! I used fists as well as the knocker.

In black from head to toe, dog-collar apart, he flung open the door in clear outrage.

'Just get your car into the garage. Now. Talk later,' I yelled. 'Do it, Andy!'

I've always liked a man who can think under pressure. Andy flipped me his car keys and sped to push the garage doors from inside. They opened sweetly. I almost brushed the second one as I nosed the car inside.

The garage had been built for a narrower car. I couldn't open the driver's door far enough to get out. Either door, actually. I could waste valuable seconds by reversing out and coming in off-centre, or I could relive my childhood, pulling myself out of the driver's window.

Unfortunately, though I'd judged the driving to an inch, I hadn't remembered how difficult this manoeuvre was.

Stuck. I got well and truly stuck. Even when I slipped the camera off my neck, abandoning it in the car.

Andy thought on his feet. He was in the garage too, closing the doors from the inside and locking them.

Merciful darkness shrouded my predicament. Or didn't.

'There's a light switch by the back door,' he managed, between gusts of laughter.

'No. Don't want anyone from the outside to see. OK, I'm nearly free.'

'Allow me.'

I could hear him shuffling down my side of the car. A mutter under his breath as he trod on something. At last, he took some of my weight and I could kick one leg free. There was no other way: I sagged sideways into his arms.

OK. Choices, Josie.

Either turn – much easier said than done in this limited space – and kiss him. Or, while never aspiring to anything like dignity, simply let him put me down and usher me as a guest into his house.

OK. No choice.

As my feet reached terra firma, he asked, very coldly, 'And now, would you be kind enough to explain what's going on?'

I matched cold with cold. 'As soon as you've locked your front door, of course.'

Which is how we came to be facing each other in the hall, lit only by the streetlight outside. 'Or maybe a better idea, from your point of view,' I said, 'would be for us to make our separate ways to the Queen's Head, where I've got a drink waiting for me.

Then I can explain quietly, and then go home without any of your parishioners thinking you're entertaining a strange woman at the witching hours of the night.' What had I said? I could feel the tension deepening, even if I couldn't see his face.

'Very well. Let me just find my shoes.'

'You mean you've done all that in bare feet? I thought it was only Hindus who walked on nails.'

'Carpet slippers.'

We didn't even mutter an *au revoir*.

When I got back the landlord's hand was ready to add my glass to his washing up collection.

'Sorry. Call of nature,' I said, retrieving it. 'Josie Welford, the White Hart. What a nice place this is,' I added, as we shook hands. 'I don't suppose you do food on a Monday?'

'None that *you'd* eat.'

'Try me.'

'I saw you in the wife's WeightWatchers' bumf: someone losing all that weight eating crisps? You'll be asking me for pork scratchings next.'

'Lead me to them. Good heavens, Mr Braithwaite! Care to join me in a tonic water?'

'Half of bitter, please, Bob. Hello, Josie – what brings you here?'

'I just fancied a quiet drive on a lovely moonlit night.'

'Lot of mist about,' Bob said, approaching

with a glass in one hand and a packet of plain crisps suspended between the very tips of his fingers. He dropped it before me and made little finicking gestures as if to dissociate himself from it.

'Tell me about it. I got totally lost. Then I tried a short cut through the woods back there and found myself on some track they could use for the RAC Rally. Scared myself silly, when I realised I could take out the sump any second. Only a Focus – not designed for that sort of terrain. And then I thought someone was following me. You know, a lone woman driver... I thought I'd be safe here,' I concluded, worried about all the garbled explanation, and smiling innocently up at mine host.

'As houses. Until chucking out time. I make a point of shutting up shop at eleven,' he said, eyeing the bar clock, which stood at ten-thirty five.

Andy and I toasted each other and him, Andy's cuff slipping back to allow me to see one of those plastic charity bracelets. At his age! I made sure no one would see my postie's version.

Bob was inclined to hover. 'Who might have been following you?' he asked.

'Someone in a white van. Maybe I'd carved him up or something. You know, caused a bit of road rage. Funny registration,' I lied. I wouldn't have had a moment to check, even if I'd thought of it. 'Looks like fowl.' I flapped my arms and clucked. 'You know, one of those personalised ones.'

Bob frowned. 'Rings a bell, somewhere. Anyway, best leave you good people to it.'

Neither of us argued.

'It happened exactly like that?' Andy asked, unamused.

'Almost. But I do know what annoyed white van man. I was taking photos of a scrapyard. I just happened to walk past it yesterday and they set the dogs on me. OK. Dog in the singular. Living daylights time, I can tell you. So I had to take a long diversion to get to church. Hence my dishevelment.'

As if on automatic pilot, Andy said, 'Dishevelled. Funny we don't use the word, "shevelled". Like "couth" and "uncouth".'

'Indeed. So tonight I had to have another look, only they must have clocked me. Hence the chase. Then, when I'd parked my car up in the least visible part of the car park, I thought of yours, just sitting there waiting to be torched, or whatever, and the rest you know.'

'Not quite. Why did you come to Langworthy in the first place?'

'Not to harass you. I told the simple truth. I was afraid the driver knew a different way out of the forest and might be lying in wait for me on the main road. Fifty per cent chance either way, of course. But not if I came straight across the crossroads.'

He nodded, as if weighing it as an excuse and not yet faulting it.

I said nothing. It was his turn, after all.

'Why should they confuse your Saab with my Focus?'

'My car is still lying low. I swapped the Fiesta for a Focus – the colour's a coincidence.' Slow down, Josie: too much data.

'I see.'

'I'll ask Bob to get me a taxi home. Safest.'
He nodded.

I suited the deed to the word.

Bob stared. 'Won't Mr Braithwaite be running you back?'

'Not if there's someone on the look-out for a Focus. Silver, you see. That's what he drives, remember.'

'Hm,' he said, as if he thought the less of Andy, as I was tempted to do, and stomped off, presumably to phone for a taxi.

I returned to the table. Andy was regarding his half as if it were poison.

If he wouldn't talk, neither would I.

Within three minutes, Bob came toddling back. 'Sorry, Josie. Bill's on a call. Won't be back till after midnight.'

And the pub closed at eleven sharp. 'No problem. I'll just have to pay extra attention to my rear-view mirror.'

'Keep your mobile on,' he urged, eyeing Andy again.

'Indeed.'

He nodded at us both, and went back to the bar, eventually disappearing with what looked like a full bin of bottles.

'Mr Corbishley came to supper the other night,' I said brightly, as I finished the last crisp. 'One of a party. They didn't half mess me about, changing their minds over this, that and the other. Poor Lorna could hardly keep up. At least they tipped her handsomely.' I drained my drink and stood up.

Staring at a beer mat, he said something inaudible to my maturing ears.

'I'm sorry?'

'I said, please sit down again. I should have explained. Bishop Jonathan received a letter complaining I was neglecting my parish duties to jaunter round the countryside with you.'

'From Corbishley? The bastard!'

'I can't tell you who from. All I can say is that Bishop Jonathan advised me to consider my position. My business is to serve the Lord, not the local police, he said.'

'Nothing to do with Corinthians? Those chapters before the one you based your sermon on the other day? The ones with a lot of advice about celibacy?'

Startled rabbit didn't come into it. His blush gave him away, but he ignored the point. 'He told me – advised very strongly, which comes to the same thing – to spend what time I wasn't doing my diocesan or parish work in quiet contemplation. He actually used the word "retreat" but can see I simply don't have time.'

'Retreat in the military or religious sense?'

If anything, he looked more shamefaced. 'Both, I suppose. And he asked me not to contact you again.'

'And you forgot you'd invited me to evensong. OK. Anyway, time for me to be off.' My smile was possibly compassionate. But my curiosity got the better of me. I pointed to the bracelet. 'What on earth is that? Ecclesiastical electronic tagging?'

'In a way. It's fashionable amongst young Christians. Bishop Jonathan told me to wear it.'

'So what do those letters stand for? I know AMGD, but not WWJD.'

'"What would Jesus do?"'

What indeed? And what would his representative do?

Not, in the event, what he might have planned to do.

From the car park came a loud bang, followed by another. Voices were raised.

The lad now gathering glasses abandoned his haul and legged it after his boss, dodging back almost immediately. 'Would the lady with the silver Focus come round the back, please?'

I grabbed my coat – I'd seen enough stolen in bars from people responding to such calls – and did as I was bidden.

Chapter Twenty-Five

There was a lot of broken glass and plastic around, including what looked like a red and orange tail-light cluster, but not much sign of anything else wrong. Something, however, had made Bob fume.

'Bloody louts. Come here taking out my CCTV camera! And why should they do that, Mrs Welford? Unless they wanted to have a go at a car? And which car might that be?' He pointed. Mine stood in solitary splendour, nursing, now I came to look more closely, a shattered windscreen. Bang had gone the fifty pounds excess.

I fumed. Not just the money: the inconvenience. The car hire people used their own repair team or the agreement was invalidated. Would they willingly come out to the back of beyond at this time of night?

Quite.

Over to Bob's taxi friend, or, indeed, to Andy. WWJD?

Bob agreed to lock his car park with the poor invalid in it, opening it when the windscreen team appeared. He was inclined to think that was enough, the loud bangs I'd heard having been bottles shattering on the retreating van and, he said, arms akimbo, 'inflicting damage'. He nodded the point home with some satisfaction, grinding some of the coloured shards under his heel.

'I suppose the camera didn't pick up anything useful?' Andy asked, materialising beside me like the Cheshire Cat minus its grin.

'We can but look. But they were canny. One got busy with black spray paint while the other did for your motor, Josie. Tell you what,' he said, checking his watch and not bothering to smother an enormous yawn, 'tomorrow is another day. You look done in, if you don't mind me saying so, Josie. How about you run the lady home, Vicar? Those lads won't be after anyone in a hurry.' What a load of interfering busybodies we publicans were.

'I could wait at the vicarage for the taxi?' I temporised.

'Yes.' Andy set us in motion.

'You want me to give Bill another shout then?' Bob sounded shocked.

'If you wouldn't mind,' I smiled. 'We'll just hang on to see if he can make it. Finish our drinks.'

Following him quietly, we practically walked into him, stock still in the doorway to the bar. After a moment's silence, he let rip a stream of expletives that would have lost him a week's wages at the White Hart. Or maybe not, given the justification.

All the squabs had been pulled from the bench seats and every easy chair. Nothing else. Just cushions everywhere.

'One man for the camera, one for the car and one to search the bar,' I said. 'Is it time to call the police? In which case we should leave this as it is, I'm afraid.'

'Bugger that for a game of soldiers. You talk to the police if you want, but not in my bar, thank you very much. And now, if you don't mind, I'd prefer your room to your company.'

'And who could blame you?' I smiled ruefully. 'I'm sorry I've brought this on you.'

'Ah,' he said, sucking his teeth with a fervour that made me fear for their future. 'And if they can do this to mine, just think what they can do to your place, if they find out who you are. Best get her back there straightaway, Vicar, if you don't mind me saying so.'

To my surprise, Andy grinned. 'I give enough advice to other people not to mind a bit coming my way. See you, Bob. Josie, your chariot awaits.'

I hung back in the doorway. 'Bob, they'll know I'm lurking somewhere: do lock up securely behind me, won't you?'

'And that,' I continued to Andy as we scurried up the vicarage drive, 'is what worries me now. They won't have gone far. Not unless Bob did real damage to their van, so much they'll want to limp it home. I do rather wonder whether calling the police might not be the best move, best friends though we're not.'

He shot a look at me. 'I understand you were very good friends, with one of them at least.'

'At least? At least! Do you "understand" I shagged my way through the entire Somerset Constabulary? You understand wrong, my friend. And just supposing I had,' I continued, grabbing his wrist, and turning it painfully, I hope, what does that say? WWJD? I rather think He'd have said something to the effect of "Go and sin no more".' Releasing him, I dug in my pocket for my mobile. Hell's bells! No bloody signal! It took me all the will of which I was capable not to fling it down and jump on it. That and the realisation that I was so tired I could hardly stand, unsurprising with just half an hour's sleep and all the evening's excitement. As I steadied myself against a porch support, I managed a self-deprecating smile, adding, by way of explanation, 'Endless prison chaplains, remember.'

'Are you sure you're all right?' Perhaps Bob's observations were just sinking in.

'Fine,' I lied. 'I'd murder for a coffee, though.'

In the streetlight he pulled a disapproving face. 'This time of night?'

'There may be quite a bit of it left,' I said, 'if we call the police.'

The vicarage was a cheerless place, cold and still stacked with boxes. It reminded me for a weird minute of Nick's caravan when he'd first settled in Kings Duncombe. Floods had washed away both caravan and contents, which is how he'd originally come to take up residence in the White Hart. Part of the deal with Social Services had been that he'd stay on as a surrogate father to the Gay kids, something he took quite seriously, with the boys especially. My theory was that he was hoping to do a better job than he had as real father to Phiz. Perhaps his illness up in Brum would provide an opportunity for the two to be reconciled, but just at the moment I could have wished him fit and well and down here. Ex-DIs might antagonise one Somerset police officer, but surely not all.

'I've not worked out how to override the central-heating timer yet,' Andy said.

'Lead me to it.'

He winced. 'You're a very practical woman, Josie.'

'When you've spent as much of your life on your own as I have, you learn to be self-sufficient.' I let him infer all he might want. 'So where's this control unit? And by the way, you need to do it, not me. Give a man a fish or teach him how to fish?'

Soon we were shivering less, but I had no intention of removing my jacket. 'They were after my camera, I should say,' I observed, applying myself to the sinful drinking chocolate he'd substituted at my behest for coffee. Biscuits too, but supermarket basics, so I stuck at one.

'I told you you should have got a phone like mine,' he said, perching on the second kitchen stool.

'You're right. I just didn't get round to it.'

'But you had time to get your hair done.'

Was that appreciation or accusation? It was safer to ignore it, even if it meant reaching for another biscuit. At the last minute I switched on my willpower. Conversationally, I continued, 'The camera's in your car, by the way. Where did you put the film for safe-keeping?'

I'd never seen him impish before, but that was his expression now. 'Guess!'

My yawn was too big to suppress. 'Indulge me.'

'In a plastic box in a polythene bag in the upstairs loo cistern.'

'Well done.' I hadn't the heart to tell him that was one of the first places professional burglars looked.

I had no memory of reaching the sofa in a cavernous living room better suited to PCC meetings than a family evening, still less of being swathed in a duvet with a purple cover – did Andy have aspirations of bishophood? But that was where I was when a couple of teenage police officers loomed over me. I felt for all the world like an invalid receiving the family doctor: they must have unearthed a long dead memory of measles or mumps.

They took solemn details, and looked distinctly more interested when I referred them to DCI Burford and the MIT. But not in a spirit of cooperation, I suspected: rivalry seemed more accurate. Tony had always stressed that he never took rural forces for granted. They might lack day-to-day experience of the worst crimes, but the officers were all multi-skilled and anxious to be bigger fish in the still small pond.

Their profound advice was to stay where I was until the morning, by which time they'd have had time to run a check on the vehicles possibly involved. They agreed that another hire car might be a sensible option. Mentally I added one for Andy, too.

'Look out for a Mercedes van with the number-plate looking like FOWL. Or,' I added, by way of valediction, 'one with a cracked driver's door mirror.' In addition, of course, to the one Bob had trashed, and another with possible damage caused by its attempt at a rally special stage.

There seemed no sign of Andy, ready to usher them out. I'd better do the honours, especially as after all that drinking chocolate I needed a loo. Not necessarily the loo with my film. As for that, some deep taboo operated against handing over such sensitive material to anyone so low in the pecking order, so I waved them off empty-handed. I didn't really want to entrust it to anyone in the police, to be honest. Mrs T used to say, *There is no alternative.* And I didn't see one now. What about Burford? He wouldn't exactly be putty in my hands, but show me a vain man who always thought with his brain, never lower down. Especially when he already fancied a woman. None of this need Andy know, however.

In search of the cloakroom, I pushed gently on all the downstairs doors. At last one gave, but not the one I wanted. This was Andy's office, though he probably called it a study. He was kneeling with his back to the door, his hand clasped on his desk. The knuckles were white in the light of a solitary standard lamp.

I didn't disturb him. I'd done enough damage already.

If this was his standard breakfast fare, no wonder he liked my food. Stale bran cereal and skimmed milk, rounded off by ordinary tea or Fairtrade decaff – not at all bad, as it happened, and something to research further. If the White Hart was green, maybe it ought to be ethical, too.

The hire car people responded to my request for pub-side assistance with complete disinterest, though that might change if the Focus were returned to them before I'd put it through a carwash. 'No racing, no rallying' indeed: did the exclusions cover running for your life?

The team they sent even brought their own little vac to suck up smashed glass. I was so impressed with their thoroughness I gave them a handwritten note promising them a free White Hart main course each. With some amusement, they also pointed out that carwashes didn't exactly grow on trees round here, and since they didn't have another shout they'd give the Focus a going over with Bob's hosepipe. A bottle of house wine was added to their IOU.

I still had to get back to Taunton to change the now spruce vehicle, of course. I took possession of the camera and the film, none the worse for its spell in the cistern; I would be dropping the film off at a Supersnap or whatever

'Shall I drive along behind?' Andy asked, without enthusiasm.

I shook my head emphatically. 'You've got

work to do. You did what was right last night,' and, judging by his pallor and the bags under his eyes, had spent a long time doing it, 'but now you must do what your boss tells you.' I didn't specify a capital letter or not. 'Just remember to keep the doors locked: use that peep-hole before you open.'

He was certainly acting on my advice when I next saw him. I waved encouragingly at the eye peering at me.

'What the–?'

'Your new transport of delight, Andy. A bit down market, but it has the virtue of being nothing like yours.'

An exchange of cash had found Sean, the brightest of the lads at the car hire depot, all too happy to follow me back here driving a pea green Nissan. Mine was a pretty blue Fiesta. No suggestion of His and Hers to offend him or the bishop.

And then home.

Which was mercifully all in one piece. And smelt richly of home-baking.

I'd probably had just enough sleep not to worry the lads with my appearance at our daily meeting. Pix went off for the morning shop with instructions to bring home as many samples of Fairtrade products as he thought relevant.

When Annie presented herself at the back

door for today's scones, I asked her in. It wasn't just news of Abby I wanted. It was any fears or suspicions she might have. I prompted her with a highly edited account of my doings the previous night, stressing Andy's positive role as clergyman offering hospitality, rather than any carnal temptations he might be prey to.

'Such a decent man. But the ladies of his parish – let's just say they're not like us, Josie. They all seem to spend all their time having their nails fixed. Have you seen the strange designs on some of their claws? They all think they're Victoria Beckham, far too posh to turn out and clean the vicarage.'

'Which reminds me,' I agreed, 'we need a working party to make the rectory habitable for the next incumbent. We can't leave it as it is. If we could get some ex-display kitchen units and bathroom fixtures, it shouldn't cost too much.'

She tipped her head on one side. 'I know you, Josie. You'll say they're ex-display, but somehow top of the range stuff will appear, beautifully fitted. You can shake your head all day, but I know you. Anyone who saw you hand over that exquisite coat jacket of yours to poor Tang without so much as a wistful sigh will know too. Generous to a fault. But if an old lady can give you advice, take care.' Grinning, I looked round ostentatiously for one. 'People can get jealous of anything, even someone else's generosity. Make sure there are at least some fund-raising activities, even if you go on to cook the books as well as you cook these scones.'

'Those are Robin's this morning. We all take it in turns. Lovely boys.'

She laid a kind hand on my arm. 'They couldn't do you more credit if they were your own, Josie. Now, I must be off. We've got a nursery to paint before the teashop opens. I got Mr Trowbridge on it, and Mrs Walker's stocktaking in the shop. And before you say you ought to be down there too, I tell you we fall over each other enough as it is!'

'So long as it's only each other you fall over. You're sure, absolutely positive, there've been no suspicious visitors? And you promise to dial 999 if there's so much as a frisson of fear? Annie, don't smile at me like that! Think what happened to Tim!'

'Mr Trowbridge is on the best of terms with those two Hounds of the Baskervilles. They lie at his feet like slippers by the fire. They don't even growl if I come near, not any more. It'd take a brave man to annoy them.' Her smile was less certain. 'But don't remind me about the geese's last end, will you?'

Burford phoned to say he was on his way back from Surrey and would hope to drop in about two, A303 permitting.

'In that case, why don't you pick up something I organised earlier?' I gave him the receipt number. It would get him one set of prints. The other set would have a different docket. He didn't need to know that. Yet.

After the miserably cold night, it was warm enough for me to don a spring outfit. I had a couple more years before I need worry whether a décolletage showed crepe, not firm flesh, so I'd make the most of them. Today at least. The sheerest of stockings, which I preferred to tights, and my lovely new shoes. What a waste.

He arrived a little after two, just as lunchtime was over. But I kept him waiting at the reception desk a few seconds longer than necessary so that he could savour delicate traces of what he'd officially missed. As I led him to the office I asked about his journey and his photographic mission.

'So you haven't eaten then?' I concluded, wide-eyed. One look at my innocent face and Nick would have been telling him to watch his back. I could hear Tony chortling. I laid a solicitous hand on the detective's sleeve. 'Oh, dear. Look, there must be something I can find for you. A drink while you make up your mind? I do a lovely non-alcoholic punch.' Casually I plucked today's menu from the desk.

I could see the words, 'Just a sandwich,'

forming themselves in his mind but his mouth refused to utter them.

Clearly I couldn't let him eat in my office, so soon he was ensconced in my living room, halfway down his second punch, which was as delicious as it was virtuous. A cheese ploughman's was on its way, with fresh bread, home-made green tomato chutney and a sliver of home-made quince paste. It was taste-heaven or calorie-hell, depending on your point of view.

While he ate, I gave him an account of my doings, enjoying the narrowing of his eyes as I talked him through the forest part. 'Being chased by a dog is one thing, Mr Burford; being chased by a white Merc. van another. Without being vindictive, I do hope a random rock took out his sump.'

He gave a muffled chuckle.

'You'll no doubt have seen from the photos that all it looks like is an innocent scrapyard. So why all the fuss? And why the smell of rotting meat?'

'I'll get on to it. I promise. This is wonderful, Josie. OK, just half a glass, please.'

Since he was driving, I wouldn't offer any more anyway. Some people would only drink a big red with cheese. Others thought a fruity white went better. This was what I'd offered him. 'Now, tell me all about your adventures in Surrey. Who wins the bet? What's the Martins' house like?'

'Expensive bland. Like a very posh hotel.'

'Very impersonal? Like the rectory, in other words?'

'Different worlds, Josie, but yes. No sense of it being home. Not even a well-used study like Father Martin's.'

So he'd clocked that, had he? Well done. 'DCI Burford – I can't keep using that mouthful, can I? Mark, is that OK? There's a little treacle tart left. Not really a full portion. And you'll be able to work it off in the gym, won't you?' My smile implied there were other places than the gym to exercise. 'Clotted cream?'

He nodded absently. 'You know how most homes, there are pictures of the kids? Little Jimmy doing this, little Jane doing that? Nothing. The daughter – she's now big in some US corporation – got a first in History at Oxford. No photos, though. Father Martin – the son–'

'Tim. Ridiculous for a kid that age to call himself father.'

'Kid? He was thirty-two. Anyway, he was top of his year at theological college, which you'd think also merited the odd photo.'

'Do they assess coming top in terms of academic achievement or of goodness? All this is such a surprise, Mark. His sermons were awful. Sub GCSE.'

'I can't comment about that.'

But I knew a man who could, didn't I? 'So

how do they make their money? Share deals? Salaries? Something illicit?'

'If only I could get a crumb of evidence, I could get the forensic accountants to go through their bank statements. But you can't do that with a pair of bereaved parents.'

'I can't imagine anything worse than losing a child,' I said. 'Tony and I never had any kids, but... Losing Tim was...' My voice started to quiver, not part of any act, believe me. I'd better shut up.

He looked at me shrewdly. 'Is this why you're so bound up in the inquiry? Because you and he were close?' He realised the other implication of his words. 'I mean—'

'I'm sure a shrink would say that he and Tang brought out my latent maternal instincts.' I changed the subject. 'Now, would you like to try some coffee for me? It's a new line I'm trying.'

'Only if you'll join me,' he said.

'Of course.'

When I came back, he was looking at one of my pictures. 'That's lovely.'

'A David Cox. Supposedly. There were a lot of imitations and School Of versions. Black or white?'

He wandered round while I poured. Looking out of the window, he said, as if embarrassed by the revelation, 'I'll put them under surveillance. Nothing heavy. Just a record of people coming and going, basically. Surrey Police will enjoy the overtime, no doubt.'

'Mark, that's brilliant!' I meant to smile coquettishly, but it came out as a frank grin. 'I suppose I couldn't see any photos – you know, a sort of *quid pro quo?*' I waved at the collection he'd picked up.

'Legally, absolutely not.'

'But you might just happen to have them on you if you dropped round for a quick bite after work.' We exchanged a quizzical – but highly ambiguous – smile.

Hardly had his exhaust fumes thickened the wisps of mist sinking into the village than I was back in jeans and trainers. Before I hit the road, however, I had a phone call to make. The hire car people. Had they valeted the Focus yet? Because I'd left a piece of glass in the boot: would they hold on to it until I could pick it up?

By now they knew I was out of my mind, so the lad – it sounded like Sean – agreed to pop it in a jiffy-bag for me.

The boys in the kitchen assured me all was fine and dandy, so I might just as well go and pick it up now. Why not? I ought to thank Bob of the Queen's Head for the trouble I'd caused. I could do that on the way back. How? I could hardly give him a bottle! And I always felt awkward about giving a man flowers. So I raided the larder for some local organic honey, some lemon cheese and a small pot of quince jelly. Laid in a pretty basket and covered in cling-film, it made a gift fit for a prince.

Chapter Twenty-Six

The piece of mirror from the broken van wing-mirror stowed safely in the blue Fiesta's boot, I drove on to the Queen's Head. Bob accepted the offering graciously, and said his wife had been grateful for the upheaval since it meant she could give the place a good clean. He walked me back to the car. This might have been a gentlemanly gesture or because, as nosy as I'd have been in his situation, he wanted to see if Andy would suddenly emerge. Once outside, however, with no Andy in view, he seemed uneasy, as if unsure what to say to me.

Perhaps the bishop had paid an inquisitorial visit and dragged off Andy, kicking and screaming, to have his toenails ripped out.

'Had a man come off his motorbike here quite badly this morning,' he said at last. 'Didn't harm himself, but he might have. Reckoned there was oil on the road, see. And I reckon he might be right. A bit of a trail, see.'

I had to squint a bit, but at last I followed the line of his finger.

'Tried following it in the car. Lost it. But I thought maybe on a push bike? Come on, Josie, what do you say?'

'They say riding a bike's something you never forget, don't they?'

Five minutes later I had to peel my fingers from the grips, one by one, I'd white-knuckled so much. And that was going uphill. And until I'd had to dismount and push. I'd already dismissed running as a civilised mode of movement: cycling had never been in with a chance. Never would be. Wouldn't live long enough. Any moment my heart would burst, and my lungs explode.

Bob laughed. 'Only another couple of hundred yards, and then you can free-wheel.'

'I might as well try to bloody cartwheel.'

At interminable last we reached the top of the hill, which gave us the sort of panorama artists might willingly die for. I was more concerned with a more limited sort of view, one featuring a damaged white van, preferably abandoned well away from dogs and thugs alike. I'd look when I could raise my head, currently collapsed on the handlebars.

And there was Bob, fat as a flounder, breathing as easily as if he'd just walked to the post. Was there no justice?

'Over there!' he said, pointing. 'That lay-by. What are you waiting for?' Suffice to say we arrived. Missing from the van, a great deal of oil apart, was a chunk of the driver's door mirror. Fancy that. Unfortunately the number was a perfectly legitimate one, looking nothing like FOWL, whichever way I squinted.

It struck me that Bob was no longer looking at his prize. Hand shielding his eyes, he was staring up the next hill – the one further away from the village. The twin of the damaged van was heading our way. More than heading – almost on us.

'Company,' he said. 'Come on, woman: on your bike.'

He might as well have told me to fly. In any case, how could a cyclist outstrip a van?

But Bob was certainly going to try. 'Just pretend you're out for a nice country ride,' he said, between his teeth.

'If they stop us, no heroics. Just go on. Take to the fields if you have to. Get help. Promise?'

It might have been the urgency of my voice, or the expression on the face of the van driver, but Bob did just that. As for me, as the van juddered to a halt in the lay-by, I waited till the driver emerged, and threw the bike at him full on. Then I took to my heels too, nipping over the stile and loping across a newly-sown crop. My target was another stile about a hundred and fifty yards away. With luck it might get me into a lane with houses: we weren't all that far from the village.

If I'd had time or energy to think, I'd have urged myself on with thoughts of non-runners who'd managed to get themselves into sufficient shape to finish marathons. But I wasn't about to pop the London event into my diary.

By now I could hear my pursuer's breathing. It sounded as if he was out of condition too. But he had legs long enough to clear the stile with a vault, as opposed to my clumsy scramble.

I was still ahead. Just. He could have me in a rugby tackle, though, and I didn't think I'd bounce. I might even get run over, the rate that car was coming towards us.

If I could just get the car between him and me. Then I could – I don't know what. My legs were burning rubber, from the thighs down. My chest was on fire. The car horn blared, the tyres squealing. Missed me. Just.

Not just missed. Had stopped, the passenger door open. Andy's hand dragged me in as soon as I'd crawled close enough. We set off, me kneeling on the seat facing the wrong way, with the door flapping.

Shut it. I must shut it. At least hold it so it wasn't damaged. The hire firm didn't mind replacing a windscreen. But I fancied they'd take exception if he lost a door.

'Where are we going?' I gasped, as we shot through the village, waving at a bemused Bob. At last he twigged and gave me a huge thumbs up.

'Taunton, of course. To change this car. I never did like green anyway.'

I tapped his wristband. 'A man for Good Samaritans, your Boss.'

'You didn't get the number of either vehicle,' a policewoman said disbelievingly.

'Nope. All I know is that one had a dodgy sump leaving a trail like a slug's and a mirror with a bit missing like one that I found at the scene of an unreported accident.' I threw my hands in the air. In exasperation, I continued, 'Tell me, is it absolutely impossible to speak to DCI Burford? He knows all the background.'

'He's in a meeting,' she replied, her mouth like a hen's backside.

'OK. The two lads who responded to my call last night.'

'They won't be back on duty till ten, Josie.'

'Mrs Welford. OK. I've got a pub to run. I'd best be on my way.' I cocked my head and checked her number, which I wrote down on the back of my hand.

'I'll just check what time DCI Burford's meeting will finish,' she said, not very coincidentally.

'He'll know where to find me.' I didn't have much to gather, apart from my dignity, but I swept out: think Mrs Thatcher late for a Europe-bash.

Andy was waiting for me, like an empty milk-bottle. 'Another car change?' he asked wearily.

'What colour would you prefer?'

He shrugged. 'Something truly invisible.'

'How about bright red?'

Was the silence companionable or strained? In my case, at least, exhausted.

Just as we arrived at the car hire depot, my legs decided to get cramp. Not just a little bit. A lot. I gritted my teeth and rubbed and rubbed. I wouldn't cry out.

'Problem?'

'Every muscle's awash with the stuff that bugs athletes – lactic acid,' I groaned.

'I thought that was what they used to make cheese,' he objected.

'It is. Oh, my God.' I'd managed to get out but now both legs gave up entirely. I sank painfully and ungracefully to the tarmac. Not cramp any more – should I be pleased? – but pure physical weakness. Was I going to have to crawl into the office? Now I knew why folk took to wheelchairs.

Sean came dashing out, dismay all over his designer-stubbled face. 'Mrs Welford? Are you all right?'

'Too much exercise,' I managed to grind out.

'Packet of crisps and a lot of water. Here, do you think you can walk if that clerical bloke and I help you?' Beneath his cheap suit he was whippily strong, and easily hoicked me upright. 'Here, mate, give a hand, will you?'

Anxious to spare the poor man, I breathed into Sean's ear, 'Leave him be. He's got heart problems.'

Andy still had to drive me back to Langworthy, of course.

Five minutes into the journey he caught me looking at my watch.

'The evening sitting will wait for no one, I'm afraid.'

'Surely you can't be—'

'Of course I've got my team to call on, but there's such a thing as exploitation. I pay them to do their work, not mine.'

'All the same.'

I turned to him. 'You do two jobs, Andy. At least two. You make no bones about it.'

'I don't dash around the countryside nearly getting killed.' He tempered the statement with a rueful laugh.

'I'm sorry it was your wheels I nearly landed under. But you didn't panic. Thanks for saving my life.'

'I didn't mean that, and you know it. Josie:

could you spare me ten minutes of your frantic twenty-four hours to talk? I owe you an explanation of – of... Of why I've let you down,' he finished in a rush.

If I'd been a counsellor I'd have asked why he felt that way, but I wasn't, so I blundered in. 'I'm sorry you see it that way. I don't. I see you as a man under enormous pressure trying to do a new, tough job, still probably mourning his dead wife, whatever the state of the marriage at the time, and trying to live up to a set of rules far tougher than I could imagine. With a worse – an eternal! – penalty if you fail. Come on, Andy: your Boss is always on about forgiveness. Try a bit on yourself. And on me,' I added, as an afterthought. 'Because up to now you've been judging me by rules I didn't even know existed, setting me a standard I don't know I want to reach. That's why we get so angry with each other, isn't it? When we just muck in as mates, we're fine.'

'The trouble is,' he said, slowing down to turn the car into the vicarage drive, 'good as that is, I'm not sure about our being just mates.' He parked, pulling up the handbrake.

Talk about unconscious symbolism. What next? Would he want to continue the conversation in the car? No, he was getting out, so I'd better too. At least I didn't fall flat this time, thanks to young Sean and his instant cramp cure. Now, if ever a lad was wasted doing a routine job like that, it was him. How would he fancy joining my team? If I had an administrator I could spend more time in the kitchen. And I'd certainly need one if I took on the Abbot's Duncombe pub.

I waited. At last he flashed a ghost of his former smile. 'Another ten minutes another day? If you've got to run the White Hart, I've got back to back confirmation classes, followed by supper with the cathedral hierarchy.'

'Another ten minutes another day,' I confirmed.

I set off to pick up the blue Fiesta, pristine in the pub car park – Bob had found a bit of gardening to do as an excuse to guard it. Not for anything would I turn back, but I was certain that Andy watched me out of sight.

The mist came down again very thickly with the dusk, and I had to concentrate on my driving. At least, that was my excuse, and I was glad of it.

Chapter Twenty-Seven

Wednesday morning, and my cycling muscles, whichever they were, were still fiercely indignant about their treatment, and were ready to bring others out on strike too. It took every stretch I knew, and a few more, to get them moving. Robin baked and biked down the scones, though he reported so many other cakes in the farm kitchen he'd been hard put to find a space on the table for them.

'You ought to have a talk with Annie,' he said, perching on my office desk. 'They've really transformed the place, by the way. Think National Trust tearoom – it's that sort of cute.'

'So all the volunteers are pulling their weight?'

'Going well over the extra mile, I'd say. Feeding the five thousand, but only a couple of hundred turning up.'

Andy would be impressed. Twang. 'Like the cake-stall at a church fête?'

'Exactly. They're beginning to have to throw stuff away.'

'Surely someone would take it into the Taunton Sally Army! Robin, do you think we should pull out of the scone supply chain? Our egos aren't involved, after all.'

'It'd make the early baker's task easier.'

'That's a good enough reason – I'd best get on the blower now.'

'I'll fix you a double espresso while you do it, shall I?'

'So long as it comes with a body transplant.'

While I waited for the coffee, I phoned Annie. Our conversation about food quickly over, Annie said carefully, 'I'd rather you heard this from a friend. They were circulating a petition in the parish about ... about the rural dean.'

'And his unsuitable friendship with me?'

'It suggested rather more than friendship. I don't think they got enough names to make it into a petition, not without looking foolish. But that wouldn't stop them altogether, would it?'

'No.' If I let on I knew I'd be compromising Andy even further.

'Shall I let you know if I hear any more?'

'I'd be very grateful – forewarned is five armed, as they say. Not that you can stop a rumour: it always makes things worse. I suppose we haven't a couple of men who ought to know better to thank for this?' *We!* How about that for a Freudian slip?

But she seemed to think I'd meant her and me. 'And men always accuse women of gossiping. And of being old women.'

'Pots calling kettles black! I wish I knew why they had it in for me, Annie. They never seemed to object to my envelope on the collection plate until the Tang affair.'

'Strong women scare a lot of men. Especially ones who've shed their own power.'

'Which was?' I wouldn't tell her about my Internet searches or my village shop pryings.

'No one really knows. Malins was a civil servant – Min. of Ag. and Fish, before it became DefRA, or whatever its current incarnation might be. Reasonably high up, but not a ministerial adviser. And Corbishley was something in industry. A captain, no doubt! As you'd expect, he always used to rabbit on about teachers having long holidays, that sort of cliché, never doing a decent day's work,' she added with a snarl.

If only she could tell me something new, something to make my ears prick. I reached gratefully for the coffee Robin parked within reach. He was mouthing something.

'Burford?' I mouthed back.

'In your living room.'

'They've always had this uneasy relationship – reluctant friends, allies, at least. I guess they knew each other from their working days,' Annie was saying.

Burford would just have to spend another couple of minutes in front of the David Cox.

'So Malins might have put Min. of Ag. and Fish contracts Corbishley's way?'

'I'd never thought of that,' Annie said, sounding worried. 'It's a big assumption to make.'

'Almost as big as suggesting there's anything untoward between a dean and a restaurateur,' I retorted. 'Annie, the police are here again. I suppose you couldn't stir the rumour pot down at the farm, could you? It's just I'd like to know where all this hostility is coming from, that's all,' I added lamely, not even hoping she'd believe me.

As I'd predicted, Burford, a natty laptop in his hand, was eyeballing the David Cox when I let myself into my flat.

'It's the sort of thing you can live with for years and still find new things in,' he said. 'Like a human being, I suppose.'

I stood beside him. 'You're right: all those subtleties...' Eventually I prompted him, 'But you've not come to discuss art, I presume. Maybe to sample a scone, however?'

'And some more of your excellent water,' he grinned.

'Give me a moment and I'll get both.' But it took more than a moment to work my way down the stairs – for some reason descent was even worse than ascent. After all that effort I deserved a scone myself. Maybe even jam and cream.

He must have registered the pain involved simply in setting down the tray on a side-table, and would, I swear, have helped me into my favourite chair as carefully as if I'd been a pensioner on a rocking bus.

'You've had another accident?' There was an ironic curl of the tongue round the word.

'Unwonted exercise, that's all. Oh, and a bit of a fall.'

'Enough to demand to see me yesterday?'

'Yes, that sort of fall. I was being chased, you see.'

'By White Van man?'

'Indeed. I can see your colleague's brought you up to speed, despite my inefficiency in the matter of number-plates.'

'I gather from Bob Page of the Queen's Head you had a lot to make you inefficient.'

'Bob? He's spoken to you?' Had he said anything about Andy?

'Of course. All about the great white van chase, the oil slick on the road, and your rugby dive under the wheels of some elderly clergyman's car.' *Elderly!* But he was younger than me! 'He even got a partial number for one of the vans. Not quite enough for us to go on, however, but it doesn't necessarily matter. We wanted to talk to this Reverend Braithwaite, but haven't got hold of him yet.'

Should I offer to try his mobile? Or try it myself later? *Elderly*, indeed!

'Anyway, I thought the least I could do was bring you up to speed. We are working hard on this case, Josie, even though it may seem that we're taking our time.' And was still, chasing a last crumb of scone around his plate.

'So there's something interesting on your laptop then?'

'A couple of photos of the scrap yard. Old tyres, Josie? Or something else?' He opened it and passed it over.

'Hell's bells! Is that what I think it is?'

'Absolutely. You said the place stank. And there you are. Chicken carcases. Birds that have died on the way to the slaughterhouse, rather than being slaughtered. Clearly unfit for human consumption, even animal consumption, most of them.'

'Isn't unfit poultry dyed blue at the slaughterhouse so people will know it mustn't get into the food chain?'

'Exactly. The carcases should have been disposed of by incineration or by rendering at a proper site, definitely not a scrapyard! And they were just left lying there, in the open.' They'd been photographed from a variety of angles, none more appetizing than another. No wonder he'd wanted to finish his scone before he'd got down to business.

I said slowly, 'So if they're dyed blue and you want to sell them on you've got to get the dye off somehow. One of my mates said the chicken supremes she bought smelt of some scent or other. And they always came ready prepared – off the bone and skinned.'

He leaned closer. 'Exactly: the dyed chicken fillets must have been bleached before being sold as decent meat. We think. We've got no hard evidence yet. Except a couple of white vans.'

'Has one of the vans lost a sliver of wing-mirror? It's in my hire car, if you want to check – belongs to a van that nearly ran me down.'

He made a note. 'We found a beat-up old Mazda at the back of the yard. Does that ring any bells?'

I struggled to the vertical. 'There are copies of photos taken of the guys who started the rumpus in my dining room in my office.'

'Shall I nip down? Give your bruises a rest?'

I eyed him narrowly. 'What, and give you the chance to search my filing system for pots of gold? They're in the second tier of the tray,' I added, using my common sense.

It took him a minute, no more. 'These the ones?'

I nodded. 'And Dan Tromans might be able to help identify them.' I didn't go into the details of Dan's conversations with me; I had an idea Dan might play fewer games with a man.

He made another note. It was so nice hav-

ing someone do my running round for me.
And then I felt Tony's hand on my shoulder. This was a policeman – wasn't I being altogether too trusting? It was always better to ask questions than volunteer information.

'I suppose you didn't find a black BMW?'

He frowned. 'Was I supposed to be looking for one?'

'Should be in your case notes somewhere. I was tailed by them – I gave them a few verbals for it. Talk to DI Lawton. She sent someone with a little laptop just like yours to help me ID them. Bernie Downs, that's her.'

His frown deepened.

'Speaking of which, have you managed to round up any of the scrapyard workers yet?'

'Yes. But they might be Trappist monks for all they're saying.'

I scratched my head in disbelief. 'Tony often said people low in the pecking order outsang canaries. Drat! I hadn't meant to use that chicken image!'

He threw his head back and laughed. 'It could have been worse – *lower down the foodchain!*' Then he became serious again. 'These lads have lost their voices and found highly professional solicitors.'

'I wonder who's paying for them.' Good criminal briefs cost a very great deal of money. 'And maybe who they're afraid of, too.' Another theory of Tony's I didn't need to spell out.

'Mr Big? Well, maybe if we find an industrial sized bleach tank, we shall find him.'

'And, with my compliments, dump him in it. Surely, though, with your DNA and all your other forensic science skills you can find where the vans have been. Somewhere with illegal Chinese labourers – unless you found any at the scrapyard?'

'No. Nor any signs of hasty exits.'

'Another yard, then. Hell, Nick Thomas must have all this on file in his office. Trust him to have a cold just when we need him.'

'He wouldn't have left his laptop in his room here?'

At least he was up to speed on something. And not making any insinuations, either.

'It was nicked.'

'Was it indeed?' He made a note, which he underlined, twice. 'From here?'

I shook my head. 'The scam where you shunt someone in the rear bumper and, as they get out to check, nip round the other side and steal anything going.'

'And what was your take on that?'

'That he was a mug to fall for it. But then, it was in Taunton, not inner-city Brum.'

'You haven't got his mobile number, have you?'

Hell: I was being sucked in deeper and deeper. 'It'll be in my mobile's memory.' I reached for it and brought up the number for him to jot down.

'Thanks. Meanwhile, I'll try tracing the vans and their movements back through possible chicken sales. Not too tricky, thanks to your list of emails.' He gave a dazzling smile, somewhat tarnished by a bit of raisin or sultana skin stuck between a couple of teeth. 'And,' he added, warming to his subject, 'we've managed to set up surveillance of the Martins, as we promised. Early days, and we can't afford as many officers as I'd hoped, but I'll get back to you as soon as I've anything to report. I promise,' he ended, with a flash of his whitened teeth, now minus the skin. He stood in one easy movement, and proffered a well-shaped hand to help me to my feet. 'Have you had your injuries checked by a doctor?'

'No need. And no time. No, there's nothing broken, I'm sure of that. Now, I'm afraid I've got lunch to think about.'

Not to mention possible food processing plants. All the same, when on duty, I had to keep the customers to the front of my mind. All my customers on diets – vegan, gluten-free, non-dairy – were there. James, the one with a severe nut allergy, wasn't, because Robin had produced a lovely Thai beef salad with satay dressing, and had phoned to warn him off. Pix found it hard to believe that the simple presence of peanuts in someone else's food could lead to James's death by anaphylactic shock, but I'd sat him down in front of the computer and set him going. Ten minutes' reading had made him the most convinced scrubber down of the kitchen you could wish to find.

So how could I find that dodgy processing plant? Nick, of course. If he couldn't get down here, he could still send his files, surely to goodness.

'Codfidedtial idforbation,' he sniffed.

I was almost convinced. 'So is Phiz going to join you for the match tonight? In Leicester?'

'I'b too ill.'

'You don't think a bit of fresh air might help? No? OK, how do I hack illegally into your work computer?'

'I suppose the police could.'

'The police'll need a warrant, surely to goodness. Come on, Nick: your country needs you.'

'I bight be well enough to get down toborrow, Elly says. But not ged back to work this week,' he added virtuously, as a female voice bellowed in the background.

'I don't think switching on your computer really constitutes work,' I wheedled. 'Just give me your password!'

'That'd be compledely udprofessional!'

I encountered Annie on my afternoon stroll – hardly surprising since I wanted to see for myself all the arrangements down at Dan and Abigail's. My eyes rounded in admirtion. What had once been as basic as a transport caff was now an attractive rendezvous, complete with pictures, plants, starched tablecloths and beautifully printed menus.

Her sudden sisterly hug caught me by surprise: locals didn't seem to go in for them. 'I'm on to our friends,' she said. 'They'll get their come-uppance one of these days, you mark my words.' It sounded rather like a promise.

On the way back, I decided I'd give her a helping hand. I'd never prompted Burford about Malins and Corbishley, for reasons I didn't want to explain to myself, but now I would. He picked up his phone first ring, sounding really pleased to hear from me. And I could almost hear him writing down their names and summoning a minion.

I was still about half a mile from home when my mobile rang. Andy! Was he ready for his ten minutes?

'I'm on to something! Bishop Jonathan commended long walks, so – not unwillingly – I tried the idea. Yours, really, Josie. And I can see why you do it. The spaces, the clear air, all the buds–'

Damn it, I didn't need a spiritual nature walk! 'And?'

'Oh, yes. My walk took me along a road – shall I give you the coordinates? – and this stinking truck overtook me. It was enough to make you throw up. And it was kind enough to leave a trail of drips along the road.'

'A name?'

'Just an average pick up. You know the sort. No attempt to cover the remains. Not even a tarpaulin.'

'Remains?'

'Dead birds, dead sheep, even. Totally revolting.'

'Any idea of the colour? The make? Andy, this is important.'

'Red. And I think it was a Toyota. No idea of the number or the driver or anything. Too busy burying my nose in my hands. Sorry.'

'So where are you now?'

'Back at my car – trouble is, I'm not as fit as you and it's taken – what – half an hour.'

'And have you called the police? Andy?'

'Sorry, you're breaking up. Talk to you later, Josie!'

Breaking up, my foot! Within seconds I was on to Burford, yelling what I could remember of the coordinates as I ran – OK, staggered – as fast I as I could back to my own car. Half a mile!

I flung myself into the Fiesta, lamenting my own car and all its extra power. Why hadn't I kept the Saab on the premises, not left it at the hire car depot? Still, the Fiesta would have to do, and bugger its poor pretty paint.

The stupid, stupid man! Did he think his clerical collar would save him? Had Tim's?

Chapter Twenty-Eight

And unlike my Saab, of course, the Fiesta didn't have a satellite navigation system. How the hell was I supposed to read a jiggling, sliding OS map and keep both eyes on the road? Not to mention check the rear-view mirror every few seconds and scan the side roads at junctions, either for heavy farm machinery or innocent motorists or even for ambush by white van? No, I was only a little paranoid, but as Tony always said, a little paranoia never did even a sparrow any harm. And they seemed to have four eyes. And could fly.

Between all this, each time I stopped to check the route, I tried Andy's phone. It was either in a mobile blackspot or switched off.

Then I had a call: Burford!

'We think we've located his car – yes, we've got a chopper up there. The pilot will be guiding us.'

And he was guiding me, too, hovering over a hill no more than three miles away. Down went my right foot. From time to time I'd catch Mark Burford's voice.

'Josie! Can you hear me? Answer, damn you! Back off. Keep out of this. Just back off.' And then he'd try again with the same message, or variants of it. Perhaps I should have responded, but doing seventy down a one-in-four track precluded polite conversation.

By now I was on what looked like an old army site – nothing as official as an industrial estate. One or two units were dotted haphazardly near the entrance: there might be more inside the perimeter, hidden by low buildings with semi-circular corrugated iron roofs. There was no sign of the police, chopper apart, or of whichever car Andy had used. A white van – and yes, this number might just be – if you had time to squint – FOWL. A red Toyota pick up? No, no sign of that, but yes, there was a trail of some sort of liquid. I'd have to follow it on foot. I abandoned the car, stopping only to pocket the key. No weapon, only the heavy torch Tony had insisted I transfer to whatever hire car I used.

Hell, the stench, and not only from the trail, either. Gagging, I told myself I'd dealt with game birds crawling with maggots, with overripe venison. There was no time for the delicacy of a tissue over the mouth. I'd lost the trail of matter, as it disappeared into scrubby grass.

Skips; five-foot high drums of something. I didn't stop to look. And all the time I ran, dragging air into aching lungs, I was straining my ears. For Andy's screams? Or simply the purposeful sound of ordinary machinery. Yes, over there. And the trail headed that way too, to a forties building that could have been anything from a Mess to a storeroom.

I tried my phone. No response. But I left it ringing: wouldn't that help Burford and his mates locate me?

I could pull that door open, and risk making a noise, or try easing it an inch, just enough to see.

Bleach. Yes, I could now smell bleach, a tart overlay on the sweetness of decay. In the everyday electric light, it seemed almost banal to see Chinese figures in overalls a size or so too large, tearing putrid skin from chicken carcases. The birds' throats and innards were intact: the creatures had died, not been slaughtered. God knew what sort of diseases they could carry into the food chain. There was a high-pressure hose for flensing meat off bones – the resultant grey-brown pulp would find its way into pâté and other processed products. Once I might have bought it. The Gay kids might have been fed on it.

And Tim and Tang had died to stop it being made.

No. That was to make martyrs of them, the wrong sort. Someone had killed Tang so he couldn't tell anyone where he had committed a crime so bad he needed sanctuary.

Had he committed it here? Had he disposed of the evidence here? It would be easy enough.

They could be disposing of Andy right now. And – if I weren't careful – I might be joining him. Even as I despaired of his life, I heard myself promising that his DNA would be found, somehow, and the workers here be nailed.

They were worse than nailed. They were shackled.

I mustn't lose control.

If they were using knives, ten to one there'd be one lying around. And if there was one thing I knew how to use, it was a knife. And – thanks to all those joints of meat I'd prepared – I knew my anatomy. If it was kill or be killed, so long as no one came up behind me, I'd bet on myself.

Evens, anyway.

Boots apart. Walking boots – heavens, had I driven like that in such insensitive footwear? – would be heard even above the thrum of the machines. Should I take them off? And risk slipping on the gory mess of the floor?

I'll swear Tony tapped me on the shoulder. My eyes found the mains power switch. This

412

wasn't the sort of place to have automatic generator back up. It'd cause chaos. The Chinese slave gangs wouldn't go fast anywhere. So who or what might I flush out?

There! The darkness wasn't complete, perhaps a bonus since I might not need Tony's torch. There was a wonderful shocking silence, then chattering, like starlings in a city. Then decidedly European voices, swearing in old-fashioned Anglo-Saxon.

My ears strained for voices I might recognise. Suddenly I caught Andy's. 'Father, forgive them, for they know not what they do!'

Boots or not, I was on the move. My torch now in my left hand, I grabbed a knife. A good one, by the feel of it, well-balanced, the sort I'd enjoy using in my kitchen, it lay so well in the hand.

'Police! The place is surrounded!'

No one would be taken in by my hollering, but a couple of Chinese kids pointed to the far corner.

My torch picked out a group. At its centre, naked, trussed like a turkey, Andy knelt at the feet of a big man – European – holding a raised knife he clearly meant to use. All eyes swivelled to me. And I pulled back my knife, and slung it, very hard, so the blade would land first. There was a scream as it sliced through flesh.

The world went black. Not just because I'd dropped the torch. Because someone had crept up behind me and–

Why was my face hurting? Soon I'd be able to open my eyes to find out. Meanwhile, my ears were full of the sound of police voices, those of people officially inured to the sort of mess they found.

I'd rather not have heard what they were saying, as they talked about the case. It seemed that a couple of weeks ago someone had pushed a supervisor into an industrial mincer in a food-processing plant, and, in the stilted lingo they used, all the evidence pointed to Tang. I tried not to gag. I tried not to laugh. For the image that insisted on presenting itself was of dismembered digits sticking out of the machine and literally pointing towards St Jude's.

Chapter Twenty-Nine

The pain was someone slapping my face. It was the one bit of my body that didn't already hurt, and here was someone laying into it as if it were steak to be tenderised.

I might as well look. A familiar face swam into view.

'For God's sake!' I spluttered. 'Lay off, Nick!'

'She's back with us. She's OK,' he yelled to someone. 'No, stay where you are, Josie. The medics are on their way. Concussion.'

'Concussion, conshmussion. What the hell's going on? Is Andy–?' I remembered what I'd done and started to retch.

'He's fine. He's in my car finding a rug. He was mother-naked, and modest with it.' Nick sounded amused, in a dry, Nickish way.

'And the guy I – I–?'

'The guy you skewered – you never told me you'd been a circus knife-thrower, Josie – he'll live.'

I found I was holding his hand. 'What's your car doing here? I mean, why are you here? And where are the police?'

'On their way too.'

I shuddered. 'Start with why you're here. No, start by getting me away from here. And – no, look the other way: I'm going to throw up.'

Bless him, he held my head and then passed me a bottle of water. 'Better out than in, as my old gran used to say.' Levering me upright, he propelled me firmly away from the shambles and nattered about Elly and Phiz sending their best and all sorts of rubbish about the football match, so I didn't even notice we had to pass all that vile mess of dead animal till he propped me against his car. He must have been a good cop in his day, even if he had somehow – mercifully –

415

forgotten all those first aid rules about not moving traumatised patients. Then he stood back and admired the distant view while Andy, kilted in a travel rug, scrabbled out and threw himself into my arms.

Assured he was in one piece, I pushed him gently away. I smelt of sick and he of blood and he had just too much baggage for me to carry just now. Just as I realised what a selfish bitch I was being, some paramedics descended and we were thrust in different directions.

'The thing is, I'd rather liked her from the start,' Nick had started by confessing, as he drove me home from Taunton A and E. All I'd got was a lump on my head that I tried to insist no one was going to get their sticky mitts on but which they X-rayed anyway. The police had insisted they needed all my outer clothes, there and then, and having made all that fuss when Tang's went missing, I supposed I couldn't blame them. So here I was tricked out in one of their spare white paper suits.

Andy, transported for some reason in a different ambulance, had had to stay in. They wanted to see how much of all that blood caking his body was his and whether any that wasn't his might be infected. I'd suggested the bishop as next-of-kin: for once in my life I had to admit to being too weary to be any use to anyone else.

'So why were you there, Nick?' I asked, trying to revive some bits of memory while firmly suppressing others. 'You're supposed to be ill in Birmingham.'

'So I am. Was, rather, if not ill. And the operation to intercept bush meat was quite genuine. But Claire Lawton got in touch–'

'*Claire* Lawton?'

'DI Lawton to you,' he flashed back. 'She was worried about her lack of progress – information not getting passed along, that sort of thing. That's why she asked to have the MIT replace her. And, since she was entitled to look at other things than the kids' murders, she decided to check out rumours of a dodgy meat-processing factory–'

'Factory! That's rather a posh term for that dump!'

'Quite. Anyway, she organised a little posse from Trading Standards and the FSA to check out one of the places on file in my office – hence my presence. Almost too late.'

I didn't want to think about the implications of that. 'So she's a good cop, really. And Burford? Is he OK too?'

'As far as I know. Any reason why he shouldn't be?'

'None. Just that – he seems too good to be true.'

Nick snorted. 'Claire tells me he's been trying to get in your knickers from day one.

417

Isn't the feeling reciprocated?'

'Nope. I was briefly attracted to him, but my heart, good sir, was never engaged.'

He laughed at my Victorian pastiche. 'So it's Andy–'

'Whoever it was must have whacked my head harder than I thought,' I interrupted him. I'd been tempted to rest my eyes, but feared they'd stay shut a long time if I didn't open them. And I clearly needed my wits about me. 'To be honest, I knew Mark fancied me so I just sort of strung him along in the hope of getting this case sorted more quickly.'

'Which may have worked, whatever the morality of it all.'

'Oh, don't you start on morality too!' I snapped pettishly.

'I gather there was some sort of problem with Andy?' he said, with that sort of lift at the end of the sentence he must have learned from his post-traumatic stress counsellor.

But he wasn't about to counsel me. 'So why did your Claire think she was losing information?'

'Because – among other things – you assumed she knew things she should have known. And she wondered why. And suspected a mole in her team.'

I would have hit my forehead in fury, but decided the old head had been walloped enough, one way and another. 'Who? Hell,

Nick, I truly don't believe it: not that nice kid Bernie? The one who was so helpful? And told me, now I come to think of it, I couldn't have ID'd the scrotes in the black Beamer.'

He nodded, waiting at a halt sign. 'Nice little Bernie Downs, a real sweetie, forgetting to tell Claire key things which made it impossible for her to do her job, poor woman. But Bernie messes things up too well, and MIT have to take over.'

'And Bernie was tunnelling away for whom?'

'You didn't see him? In the hangar?'

'Would I be asking you if I had? OK, give me a clue,' I suggested, my voice honeyed with sarcasm.

'Actually, it was a straight question. I wondered if you had seen anyone to arouse your suspicions.'

'Nope. But then, I wasn't looking. All I thought about was stopping them slaughtering Andy. Are you sure that that knife didn't do too much damage?'

'I wouldn't give it a second thought, Josie. You saved Andy's life, at the certain risk of your own.' He pulled on the main road.

'I wonder who clobbered me. I'd like it to be Malins or Corbishley. Or one of Tim's loathsome parents. The world would be a better place with them all doing a long stretch, preferably together, like in that

French play. *Huis Clos*. Hell is other people,' I explained, when he clearly didn't pick up the reference. 'But I can't see them running an immigration scam. Any of them, to be honest. And Downs surely wasn't running the whole shebang on her own.'

'I wouldn't think so.' He sounded very restrained, all of a sudden.

'She was in cahoots with someone I know? One of my catering colleagues? Come on, Nick, I'm a big girl.'

'I never know how involved you get with these blokes dancing attendance on you,' he grumbled.

'First rule of flirting: don't get involved. And you know how I feel about Tony – he's still a far bigger player in my life than any of these hunks.'

'He's also dead, Josie: one day you'll have to move on.'

'I don't see why!' I fired. But I could see him preparing to tell me, so I continued, as if there'd been no digression, 'I'd quite like it to be Rousdon, because he wouldn't tell me where he got his samphire, but I'll bet it was Nigel Ho. All that business about getting Tang into custody – where no doubt Bernie Downs would have managed somehow or other to get to him?'

'Let's see what Burford comes up with, shall we? Come on, Josie, you know you can trust my driving. Why not have a little snooze while I get us home?'

Why not indeed? But Tony squeezed my shoulder in warning. So I saw why not.

'Pull over. Now!'

Without arguing, Nick obeyed, every tyre protesting – almost as much as my body, come to think of it.

'Why?' he asked.

'I think that's Michael Rousdon's car. What would he be doing round here?'

'Come on, Josie – a man's entitled to drive anywhere.'

'All the same.' I told him about the photos Andy had taken, light years ago now. 'Mobile!' I demanded. 'Have you got DI Lawton's number in the memory? Oh, call her yourself and tell her to get a fix on him. Just do it, Nick. And tell her to get a reception committee waiting for him. In Starcross, of course. Where he lives.'

I heard Claire's tinny voice, then somehow Burford's.

'That's very interesting,' Burford said, repeating the map reference Nick gave him. 'Because a witness places him in the vicinity of that factory. We'll get on to it.'

Nick cut the call, 'Hell, what a shambles.'

'Curiously enough,' I said, flailing desperately for normality 'you've picked on almost the right word. A shambles used to be the street where there were slaughterhouses and butchers' stalls. There's a street called that in Worcester to this day.'

'Wow,' he said, sounding completely un-impressed. 'Are you sure that bang on the head didn't do more damage than the hospital picked up? And one of these days, Josie Welford, you can explain why you signed yourself out against their advice.'

All these people interested in my welfare. There were days, more than I'd ever admit, even to myself, when a bit of pampering and spoiling, the odd cup of tea in bed, that sort of thing, was what I craved. But not inter-ference.

'Now,' he said, starting the engine again, 'I'm taking you home. OK?'

'But Michael Rousdon. We should be tailing him. We should–'

'Are you sure you should be doing any-thing, dressed as you are?'

'Bloody hell. OK, the White Hart it is. I should be getting ready for the evening sitting!'

I called Robin.

'Pix and I are on to it already. When you didn't turn up and didn't answer your phone, we got on to a couple of the better work experience kids we've had and offered them real money for real work. Wendy and Lucy are primed. We've cut a couple of specials. Don't worry, Josie: we're motoring.'

'I'll be with you as soon as Nick can get me there.'

Which wasn't very fast, because every bump in the road hurt my head.

Once Nick had been the most timid of God's creatures, incapable of saying boo even to the decapitated Samson and Delilah. Increasingly I could see him as he must once have been, and as Claire Lawton presumably saw him most of the time. In my mind's eye I already had them tying the knot at St Faith and St Lawrence's, with the most slap-up wedding breakfast at the White Hart it was within my power to give. The only fly in the mental ointment was the officiating clergyman: I'd bet my boots Nick would insist on Andy, with whom he'd got on quite well.

I suppose I must have dozed off during this little flight of fancy, because I heard someone snoring and found it was me.

'Here we are,' Nick said, pulling up right by the staff door, bless him, so no one would see my snowman outfit. 'Get yourself upstairs and I'll come and make you a nice cup of tea.'

Chapter Thirty

Imagine me sleeping the clock round. But that was what happened. My team had managed perfectly well without me, and Nick had brought me breakfast in bed and the news that a whole lot of knots were being tied up. If I felt well enough to ID a few people via mug shots on a computer it would speed the process.

'So long as you can guarantee a pukka officer,' I grumbled.

It was Mark Burford himself who did the honours, and for once I let myself share the Danish pastries and fresh rolls while he updated me.

'Did you pick up Michael Rousdon?' I asked, wondering if I was strong enough to eschew fresh butter.

'Yes. Not in Starcross. Our helicopter found him in a little place called Cockwood. Do you know it?'

'A darling little hamlet on the coast? Two pubs in a to-die-for location and little else?'

'Right. An ideal location for a man to do a spot of fishing and keep his boat.'

'He always boasted he caught his own.' My brain got into painful gear. 'I suppose

you could catch other things beside fish...
Like the odd economic migrant?'

'Illegal immigrant, indeed. Now, are you
ready to look at a few ugly faces?'

I was. And there they all were, an unlovely
collection. White van men; the BMW driver
I'd threatened with Tony's revenge; the man
with the vicious dog.

'But these are small fry,' I sighed.

'And you're used to Mr Bigs, aren't you! Is
Michael Rousdon big enough? He kept his
most recent boatload of Chinese lads in his
boatshed. Shackled,' he added, his voice
mingling pity and anger. 'Unlike the two we
found working in his kitchen.'

'Chinese workers! No wonder he tried to
keep me out: he told me it was because I
would steal his pickled samphire!' I
squeaked. Then, regaining my normal voice,
I asked, 'Why did Rousdon involve himself
in people smuggling? Why should an
ordinary English crook dabble in a Triad
preserve?' I'd have scratched my head
except it meant moving too many muscles. I
thought briefly of going to a health spa to be
massaged into comfort, then I remembered
the awful food at the last one.

'Money. What else?'

At this point Nick knocked and came in,
followed by Claire Lawton and a worryingly
pale Andy, who'd been kept in hospital
overnight and looked as if he could have

425

done with a longer stay – though perhaps his pallor owed something to a very black clerical shirt he wore buttoned down to the wrists. Clearly the bishop's choice, not mine.

'No. Josie's right. It doesn't make sense. Too dangerous,' Nick put in, as if he'd been on the conversation all along. 'He's got to be a middle-man, hasn't he?' He sat down, eager to continue.

The others sat too. I ought to have got up and found more plates and mugs, or at very least asked Andy how he was.

Mark shook his head. 'All the people we've picked up so far insist he's the boss: Andy's would-be executioner, who might also sue you for assault, I suppose; the lads from the scrapyard, who've now found their voices; the Chinese labourers as translated by an officially accredited interpreter.'

Nick and I exchanged a look with Andy. This conversation was taking on an uncanny echo of one in St Jude's light years ago, when I'd mooted one of Nigel Ho's employees for the role.

Andy spoke softly, as if his throat hurt. 'Have your forensic accountants checked Rousdon's books? Not the recent ones. I'm sure they balance perfectly.' He shot a look under his lashes at me. 'But in the past. To see whom he owed money to when he started his life of crime.'

426

Burford raised an eyebrow, but wrote it down. With a grin at Nick, Claire Lawton excused herself, fishing her mobile from her pocket as she left the room.

'I don't suppose it'll be any of my *bêtes noires*,' I grumbled.

'You never know,' Burford said, surprising me. 'We've maintained our surveillance operation on the delightful Doc Martins.'

Andy was suddenly bolt upright. 'On a bereaved family!'

'Come on, Andy,' I said, not as sharply as I could have done, 'you thought them as loathsome as I did. Has anything interesting shown up?' I asked Burford.

'Did you know they were acquainted with Mr Corbishley?'

'Corbishley! The churchwarden!' Andy's shock turned to interest. He slumped again. 'But they neither contacted nor referred to him while they were down here. To the best of my knowledge,' he conceded. Then he got into full flow. 'Never have I seen such unnatural parents. All right, they might have been exhausted, jet-lagged, whatever, but not an iota of emotion did they show. Not for one minute. The only interest they showed at any time was in some of poor Tim's books.'

'Are they still there? The books?'

'I didn't see them remove any.'

Burford was on his feet in an instant. 'I take it you've still got the rectory keys, Mr

Braithwaite? And no, with all due respect, none of you is coming with me.'

'Would there be any point?' Andy asked wearily. 'It was most possibly something left in the book that they wanted, not the book itself. Why not do the simple obvious thing and talk to the church wardens direct? Corbishley at least? He'll bluff and bluster, but he can't have worshipped at St Jude's for thirty years without some good rubbing off on to him.'

To describe as cynical Burford's expression would have been a massive understatement. However, he shrugged. 'Why not? But why don't you go and check out Tim's study? See if you can see where any books might have been removed.'

'Four eyes are better than two,' Andy replied, surprisingly. 'What about Josie coming too? After all, she dusted the study and put everything into some semblance of order.'

'Disorder, more like. I tended to put big books with other big books, small ones with small ones.' And I had a strong reluctance to spend the ten minutes I promised Andy until we'd both recovered our equilibrium.

'Even so,' Burford put in thoughtfully. 'I'd be very grateful – I'll organise transport.'

Andy coughed, ironically. 'It's a most beautiful day out there. I fancy that, our various injuries notwithstanding, Josie and I might be trusted to walk the three hundred yards there without keeling over and expiring.'

I gave my most non-committal nod. 'I'll get my jacket.'

Feeling middle-aged is not something I do. Hardly ever, anyway. But I certainly didn't have much youthful spring in my step as we strolled down the village street. For a weekday, there were plenty of people around: we could almost hear the jungle-drums pulsating as we greeted anyone we knew. Was this what Andy had intended? A silent snook at Bishop Jonathan?

'I wanted to thank you for saving my life,' he said, slowing to an amble.

I'd prepared my response. 'Anyone would have done the same.'

'By throwing a knife? Quite a skill! Did you run away to join a travelling fair? Or is it another accomplishment your late husband taught you?'

I wished I didn't always suspect a flick of the tongue when he spoke of Tony. 'Blame my gypsy blood. What are you expecting to find tucked in one of Tim's books?' Once I'd started to exercise regularly I'd found it easier to walk briskly than slowly, so I steadily edged up the pace.

'I've truly no idea. Probably nothing. I just needed some air, and thought you might.

But we might as well see what shows up. If anything.' He gave one of the smiles I'd have died for a couple of weeks back, before we got angry with each other.

Despite all the air-fresheners, the rectory was as musty as ever, just with a sickly air-freshener overlay. Without speaking we flung open windows before going into Tim's study.

The books seemed to be exactly as we'd left them. They weren't all theological tomes by any means, though they predominated. It seemed he was interested in natural history, and had for some time collected – and read! – standard editions of biographies of celebrated Victorians. Not a lot of light reading apart from a few books on cricket tucked away behind his desk, as if he took secret dips into them when he should have been concentrating on his next sermon.

'All those student books,' Andy said sadly. 'Prefacing a life dedicated to God.'

'And achieving that end, if you think about it. Laying down his life for a stranger.'

'Tang had become a friend,' he corrected me.

'Tim knew he'd bitten off too much. There were times he regretted it, but he stuck to his task. A good young man.' I gestured. 'All these: did he leave them to someone in a Will?'

'I don't know anything about one. The

young rarely bother, do they? They think Wills are for old people. And he'd precious little to leave anyone.'

'If he died intestate,' I pursued, 'I suppose his parents would get everything. Or that sister of his.'

'Sister? He never mentioned a sister to me!' As if he'd admitted a personal failure, Andy drifted to the window, peering out at a garden refusing to surrender completely to neglect – wherever you looked bulbs intended to break into flower at any moment.

'Nor to me. Burford dug it out of the parents. She's emigrated to – God, my memory! You'll have to ask Burford, who only found out when he visited them at their house. He said it's not like a family house at all. No clutter. No photos. And you can't say Tim exactly celebrated his parents – not a single family snap around the place. I should have clocked that before. It's as if parents and kids have settled for a divorce from each other.'

'Something terrible or something entirely trivial: that's how rows flare up,' he said, but not as if he was alluding to our contretemps. 'Especially family ones.'

'How about we go for the terrible? Would there be something in one of these books to give us a clue?'

I made us instant black coffee – I drew the line at milk granules – and Andy settled to open and shake every single volume. We ended dusty and tired and irritable. With nothing.

'But it's something Corbishley knows about,' he said. 'He couldn't – he couldn't have been blackmailing the parents, could he?'

'Which argues they've known each other a long time.'

'Captains of industry, all three. Their paths might have crossed. And it also argues he'd known Tim a long time.'

'Or *of* Tim. Maybe he didn't expect such parents to produce such a dedicated young man – any more than they did!' I added, with a dry laugh. Almost as an afterthought I said, 'Tell me: how were they searching? Desperately? Leafing through books and throwing them down? Or deliberately? Show me. No, relax: don't think about it. Just do it.'

He closed his eyes, picking up a book and restlessly riffling through it, rather as I skim magazines at the dentist's.

'Andy, are you sure they weren't just killing time? Doing something with their hands? Doing something till it was decent to leave?'

He drooped. 'You mean all this has been a wild goose chase. I'm sorry. And I'll bet you're needed at the White Hart.'

'I am. Look, why don't you have a bite

there too? If you'd rather, you can have a rest in my flat until the rush is over and we can eat together.'

I should have said, 'All eat together.' Because that's what happened. I allowed myself a very swift shower before dashing down to supervise the bar meals. The lads tried to send me away, but the weather had brought a huge rush, so they let me stay.

Meanwhile, Andy had a bath and then presumably a snooze, because when I saw him next he looked much less funereal. Or perhaps that was because he'd cadged a light coloured shirt from Nick. He'd turned back the cuffs to just below the elbows, something I find for some reason very sexy. Perhaps I'm a forearms woman.

The sun was so warm I decided we'd eat in the garden, so I set about organising all those highly qualified professionals into dusting everything off, laying the table, slicing bread and tossing salad: I wasn't going to ask Robin and Pix to work yet more unpaid overtime with all those idle hands around. Nick, as I could have predicted, manned the bar, pulling pints of my very best bitter and finding champagne – vintage! – for those who preferred it.

'Let me guess,' I said, taking my place at last and lifting the embargo on news. 'Corbishley went to see the Martins because when he'd seen them around the village it dawned on him that Tim must be his son. Poor bugger.'

There was a satisfactory gasp, which told me my wild theory had some truth in it.

'Funnily enough you're right. He confessed everything. I think,' Mark Burford reflected, 'he was glad to get it off his chest after all this time. He got Celine pregnant just before she married Thomas. It never was a marriage made in heaven, but they rubbed along and then had another child, who took up a high-flying job in the States the moment she could.'

'At least one of them was an achiever, then – if not a grateful loving child,' Andy observed.

'But they stayed together? Even had another child! Although there was nothing in these days of swift and easy divorce to stop them going their separate ways?'

'As you know, Josie, marriages take different forms,' Andy smiled. 'On another level, think of trying to disentangle all that money without one of them feeling hard done by and involving expensive lawyers – I can't imagine them wanting anyone else to sniff their money, let alone get their hands on it.'

Nodding, Burford continued, 'And we found nothing, absolutely nothing, in their background or in their business dealings to suggest that they are anything more than hard-working, high-achieving business people. I loathed them as much as you two seem to have done. But that doesn't make them criminals.'

'So, having got the young woman pregnant, Corbishley retires to the country and pumps huge amounts of money into a village church,' Andy ruminated. 'A form of expiation?'

'You're the one to ask him about that,' Mark Burford said, adding awkwardly, 'Though I did rather sense that you might not be the person he'd choose as a father confessor.'

'No one as puritanical as the reformed sinner,' I said as lightly as I could. 'And he certainly hated me and all associated with me. He and Malins would have had me whipped at the cart tail if they could. Unless – I'd really love it if Malins were our Mr Big?'

'Sorry, Josie,' Claire Lawton said, dabbing the last crumb of cheese from her plate, 'not if my information is correct. A quick scan of Michael Rousdon's accounts suggests he owed a huge amount to a Chinese guy in Plymouth, a chef, as it happens, who in turn is trying to finger Nigel Ho. But there seems to be no direct link. Not an obvious one, anyway.'

I shook my head sadly. 'Nigel it may be. He said someone had approached a chef in his

Plymouth restaurant with cheap chicken. He could have been bluffing.'

'Or he could be telling the simple truth.' Did I detect the flicker of a blush cross Claire's cheek? 'Nigel could charm the ducks off the water, couldn't he? And I'd never trust a man who oozes honesty and good advice from every pore as he does. But it'll take more than half a morning for our forensic accountants to nail him.'

'In the meantime,' Nick said meaningfully, though whether to me or to Claire it wasn't clear, 'a man to be kept at arm's length.'

There was a tiny pause.

Andy filled it. 'So Malins is just a miserable bugger who likes sticking his terribly pious nose in other people's business? The sort of man who gets Christianity a bad name?'

Mark looked taken aback, but Nick gave me a sly wink.

I jumped in. 'The sort of man who cadges free meals with the bishop and later makes sly remarks about people who cadge even bigger freebies. How did you describe him, Andy? As a Pharisee?'

'I think "miserable bugger" is accurate enough.'

'But not evil, like Rousdon and his boss,' Nick reflected.

Andy, his voice a little less secure, said, 'Evil indeed. Evil enough for Tang to be driven to kill someone and take to his heels. Evil enough to pursue Tang and kill two young men. May God forgive him.'

'Rousdon may have to wait till the hereafter for his forgiveness,' Mark said dryly. 'I can't see the English justice system being compassionate.'

'The words "locking" and "throwing away" seem to fit naturally in the same sentence as "the key",' Nick said. 'And though I never was a cop who advocated long jail sentences as a matter of principle, I don't want people like him wandering round.'

Mark shook his head. 'After the disgrace of being found out, he won't survive long, not if I know Chinese gang leaders.'

'Where did he bring the slaves in, by the way?' Andy asked. 'The ports have got all this clever equipment for checking vehicles, I thought.'

Mark moved slightly so that the sun no longer shone directly into his eyes. 'Right on his doorstep. He had a reputation, Josie tells me, for freshly caught local fish and made a point of being seen in his boat pottering in and out of Cockwood at all times of the day and night. Most times he'd be alone; others he'd have company. So there it all is. My colleagues and I will move mountains of paperwork, see if we can finally nail a Mr Big, and move on to the next case.' He got to his feet. 'Can I give you a lift, Claire?'

'No thanks. I've got my car parked round the corner, ready for when I've sobered up. And I'd have thought you were over the limit, too.'

And just to make absolutely sure everyone was, Nick produced another bottle of bubbly.

Epilogue

'Hot work, cricket,' Nick declared, sinking into a deckchair in my private garden, not the pub one, and reaching for the cold beer he still preferred to cider, even though his long-term stomach ulcer was now officially healed. He'd been coaching the Gay kids, all of them, not just the boys, in the hope that Lorna and Dean would make it to the village club's colts eleven.

I wasn't sure whether he'd taken it up for love of the game, for love of the kids, or in the hope that it would trim his figure and keep love burning in Claire Lawton's eyes. Personally I thought the age gap – fifteen years – too wide, but for once I said nothing and let him get on with it, especially as both his children were now regular visitors and always ready to give him grief over his love life.

I sipped my champagne and we lapsed

into companionable silence, until he said, 'Are you expecting any visitors tonight?'

That was his way of asking if Mark or Andy would be round. 'I should think they're both working,' I said idly, swatting a midge. I appeared to have settled into a sort of friendship with them both.

Bishop Jonathan had found a whole series of vitally important tasks for Andy to do, including liaising with an African bishop – it seemed you could twin sees, like twinning towns. This particular bishop was known for his hard-line views about everything from women priests to gay marriages, and was no doubt expected to stiffen Andy's moral fibre. Andy did what he was told, each time returning to the White Hart to be cosseted. I made sure I always tempered the extravagant food and drink with a cash donation to one of the underfunded schools in the desperately poor African country. What poor Andy's conscience made of it all, I never asked.

Mark had been promoted to superintendent in Yeovil, and was working as many hours as I did, more when there was a murder on his patch, although technically he was supposed to be an administrator, not a hands-on cop. When he came for a meal, however, it was always alone, and usually in my flat, where he'd talk through his day as if we were Derby and Joan and always leave at chucking out time.

Before he'd moved to Yeovil, he'd tidied what he always called the St Jude's case as best he could. The forensic accountants were still beavering away trying to link everything to Nigel Ho. I never asked how they were getting on, but had never quite got round to renewing my relationship with Nigel, nor had he been in touch with me.

The DNA the forensic scientists had extracted from poor Tang's clothes had confirmed links with the meat-processing hut: try as we might, we could think of no other term for it. The scientists had also managed to pick up traces on Tang's clothes that matched DNA from a missing worker's clothes. The interpreters – nothing to do with Nigel Ho! – discovered that Tang had indeed broken free of his fetters, strangled the overseer and shoved him into the industrial mincer. Naturally Andy had not dwelt on this fact when he'd taken the memorial service to the lads, the bishop in attendance, at St Faith and St Lawrence. The choir had done us proud, an old friend of Tim's now an organist at a Midlands cathedral had played and every last one of the villagers had turned out, both the shop and the pub being closed for the event. I'd offered to provide the wake, but the village hall committee would have none of it. It was village tradition that every family coming would provide enough food and drink to share. I could underpin the offerings if I wished.

I did. As unobtrusively as I knew how. As I would the church fund.

Somehow I'd been coopted on to a committee to decide the future of poor St Jude's. Building inspections had shown the fabric to be irretrievably damaged. I was all for pulling the place down – the altar removed to another church! – and leaving a simple cairn to record what had happened. The insurance money would pay for a parish minibus, which could ferry any parishioners without transport to another church in the benefice, probably St Faith and St Lawrence. The remaining money could rescue St Peter's in the Combe.

Not everyone saw it that way. Not by any means. But for once I had the bishop's support, and I suspected that after a summer of haggling at many meetings, to many of which I had sent my apologies, Corbishley and Malins would accede to the will of the majority. I almost found it in me to be sorry for Corbishley, given all the circumstances of his life: imagine having been locked in furious dispute with a young man you only discovered after his hideous death was your son. I tried, anyway.

'Have you thought any more about opening another restaurant?' Nick asked, dragging me back to the present.

'I'm torn,' I admitted. 'Without a pub or a church, there's no heart in a village. But the sort of place I'd want to run would hardly cater for locals and would bring a whole lot of disruption to the place. When the St Jude's business dies down, Robin, Pix and I will discuss it all with the villagers.'

'Is that what Tony would have done?'

Nick was the only person to mention Tony in that way; I could never tell if he was serious or mocking me.

'He'd have done exactly what he wanted and ridden roughshod over those who were unwise enough to object.'

He nodded, not needing to point out I was moving on. 'The lads are committed for another year?'

'Maybe longer now they've got girlfriends in the village. And they're both starting courses at Exeter Uni in October. They'll only be able to work for me part-time, but even that will help with their fees.' And of course, they wouldn't have to worry about paying for their accommodation, though I didn't tell anyone that. To supplement the staff I was taking on a couple of young women with their baby: what had been temporarily the Martins' quarters would house a proper family.

'You won't get bored, will you?'

'Not with the christening coming up!'

There was no need to be unobtrusive for

the forthcoming christening of Violet and Tom, Abigail and Dan's twins, at which Andy would be officiating. I would even breach my free Sunday evening rule so they and their family and friends could hold the post-ceremony party at the White Hart. It wouldn't be just me and the lads cooking: all the people who still kept the farm shop and tearoom afloat wanted to support the babies in whom they took the proprietorial interest of quasi-grandparents.

'Have you made up your mind about being one of Violet's godmothers?' he asked. He'd agreed to sponsor Tom.

'Well, there's a snag, of course. Only baptised and confirmed members of the church can be godparents.'

'Oh, I'm sure the rules are broken all the time! Think of all those *Hello!* christenings.'

'Sure. But a dean could hardly condone it, could he?'

'Surely there's a way round it? You know nothing would give Andy greater pleasure than to baptise you.'

'It's the thought of Bishop Jonathan's greasy hands on my head to confirm me afterwards that puts me off.' It was also the thought of what I was committing myself to. Not the godmotherly duties: everyone knew I'd make sure little Violet never shrank, official godmother or just friend. It was Andy himself.

'Come on – there are worse things than a pair of bishop's hands, aren't there, even if they are greasy?' Nick pursued.

But he didn't wait for an answer. He heard the footsteps approaching the gate, took one look at my face and knew when to make himself scarce.

This Large Print Book, for people
who cannot read normal print,
is published under the auspices of

THE ULVERSCROFT FOUNDATION

... we hope you have enjoyed this book.
Please think for a moment about those
who have worse eyesight than you ...
and are unable to even read or enjoy
Large Print without great difficulty.

You can help them by sending a
donation, large or small, to:

**The Ulverscroft Foundation,
1, The Green, Bradgate Road,
Anstey, Leicestershire, LE7 7FU,
England.**
or request a copy of our brochure for
more details.

The Foundation will use all donations
to assist those people who are visually
impaired and need special attention
with medical research, diagnosis
and treatment.

Thank you very much for your help.